Praise for *Stay with Me, Wisconsin*

Tough, yet tender and thought provoking, this elegantly-paced collection brings a wide cast of characters to life in celebration of the restorative power of love. Beautifully written and honestly rendered, these stories are both intimate and universal.

Thomas Trebitsch Parker, author of the novels *Anna, Ann, Annie,* and *Small Business*

With the deft touch of a natural storyteller and a brilliant ear for dialog, JoAnneh Nagler's enchanting short stories get to the quickening heart of relationships—each of her unique and compelling characters in search of an authentic connection and a place to call home.

Marcia Kemp Sterling, author of the novels *Tangled Roots* and *One Summer in Arkansas*

JoAnneh Nagler's Stay with Me, Wisconsin *weaves together poignant, tender and riveting tales of unforgettable characters grounded in a profoundly strong sense of place. She vividly captures the flavor and magic of the glacier-scoured landscape of Wisconsin—both emotional and scenic—in a way that is absolutely unmistakable to those who know the hearts, towns and sensibilities of the spirited Midwest.*

Fred Schepartz, Publisher and Editor *Mobius: The Journal of Social Change,* author of the novel *Vampire Cabbie*

Richly drawn characters find themselves in provocative and complex situations in this collection of modern short stories built around the drive we all have to connect. A lush, textured, unforgettable dive into life.

Holly Brady, former director, Stanford University Publishing Courses

Upon reading the last sentence of Stay with Me, Wisconsin, *I lingered long, not ready to say goodbye to these wonderfully realized characters. They wound their way into my heart and thoughts—so much so, that long after I closed the book, I found myself wondering how they were faring in the world, as if they were people in my life. As a native Midwesterner, I can attest that JoAnneh Nagler has perfectly captured the unique blend of reserve and friendliness inherent in our lineage. I envy the reader lucky enough to be reading these stories for the first time!*

Jaime Love, Artistic Director and Founder, Sonoma Arts Live Theatre Company

Stay With Me, Wisconsin

JoAnneh Nagler

COYOTE
POINT PRESS

An imprint of Flying Ketchup Press®
Kansas City, Missouri

Appreciative acknowledgements that several stories in *Stay with Me, Wisconsin* were previously published in literary journals, including Ponty Bayswater (*New Haven Review*), Asa at the Foundry (*Glimmer Train*), Claire Rose (*Mobius*) and Fishing (*Gold Man Review*).

Cover Art based on Photograph *Couple* © 2015 Wyatt Fisher
www.drwyattfisher.com

Flying Ketchup Press
11608 N. Charlotte Street,
Kansas City, MO 64115

FLYING KETCHUP PRESS ®

Library of Congress Cataloging-Publication Data
Stay with Me, Wisconsin / JoAnneh Nagler
Library of Congress Control Number: 2021944262
Softcover ISBN-13: 9781970151-93-0
Hardback ISBN-13: 9781970151-94-7

Also by JoAnneh Nagler

Naked Marriage

How to Be an Artist Without Losing Your Mind,
Your Shirt, or Your Creative Compass

The Debt-Free Spending Plan

To Michael, for every beautiful and loving thing you bring to my life

Stay with Me, Wisconsin

By JoAnneh Nagler

—✳—

Contents

Don't tell your father, Ponty.
He doesn't like me anyway and profanity
will not help my cause.

Ponty Bayswater

Ponty Bayswater was ninety-one when he finally changed his name. Christened "Pontius"–an old Alabama family name on his mother's side–all his long life he had dodged the blows and taunts of playground bullies, dolled-up teenage girls who wouldn't get near him, and business colleagues who assumed he had some "in" with a Christ-bashing mission. It didn't help that he was half-Jewish.

Bayswater was the family name his father took instead of Brenowitz when he immigrated through New Orleans in 1905–the name had been printed on the side of a cracked, wooden crate dumped off on the harbor-side of an ocean liner, which was then left behind. His father claimed the name. It figured. The family legacy was a splintered and abandoned crate.

At age seven, he coined the nickname "Ponty" and would refuse to tell its origin until some little ape outed him for the Christ-hater he would inevitably be accused of being.

His teachers were of no help. Stuck deep in the belly of the Bible Belt, they most often looked at him askew and then shuttled away any mouthy children who were bellowing out the brainwashing of their small-minded parents.

"Jew-boy!" "Christ-killer!" "Pontius goes to hell!"

Never mind that Pontius Pilate was a Roman, Ponty thought. Never mind that it was the Romans, not the Jews, who really pulled the trigger on that cross-hanging thing–a verdict as sinister as any he had ever heard. And what the hell did he have to do with it anyway?

But in Alabama in 1929, accurate history was just a lot of side-chatter. Doctrine mattered, and where you fell on the line between Christ Jesus and the town's loyalties to that martyr determined the treatment you'd receive from even the lowliest of the town residents.

Ponty learned to hate "Alabaman idiocy," as he dubbed it, and became a precocious and prolific reader of history books, a combatant of all manner of inaccurate attributing.

"Accuracy matters," his mother would say to him after he had narrowly escaped another attack by the "trolls," as he called them–bullies from his third-grade class who regularly attempted to beat him up on the wooded trail which led to his neighborhood.

"You are not a Christ-killer because your name is Pontius," his mother intoned rather stiffly. Ponty was a late-in-life baby for his mother, an only child.

"I know that, Mama," he would sigh, "but can't we please change my name?"

"We do not give in to ignorance, Pontius," she would retort. "It was your grandfather's name, and that's that."

When he was ten, his father got an important engineering job in Green Bay, Wisconsin, designing roads and highways (the state was in the midst of major construction), and he moved the family north. By then, even in a school with a whole new slew of beastly bullies and name-callers, Ponty could refute any nastiness with a quick verbal jab that left his accusers stunned just long enough for him to run as fast as his asthmatic lungs could carry him.

"You're parents are *Huguenots*!!" he would shout at his fifth-grade attackers, freezing them in their tracks with their ignorance of the word long enough for him to backpedal and beat a path back off the footbridge, down into the river-bed under the heavy brush. He often came home wet.

For his entire twelfth year, he refused to go outside after school, preferring instead the company of his loopy Aunt Violet, a former schoolteacher who lived with his family, never forgot a date, and could tell him the dirt on any historical character who ever lived.

"They're all dead anyway," she'd say, squeezing out a steaming orange pekoe tea bag into her cup, swearing as she burned her fingers, "so who gives a good God-damn if I gossip about them?" She wore pink cat-eye glasses with fake diamonds, had a head of tightly curled gray and black hair and wore bright red lipstick, even at home.

Ponty loved it that she swore, that she said "shit" and "piss" and even "fuck" from time to time.

She'd look down over her glasses, and with a nicotine bark in her voice she'd say, "*Don't* tell your father, Ponty. He doesn't like me anyway and profanity will not help my cause." She was the only one in the family who called him by his chosen nickname.

Ponty loved her. He basked in her tales of King Henry's affairs, Marie An-
toinette's sex life, and of some obscure nobleman whose wife had come to him
and told him that she was in love with another man, and they had all three lived
together as lovers for the rest of their lives.

He hungered for her stories of outsiders, too; people who were ostracized
in their hometowns but who made good by leaving forever. He loved tales of
people who invented things: engines, planes, the discovery that the earth was
round and not flat. It was even better if the protagonist had suffered ridicule or
had been put in prison for telling the truth. Galileo, the Wright brothers–Or-
ville and Wilbur–and Leonardo di Vinci were some of his favorites.

His aunt told him that Leonardo was a homosexual. Ponty hadn't even
known what that was or that it existed.

"Men can have relations, Ponty," she insisted, looking unabashedly into his
eyes.

Ponty was stunned. He asked how it worked.

"Think, boy!" she said. "What would feel good to you?"

She was the one who told him about sex, the actual mechanics of it. "We'll
just get down to business and talk the real truth of the thing, shall we? No *euphemisms*," she'd say. "I *hate* euphemisms."

She had explained to him the varieties of how women's bodies worked, how
men and women worked together–not just the biology, but the how-to prowess
of being a good lover, too–and then, also, the inner workings of homosexuality.

It was an education he appreciated–facts and tactics he was sure the sad little
trolls at his new school would never get, and it made him feel superior enough
to get through the blockhead-infested school day, then propelled him home,
rushing to prod and query Aunt Violet some more.

———

Ponty had his first love affair at the age of eighteen, just when the U.S.
entered the Second World War and he was about to be shipped off to the Phil-
ippines. Five weeks before he was scheduled to board the USS *Alabama* out of
Casco Bay, in Maine, a WASP of a girl named Juliette Whitaker planted her
body between him and the men's room at Jasper's Supper Club, then landed a
big, sloppy, wet kiss on his lips.

"I'm gonna marry you, Ponty Bayswater," she drawled.

"No, you're not, Juliette–you're just drunk," he said, throwing an arm under
her collapsing frame. It was July, still sticky and warm at eleven at night, and
she was sweating under her armpits, the light blue taffeta of her off-the-shoul-

der dress slipping slightly down her upper arm. He had liked Juliette; had admired her, too. But he hadn't thought much beyond that. Her parents were the high and mighty type–everybody knew that–and he was certain they thought well enough of themselves and their bloodline that they wouldn't want their only daughter gallivanting around with a half-Jewish young man.

Juliette stumbled towards him.

"Nope. Ponty. You're–*uh-oh…*" she said, tripping over the heel of her shoe. "You're *myyyyy* man. Always wanted you." Her head took an intoxicated roll towards his shoulder and then plopped there, with a rather hard thump. "Just had to get drunk enough to say it."

It landed on him like a bag of coal to the head. She meant it.

Ponty did not think of himself as handsome. He was thick-built, on the short side and masculine enough, certainly, with a warm-colored brown head of hair and bulky forearms. Juliette was an inch taller than he was, even in the flats she wore, and the fact that she had never cut her chestnut hair into the overly swept-up, curling-ironed styles of the era charmed him. She wore her hair parted on the side and flowing to her shoulders, and she was shapely besides–small breasts, flat belly in cinched-waist cotton dresses, and lovely gams peeking out under her skirts.

Ponty walked her home and waited on the sidewalk while she wobbled up the front stoop.

"Bye-bye, Ponty!" she drawled, not turning, but waving her fingers at him from the side of her curvaceous hip.

The next day he came to call, stood on her front porch while she faced him through the screen door–she was standing much too close, almost within kissing distance–and asked her to go for a walk with him on the green.

"I would love *nothing more*, Ponty," she whispered through the tight metal grate of the screen. He could feel her breath on his cheek as she spoke.

Her mother sat still and tight-lipped in the front room as Juliette walked out, and Ponty got a good glimpse of the woman's expression as he held the door and balanced the screened-in. Her mother didn't get up to say hello, and Ponty didn't go in.

"You sure you want to do this?" He nodded his head toward her mother and looked Juliette in the eye.

"Wanted to *forever*," she said, and then leaned in and kissed him on the cheek. Ponty let the screen door slam good and loud and turned to escort Juliette down the steps.

Two days later, they were touching each other in the grass next to Siber's

Creek behind a big grove of trees, and Ponty was taking his time exploring her every crevice.

"Well, Ponty Bayswater!" she said, laughing into his armpit. "Who would've thought that you'd be such a Casanova!"

He spent two hours delivering as much pleasure to Juliette as he could muster, never entering her. Her breath came hard again, and she panted into his ear, "Where did you learn to…?"

"My aunt…" he said as his tongue found her earlobe.

Juliette pushed him back and sat straight up, almost jumping. "You mean *she*–and *you*–"

Ponty laughed out loud–a big, hearty guffaw. "No, no, no! Juliette, she *told* me how to touch a woman…"

"Isn't that a little…*inappropriate?*" Juliette sniffed, trying to regain her composure.

Ponty smiled a sweet smile. "Do you like it, Juliette? You tell me the truth now…"

She smiled back, looked down at her naked body, and then blushed bright red.

Ponty began kissing her belly. "Then we'll have to pay a visit to my Aunt Violet and tell her thank you, now won't we?"

–––

Ponty boarded the train in Green Bay five weeks later, heading for the USS *Alabama*, without "jumping on the pre-combat matrimonial bandwagon," as he dubbed it–much to the chagrin of Juliette.

"But what if you die?" she sniffed, her big eyes filling up watery and red-rimmed. They were alone on the train's platform; all his family goodbyes–misty-eyed hugs and firm handshakes–had been said on the wide front porch of the Green Bay family house. He'd had a private moment with Aunt Violet that morning, and tears were shed.

"All the more reason you shouldn't sit around waiting for me," Ponty said to Juliette stoically.

"I know you love me Ponty Bayswater," she pleaded. "I can see it in your eyes."

He took her by the shoulders and pulled her slim frame close to him, her face just inches from his. "Juliette Whitaker. I love you with all my heart, and if I come home whole and safe, I will you marry you that same day. I promise." He kissed her hard on the mouth, pulled her into his chest, and then swung his duffle over his left shoulder, hopped aboard, and didn't look back.

—⁓—

A week later, Juliette packed her bags and moved into Ponty's parents' house.

She knocked at the front screen, and red-faced and sweating from the humid August heat, said to Ponty's mother, "I'm going to marry your son when he comes back, and I need a place to live."

"Let her in, Maxine!" Aunt Violet yelled from the parlor.

Ponty's mother cracked the screen door open, but Aunt Violet was suddenly right behind her and reached in and pulled it wide.

"Your mama threw you out? Over Ponty?" Aunt Violet said pointedly.

"Mmm-hmm," Juliette sniffled. Her eyes were wet. She put her brown leather suitcase down on the porch, wiped her eyes.

"People do the most asinine things, Maxine!" Violet said to Ponty's mother. She placed both of her hands on Juliette's arms and looked her straight in the eyes. "You're *family* now. You stay here as long as you like, you hear me?"

Juliette got a job at a paper-processing factory working part-time on the line, and volunteered for the Red Cross making bandages for the war effort. She thought about Ponty every day, wrote to him weekly, and though she got on fine with Ponty's parents, her preference was the kind and bawdy company of Aunt Violet.

Aunt Violet told her stories of Ponty's childhood: how he used to carry a fish or two in his pockets after spending the afternoon at the river with his fishing rod; how his hair changed color from sandy to auburn to dark brown as he grew; how he ate fried egg sandwiches on white bread every day of his eleventh year.

How his name had made him suffer, made him different, special. "He's a man with real *heart*, Juliette, and don't you forget it."

"I won't," Juliette replied, tearing up.

She told Juliette how she had kept a post office box for Ponty when he was sixteen, so he could mail-order lusty, school-banned novels.

"Old Florence down at the post would get all huffy every time she'd see me pull one of those books out of Ponty's box. I'd rip open the brown paper, standing right there, lookin' dead-on at that scrunched up face of hers and say, 'How's your *Sunday School* teaching was shaping up, Florence?' Laughed all the way home every time!"

Juliette adored Aunt Violet and yearned to tell her all of the secrets of Ponty's sexual charms. One day she blurted out, "Thank you for teaching him the way to…" Juliette ducked her head and blushed, unable to choke out the rest.

"Look me in the eye, dearie," Violet said, pulling Juliette's chin up level. "No woman should ever have to apologize for taking pleasure from the man she loves."

"I *do* love him, Aunt Violet," Juliette said.

"Then that's just that," Violet said, grinning at her.

From then on, the two women sat upstairs each evening in the sticky heat of the screened-in porch or the chill of the autumn rains, wrapped themselves in blankets near the upstairs heating vent when it was snowing, talking about all manner of intimacies.

"Practice on yourself, young lady," Violet would say in her pointed and gravelly voice, puffing on a cigarette, and Juliette would giggle, half-trying to hush her on the porch as neighbors strolled by on the street below.

But each day after work, Juliette would go upstairs into her small room and practice, as instructed by Aunt Violet, as best she could. She was delighted to discover that she was not at all rigid or reserved. No. She was hungry and curious for every variety of private pleasure that her own mother would never, ever have given vent to, let alone have participated in or shared.

—᷍᷍—

One night, sitting on the porch after dinner—it was late spring, and unusually warm—Juliette felt herself drifting off, staring at Aunt Violet with a sadness welling up in her chest.

"At least three times a week then, honey," Violet was saying. "Keeps the desire fresh and the libido in check."

"Aunt Violet," Juliette ventured tentatively. "Don't you ever want to—*you* know—have a man again?"

Violet took a sharp breath in and quickly looked away.

"I mean," Juliette stammered, "you of all people—of all *women*—should have a—"

"I'm too ol—"

"No, you're not!" Juliette sat up straight in her chair and leaned in. "You tell me all the time to stay *interested* in my own desire…"

Violet turned and looked Juliette in the eye. Her face had gone soft, almost vulnerable. "Edward was my third and I loved him best. I had him for a good long time, and when he went, I knew I couldn't stand to have a fourth one die on me. So now I tell tales, and I don't do the act."

"You miss it?" Juliette asked, angling her face in Aunt Violet's direction.

Violet winked at her. "I know how to take care of myself, dearie. And don't think I don't."

―⁂―

By the time Ponty returned three-and-a-half years later, Juliette had had a thorough and unabashed sexual education.

On the day his train arrived home, Juliette waited on the platform with his mother, his father and Aunt Violet, standing near the heaving and braking passenger machine as it screeched to a stop. Ponty came down the steps of the train, shook his father's hand, kissed and hugged his mother, lifted Aunt Violet in the air, and then placed both hands on Juliette's shoulders, as he had on the day he had left. He kissed her tenderly on the lips, and without a word, took her hand and walked her through the crowd until he found a justice of the peace. He married her that day, just as he had promised.

―⁂―

Ponty and Juliette lived with his parents and Aunt Violet for twelve months, and the whole house hummed and buzzed with the electricity of their loving. It was impossible not to feel it. Aunt Violet gloated, as proud as punch—and since it had been her instruction, after all, that created their marital and sexual happiness, Ponty and Juliette felt she was entitled to it. When Juliette became pregnant, Ponty moved them into a little yellow bungalow with a trimmed green lawn a few miles away.

Fatherhood did not scare him. All he had ever wanted was a woman who truly loved him, his own family, and some day, a business with his chosen name—*Ponty Bayswater*—painted on the side of the building.

Ponty became a good husband, a doting but firm father, and after several years, an ample provider. Juliette was an easygoing mother with a delighted and realistic approach to raising her children, an organized homemaker, and active in all manner of secular volunteerism. They were happy.

They had three children, two boys and one girl, and named them, at Ponty's insistence, "normal American names." Terence, Daniel, and their ten-years-later surprise, Ellen, would never have to fight off the "trolls" in their third-grade class because of their names.

When Ellie was two, Ponty started his own insurance firm (farms, crops, heavy equipment), and though not a salesman by nature—it never ceased to amaze him how the introduction of his full name could bring a quick and sometimes fierce revulsion in people–his easy wit drew him many appreciative clients.

After the war, some of his Green Bay neighbors were chagrined enough by the travesty of the holocaust–as was the nation, at least in the places where those horrors were admitted to–that the combination of Ponty's half-Jewish-ness and his Christ-killing first name were rather overlooked. Fewer neighbors balked at his and Juliette's "interracial" marriage, and they were even offered dinner invitations from regular churchgoers.

When the subject of Christ, God or religion came up at one of these din-ners–particularly when it became clear that Juliette and Ponty had no intention of subjecting themselves or their children to doctrines of any stripe–he would say something pithy in a merry tone like, "You all go on ahead and brainwash those kids however you like. We're stayin' out of the pool," or, "The only church or temple we need is the one in our bedroom."

They were tolerated as the "funny" couple, the off-beats in a sea of homog-enized, up-and-coming Wisconsin middle class, the "we-have-friends-who-are-Jewish-so-we-can't-be-anti-semitic" token dinner guests.

Though Juliette's parents, Alice and Joseph, never got over the shock of her marriage and subsequent willingness to have children by Ponty (especially with regard to their lack of a christening), they grudgingly came to enjoy Ponty's wit-ty company on holidays and family birthdays. Joe, Juliette's father, could not form the sounds of Ponty's full name without wrinkling up his face in distaste and disgust, and took to calling him "Son," much to Juliette's delight.

—⁓—

Aunt Violet began to falter the year Ponty turned forty-five, just five months after his father had died, and when his mother Maxine was recovering from long-term pneumonia. Ponty and Juliette moved Aunt Violet in with them without so much as a hiccup of hesitation.

"Ponty, leave me be!" Violet hollered as he lifted her into his paneled Ford station wagon the day he came to get her. "I'm a banged-up old wash-basin of a woman, and I'm gonna kick the bucket as soon as—"

"Hush now!" Ponty interrupted. "If it weren't for you I wouldn't have Ju-liette, or my kids either."

"I'm not going to be of any use!" she protested, flailing her hands at him.

He dropped her in place on the red leather front seat. "You've already been all the use you need to be! Now you're comin' with me, you mouthy old broad, and that's the end of it!"

He kissed her on the cheek. She smiled broadly, wrinkles crackling across her thin face.

When Terence, their oldest, asked, "How come Aunt Violet lives with us and not Grandma?" Ponty answered, "Because Mama doesn't want to, and Aunt Violet cared enough about me to teach me how to love."

When Aunt Violet died two years later, Ponty and Juliette wept bitterly. At the gravesite, Ellie, age nine, turned to Juliette and asked, "Did she teach you how to love, too, Mama?"

Juliette's eyes went wide, and hot tears fell down her cheeks. "She did, my love. She absolutely did."

—⁓—

Several days after Aunt Violet's death, Juliette came upon Ponty hunched over on the stairs of their front porch with his face in his hands. His hair was thinning, and his sides had become a bit fleshy. She touched him lightly on the neck, her fingers barely brushing the suntanned skin at his collar-line.

"You miss her, don't you Pont?" She said, gently lowering herself onto the stair next to him.

He pulled her into his chest and kissed the top of her head. "Terribly, my love," he whispered. "I miss her terribly."

—⁓—

Ponty and Juliette lived another thirty years together "without a hitch," Ponty liked to say. Their desire for each other never diminished, and their friends and children took to calling them "The Romantics."

Even after their children had grown up and moved out, they still kissed in public. They held hands whenever they walked anywhere together, and always when they walked on the green. Juliette sat on his lap at picnics, even at insurance events (he owned the place, after all), and he still asked her to dress up and took her out for cocktails each weekend, like a first date. In bed, they continued to explore and laugh and please each other.

As happy as he was, Ponty thought being called "The Romantics" was hogwash. Aunt Violet would have set them all straight, though, barking out some raspy-voiced remark, like, "Romantic—ha! Euphemism! It's sex between the two of them! They please each other and they both like it—that's what you're seeing!"

Because of Aunt Violet, all of their long life their intimacy had come easily. Ponty could twinkle his eyes at Juliette from across a room, even in the middle of a party, and she would know that he wanted her. Juliette could slide her hands over her hips and lift her breasts ever so slightly at dinner, and he would feel her arousal. Age, wrinkles, spots on the skin—nothing diminished their wanting. They held tightly to each other for more than fifty years.

When Juliette died, Ponty was seventy-six. He grieved slowly and patiently, refusing the company of all except his children and grandchildren. He had had a full life with Juliette, and his gratefulness filled him. Each morning he got down on his knees and talked to her, speaking out loud the things he planned to do that day, the things he felt, how he missed her.

"Your daffodils are coming up again," he'd say, swaying a bit as he spoke, "and you're going to have a lovely patch of strawberries this season."

He dreamed of her; he could feel her near him daily. He felt, now, in her death, that she was next to him always, in an invisible way, something he could not express or explain in words.

After she had been gone for a year, he cleaned out her clothes and personal objects, saving from the Goodwill pile several articles of her cocktail-wear and lingerie that had always aroused him, even after years of being together. He did it alone, crying through the days until the task was done.

He found things she had hidden in small boxes—a note from 1945, when he had returned from the war which read, "P.–My one and only. Love, J." in her handwriting, and his own answer scrawled on the bottom, reading, "Dearest J.–I'll never, ever be away from you again. Your P."

He found a sock filled with trinkets he had bought for her—junk jewelry in chipping bright red plastic that, in a flush to his chest, brought back a hot, sticky night they had made love in the dark behind a lean-to at the county fair.

In her underwear drawer, he found something that caught his breath in his heart—a tiny journal of Juliette's in small, almost illegible scrawl, with notes from Aunt Violet on how to pleasure herself, and how to show him how to do the same for her. He sat with the journal for three days, and when he had finished reading, he went to the cemetery and covered his wife's and his aunt's gravestones with pink lilies and yellow daffodils.

—*m*—

One morning as he was cleaning out the back of their closet, he found a wooden keepsake box full of old photos—his own from years ago, almost forgotten—then lifted them out and set them on the bed.

There was a black-and-white photograph of Juliette as a young woman in a smart, gray, 1940's-style suit with dark piping, and another of her in a see-through black nightgown, well into her years. There was a snapshot of himself on his parent's front porch in 1941 with broad white borders on the Kodak paper, one that he had given her when he left for the war, which she had covered with lipstick prints.

His eyes lighted on a small upside-down snapshot at the bottom of the box with writing on the back that he recognized. George Chesapeake, from his Navy war days, smiled broadly out from the black-and-white, his arms wrapped around Ponty's shoulders from behind, leaning in. Ponty was laughing in the shot, holding a glass of beer and looking up at the camera with joy in his eyes. George's writing on the back read: "Anything you ever need, I'll be there. Love, George."

The script, in George's hand, sent a rush of warmth through his limbs. A split-second of longing, as if something long buried had pushed up from under the earth.

George had come from the Tennessee Valley and was a year younger than Ponty. On their first day aboard ship, George came right up behind him and dumped a bucket of ice water over his head and said, "Welcome to the USS *Alabama*." Ponty howled with laughter, and they quickly became inseparable friends.

Full of wit and both pranksters, their troublemaking was bombastically punished and hugely appreciated as an antidote to perilous combat missions. Finding his chair glued to the floor, or his file cabinets filled with sand, or his desk flipped upside down, their Lt. Commander would scream, "Chesapeake-Bay! You two get in here!"

―~~~―

It took two months to find George, looking through Tennessee phone books at the public library and calling long-distance. When Ponty finally got him on the phone, he said, "George? George Chesapeake?" The hopefulness in his voice surprised him.

"It's me, Ponty." George said warmly. "Long time. You're feeling well?"

"Juliette died, George. Year ago now." Ponty was quiet for a long moment.

"So sorry, Ponty," George said softly. And then, steadily, "Should I come?"

"You're on your own now?" Ponty queried.

George sighed. "Yeah, I am."

Ponty's eyes went watery. "Why don't you come then?"

That night Ponty went into his and Juliette's walk-in closet and stood still for a long time. It had been the right thing to do to clean out her things–surely it had been—but now it made him feel empty.

He had spent many lingering moments in their closet over the years, when he knew his wife was elsewhere, ensconced in the scent of her and surrounded by the femininity of her clothing. He loved fingering the fabrics of her cocktail dresses and the see-through things he had bought for her. He loved to pick up her high heels and even smell the sweet-and-sour scent of her sweat in them after a night out dancing.

He had had an intimate relationship with her things as well as her person: a dress, a blouse, a stocking, or a négligée recounted for him a precious moment of intimacy, his kisses moving down her belly, her hand sliding up his inner thigh, places and positions and nights they had gone at it so hard they made the four-poster move across the floor.

"God, how I miss you," he breathed into one of his now keepsake objects—a sheer red nightgown.

Later, he lay awake in his bed for a long time, closing his eyes and pretending that Juliette was lying next to him. For the entire year since she had died, he had filled her side of the bed with pillows so that if he woke in the night, he would not feel the emptiness of her missing body. He had stuffed in earplugs so he would not long for her early morning laughter, the snippets of songs she used to sing before she opened her eyes.

On this night, though, he left the pillows on the armchair, and reached out into the dark to feel the still-indented place where she used to lie. He listened—all quiet—her voice missing now. It filled him with longing to try to feel her, to remember his hands reaching around her hips in the darkness, to feel her open her body to him easily and automatically, ready for pleasure, even when she was half-asleep.

⸻

The morning George was to arrive, Ponty sat upright in his bedroom armchair, staring at the bed. He tried to remember his time with George—not generally, but in detail. It had taken fifteen months of Navy shenanigans and side-by-side combat for Ponty and George to consummate what had begun as simple camaraderie, but what had grown into a genuine and pressing attraction.

"No," Ponty said out loud. "*Euphemism.* It was more than attraction. I loved the man."

What had made them do it? Was it the daily shelling, the very real possibility of death banging on his heart at every single hour? Was it knowing that he could lose his life at any moment of the day or night and might never love Juliette or anyone else again? Was it Aunt Violet's ability to make him feel that exploration was allowable and human, even between men?

He did not believe that his wife had suffered at his hands. He had given all of his love to her, warmly and with genuine affection. He had had a ferocious passion for her, had made her happy, and been made happy in return. He had not held back and had not held a torch for anyone else—not even George.

He heard Aunt Violet in his head, saying, "Ponty Bayswater, screw that namesake! You are honest and good and true. And you love who you love."

Could he now, at the age of seventy-seven, begin again—*all* over again—and live a completely different life?

When George's cab arrived, his old friend got out of it carrying two small suitcases. He took a long time walking up the path and set them down on one end of the wide porch. George had been stocky and well-built with trimmed blond hair atop a wide-jawed face, punctuated by shimmering green eyes and a sly smile. Now his hair was white and thinned with a bare dome on top, and his once-thick thighs were spindly. But his eyes still shone.

Ponty stood in the doorway watching his old friend, and then propped the screen door and reached out for George's hand. A zapper toy which George had hidden in his palm gave Ponty a zinging shock, and they both bellowed with laughter.

"Chesapeake, you old son-of-a-gun! You're still the same." Ponty moved in to hug him. "Kept that smirk, I see."

George stepped back. "So, we're gonna dive into this pool then, are we?"

"If you want to," Ponty said. His eyes were warm.

George's eyes welled up. He breathed in hard. "Ain't going to be easy now, Ponty," he said, moving back to get a look at his old friend's face. "Both been married. Both have kids—and grandkids."

"Know that, George." Ponty wiped his brow with the back of his hand. "Waddaya say we just do our level best from here on out?"

—⁓—

Ponty moved George into Terence's old room so he had a place to set up his personal things, but they both slept in the master bedroom, in the bed that Ponty had slept in with Juliette until she died. They kept house rather simply—retirement meant plenty of time for reading and making meals and taking in a movie.

The neighbors queried, but all Ponty would say was that an old war buddy had come to stay, joking that his house was a "bachelor pad" now and they would "live like slobs and be damn happy about it." No one pressed him any further.

George was quick to laugh and had a relaxed demeanor, and Ponty found his company joyful and comforting. In bed, they joked around at first to get comfortable—lots of wisecracks about not knowing where to put things, and body parts that seemed to have meandered off their usual path—but very quickly they settled into an easy intimacy, much like the first time they had been lovers on the ship, years before.

More than sex, Ponty found it relaxing to his heart to wake up and find George next to him. Somehow with George with him, Juliette felt *more* present, instead of less. There was love in the house, the way there always had been.

After several months of living with George, Ponty decided to sit each one of his adult children down and tell them about him. He wanted to do it in person, not on the telephone, to help avoid misunderstandings. He drove across the Wisconsin landscape, visiting each of his kids in turn. Terence took it best; Daniel, not so well; and Ellie not well at all.

Daniel asked him if he had ever really loved his mother, and Ellie assumed he'd been a homosexual all his life and had hidden it from his children and his wife.

"You're betraying her!" Ellie yelled over her kitchen table. "It's almost as if—"

"Easy, babe," Ellie's husband James had put a firm hand on her arm to stop her. "It's his life."

Ponty had known what that 'as if' had meant. An accusation—his namesake; Pontius, the betrayer—and almost uttered from his daughter's own lips. It hurt terribly.

"They'll come around," George said on the phone when Ponty called from the road. "Let 'em get over the shock, and then we'll see."

"How'd it go with yours?" Ponty asked, exhausted.

"Same, same." George choked out a laugh. "My daughter wants to know if we'll be wearing leather at Thanksgiving."

"Ah, George," Ponty chuckled. "Always made me laugh. Even in combat."

"This *is* combat," George said. "A fight for our freedom, Ponty."

———

At home, Ponty took George up to the cemetery to visit Juliette's and Aunt Violet's gravesites. He walked across a bright green lawn with flat plaques in metal or stone, placed equidistant and embedded into the uncut grass. Ponty moved from one marker to another, orienting himself and searching for his loved ones. Gray clouds began to move in along the horizon line, and the sun began to set in brightly pink hues behind them.

"Aha! There you are!" he stepped over several metal markers to Juliette's. The plaque read, "Juliette Bayswater, 1921-1997. Devoted Wife and Mother. May the Happiness You Gave Be With You Forever."

George stood back as Ponty bent down low to talk to her, hushed and quiet. After several minutes he got up slowly and began to walk again, searching the markers once more.

"How come you don't visit your folks' sites?" George asked, trailing behind.

"Do. Once a year—watch your feet," Ponty said, marching through the too-tall tuffs of grass toward Aunt Violet's headstone. "Visit the two who loved me the most every month, though."

When he found Aunt Violet's headstone, Ponty gingerly eased himself down on his knees onto the grass and began to whisper again.

"What you sayin', Ponty?" George asked him. "I'd very much like to know."

Ponty turned on his left hip and looked up at George. The wind was lightly blowing, and the sky had turned a beautiful gray and watery blue with gold tinges above the clouds at the sunset line. George's face was backlit from behind, his thin hair sparkling.

"George, I was telling her that I love a man now, after I've fully loved a woman."

George tugged on his right ear lobe. He looked down at Ponty on the grass. "And what'd she say to that?"

Ponty smiled. "She said, 'No man should ever have to apologize for taking pleasure from the man he loves—even if he's already loved a woman.' "

George wrinkled his nose and turned up the corners of his mouth in a sly smile. "That sounds right to me," he said.

—⁓—

George had been right: his and Ponty's children did come around, and by their second Thanksgiving the whole family gathered at the house for the holiday—George's two children and five grandkids, and Ponty's three and eight grandchildren.

The morning after Thanksgiving Day, Ponty sat across the kitchen table from Ellie, his daughter, drinking herbal tea.

"Ow! Damn it!" Ellie said as she queezed the just-boiled bag, burning her fingers on it.

Ponty laughed out loud.

"You're laughing at my pain, Dad?" Ellie said.

He chuckled. "I'm remembering how Aunt Violet used to burn her fingers on her orange pekoe and swear like a sailor. That was just before she told me how to sleep with a man."

"So it's her fault," Ellie smiled and put her fingers on the back of her father's hand.

"You could say that Ellie. You truthfully could." He stared down at his daughter's fingertips touching his own veiny and purplish flesh.

"How did I get so old? Wasn't it just yesterday I got off of a ship and married your mother? And only a week ago, you were a tiny little thing…"

Ellie looked into her father's eyes. "I'm sorry, Dad. For how I acted. I'm glad you have someone now, I really am."

Ponty flushed with warmth, and tears sprang up under his wrinkled eyelids. "I loved your mother with every ounce of breath I had, Ellie. I miss her every day. You know that, don't you?" He turned his hand over and grabbed his daughter's fingers tightly.

"I do, Dad." She leaned over and kissed him on the forehead. "I honestly do."

———

Ponty turned ninety-one the month that he and George celebrated their fourteenth anniversary. His grandson Jake stayed with them all summer long, and Ponty and George sat up every night with him on Violet's favorite old couch after dinner, available, in her old tradition, for questions about love and sex.

"Truth, Jake," Ponty would say, rocking his legs against a wooden chair propped in front of the couch, "That's what we're here to tell you about. No *euphemisms*. Just say it like it is."

"Grandpa…" Jake would begin. "What if the girl wants to sleep with me and another guy too?"

"Hmmm. Well, let's see," Ponty would say, "First off–do you love her? 'Cause if you do, then that's a whole can of worms by itself. I loved your grandmother, and once she was gone, I loved George. Never wanted to share her–or him."

"One at a time, son, I say," George said. "Key to happiness."

Ponty's children and grandkids had done well, and he was proud of them. Ellie's husband was a particularly kind man from Wild Rose named James Krawitzky, a professor at Madison, and they had three lovely kids. Daniel had a partner named Jewel and they ran a gardening business in Fox Point. They never married, had a fiery, redheaded daughter named Alisa, loved each other fiercely. Terence, Ponty's oldest, took over the farm insurance business, made it grow. Terence's wife, Claire Rose, had birthed a baby on a farm out in Omro when she was fifteen, and the young husband had caused the child's death. Ponty knew that it had only been with Terence's kind and patient attentiveness that she had come back to herself. The two had four children, including Jake, Ponty's favorite, and Claire Rose laughed with them, held them close and let them be. *Funny, the things you contribute through your children,* Ponty thought. *A repairing of the world that you never expected, achieved just by their generous presences.*

Their children and grandchildren threw them a small dinner for Ponty's ninety-first birthday. After it was over and he and George had settled into bed for the night, George turned to him and said, "A full life, Mr. Bayswater. You're a lucky dog."

"There's still one thing…" Ponty said, pressing his lips together and rolling over gingerly on his forearm to squint at George.

"What's that, Pont? Skydiving? Twenty-mile marathon? Harem?"

Ponty jabbed at George's side, upsetting his own balance on his arm, then fell onto his pillow.

"Easy there…" George chuckled.

"Nope, not a one of those things," Ponty said, staring at him with a steady gaze, righting himself. Then, in a determined tone: "George, I want to change my name. No more *Pontius*. I'm all through being that man's whipping post. I'm ninety-one, and I want the name I chose on my gravestone."

The next day Ponty and George called a cab and went down to the county clerk's office, stood in line, and asked for the forms. When he had filled out his name, address, and social security number, and when all of the other attendant lines and boxes were filled in, Ponty paused, looked at George, and said, "Here we go. Should've done this a long time ago."

"Never too late—we're still a-kickin'," George said, adopting a John Wayne swagger and faking a gunslinger's shots.

Ponty laughed and then filled out the last two lines. Under "previous name," he scribbled in "Pontius." Under "new name," in delicate print, he wrote, "Ponty." George took out his old, leather-encased camera and took a picture of the page, even though the clerk said that they could have their own copy.

Ponty sent out announcement cards to all of his family members and several friends who were still living. They read: "Pontius no more. It's legal. Love, Ponty."

Three nights later, Ponty awoke shortly after 3:00 am and opened his eyes. He could feel George's heavy breath on his back, and he was sweating, overheated by the too-thick comforter. There, at the end of the bed, was Juliette. She stood, clear as day, in her smart 1940's suit with the dark piping, and she was angry with him.

"Ponty," she said. "I'm waiting, and I don't want to wait." She crossed her arms, and her eyes went wide with irritation.

"Juliette–" he cried out, reaching a hand towards her apologetically. "I'm sorry–I–I…George is–"

"No, no–none of that Ponty Bayswater. George is a good man. But Aunt Violet and I are here–we're waiting for you…"

"Juliette–I–I–"

George sat up and put his open palm on Ponty's back and calmed him, waiting.

"You saw her, then?" George said steadily. He reached for Ponty's left hand and held it tightly.

"Yes. She was right there." Ponty pointed, looking confused.

"Then I guess it's time, Pont," George said solemnly. "If Juliette's a-callin'."

———

Ponty lived another two weeks, began to lose his sight, and had time to say his goodbyes. George helped him make phone calls and write short notes to his children and grandchildren, telling them how much he loved them. He died in George's arms on a spring morning on the same date that he had returned from the war, the same date he had married Juliette.

He awakened after six in the morning that day, turned to George, and with a heavy rasp in his voice said, "No one should ever have to apologize for loving who they love, George, and I love you, just like I loved Juliette."

"Shall we say a little thank you to Aunt Violet?" George said, reaching an arm under Ponty's frail frame.

"You betcha, George–let's," he whispered, and then he closed his eyes. ❧

Asa Krawitzky, you look me in the eye and tell me you're not even gonna tell me what I can and can't wear! It's my damned body!

Asa at the Foundry

I never wanted to work at the foundry. But then Josie got pregnant—not like it happened by accident, I'm not saying that at all. It was *me*, plain and simple. *And* her. Couldn't wait. Didn't want to wait. Like to think I wooed her, us seventeen and all, and in 1959 that was old enough alright, especially in Wild Rose, Wisconsin.

Got her out past Loopis's farm—that dirt road out on Highway K—then took her down to Kopinski's Creek behind the dairy. Took all her clothes off one by one; felt like we were dancing, a big-as-a-cow's-backside yellow moon hanging low in the humid sky, and me moving 'round her white, sticky body peeling off a shoe, a checkered blouse, a yellow cotton skirt, a peach-colored slip. I remember thinking, *how the hell is she wearing that slip in this damnable heat?* It stuck to her like the slick sheen on a baby piglet's slippery belly when it's being born, pearls of sweat beading up on her skin and cementing the skimpy fabric to her body, and for once I loved Wild Rose for its stupid summer heat, never lettin' up on its mugginess, not even at night.

Air was thick, feeling like you were moving in a slow-motion movie picture—and a few minutes later, us just laughing and bellowing, naked as jaybirds.

Josie was lean without being skinny, and she had a fine rear-end—curvy and high-set; full and fleshy—and though I was trained by my mama to look a woman straight in the eye and not at her parts, from the first time I saw Josie I couldn't keep from looking at that round shape of her backside. Once she took off that slip and stood there right in front of me naked and shameless and the way God made her, well, I just had to have her.

I took her right down into the creek, made love to her standing up, water rushing up between our legs, the coolness of it like a yoking invitation to everything that was about to come after.

First time we'd done the act, and boom! Knocked up.

In those days you did what you were supposed to do. My daddy told me, "Son, you get yourself into any trouble, you marry it. You understand?"

Well, that's what I did. I married Josie.

First day on the foundry job I got scared half outa my wits. Yeah, I'd seen farm equipment plenty, and I'd known men who'd got an arm caught up in a combine, trying to pull a jammed-up clump of corn stalks out of the way, and then—like a shot—the arm plucked up and sucked in by those teeth-like, grinding choppers, chewed up like corn stalk residue. Tom Jorgenson lost his left that way, and Avery Olson the same.

But I'd never been in the foundry. I'd just turned eighteen that day, and I'd seen the place a thousand times—it was a few miles down the road in the next town over, in Waupaca—a factory for making cast iron, that's what it was. Somehow, even with all of that smoke and soot blowing out over the nearby farms, I'd never thought about what they were doing in there. Stupid.

First day I walked that floor I felt the heat coming off those boilers—huge iron furnaces in those days, and just walking by nearly singed off my eyebrows. The foundry was making semi-truck brake drums and heavy axles, and some other industrial parts, too—"odds and ends" we called 'em—and it was our job to get 'em in and out of the sand molds. The old-timers—all of them, it seemed—had got one mark or another on 'em. A melted patch of skin across a forearm, a squashed and flattened side of a face, a scarred up and mangled body part. But there wasn't any choice in the matter. Josie was pregnant, and that was that.

My daddy and mama coulda helped us a few years back, but they lost their farm the year we had the blight, both working down at Lundt's Hardware for no money by then, the three of us livin' in a little one-bedroom trailer on Olson's land out next to the Veteran's home. Josie's father was dead, and her Mama was leavin' to go live with her sister in Racine soon as Josie finished high school, so there wasn't any help coming from either side, and we just had to buck up and do it ourselves.

When the baby came, we called him James. I'd been at the foundry by then nearly four months, and the day he was born I cursed my town—a God-forsaken and freezing mid-Wisconsin morning in a place with nothing else to choose from besides dairies and corn and the hellfire of a foundry full of white-hot, boiling metal.

We got us a little apartment on the backside of The Chatterbox Café. Was called something else back then, but I can't remember the old name. Lupin owned it, and our apartment above it, too–changed his name from Lupinski to Lupin for some stupid reason when he bought the place; not like we all didn't know he was Polish, and most of us were, too. The café was the only thing in Wild Rose, really, 'sides a few feed stores, a hardware, a bank, a makeshift hospital and a handful of beat-up taverns sittin' on the edge of Mill Pond on the main street.

It was freezing cold February the day we moved in–close-to-the-ground clouds like a too-low ceiling pressing on my head, making me feel claustrophobic. It was lightly snowing, little flakes landing on my son's bald head, Josie smiling all to get-out, and me wondering how the hell I ever landed where I was standin'.

We walked up a battered wood staircase on the backside of the building– nothing nice about it, rickety slats set over the café's tin garbage cans–leading up to a four-foot-long covered entryway with the overhang sagging a foot too low, blue-speckled tiles made outa tar hanging over the edge. Inside, the place was bare: beat-up wood floors, a dirty, burned-to-hell cast-iron stove that Josie got to scrubbin' the first afternoon, which was the only thing we had for heat in the whole blasted place.

That first minute standing there, Josie with little James in her arms, she just smiled her biggest grin at me and said, "Look at this, Asa!"

"I see it," I said, not very happy about it.

She walked over and gave me a kiss–wet and full, our lips soft, the way I liked to kiss her–the baby squeezed in between us. She wrapped her lean leg around my right ankle, snaking it around me.

She laughed, full and throaty, then whispered in my ear, "It's *ours*, Asa."

———

It happened the day James was set to crawling. He took his fat-bottomed little body and rolled himself over on his belly, then pushed up like a hog on its hocks and took off across the knobbed, battered floor of our place. Something about his chubby little knees sliding across that wood made tears sting in my eyes. I never knew something so simple and beef-witted as that–my baby crawlin' across the floor–could make me so happy.

I got to work that day and was set to my line with a six-foot hook, my arm protectors on–we called 'em "oven mitts"–and I wasn't, God help me, keepin' my mind where it shoulda been. My baby boy was crawling through my heart and the goddamned piece of cast iron–a boiling hot brake drum–just slipped off the hook and fell, clipping me on the right thigh. I never thought I could scream like that. 'Nough to take the whole building down with my hollering and cussing.

They got me to the hospital alright, but here in Wild Rose it wasn't much—a little cement block building with some hardly-older-than-me kid barely graduated from medical school working on me, patching up the burns.

Josie wouldn't come by the hospital 'til the third day. She called from the payphone in town and told the nurse to tell me she wasn't gonna look at my leg 'til she could breathe without wanting to burn the whole damned foundry down. Daddy came, and Mama, but not Josie.

She had little James in her arms when she finally showed up, and as soon as she saw me she started weeping something awful, standing next to the little dresser that sat by my hospital bed, kicking the thick block leg of the thing—*hard*—with her shoe. I was afraid she was gonna drop James, so I reached out for him, pullin' him to my chest, away from my bandaged thigh, and she stood there over the two of us, wipin' her eyes and bawling.

"Oh, Asa," she sputtered. "I gotta get you outa that damnable, *fucked up place*—"

"Shhhhh now, Josie," I said, rocking our baby. "I'm gonna be careful. It'll be alright. You'll see."

They kept me there four more days, dressing and undressing the wound, then dressing and undressing it again, 'til I finally told them all to stuff their goddamn dressings and went home. Felt like a rat in a cage in that place and swore I was never going back.

Learned my lesson, though. A foundry ain't no place to think; no place to drift.

—————

When he was small, our boy's nickname was Jamie, and at five-and-a-half—he woulda wanted me to say the *half* part, even then—he had a swagger about him, like he thought he was as big a man as me. Bossy and demanding and speaking out like he was the opinion-maker of the *Waupaca County Post*. I loved that boy like I never loved anything in my life. He was strong, even then, but with a kind soul, that's what you coulda said about him. Boisterous sometimes and smart as a whip. Josie loved him something awful, too. I knew that boy would never suffer at our hands.

When I'd wake up in the morning and see that patch of skin, melted and scarred all to hell on my right thigh, I knew who it was for.

I had to go back in there, to that iron and metal-chucking hot house, and every time I'd walk through those doors there was no doubt who I was doing it for.

—⁓—

Josie kept her shape. God knows, when I say that to myself now it sounds sort of mean–like I was looking at her like some kind of *thing* and not a person–but I loved her true then (still do), and it was a gift to me that she had that body and kept it up. She made me laugh, even in those early days when we didn't have a penny to shine or spit on, when if we were lucky, we'd put a meatloaf on the table, and there'd be creamed corn out of a can if we weren't.

After James, we wanted to wait and see if we wanted another one, and then we couldn't have another one–something fouled up somewhere–and in those days no one was going to fertility doctors and that sort of thing. You just lived with it as if it was a law that was handed down to you, and you had to make the best of it. So we did.

—⁓—

When James turned ten years old it was 1970, and the world was upside down, even in Wild Rose. There was a rock concert out in some field in Iola, and all the little towns around were overrun by hippie-types for a couple of months after.

We'd gotten a little house by then, a two-bedroom box of a place on Kusel Lake that was covered by fake-brick tiles made outa tar that clung to the side of the house like glued-on flaps, lookin' like bad dark-red wallpaper. The roof was tin and pitched sharply so the snow would slide off in winter, and the place had a front and back door–seemed like a luxury to us–and after a few years, Josie took to building a big deck out the back side, facing the lake. I didn't know she could build (her daddy had taught her before he died), but she had the gift; more than slappin' some wood together, she could *engineer* things.

It was a funny time. At home, Josie was usually in an old pair of OshKosh B'gosh overalls (this was men's farm attire, bought at The Fleet Farm store down the road, long before the company made a fortune makin' cutesy little baby clothes), and she'd be re-tiling the front porch with those big Mexican tiles (nobody had ever seen 'em in Wild Rose; she had to order 'em special), or pulling those nasty tar tiles off the house and hammering clean wood siding in its place. I was working heavy hours just then, the foundry short of men, and when I came home from chucking steel and iron I could barely lift my arms, so there was no arguing or taking over like I thought a man really ought to.

Josie said, "Never mind that *sexist bullshit*, Asa. I can build as well as any man, and you need the rest." I didn't fight her. But I noticed she was talkin' stronger–growing up, you could say–being a woman now and not a girl.

When she'd go out to shop or up to town with me, she'd be wearing short skirts and knee-high boots–it was "the look," she said–and I had nothing to say about it, not just 'cause I liked lookin' at her legs, but because she wouldn't have it. Sometimes she took to wearing a red bandana tied across the top of her head like the hippies did, with big silver hoop earrings and tiny, wire-rimmed sunglasses with blue tints in them perched up on top of her head.

"Asa Krawitzky, you look me in the eye and tell me you're *not even* gonna tell me what I can and can't wear! It's my damned body!" She looked like a picture outa *Life* magazine the day she shouted that at me, some young hippie woman at a rock concert.

"Did I say anything?" I blurted out. She was on her way to do her monthly "big shop," as she called it, probably taking the truck into Waupaca or maybe all the way into Stevens Point to stock up on groceries and stuff.

"You're giving me that *look*, Asa–you know you are!"

"Mama," James piped up. He was whittling–something I'd taught him to do; a good thing for a ten-year-old's concentration–dropping strips of wood onto the kitchen floor. "People are saying you're wearing your skirts too short. That's why Daddy's givin' you the look."

Josie turned to James with fire in her eyes. "Oh yeah? *Which* people?" she blurted out, then whipped her head around to face me. "That's why you're eyeballing me, Asa? *Daddy doesn't like it* that James has to stand up to some stupid little small-minded idiots at school?"

"I am not your *daddy*," I said levelly.

"You're damn-well *not*," Josie said, stomping her feet in her burnished brown suede boots–something she did when she was getting up a full head of steam. "It's a *style*! Nothing more!" She whipped her head around to face James. "Now you listen here, James. Nobody knows nothing in this town! You understand me? Just 'cause your mama looks nice and dresses *fashionable*, and people in this godforsaken place got to have something to harp on, doesn't mean they know anything!"

James' eyes went wide. "I guess…" he stammered.

"For Christ's sake Josie, he's ten years old," I said loudly.

"And that's old enough to know that those blabber-mouths who're babbling away are up to no good." She stepped out from around the kitchen counter in two giant steps, hovering over James. "What're they saying, James?"

James sighed, then looked down at his whittling. "They say, it's *devil's work*, wearing short skirts."

Josie stomped her feet harder. "Oh my god! *Who* says that? Those damned Assemblies-of-God kids? Those Lutheran, pious, stick-up-their-asses preacher's kids?"

"Leave the boy alone, Jose—" I went over and pulled up a chair behind James and leaned on it, standing by him as best I could.

"They got no right to be badmouthing women for their *clothes*, Asa! Jesus!" She flipped her gaze to James. "*Who*?!" she demanded, her hands on her hips.

"The Lutherans," James muttered.

"You see! *There*!" Josie hollered, with a razor-gaze at me. "Small minds, Asa! Mean-spirited, miniscule, small minds trying to make trouble where there isn't any! I can't *breathe* in this town, I swear to God!"

"Alright! Drop it!!" I hollered. "James, your mama gets to wear whatever she wants to wear, and you're gonna stay clear of kids who got nothing better to do than blab out their parents' nastiness, you hear?"

Josie stared at me. "You're still lookin' at me that way, Asa," she said, narrow-eyed and testing me.

"I'm doing nothing of the sort. I'm simply admirin' you."

"You'd better be," she said, breaking into a smile. Then she grabbed her leather bag and headed out the door, the fringe slapping her bare thigh under her skirt.

—◦◦◦—

At the foundry three years later, Old Murph got killed.

We all knew each other in there, and some of the men better than others, just like anyplace you'd work, but Old Murph meant something to me. He was Gavin Murphy's daddy, my best friend in high school and for a time after. Gavin went up to Menomonee to work and then, one winter, fell through the lake ice fishing and died from frostbite. He was out there fishing by himself—stupid; I always told him not to go out alone, but he did it anyway, even in high school. I missed him somethin' terrible. I liked to take special time with Old Murph, his wife gone, and now his son, too—have a beer every once in a while, bring him some soup that Josie made.

There was a rumor spreadin' around the foundry—the men were sayin' it was management trying to instill some doubt, 'cause the insurance people were coming to investigate—that Murph was depressed, that he drank too much, that maybe him getting killed was suicide. It was a nasty rumor, since though Old Murph drank, he never did it on the job, only on Saturday nights down at JR's roadside tavern out toward the little town of King. Yeah, you'd find him in there drinking too much for sure on a Saturday night, but who could blame a guy who'd spent his whole life stoking a metal-burning furnace, losing his wife to some blood disease when he was forty and his son dropping through the ice as if nobody could stick to him. But suicide? I didn't believe it for a second.

That was the year—1973—I started getting itchy and anxious, worryin' for myself and Josie and James, knowin' it coulda been me standing there stoking that oven with gas (it used to be coal), then getting caught in a gas eruption—a bubble in the line, I was guessing—one minute alive-and-kickin', the next burnt to a crisp like a chicken leg left to burn on the barbeque.

Old Murph had always handled those temperature gauges just fine, but the bosses were saying he spiked it, that it wasn't meant to be torqued up that high so quickly, but we all knew that was crap. Murph knew how to handle that burner. He'd done it for twenty-odd years.

I saw it all a few seconds afterward—we all did. I heard the *pop* of the irregular gas surge blowin' up; saw the flash of it. When somethin' happened in that foundry, we all rushed over like rubberneckers at a roadside crash, staring and knowing it was a total crapshoot who was next. Old Murph was unrecognizable. Still to this day I got no words for how mangled he looked and how scared I was.

———

A few years later some of James' buddies were quittin' high school and getting jobs at the foundry—fifteen, sixteen and seventeen they were, and James just comin' up on sixteen. James liked school, but there was pressure to grow up fast in Wild Rose, and nobody thought anybody was gonna need college from where we were all sittin'. James was smart, and he liked school mostly and got good marks every report card, but I was afraid those boys were gonna get to him, so I brought him into the foundry one day and walked him through, talkin' to all the men I worked with. I let him ask them what happened to each of 'em, what injuries and pains and melted skin they'd got hidden under their work-shirts.

It was a hard day for all of us—for me, for James, and for my pals at work who I asked to help James see why he had to go to college. Some of the guys teared up when they were telling him about their time in there, or what they had wanted for a job instead, saying their piece like working at the foundry had been a prison sentence or something.

Amos Jones told him, muttering with his voice breakin' up, "I got my backside whopped good with a set of tongs just come out of the oven ten years ago, and I couldn't do right by my wife after that for three years. Didn't think it was comin' back, and lost all faith in God and everything else, too."

James was kind, and he put his unmarred, sixteen-year-old hand on Amos' chapped, red forearm and said, "Yeah, but it did come back, right? And you did right by her by workin', didn't you?"

Amos got all emotional, tears fillin' up in his lower lids, and then he put his hands on James' shoulders and said, "You listen to me, Jamie-boy. You do whatever you have to do to stay out of this oven. I mean, *whatever* you have to do. Run, steal, catch a train to nowhere. You stay the hell outa here."

—⁓—

It was 1977 when my shift changed and I started leavin' the house at five a.m., getting back about three in the afternoon every day. I hadn't told Josie about the change, just that I had to work some extra hours in the early morning, wanting to surprise her with a little "afternoon delight"–a phrase we stole when we did it in the afternoon from the *Starland Vocal Band's* song that was all over the radio waves that year.

The first afternoon I came home early, she was gone, and I didn't think nothing of it. She came back in the old green Ford pickup she liked to drive (it had been her daddy's before he died, a 1958 rattle-trap thing), with groceries in paper bags, and then made us a nice dinner. James was a junior in high school by then and he was playing basketball about every night, me drivin' over in my burgundy-colored Camaro to the school gym–my first new car ever; my pride and joy–to pick him up after nine.

But then the rest of the week Josie still wasn't home in the afternoons when I got back, and not the week after either. I took to worrying–everybody was talkin' about affairs and "open marriage" and "free love" and all that rot about that time, and I was nervous Josie was indulging. I'd be edgy when she got home, picking at her like I was plucking the feathers off a dead farm chicken held by the feet and dunked in boiling water.

She made me venison one Tuesday night–my favorite; she was a good cook– roasting the parts with apples and apricots and a little brandy.

"You got the apricots wrong," I said to her kinda snippy, staring into my plate. "They're chewy."

"Since *when*, Asa Krawitzky?" She always used my last name when she was flarin' up at me.

"I'm just sayin'," I said, eating it anyway, finishing my last few bites.

"And I see that flavor *faux pas* hasn't kept you from inhaling it," she snorted, leaning into me, big-eyed.

"Since when do you speak *Italian*? And what the hell is a *Fo Paw*?" I bellowed.

"It's *French*, Asa, and I just learned it. It means a *social error*, and you've been a *giant pain in the ass* one all month long. What the hell is wrong with you?"

We'd had sex four or five times that month—I had needed to know she still wanted me—but it had been edgy and intense. I was going back and forth in my head, worrying something awful that she was cheating, then sure she never would, the comin' home in the afternoons and finding her gone makin' the whole thing worse. I knew that standing on the line, worrying at the Foundry was a dumb-ass, idiotic thing to do. But I couldn't stop myself.

"You're changing..." I said.

"So what?" she said directly, but not meanly, aiming her fork at me over our plates. "Everybody changes! You're changing, too! You think we're not going to get *older*, Asa?"

"That's not it...it's just..."

"What?" she said, locking my eyes in a tractor-beam.

I clammed up. Sat there, staring at her, not sayin' a thing.

"What the *hell*, Asa? You've been all bound up for weeks and now you got nothin' to say?"

I just looked at her, dumb.

"Alright, that's it!" She stood up and went to the refrigerator and came back with a bowl full of green grapes, plunked them on the table, then standing back from her chair, picked 'em up one at a time, pulling 'em off their stalks and started throwing 'em at me.

"*That's* for being a grouch!" She threw hard, at my face. "*That's* for being cold!" She aimed for my gut and the grape burst on my T-shirt. "And *that's* for not tellin' me what the hell's the matter!!" She slammed another handful into my body, one after the other, rapid-fire.

"Josie, knock it the hell off!" I shouted, standing up and covering my face.

"Not a chance, Asa! You're gonna damn-well tell me what in God's name is the matter!" She pelted me with six or seven more grapes while she hollered.

"I'm not gonna tell you!" I yelled back, little mashed pellets of lime-green fruit rolling off my body.

"Eaaahhh!" she screamed.

She reached into the bowl to grab another handful, then stepped back and wound up like a baseball pitcher, gaining a little more velocity and winding her arm with some real heft, pelting me with the fruit.

"You–make–me–*in–sane*!" she shouted, each syllable punctuated by another pounding.

The grapes were comin' faster and faster, smashing into me–Josie had an arm on her, I had to give her that–and pretty soon I was laughin', couldn't help myself–covered with green mush, watchin' her face go bright red and her all outa breath, those damned little grapes breakin' and splattering on my jeans, my arms, my T-shirt, my face.

"Okay, okay!" I said, "*Uncle*!! I give up!"

"Good," she said, fire in her eyes, leaning in. "Now *tell* me."

I stood, facing her across the kitchen table, my hands gripping the edges of it, both of us in a stand-off at opposite ends. I blurted it out. "I'm comin' home at three in the afternoon and you're never here and I'm afraid you're havin' an affair…"

"A *what*?" She looked incredulous. "Since when are you here at three?"

"Since last month," I said, a bit shamefaced.

Her face softened, but she still shouted. "Why didn't you tell me?"

"I wanted to surprise you…have a little *Afternoon Delight*…"

"Oh, Asa…" she sighed. "You're so bull-headed half the time…I thought if I told you–"

"Told me *what*?"

She shook her head, then looked at me dead-serious, staring me in the eye. "I'm going back to school. I'm drivin' to Fox Valley Tech every day and I'm studying COBOL."

"What the hell is *that*?!" I erupted, my anger and hurt boiling up all at once.

"It's computers! It'll teach me how to make 'em work!!" She looked down at the boots she was wearing and stomped both of her feet a couple of times, then looked back at me. "I didn't want you to feel bad that I want to learn this stuff! I want a *job*, Asa!!"

I blinked back a few tears, starin' at her. I felt a shudder of relief run through me, all the way down to my toes.

"That's *it*? You're goin' to school?"

"Yeah. That's it! I got a scholarship, Asa. I've been there six weeks."

I started laughin' and cryin' all at once, went over and put my arms around her, then laughed some more. My Josie was going to school. My Josie wanted a job.

She put her head on my chest and said softly, "I shoulda told you, Asa. I'm damn-well gonna get you outa that foundry, I swear to God."

"Jose. I'm alright–" I said, pulling her closer.

"I *will*, Asa," she said into my shirt. "Even if I have to do it all by myself."

—⁓—

When it came out that Josie had been going to school, James got all puffed up about it, saying his mama was the smartest mama in town, that he had to go to college to keep up with her. That was fine by me.

He'd sing it out sometimes when he was doing the supper dishes. "My mama's smarter…stomps her boots and she's *smarrrter…smarrrrrter* than any-body's mama could be…" making up tunes while he washed.

"Just don't go singing that out to the Lutherans, James. They're gonna tell you a woman's place is at home and that a mama going to college is *devil's work*." Josie had her head in a book that night with a bunch of math in it (noth-ing I could decipher, even looking over her shoulder at it dead-on), studyin' and flippin' pages faster than I could comprehend whatever I was looking at in a book even if I liked the topic.

James sang some more, stomping his feet and pounding out a beat with a wooden spoon on a pot. "I ain't listenin' to no Luuuuu…listen to my mama, but not no Luuuu…get no *sat-is-fac-tion* singin' to no Luuuuu-therans…"

I laughed out loud at my little family, the three of us come from nothing at all but me and Josie wanting each other one hot, sticky, humid night out by Kopinski's creek, and here we all were just being ourselves and having a good time of it.

I got all teary, and Josie looked up at me and said, kinda sweet, "What, Asa?"

"I'm lucky, that's all," I said, wiping away a tear.

Josie put her book aside, walked around and slid herself on top of my lap, then kissed me on the mouth.

"Yep. I'm outa here," James said, wiping his hands with a checkered dish-towel. "Basement."

We had set up James on his own floor in the basement, Josie building it out from a cement slabbed and wood-beamed musty place into a red carpeted, paneled room for him–"the cave," we called it–complete with a used pool table and a ping pong set. He had his own TV, too, the old black-and-white with an antennae that we'd bought a few years after we'd had him.

That night in bed, I was looking up at the ceiling, thinking about things.

My hair was startin' to streak grey, above my ears, and though I was still plenty strong, my body was getting fleshier and tired more easily. I was getting older, no doubt. Josie was about to go to Marquette University, in Milwaukee–she'd get her degree in two years–meaning, she'd be gone five days a week, and then drive that damnable truck a couple of hours every Friday and Sunday to get back and forth to see me. Next fall James was going to college, too–however the hell we were paying for it, if he didn't get a scholarship, I didn't know, but I was guessing we'd have to sell my Camaro either way. I was hopin' to all hell that he'd choose Madison or someplace close, so at least I could go down and see him on weekends, and then have Josie close by in Milwaukee, too.

I was feeling emotional, and Josie rolled over to me and said softly, "What do you want, Asa?"

"What do you mean, Jose?" I knew what she meant. I was stalling.

"I mean, for you–what do you *want*?"

I took in a quick breath, felt a sour taste come up in the back of my throat. "Honest?"

"Yeah. Honest," she said.

I breathed in hard. "I don't know. I've been at the foundry so long I've just stopped thinking about it."

"Well, think about it, will you please? It's your turn." She kissed me and turned off the light.

I lay there next to her, staring into the dark, wondering how the hell it could be my turn with my wife in college and my boy about to go, too, and us needing the money, and as if she was reading my mind, Josie rolled over and said, "Asa. There's nothing that can't be done with a little will and a bit of grist from the mill."

—∽∽—

My boy went to UW Madison–got a scholarship for two years, provisional for the third and fourth if he did well, which I knew he would. He wanted to study anthropology.

"That's digging up stuff, right?" I said when he told me. We were standing in front of Bascom Hall on his campus, a big Colonial building with huge columns, and it was snowing. James had got facial hair by then, and he was tall and lean and strong, his mama's body in a man's form. It was about seven o'clock and I looked over and saw the shadow of a beard on his face, and it touched me.

"Yeah, Dad. It's that, and it's looking at social systems through the lens of history and culture. It's a philosophical approach to making peoples' lives better."

"Sounds like you got that definition out of a book."

"I did," James said, grinning at me.

"Well, that sounds fine, James," I said, grinning back. "Just make sure there's someplace you can work that isn't no foundry and I'll be happier than a pig in its own slop. You're a man, and you choose your own way, but I need you to stay out of the ovens. You do that for me, will you?"

"No ovens, no coal mines, no caves or hard labor, okay Dad?"

"Right as rain," I said, wrapping my arm around his shoulder. He smiled at me, big as life, and I was happy he was my son.

<center>~~~</center>

Josie kept askin' me, and I kept dodging her—*what did I want? Wasn't there something else I wanted to do?*

By then, Amos Jones and I had become good friends. The first few years of working near Amos I hadn't really known him much at all, but then, after the day he took James aside and told him to run, steal or do whatever it took to stay out of that damnable foundry, we sorta bonded with each other, and stuck nearby.

I would sit with Amos in the break room, havin' coffee or lunch, trading funny stories with him about our wives, our kids—Amos had two, now grown and gone—and I liked his company. He worked on the other side of foundry floor from me, but about every hour or so, he'd step back from his line and wave at me, lifting his arm in his gear, me waving back at him. I would hang out with Amos and his wife Angela on weeknights when Josie was at Marquette, me lonely as all get-out for her, the two of them takin' pity on me and having me over for supper.

When James came home from school one weekend, Amos took the three of us out to an old, abandoned farm on the north side of town, and tromped us through the fallow fields to where the family had dumped their garbage back in the late 1800's. He handed us each some trowels, forks, and fish-filleting knives, and then headed us down the steep side of a densely wooded hill.

"Here's what you're gonna find, James…" Amos said, kinda giddied-up from bringing us out there.

"We're gonna find *garbage*, right?" I snorted, playing with him.

"Dad, come on…" James said, my son's kindness making me shut up, gettin' the better of me, as it always did.

"Not just *any* garbage, Asa. This here is a Wild Rose *archeological dig*. There's stuff in here that's gonna rattle your cage, James. You'll see."

It was true. We spent the day digging through that farm family's old tossed-away objects, mostly finding tinted turquoise and green glass bottles that had once held everything from medicine to perfume; big wooden bins that were somewhat petrified now, but probably once held flour and sugar and corn; rusted metal tools that looked like nothing we'd ever seen; and then pieces of jewelry that had somehow got dumped in the muck at the bottom of the hill. Amos said the muck preserved 'em, and he was right. I brought home three strands of pearls for Josie—tiny little pearls on thick, stained thread—and had 'em cleaned up as best they could do in the next town over at Courtland Jewelers, and they'd come up peach-and-gold colored, gorgeous.

It was a month later, on a Sunday—overtime, the plant short of bodies that month—when Amos fell down, dropped to the ground under his line. By then everything was automated enough to cool without us digging red-hot parts outa the sand flasks with a hook, balancing the metal by hand, but we still had to shove the stuff along, make sure it wasn't sliding or rattling as it moved down the line. I didn't see it, so I don't know what happened for sure, but I heard the scream, and I just ran.

Amos was under a section of his line that had fallen—God knows how, but the line was tipped enough to figure something had not held—the red-tinged pieces of composite iron brake drums rolled on top of him. I heard him hollering something awful as I was runnin' toward him, but by the time I got there, he was just quiet, in shock. The cement was grey underneath him, making those red-hot parts look like they were on fire, burning into his body. For a split-second Amos' eyes caught my own, then they emptied out, went blank.

I screamed out, "Noooooooo!" and leaped towards him, wanting with all my might to pull him out from under all that metal with my bare hands, but Jeff Kemp jumped me from behind with his full body weight and pulled me back, me screamin' and bellowing and cryin' all at once. It took four hours for the cleanup and the questioning—everyone had to stay when there was "an event," as the management called it—answering questions and saying what you saw or heard or knew.

Josie was home that day; it was four days before she was supposed to graduate. I had been crying a solid four hours since it happened, not being able to control myself, and sure as shit not enough to drive. Kemp said he'd drive me home, and I let him.

Josie came walking out the front door when she saw Jeff's car pull up, and she took one look at me through the windshield, and started crying herself, saying to Jeff, "Jesus *fucking* Christ! Who was it, Jeff?!"

"It was Amos," Jeff hung his head. "He's dead."

"No *fucking* way!" Josie screamed at him. "His *best friend*? Screw that damnable, goddamned place all to *hell*! Oh my God, Asa…" She ran to me, opened the car door, and fell to her knees, cryin' into my lap, me sittin' there in Jeff's passenger seat comatose and staring.

The tears started comin', Josie's head in my lap, and it took another twenty minutes for us to get ourselves outa Jeff's car, all of us weeping like our guts were comin' out of us.

———

Josie didn't want to go to her graduation ceremony, didn't want me to miss Amos's funeral, but I said to hell with that. We were going, come hell or high water.

"I want something to be hopeful for and I ain't gonna be argued with on this," I said.

Josie nodded and said softly, "Okay, Asa–alright then."

James came home and we all three had a private service on our front porch for Amos, saying the good things we remembered about him. Then we planted a few flowers in our front walk for him, and a pine tree shaped like Christmas out past the back deck.

On the drive to Marquette for Josie's graduation, she and James started in on me.

"Dad," James said. "Enough already. Get the hell out of there. There's gotta be something else you can do."

"I've been saying that to your father for years, James!" Josie said, spinning the steering wheel around a sharp bend in the road. I was sitting in the back, James and Josie in front. I was slipping around on the used Dodge station wagon back seat, a bland brown color–"shit brown" Josie called it–my Camaro long gone to pay for James' college expenses.

"I don't want to talk about it right now. Let's just get your mother graduated," I said to James.

Neither of 'em pushed me much then–it was only a few days after Amos died–but on the way home, they started in again.

"Look, you two," I said to my wife and son. By then I was steady enough to take the wheel, and I'd gotten us an hour-and-a-half outa Milwaukee, reeling through the backroads up toward Wild Rose, a gorgeous early June day outside my open window. "I got to make this decision on my own. What to do. I can't just up and quit; I've been there too long." I was afraid, though, truth be told. Without the foundry, what the hell else would I do?

Josie and James gave each other a look and went quiet. After a minute or two, Josie spoke.

"Now Asa, you listen here. I have never once told you what to do—"

"You're kidding me, right?" I blasted back, a little too much blow-back on my reply. "You're always telling me what to do!"

"Dad. That's only if she's telling you to pick up your socks and get the trash out. She's talking about something *bigger*."

Josie chuckled.

"What?" I said, irritated.

"Don't you love it when your twenty-year-old son gives you marital advice…and he's *right*?"

James laughed out loud, and Josie turned and reached across to the back seat where James was sitting and high-fived him with one hand.

I went cold inside, thinking about Amos. Josie looked over at my face, watching the mood pass over me.

"Okay, now, Asa. It's alright." She put her hand on my forearm, and I thought to shake it off, but I didn't. Her touch felt sweet and light, and I needed it just then.

To be known by someone, someone you truly love, I thought. *To have a good son, and to have had a fine friend.* My eyes filled up with tears and I couldn't see for shit–the sunlight in my eyes and the water running down my cheeks–and Josie gently leaned over and took the wheel outa my hands and told me to pull over. We were on a two-lane road with a corn field on one side and soybeans on the other, and I managed to get over to the edge of the road, staying clear of the ditch running alongside. Josie got me out of the driver's seat and slid in to take the wheel. She pulled onto a tractor path, a little dirt road running between the corn rows in the next field down, and stopped.

"Everybody out," she said steadily.

"What the hell, Jose," I said, being ornery.

"Just get out, Dad," James said, coming around to open the door. He grabbed me by the underarm, guiding me out of the car.

We stood there, lookin' at each other for a long while, the three of us, and then Josie spoke.

"Asa, this is what's gonna happen now. You're gonna walk into that godforsaken, man-killing, boiler room of a metal factory and you're gonna say 'I quit!' And you're gonna do it *tomorrow*, Asa, you understand me?" She was speaking calmly and quietly, in a level tone, with none of her usual banterin' and flarin', and though I couldn't remember ever hearing her talk to me that way, I knew she meant business.

She kept on. "I'm gonna get a job, and you're gonna *rest* until you figure out something that you like to do, and you're not gonna set *one foot* in that goddamned place ever again. This right here," she pointed to the ground, "this is the *end* of the road for you in that hot house. James and I are not gonna lose you to that furnace—not now, not ever."

"That's right, Dad," James said. "I'm driving you down there first thing tomorrow. And I'll be standing there with you when you tell 'em."

I did just what my wife and son told me to do. I walked in to old Dubrowski's son, who was managing the place, and told him I was done, that I wasn't comin' back, ever. He didn't say a word, just shook my hand, and then I went out on the line and said my goodbyes. It was hard sayin' so long to those men, especially the old-timers. We'd watched out for each other so many days in that foundry, all of us lookin' out for the new onslaught of high school-aged boys comin' on each year, knowing what was ahead for 'em. I knew I'd see some of 'em—old and young—in town from time to time, or maybe out on the lakes in summer, but I wouldn't be in there with 'em anymore, up to our necks together in boiling cast iron, holding each other up for the sake of our families.

I was feeling pretty stirred up after that, so James took me over to the Waupaca Café and we had four pieces each of their homemade pie for lunch, needin' the comfort of it, and then we brought home a bunch of fried chicken for dinner.

Josie got a job right away in Appleton, working in "industrial engineering," whatever that meant, but she was happy and making good money. I worried sometimes about her workin' around all those men, but she knew how to hold her own, and she was smart as a whip besides, advancing each year or so, getting higher up in her company.

I didn't do much for a good while, just sat out on the back deck watching the pine tree grow that I'd planted for Amos. *Resting*, as Josie said. It rattled me a bit, not feelin' the need to work (seemed like that's what a man ought to do; get up and work at *something* every day), and I'd done it so long I didn't know anything else.

I got a little quiet for a time, mowed the grass in summer, cleaned out the garage in winter, did the shopping, went into town for some pie and coffee, shooting the shit with the old-timers in their beat-up overalls and hand-knit caps and gloves. I learned to cook so Josie would have something to eat for dinner when she came back from work at night, and I found I liked doing it.

I kept thinking, *I spent twenty-one years in that damnable foundry and I'm not dead and I'm not maimed. I can breathe. I can walk. I've got my parts.* But then that's as far as I'd get, ending up in a chair in the backyard, reading some mystery novel or a stupid magazine.

My son became my friend that first year I was at home, him callin' me up long distance from college to tell me what he learned that week. He'd make it simpler for me, for sure, all that anthropology stuff—but without all the fear I'd been living with churned up inside me from working in that furnace, trying to keep from getting maimed or killed in there, I listened better, learned more.

A year after I left the foundry, it occurred to me: I'd become a house husband. It was headin' into 1982 and the world was all hyped up on business and money and "success," and I couldn't of given a good goddamn. I was doing all the things Josie used to do for me and I didn't mind it a bit. Sure, I'd think sometimes I wasn't doin' my part as a husband, that somehow I shoulda been the one doing the earning, but Josie said, "You never mind about all of that crap, Asa. You've done your part, and you deserve a little *reclining.*"

She would come home, drop her briefcase with a *thud* in the hallway and holler, "Asa, honey, *I'm in our house!*"

I'd go to her, kiss her in our mud room by the back door, and she'd reach down to take off her shoes, still kissing me, throwing her business pumps over my head, landing them on the kitchen floor.

We laughed a lot more then, we worried less.

Josie looked over at me one night and said, "Asa Krawitzky, I love you more and better now than the day you knocked me up. You're everything I want."

If that's how she felt about me, well, I knew I could live with everything else; all of the upside-down changes that I never saw comin'.

——⁓——

My life settled kinda peaceful after that—Josie working and pleased with herself about it and me taking care of our house and her.

For a while I tried raising rabbits, selling 'em to a high-end butcher in Appleton. Then I repainted the house—took a year, sandin' and scrapin' and applying paint with a single brush, doing the trim line with an art brush, so it was clear and exact. I worked at the Rec Center in summer, takin' people—mostly older folks—on canoe trips on the Chain of Lakes. But after a while I gave in to lettin' Josie do the earning, me keeping her steady and working well, doing the housework and reading and noticing what it is to be alive every day, loving my family, being what I guess you'd call *happy*.

My son James married a good woman named Ellie Bayswater from Green Bay, stayed on at UW where he's been a professor for years. Three grandkids, all grown now, and me going back and forth to Madison to see 'em, even more than Josie, since I had time on my hands. Ellie's father, Ponty (I always loved that name), had a relationship with an old navy buddy named George after her mother died, lived with him before he passed on himself. Times change, even in Wisconsin, and I've changed with them. Makes me think how if we're lucky in life, the unexpected things that show up recast us for the good, make us more *inclusive*, as my son would say. James' best friend at the university, Maximus, came from Mexico, his wife Nori from Japan. We spend every summer out on Kusel Lake with them, my family and theirs. Josie calls it *chosen family*. I call it looking out for good people, keeping them close.

It was something to watch my grandkids grow up and see their soccer matches and baseball games–to read to 'em and teach 'em things and just be there. I'd sit in the crowd at a track meet or a school play thinking that all of this, my family–birthed and chosen–started from nothing more than me and Josie needin' each other on a sticky, humid, Wild Rose summer night.

—~~—

Josie and I are seventy-seven now, our birthdays two months apart, and all of that foundry nonsense seems like a century ago or more. I was thirty-nine when I left that oven, and I've lived a lot of life since I got outa there, no doubt.

But still, even now, the foundry is at the heart of what I've got to say about my life–it's the story I've got to tell–that what I did for love mattered; that though I wouldn't wish a life in those old-time furnaces on anyone, it did me alright. I learned to stand up for something that mattered to me, to dig in, to be a man. It was the time of my life that made me.

I drive by there now, just to see the look of the place and remind myself what it was like back then. Last Tuesday, I went by as the first shift was lettin' out, and I saw some of James' friends' boys–girls, too now–they're in their twenties, as old as my grandkids–all of 'em heading for their trucks and cars, and I pulled over and watched. They were jokin' and hollerin' to each other like we used to, probably not thinkin' much at all about which of 'em was gonna get worn down, worn out, their bodies accidentally harmed in some awful way in there. Yeah, I know it's different for them now–a lot safer; not nearly so risky as when I was startin' out, the foundry gettin' awards for doing more than their share to protect their workers—but I still felt for 'em.

When I think about those men I worked with back then who did something hard for the people they loved, I know there's a lot to be said for the camaraderie between men who are suffering together; for the families who are propping them up so they can do what they need to do. The men I worked with stood up to support their families as if it was a charge they took up with a sword and a shield, battling the awful forces of hard labor every day of their lives. I don't wish that old foundry life on anyone, man or woman—the worrying, the fear, the dread and the exhaustion wearin' us down to our very bones. But I've come to see it now as something good. I stood up. I loved my wife and son. I gave what I could, with all my bones and flesh, my will and heart and soul. And they loved me back for it, then got me the hell outa there when it was time.

Josie and I celebrated our sixty-first wedding anniversary last month—hard to believe—and I took her down, late, to Kopinski's creek, after dinner at that fancy place Simpson's, in Waupaca. I didn't have it in my head to do it, but then it was all muggy outside, and I felt the humid heat under my arms and between my legs, and it all came rushing back to me, and I pulled the car down highway K and started drivin'.

Josie looked over at me and saw the smile on my face and she didn't say a word—just rolled the windows down and turned off the rattlin' air conditioning, us getting' good and sweaty on the ride over, the sticky humid heat not lettin' up, even at ten o'clock at night.

I took a flashlight outa my glove box and guided her down the path, a half-moon that night, which seemed just right, us well into the used years of our lives. We got down there by the creek—over ninety-five degrees and muggy as all get-out—and I stood there in the half-light peeling her clothes off one by one: a chunky-heeled sandal, a sleeveless cotton blouse, a wrap-around print skirt that I enjoyed untying, a bra, some cornflower blue panties.

When we were both standin' there naked as jaybirds, smiling and giggling at each other, I got us down the sandy bed into the soft dirt of the creek, standing up with the cool water rushin' up between our legs, and we made love just like the first time, kissin' and holdin' each other like there was no tomorrow. ༄

You better watch out, Claire Rose.
That one's got a mean streak.

Claire Rose

The barn won't be warm tonight, and not the house neither. Not for a girl like me who's lost everything. Everything that matters, anyway. Cows been fed, chickens too. Nothin' to do out here but look at the hay piled up too high, waiting for it to fall. Building a fire won't do no good. I been cold these six months now, down to the bone, ever since he done it. Can't get warm no matter what. No use trying after dark.

I got my mama's old lambs-wool on. I was thinkin' that maybe if I was in her clothes, I could feel her some. That she'd come 'round a bit, a spirit up from the dead, and help me stand up, keep me walking. But it ain't no use. Evil is evil and you can't make it go away with an old sweater.

I been staring at it all day long for months now—that hole in the barn floor. Just a square with a hatch of battered wood for a lid, leadin' down from the hayloft to the stone stalls on the ground floor where we keep Daddy's milk cows. The light's on down there for the cows, and it's glowing up through that hole so's all I can see, sittin' on the barn floor, is a bright square of yellow, blarin' up at my eyes. The whole hay-stacked place is pitch-black 'cept for that yellow square, burning a hole in my heart.

When we were kids, me and my big brother Les would crawl up and down the wooden ladder nailed to the wall just underneath that hatch, pitching hay and grain to the cows down below. Les could play with me all day long and never get tired of me. He teased me and chased me and hauled me up in the air, landing me light as a feather. He showed me pretty things—how the mist come up over the pond after sunrise, where a patch of pink flowers was sprouting by the woods where they weren't s'posed to be growin'. He was good to me. That's what I thought men were like.

"Claire Rose, you come on over here and see these pink flowers, now! You won't see a prettier thing come out of the ground ever, and 'specially since nobody planted 'em but God." I'd run over where he was standing, right near the cleared-out place on the edge of the wood, and look with him, those pink flowers standing on tall greens stalks, wild lilies sprouting up outa hay.

"Stick your face in there, Claire Rose. It smells something sweet, I'm telling you." I'd do it and as soon as I bent over he'd start to tickling me, rolling me around on the ground and making me laugh so hard tears would come outa my eyes.

I used to run out to the barn after supper with him, before he grew up and left home, joining up and livin' someplace overseas I never heard of. I'd leave the light on downstairs for the cows, open the hatch, and dare Les to get up high on a stacked bale and jump off in the dark with me, caught by nothin' but a pile of loose hay. Just the glow of that yellow light in the hatch for seeing. We'd be screaming and laughing for an hour before Mama would come out and make us stop it, afraid we'd get hurt. That's what that square of light used to mean to me. Me and my brother Les, laughing 'til we cried. Not now. Not anymore.

The man I had wasn't like Les. He said he wanted me, then one day just started hating me. Felt like it happened overnight. I looked over and saw it in his eyes: hate.

My daddy says that any man that done what he done ought to be locked up forever, or better yet, shot. But he got himself a city lawyer who come out to Omro where our farm was, askin' questions. Then at the trial in Oshkosh, the two of them said what happened was a terrible accident.

But I know. And he knows, too. Don't do no good, though. 1960 in Wisconsin, nobody was listenin' to a skinny farm girl.

Daddy says that's what comes of not gettin' married first. Pain, hurt and bastard babies. He says that man never really loved me at all, that it was all for lust and nothin' else. I can't say that I knew any better. I thought that's what you did when you were with someone. I never seen nobody givin' me lessons on loving a man, and living on a farm in the middle of nowhere, nobody woulda thought I needed telling. Things were how they were.

All I want now is to sit on the edge of that hatch and dangle my feet like I used to, jumpin' ten feet down to the stone floor of the animal stalls like the girl I used to be. But I can't get near it. I just come to stare at it, not believing.

I was fifteen when he first come around—he was seventeen, a boy from school in town named Vance. I guess I was surprised he liked me; nobody else had paid me much notice. I'd always been a skinny thing, hair like straw, big eyes and on the skittish side. Never thought much of myself, but he kept coming by, riding his bicycle six miles to see me. Then he bought a beat-up old car and took to driving me around a bunch, and my daddy said I had a steady man. Daddy looked mad when he said it, but Mama said not to worry, daddies never like their daughters' men.

One night, I was fiddlin' with the light bulbs in the chicken coop and Daddy come up behind me and said, "You better watch out, Claire Rose. That one's got a mean streak." But I didn't believe him. I just saw what I wanted to see.

I liked his smell. He had a smell like corn and oats mixed, kind of dry and fresh, like somebody was about to make something special outa him. He had a mess of dark brown hair; strong, working man's hands; and eyes that could pierce you through with their darkness. I gave him my body, didn't think it was wrong. Thought I loved him. I thought that's what you did with a steady man. You gave him what you had and expected he'd do the same.

After he had me, he always cried a little, like somethin' was breaking in him, and then he'd hold onto me hard like he was tryin' to keep me from getting away. The crying made me uneasy, like I should be seeing something about him I wasn't seeing.

He liked to sit with me outside on the grassy slope in front of the barn. Our barn sat kinda funny, on the side of a hill, the way Wisconsin barns always do—the front side a rise of sloped soil and grass for the flatbed truck that Daddy drove in there to unload hay into the loft; the animals coming on in from the backside to the stone stalls below, like a basement, big sliding wood doors down there that we kept open in warm weather. He'd lean back on that pitched drive in front of the barn and kiss me when Daddy wasn't looking, sayin' that this was the best place on earth, then jump up all of a sudden, runnin' like he got a wild hair and tearing all the way around the barn, hollering how he loved me and he wanted to live here someday. He'd come back 'round and throw his body down on the ground next to me real hard, almost knockin' the wind outa himself. Reminded me of a chicken we had once, kinda touched in the head, used to flap itself in crazy circles every time it was outa the coop, spooking the other birds. I laughed every time though, with the chicken, and him, too.

Mama said he didn't have two dimes to scrape together, and to watch out for a man who come from nothin', wanting in on our farm—we had forty acres, that was a lot around Omro; corn and cows and sometimes pigs—but we were still poor, no matter what it looked like, so I put that stupid idea outa my head. Nobody'd come chasing after me for money.

When the baby was in me everybody acted as though we did somethin' terrible. Looking the other way if they saw me, big as a house and pregnant, walking around in town. Being nasty to my mama in the feed store. But when the baby finally came, all that changed. People said she was a beauty. Took one look at her little smiling pink face, an' they just smiled right back. Mama and Daddy were happy we give 'em a grandchild. Seemed everybody loved her, and all that stuff people were sayin' passed on like a bad windstorm come to a halt.

Except for him. His meanness came when everyone else's went. A girl knows when she's hated, and I knew. But I pretended I didn't. I thought it would go away, that he'd get past it like an old dog that has to get over sharing its attention with a new pup.

I guess I shoulda known that meanness is meanness. But I never seen nobody turn like that, as if the sun froze up in a day and the cold seized up everything.

I been praying to whatever God there is that if I shoulda known better, that He'll let me make it right somehow. I don't know how.

—⁓—

I didn't count on the kind a' love I was gonna feel for my baby girl. When she was in my arms, it was like the whole world could disappear under a pile of crushing soil, and I wouldn't a' cared. I'd look into her bright blue eyes, lettin' her wrap her tiny hands around my fingers, and I could go on staring at her like that for hours, not being bothered by nothin'. Not even him being awful to me.

It was like love came up underneath my skin and warmed me inside and out, all the way through my soul. I never thought nothin' about having a soul 'til I had her. That there was something in me–deep–that could love her so strong it'd go and make my heart burst from all of the feeling rushing through me.

I'd sit in Mama's beat-up rocker on the front porch–the same rockin' chair she rocked me in when I was a tiny thing–and I'd look out off the rise of our farm's hill, holding my baby, rockin' her, staring at her pink cheeks. She liked me to hold her up in the air, raising her from side to side like she was flying. She'd laugh and drool on me as if she'd never know a better thing, ever. I'd see the green fields full a' hay all around us, or the sun setting over the one-lane road comin' up to our farm, and I'd feel more love than I'd ever felt welling up inside me, sittin' there, holding her. More than I'd felt for my brother Les, who

I loved best of all.

My baby girl's little face would flush kinda red when she was wanting some-thin', but even when she was hungry, I could calm her to still by stroking her pretty cheeks with the back of my fingers. It was what Vance used to do to me when he was first tryin' to get me to love him. He'd lay me down in the grass, away from the house on the other side a' the woods, and stroke my cheeks, takin' his sweet time, saying how he never felt nothin' like this before. Like love was welling up inside him. I believed him.

—◦◦◦—

At first it didn't seem like nothin' at all. It was just after the baby–him being in me the first time after, and me all tender inside. But I wanted it. Wanted *him*. He was on me in the upstairs bed and he flipped me over and pinned my right arm behind my back, pulled on it so it stung and pinched. You coulda said it was excitement, a thing men do when they're all riled up after they hav-en't had it for a while. But I squirmed under him and pushed him off, twisting sideways to get a look at his face. Those dark eyes of his were cold.

Daddy'd made him take me down to the justice of the peace, sayin' if he wanted to work the farm and earn like a man, then he better stand up and be one. Why he went along with it, I don't know. I guess he had nothin' and stay-ing was better than nothin'.

Then he heard Daddy talking low one night to Ponty, that man from the farmer's insurance company, about us not making our mortgage. Vance said he was hiding under the stairwell, that's how he heard. I didn't know to believe him or not. That mean look was in his eyes. Then he come upstairs and woke up the baby, yelling at me about who did I think I was, trapping him with a baby and now there's no money. When I didn't say nothin', he went over to the crib and started shaking her–hard. I jumped in the crib and got myself writhed up under him and covered her with my body. My skinny body wrapped around her, my back takin' the blows.

I remember thanking God my daddy built that crib strong, outa oak. Like the crib breaking woulda been the worst thing.

—◦◦◦—

He started yelling at me mean after that. Screamin,' really. He'd do it when Daddy was in the barn with Mama, or up to town at the farm supply or at the A&P.

"You skinny little bitch! You trap me into marryin' you and now you got no money?"

He'd try to slap me or pull my hair when he was like this, and sometimes I would run. But I always tried to keep my body between him and my baby girl—between him and the house if we was outside and she was in there, or between him and the bedroom door if she was sleepin'.

He yelled all kinds of awful things, but I just figured I had to take it. That it was my fault what I done, getting pregnant with him, and takin' this was what I had to do to make up for it.

Sometimes he would goad me. "You got nothin' I want! Nothin'!! You're a skinny, good-for-nothin' rope around my neck!"

I'd back away, watching his hands. I never cried. I just watched, never takin' my eyes off him.

"You gonna duck and bob like that all day? I can break you in *half* if I want to!" His eyes would get wild and crazy-looking then, like a hog that hadn't eaten for weeks, wantin' to rut its full, ornery weight towards you just to get to your flesh.

Most of the time he would blow up and spit all his ugliness out on me, and then he'd peter out and be done with it. Come back later and try to touch me sweet, like nothin' had happened. Reach out to hold my hand or kiss me like he did when he first come 'round; then being all nice with Daddy and Mama. But not always.

When I was pregnant, he'd started slappin' me on my arm or my back—hitting me like he was trying to get me to listen, but harder than he should: harder than a man should ever hit a person with a child in her belly. I shoulda known then.

Truth told, I never should've let Daddy make him marry me. I should've told someone—anyone—what he was doing. Shoulda let him go, told him to get on his way, no matter what people thought.

My baby girl was four months when Vance stopped going into town at all, just hanging out on the farm smokin' his cigarettes out the backside of the chicken coop or sitting on the grassy ramp leadin' up to the barn door, starin' and not showing up at our table for supper.

"Get your stupid farmer food away from me!" he hollered when I came out one night to bring him a plate. He grabbed it and spit on it, then chucked it into the grass.

He was barely pretending with Mama and Daddy, and never touchin' our baby girl, ever, not even when he was in one of his good moods. If she cried at night, he'd hiss at me to make her shut up, whispering low like a growling dog, tryin' not to let Mama and Daddy hear him.

One Tuesday, that insurance man Ponty came back to say he had a way we could keep the farm and not go under, but Daddy said we might be too far gone. Ponty brought his kids out to have a look at our place–they were nice, all three of them, and said the farm was real pretty. "Well-behaved," my mama said. "Raised right, you can tell." She thought the older boy, Terence, took a shine to me, but I didn't pay attention to that kind of thing, me being in the middle of the mess I was in. There are things that come about–split-seconds of them–that you have no idea are gonna come around years later. But that's what happens.

Mama was already looking at me sideways by then anyway, askin' in a low voice what's going on with Vance and me, but she'd blush bright red saying it. Nobody talked 'bout those kind of things. I didn't know what to say, so I just kept quiet.

I tried, but talking to him was like trying to get a Pitbull out of his corner without getting bit, so I let him alone. Why I didn't tell somebody, I don't know. I just kept hopin' things would change.

Sometimes he went up by Lake Winneconne to get drunk at a tavern up there, but only after we were already asleep so he could steal Daddy's keys and take the truck. Those were bad nights.

I'd hear him pull up on the gravel and I'd lock the bedroom door where my baby was sleeping, climb out the window and try to head him off at the back door. Sometimes he'd swing at me, lettin' a punch fly, and I'd duck, thanking God for my good reflexes. Other nights I wasn't so lucky.

The night he done it I didn't see him take the baby with him. It was dark outside, and I was doing the supper dishes. I went upstairs and saw the crib empty–my stomach came up in my throat and I just *ran*. The barn door was closed, but I could see the square of light beaming from the hatch through the broken slats in the wooden door. He was standin' over that hatch, holding her out over the stone floor below, ready to let go.

I screamed a scream I never heard come out of no one before. It sounded like it came from the bowels of a place so awful and full of pain that I couldn't believe it was me screamin'. My arms slammed the weight of the barn door to the side, and I saw him do it. He dropped her with one flash of his cold, hateful eyes.

My mouth went dry, and I felt every bit of warmth that ever was in my body get sucked out, like a sink hole ripped open the inside of me. I heard her cry out below me. Just once. I remember falling down hittin' my chin hard on the wood-beamed barn floor, feeling the blood gushing out of it. My heart went ice-cold, like the pond had broke in winter and I had dropped like a rock to the frozen bottom.

What happened after is nothing I can tell for sure. I sat in the barn for days straight, my daddy says, not eating or drinking nothin'. Going out back to the old outhouse when I had to, refusing to come in the house, then going back in there, sittin' on top of a pile of hay on the cold barn floor. Staring.

Only thing I remember from those days is feeling like my eyes had come out of my head, as if I had suddenly gone blind to everything 'cept the yellow light in that hatch.

My mama died a month later—they said from her diabetes, but I knew it was from a broken heart. All Daddy does now is sit and look at her empty chair at the supper table.

There's a preacher in town who came out a while after we buried my baby girl. He said, "Time will heal." He said I ain't got nothing to feel guilty for, that the guilt ain't mine to carry.

My man didn't go to jail, that's true; but the judge said that he can't get anywhere near me for his whole life. He don't want to I'm sure.

My mama got buried in the cemetery, but my baby girl is buried in the little patch of hay by the woods that my brother Les showed me, that place where three or four pink flowers come up every spring without ever being planted. Where the soil ain't no good for flowers, but they come up anyway. I been looking for those flowers every spring since I was a little girl, and when I find 'em it lifts up my heart.

—⁓⁓—

That preacher come out again a couple of nights ago and sat down next to me with his Bible, right there on the barn floor, on the pile of hay I'd been sittin' on for months.

"It's been six months, now, and it's time to come on outa here," he said, putting a hand on top of my skinny shoulder. "This isn't what God wants for you."

I turned and stared at him, like he was the first thing I saw with my eyes since it happened. I don't know why it was him I saw, and not Daddy, but it was.

"It's time to stand up," he said, offering up his open hand.

I took a long time tryin' to speak. I was cold in my thin cotton dress—a yellow dress with tiny white daisies on it my Mama had made me with her old black Singer machine—and I looked down at my arms and legs all red and pockmarked from sittin' on the poking edges of loose hay for so many days and nights.

My voice broke and cracked. "I can't," I said.

He breathed in hard and looked me in the eye and said, "Yes, you can."

I wanted to reach my hand out—I felt myself reaching—but I stared at him instead, my fingers frozen at my sides and closin' tight around fistfuls of hay. I turned and locked my eyes on that hatch, waiting for him to go. I sat there 'til mornin', never moving.

The barn ain't no different tonight than it was two nights ago when that preacher left, no different than the night before that or the night after. That square of yellow light is still blarin' up at me, cutting me from across the room.

I been sitting on my pile of hay thinking about Les, about the days we spent in here running and laughing, doing our chores, bein' brother and sister. About how love is something you can feel and see, and how it's up to me to see it. How evil is evil, and how I shoulda known it when I seen it, an' known better to run from it.

That yellow light has got to flickerin' all of a sudden, and it's like somebody's searing my skin as it sputters. Bile comes up bitter in my throat, something in me wanting to scream and cry and burst open. It hits me maybe that preacher is right: maybe the only thing I have to do is get up again, and help my daddy get up, too, if he'll let me. Try to live some and find some way to get on in this life if I can.

I'm breathin' hard, and I stand up and walk to the house, my legs wobbly like I'd never used 'em before, like a fawn takin' steps it don't know how to take yet.

I take my daddy's hammer from under the kitchen sink, grab a handful of thick iron nails. I sink them deep in the pocket of my dress and head back outside before Daddy can hear me.

When I come back in the barn that hatch is still blaring, a beam of wicked light shining up like a fire that can't stop torchin' itself, burning and destroying everything in its path.

I walk over to that blaring hole, reach down for the latch on the top of the thing—the square wooden lid on the hatch that I've almost never seen closed my whole life long. I slam it down. The thing smacks the wood, and the sound stings my ears. I stand over it expecting the roof to fall in or something, but nothin' happens.

I take the nails from my pocket and hammer them in, one at a time, banging as hard as I can, my tears coming up fast. I can't stop it—the crying or the hammering—but it's alright with me. I am stoppin' up that hole.

Tears come hotter now and they're stinging like a hailstorm pelting down on my neck and dress, my fingers blistering from the pounding. A moan comes outa me, and it feels like coarse, nubby sandpaper scratchin' across my heart, but I don't care. I'm closing off this thing if it's the last damnable thing I ever do.

I bang those nails until every single one of 'em is slammed in good, pounded and flattened.

———

The wind has got up this morning. I'm standing out in the field near the woods over my baby girl's grave, lookin' back at the house, Daddy's rusty pickup with the paint peelin' off parked out by the back door. The leaves have all gone off their branches, most of 'em crumpled brown against the fallow ground.

My fingers are still swelled up from all that banging, new blisters makin' it hard to hold onto anything. But it doesn't matter. Something has let loose in me and I feel like I can stand up now.

I stayed up the rest of the night cleaning things for Daddy and gettin' ready, the two of us figuring what to do. Leaving him seems like it ain't right, but he said that preacher told him to help me get on my own way, so's maybe I have a chance somewhere away from all this.

I get down on my knees next to the small stone I'd carved for my baby girl, a tiny flower I painted on it, my mama's old suitcase in my left hand. Those pink wildflowers are still growing—a little faded, but it being autumn I don't know why they're still here at all.

Daddy said he'd gone and sold all the boards on the barn to some city people for siding—it'll be down to bare studs in a week—and he's putting the whole place up for sale. Funny somebody wantin' them old beat-up barn boards.

At the cross-road, I start down toward the highway stop, to wait for my bus. I picked a spot on the map, got the money my mama hid for me behind the slats in her closet floorboards, and I'm buying a ticket.

I got my mama's old lambs-wool on again, and I pull it tight to my body, takin' the wind in my face as I walk, but all I'm thinkin' about is those pink flowers, rising up every year, not being asked to, but rising up anyway, no matter what.

When I step up on the bus stairs, I'm shaking, but I get on. I got nothing but a few pieces of clothes and a little money. Nothing but my grief and the preacher's voice in my ear, tellin' me to stand up.

I'm guessin' that if the froze-up ground can melt and grow into something where pink flowers come up year after year without being asked, in a place they're not supposed to grow, then maybe there might be something in this world for me. There just might be. ❧

How the hell did you get a first name like Maximus?
There's a good goddamned story right there for damn-sure!

Maximus

Maximillian was his given name, but his family called him Max-imus, after an old great-grandfather in Mexico who had once, when he was a young man, avoided a gunslinger's challenge by simply dropping his pants in the middle of the dirt street in the tiny town where he lived outside Lake Chapala. A well-to-do young lady in petticoats came out of the local hotel, saw Great-Granddad naked to the shins and, finding herself ten feet away, said brightly to him in Spanish, "Oh, *carino*—my darling, that's a *maximus* appendage you have there." The name stuck, and within a year, the two were married. They had eight children and stayed together for more than sixty years. They were still alive when Maximus was born in 1965, and to hear his mother tell it, Great-Granddad had sauntered into her room after she gave birth, hobbling on his knobbed-stick cane, then pulled Maximus's *panal*—his diaper—aside, took a peek and said, "He'll do as a namesake."

Maximus thought it was a good legacy: profligacy, nobility, way-out-west romance, and of course, the virile reference to his manhood. He loved the name.

How his family ended up in San Francisco, then migrated to a little town in Wisconsin called Mayville, was another legacy story.

When he was ten years old, in 1975, Maximus's mother, Magaly, and father, Mauricio—then just twenty-seven and twenty-eight years old—gave an American café owner named Rocky a few pieces of family jewelry and six years' worth of saved pesos to smuggle them over the border in the back of his dusty brown Pontiac coupe. The thing had a huge trunk with two fake panels in it—one built out low under the level of the car's trunk in the spare tire well, and another in a false-back that was pushed out from the rear seat—with barely enough room for four small people compressed into fetal positions.

They had taken a single bag of clothes for all of them–Mauricio, Magaly, Maximus, and his younger brother Manuel–his mother had a thing about the letter "M"–and had arrived hours later in the little beach town of Long Beach, California.

The café guy, Rocky, was known all over Lake Chapala as *el unico bandido honesto*–the only honest bandit, the man who could get a family across the border illegally in one piece. The guy had an ulterior motive for sure: he made the trip to Chapala a few times a year, trading the border-crossing and the small pittance he got paid by the families for a few years of under-the-table wages to work in his café in Long Beach. Rumor had it Rocky's father-in-law was Mexican and had been sick years ago, so when he smuggled the old man over to care for him, he'd also figured out how to get good labor for his café in exchange for the crossing.

When Rocky packed Maximus and Manuel into their hiding places he said, "I'm not shitting around here. Do not make a sound until I open this trunk in Long Beach. *Lo entiendes?* You got it?" The guy was burly, with a ratty brown beard, a half-bald head, and a spare tire of fat around his middle, but he had an honest-looking face. Soft eyes that looked right at you with no fear. He had drilled holes in the floor of the Pontiac's chassis for air, but it was still terrifying to Maximus, curled deep down inside the secret compartment of the spare tire well with his brother.

"How long?" Maximus asked, in English. His mother had taught him. His parents were already packed into the back panel compartment, bolted-in behind a piece of wood and a fake Naugahyde seat-back, and it sent a pin-pricking sensation of fright through Maximus's brain to open his mouth and speak.

"It's gonna be about five hours 'til we stop, so don't freak out. When we get to the border, they're gonna open up the trunk. I'm gonna have gallons of canned cabbage in bins on top of you–it's heavy. *When you hear them, don't move.* They're not gonna want to pull all that shit out, I can tell you that for damn-sure."

Silent and unmoving, Maximus was so afraid to breathe that he almost passed out in the first few miles on the road.

His brother Manuel was just eight, and he slithered his hand through the dark in the inch-wide space atop their heads, tapped Maximus on the face, then pinched him.

"Maxy," Manuel hissed. "*Respirar.* Breathe. It's okay."

"*Ay*–ouch! Stop!" Maximus hissed back.

Maximus was certain they would all die, that the café owner would leave them on the side of the road in the desert to perish, abandoning the car with his whole family locked in the trunk.

The road noise from inside the belly of the Pontiac was constant, an annoying whine from the tires. When a car behind them would speed up to pass, the high-pitched and insistent exertion of the other engine sounded like someone crying too loudly–a child who couldn't stop wailing. It rang in Maximus's ears.

His brother's head was perched within inches of his, both of their bodies crunched tightly together in the fake panel space. "You're not breathing, *hermano*. Come on! You gotta *be cool*, now." *Be cool* was a phrase Manuel had heard on the American radio station in San Diego that their father had patched into to help them learn English.

"Shut up!" Maximus spit out in English. "*No quiero morir*! I don't want to die because you're *estupido*. Don't talk to me!"

Manuel, his little brother, had always been calmer than Maximus. He could shimmy up the thin trunk of any rosewood tree near their tiny, yellow-painted concrete house in Chapala–no branches on the trees, just the rough bark of the trunk–often climbing up a full story over the rooftops, or even more, depending on the tree's shape, staying as cool as a cucumber.

Maximus couldn't even watch him, let alone climb himself. He was terrified of heights. He'd turn away, looking away from the tree and towards the house–two battered rooms and two tiny closets–pushing his palms to his eyelids. "Get down!" he'd holler as soon as Manuel started climbing.

"Ah, Maxy, I can see the lake for miles!"

"Mama is gonna *golpear* your hide, *hermanito*!"

It never worked. Manuel hummed when he climbed trees, and Maximus would stand listening with his eyes covered until Manuel finally came down and the humming stopped. Maximus never told on him, never told their mother.

Packed in the Pontiac's tire well in the blackness, he felt his little brother blow cool air on his head, lifting Maximus's straight brown hair slightly off his forehead with the movement of breath. The hum and groan of the Pontiac's engine rattled his limbs, but the feeling of Manuel's breath on his forehead felt calming. "Be *coooool*..." his brother said to him, whispering and blowing air.

The sensation was sweet, and Maximus felt a wave of warmth for his brother wash over him, the way the clear heaviness of Lake Chapala enveloped him on a hot summer day when he sat on its sandy bottom and looked up through the water to the sun. He felt covered, suddenly, by his brother's love. Somehow, with Manuel blowing on his forehead, he knew they would be alright.

"They have farms, Maxy, in America. Green places, with corn fields and cows. Places where it snows in winter and there are lakes to swim across in summer."

"Like Lake Chapala?" Maxy whispered.

"Better. Clearer, where the water is cool. Like this." He blew on Maximus' face once more. "You'll see."

—⁓—

Instead of leaving them to die in the desert, Rocky, the café owner and Pontiac driver, set them up in Long Beach in a peeling-paint lime green room with a hotplate and a bathroom, in a neighborhood that was full of Mexican immigrants. The place had two tiny twin beds with worn plaid bedspreads on them, and two thin canvas cots set on blond, wooden slats. The shower was a tin bin of a thing that made banging noises when you stepped inside it or leaned on the walls, but it was indoors, with a thin plastic sheet as a curtain–a revelation to Maximus since in Chapala they had bathed under an elevated spigot outside the back door with only cold water.

Their new neighborhood was littered with closet-sized, south-of-the-border shops, liquor stores, ice cream stands, corner markets with Mexican canned goods.

Rocky gave Maximus's parents jobs in his café–Mauricio was a "busboy" at first, which Maximus could not understand; his father was not a *boy*, after all– and then, when his English became good enough, his father became a waiter. Magaly, his mother, cooked. The place was called *Rocky's Blue Rose Cafe* and served stuff like avocado burgers, three-cheese omelets, corned beef hash. It had a gazebo on the back patio, a favorite breakfast and lunch hang-out for the local university students. There were no blue roses, but there were irises and blue and purple morning glories winding around the crisscrossed gazebo walls. But even though Rocky paid for everything–rent, utilities, even medical care once when Magaly cut her finger in the kitchen and needed stitches–Mauricio and Magaly had more in mind for their family.

"We stay here *poco tiempo*," Maximus's father said to him with a hand on his shoulder one night after they had been in Long Beach a few months. "Then *norte. Vamos.* Then we go, Maxy. This is only a beginning."

For three years, his parents worked for Rocky and picked up side jobs. His father built decks on weekends, sometimes taking Maximus with him to teach him how to build. Four nights a week, he cleaned and power-washed the back end of semi-tractor trailers that had been hauling produce. His mother cut hair in the neighborhood, and on days off from the café, took in sewing alterations from a local dry cleaner.

Maximus got on alright at his elementary school, then later at his middle school, but his brother Manuel fared better, picking up more than a better English vocabulary. By the end of the first year, Manuel had mastered pronunciation and spoke with a regional accent, and he was in love with farm equipment. Other kids had magazine pictures of hot rods and movie stars taped to their walls, but Maximus's brother had tractors, corn fields and tall Wisconsin silos pasted up near his bedside.

"It's *break-fast, hermano*. Not *brefast*," Manuel would correct in between bites of eggs and fried bread cooked on the hotplate in their tiny lime green room. His mother and father left for work by six in the morning, so Maximus had to cook for both of them before school.

"Yeah, no *puedo hablarlo perfectamente*! I can't speak it perfect! It doesn't mean I'm dumb…"

"You can't mix English and Spanish, Maxy. You can't. Speak *American*."

"It means *nada* about me…*Cero*!"

Manuel reached over and twisted Maximus's arm behind his back, until he gave in. "Say it! In *English*!"

"Nada!!" Maximus squealed, trying to untwist his arm. But his brother pinched and corkscrewed his arm tighter.

"Say it, Maxy!"

"Alright, alright, *pinche*! It means *nothing. Nothing*! You happy now?"

"Yes," Manuel grinned, then sat back down to his plate of eggs. Manuel was the stronger one, even though he was two years younger.

"You speak their language, you get along," Manuel said, chewing on his bread. "Otherwise, you don't."

In late April, when his parents had saved just over five thousand dollars–a fortune to them compared to the Mexican pesos they used to earn–they pulled Maximus and Manuel out of the neighborhood schools and took the family to San Francisco. Maximus was thirteen and had started to feel at home in Long Beach, even though the neighborhood had gotten rough and he knew to watch his back whenever he walked alone to the lime-green apartment. They had not said goodbye to Rocky or even told him they were leaving. They packed their clothes and a few pots and pans, bath towels, a pile of maps and then took the local Greyhound bus north. It seemed wrong to Maximus that the man who had helped them leave Mexico should get left without a word.

On the bus, his brother was full of questions. "Mama. Why are we leaving at night? It's midnight."

"*Shhhh. Sueno*. Sleep, Manuel," Magaly said to her son. Manuel drifted right off as soon as they sat down, leaning his cheek against the Greyhound's charcoal-colored fabric headrest, but Maximus was wide awake.

The bus smelled like exhaust fumes, and the minute the metal Greyhound heaved itself into the northbound lane of the 405 freeway, the smell got worse. All at once, Maximus found it hard to breathe, as if the fumes from the bus could force him back into the tight and panicked fetal position he'd been in, packed in the wheel well of Rocky's Pontiac three years before. He began to shake.

"Papa," Maximus whispered to his father, his voice wavering. "Why did we leave and not say goodbye? What's wrong? Why are we running? *Corremos!*" His hands trembled. Maximus sat on one side of the aisle with his father, his mother and brother across the rubber-tuft, foot-wide floor space between the seats opposite.

At the sound of Maximus's frightened voice, his father exchanged a quick glance with his mother.

"Tell him, *mi vida*," his mother said to his father, leaning over the aisle toward her husband. *Mi vida* was always what she called Maximus's father. *My life*. It moved him, even at the age of thirteen.

"Because Mister Rocky is getting arrested…for bringing people here, like us. He wants us to go. He told me, 'You go in the dead of night. Go and don't tell me.' He helped us, Maximus. Someday maybe we help him." His father wrapped an arm around his shoulder, sliding it against the rough gray fabric of the bus seat.

His mother reached long, all the way across the bus aisle, for Maximus's knee and squeezed it, her eyes watery, lips turned down the way they always were when she was about to cry. Maximus took her hand from his knee and kissed it.

———

For nine months in San Francisco, Maximus's parents rented a small, rusted trailer on the backlot of a battered Victorian in the city's Mission district–a run-down and claustrophobic (so Maximus thought) neighborhood full of immigrants from all across Central and South America. There were Mexicans, Guatemalans, Hondurans, Peruvians, Salvadorans, Colombians and more. Every store owner spoke a variant version of Spanish, and though there were occasional and stupid turf wars in high school and on the streets–usually a handful of El Salvadoran punks wanting to fight anybody they could lay their bruised and tattooed fists on—mostly everyone got along in the neighborhood.

Maximus had a favorite purveyor—Alejandro at *El Contadore*, a tiny Peruvian counter spot at nineteenth and Mission, who would, if Maximus would wash dishes for an hour or two, feed him ceviche plated on a bright yellow puree of Peruvian chilies. Sometimes, on a special day, he would fill a bowl of roasted lamb shank for Maximus to take home.

"You take that home to Mama," Alejandro would say. "I saw her yesterday, and she getting *flaca*. Skinny, Maximus. You feed her, you hear me? Make her eat." He'd hand Maximus a large ceramic bowl—thick and rough brown clay, fired someplace locally—and drape a kitchen towel over the food and shove it into his arms. "Go now, before it's cold. *Espantar*—shoo!"

Maximus's mother had gotten a job as a child-care worker—she called it *babysitting*—from seven in the morning to eight at night for a "career couple" on Russian Hill. They were both lawyers and had three small children, and it was true: the work seemed to be wearing his mother out. She looked tired all the time.

Maximus's father got a job as a luggage carrier—called a "busman" by the office bosses; a "grunt" by the staff—at the Sir Francis Drake Hotel on Powell Street off Union Square. The plum job was becoming a *Beefeater*—one of the red-and-gold-corded uniformed men (gold-trimmed epaulets on their shoulders) who greeted hotel guests at the front door, hailed taxis, dumped off the luggage into the busmen's hands, and generally became unofficial mayors of the street scene.

On Tuesday afternoons, the hotel's slow day, Maximus's father would take him to the Drake and let him haul bags for a few hours, earning a small wad of dollar-bill tips under the table, and then send him off to go and spend it. Sometimes they'd bring Manuel, too, who, at age eleven, would pretend to get tired so he could sit in the grand lobby of the Drake and read books on Wisconsin. He was fascinated by farms, silos in particular, and loved to sit on a red velvet chair in a luxurious corner of the lobby with a book in his hands. The Beefeaters stuck their heads in every half hour, along with his father, to check on him.

"This is what you will be, Papa—a *Beefeater!*" Maximus said to his father one day as the rain drizzled down on their heads outside the hotel.

They were carrying seven bags between them, and his father nodded in the direction of Ernie, the nicest of the Beefeaters.

"You will be an Ernie!" Maximus yelled, loud enough for Ernie to hear.

Ernie threw back his head and laughed. "Mauricio–*baby*–you will be the *best* of them! A groovy and *boss* Beef-man! Just wait and see, man!" Ernie had a full, red beard, a pot belly and huge hands. He loved to smoke pot, used the word *boss* to refer to any good thing, and came to work high every day. He always had a kind word for Maximus. "You're good, Maximus–right here–" he'd slam his fist into his chest at heart-level, "right here, in the *ticker*. Like your *daddio*."

"Yes, Papa? You will be a *Beefeater*?" Maximus said, straining with two large black velvet suitcases and a white Samsonite overnight bag under his armpits.

"We will see…" Mauricio said, raising his eyebrows at Ernie and lugging three psychedelic-printed cases and another bright pink one up the lobby stairs.

After working at the hotel, Maximus would wander the few blocks into Chinatown and then through the Financial district, knowing he'd end up having a bowl of soup or some shrimp dumplings from a closet-sized restaurant, or a plate of spaghetti if he felt like walking all the way to North Beach's Italian neighborhood. But each time, after he ate, he'd find himself standing in front of Le Central on Bush Street watching the businessmen, the politicians, and the *San Francisco Chronicle* reporters sauntering out the door after a late afternoon lunch.

Something about the place fascinated him. The weathered brick facade, the glimmering plate glass windows, the white tablecloths glimpsed from the street, the smell of fresh fish sautéing. Even the rounded and scalloped-edged awning over the front door moved him. It felt off-limits. It felt *American*.

One day I will get up the courage, he thought to himself on a graying and fog-enveloped Tuesday, standing in front of Le Central's swinging front doors. The sky was going dark, but the last bit of gray light reflected off the fog. *My father will be a Beefeater, and I will eat at Le Central. A fine fish dinner at a fine table.*

Three beefy men in suits pushed through the restaurant's door, guffawing and high from their meal and their alcohol, and bumped Maximus off to the side of the entrance, landing him against the restaurant's outer wall. They brushed past him as if he wasn't there.

One of the men turned, ten steps into his pace with his cohorts. He had a bald pate and curly, close-cropped grayish-blond hair natted above his ears. "Hey kid," he called out over his shoulder. "Just go the hell *in*, why don't you! They're not gonna bite your ass!"

—⁓—

Maximus went to Mission High School—not the best of the city's schools, but enough of a school to get a decent education, so his papa said.

"You don't worry about no knife-flashing gangs or no *pinches* trying to make you do things you're not supposed to do, you hear me?" his father said the first week after he'd been at the high school. "Keep your head out, Maximus."

"It's 'Keep your head *down*,' Papa," Maximus said.

"You know what I say," Mauricio said, opening his eyes very wide. By then, they were living in a fourth-floor walk-up with two full bedrooms and a back stairway as well as a front door, on an alley two blocks off Dolores Park. "We come to America, to this place, for you. For you and Manuel. You *be good.*"

Later that year—1979—his father paid seventy-five dollars for the social security card of a guy who was dead, and he took a new name.

Arturo Avila was somewhere in heaven, his father said, and now they'd be legal. "Now I get a driver's license as Mr. Avila, then I marry your mama at City Hall, and then we are all legal."

"What about *birth certificates*?" Manuel said. "What about us?" The skin of Manuel's nose pinched when he was angry. By now, he had a polished regional San Francisco accent and had excelled in school—he was smart, and because he had light, creamy-tan skin and a strikingly good-looking face, no one beat him up for being Mexican. When Maximus looked at him, he knew his brother would grow into an exquisite-looking, dark-haired man—statuesque, square-shouldered, and quick-witted. He already had the mysterious-looking eyes of a lover: the high school girls called him "Bedroom Eyes," and he always had a girlfriend. Manuel wanted, more than anything, to be American. He talked incessantly about owning a farm in Wisconsin, wanting to raise corn and cows, having "an empire." He wanted a sign that said *Manuel's Farm* painted on his very own silo.

"I will take care of the papers," Mauricio said to his son. "You don't worry. We will say you were born at home, in Modesto, or someplace near here where Mexicans go."

"*Ay, mi vida*...is it right? I fear the angels come for me at night with this..." Magaly said to Maximus's father. She pointed to her chest. The worry shot across her face, wrinkling it like creases in cream-colored linen.

She was even thinner now and had been being *visited* at night by "spirits." Angels. They told her things.

She caught the concern in Maximus's face, then smiled at him and said, "Do not worry my son. A good life and an angel of a woman is coming for you."

Maximus flushed red, the way he always did when she talked about him finding love, but his concern for her resurfaced in seconds. She seemed worn out in a way he could not understand. Some days it seemed she could barely make it up the stairs to their fourth-floor apartment at the end of the day.

"Mr. Avila is not using his name—*muerte es muerte*—dead is dead, *mi corazon*," his father said to his mother. "He can't do anything with it now, and *we* can…to help our sons…" His tone was as level as a saint's.

Maximus knew that tone. It meant something was wrong. Something *bad*. Maximus held his breath, staring at his mother intently.

The next Tuesday, Maximus went straight to Le Central after working with his father and Ernie at the hotel and stood across the street outside, staring at the front door. He had money. It was four-thirty in the afternoon and a rare sunny day downtown. The beams of light came in at a soft angle off the roofs of the financial district buildings, the fog beginning to creep in in wisps. He dug his hand into his pocket and fingered the rolled bills there. With his body eased against the painted brick building behind him, he closed his eyes, swooning for a moment with the sun on his face—a moment of pure pleasure in the day, leaning in the light. He suddenly saw, like his mother saw things now, a flash of himself, older—twenty-five, maybe—in a white shirt and a tie, a long white apron, walking the length of a high-ceilinged, wood-paneled restaurant with a tray in his hand and chicken-wire tile under his thick-soled black work shoes.

"Hey, kid!" someone yelled from across the street. "Wake up!!"

It was the bald guy with the matted gray hair over his ears. He was yelling at Maximus.

"Yeah—I mean, *yes*? Um…*yes*, sir?"

The man laughed—a robust, truly-amused guffaw. He was barely portly, and his shirt pulled a little at the buttons under his tie, but his suit was expensive: a polished gray fabric with tiny stripes, and a red kerchief in his suit pocket. The man crossed the street and stuck out his hand. "Whatdoyousay we get you *inside* the damn place, alright? You've been standing out here for months. How 'bout I buy you a bowl of French Onion or a shrimp cocktail or something?"

Maximus reeled back a bit as the man pumped his hand.

"What's your name, kid?"

"Maximus. Avila. That's—that's—that's my *last* name. Avila."

"Well, it's a good solid last name. And how the hell did you get a first name like *Maximus*? There's a good goddamned story right there for damn-sure!"

"Who're you?" Maximus said, taking in the man's broad, smiling face. He looked honest enough. He certainly wasn't dangerous.

"Yeah, yeah, let's not worry about who I am right now. You'll find out soon enough." He put his hand around Maximus's back–a midsized paw of a hand with short fingers–and guided him across the street to Le Central's front door. "Come on in, then."

Maximus had waited so long to enter the place–had dreamed of walking in a thousand times–trying to get up the courage to saunter in casually, take the place in, see what it looked like. But within two seconds, entering with the bald guy, the whole place seemed to erupt into a kind of party–middle-aged men and women yelling over at the man; people coming up to shake his hand, patting him on the back; the bartender yelling something in Italian.

"Herb! *Baby!*" A woman in a puffy-shouldered, unbuttoned red blazer said, then leaned her low, scoop-necked breasts into his chest and kissed his cheek, lingering there. "So nice–oh, you are, you are!" she said.

"Get the man a *table*," a customer who clearly knew the man shouted, interrupting and patting him hard on the back. "Herb! What've you got to say for yourself?!" the man bellowed.

Herb reached behind his back and stuffed a five-dollar bill into the maitre d's hand–*five dollars*! Maximus thought–and leaned into the guy. "Sit my friend down, will ya, Dickey?" Then, "I'll be right back," he said to Maximus, trumpeting his voice above the din.

The whole hollering entry onslaught took less than five minutes, but it was a whirlwind–a tornado of energy coming at the man–at Herb–and at Maximus, too. When the maitre d' tried to guide him to a table, Maximus's feet were frozen to the floor. The maitre d's hair was jet black and slicked, like a 1960's movie star, and his voice was as smooth as a TV game show host's. "Right this way, sir. *Sir*–this way…"

Sir, Maximus thought. *The man called me Sir.* The maitre d' nudged Maximus on the forearm, and then guided him to a table for two along the side wall.

"Old Herb's gonna *schmooze* for a while. He'll be back before 1980's over, don't you worry," the maitre d' said, laughing into Maximus's nervous face.

When he could breathe again–things coming at him fast gave him an instant sensation of breathlessness, like the first few minutes of being stuffed into Rocky's old Pontiac, crossing the border–he looked around. Le Central was smaller than it had looked from the outside, and a little less shimmery without the glimmering glass of the windows between him and the room. But it felt *right* to finally be inside it. The small tables were covered with white linens, a pristine white that was smooth to the touch. There were white-tiled floors that made a scraping noise under the rough, wood-backed chairs, and bottles were lined up against a thick-edged walnut bar. A couple of beer taps were built into the bar's surface, and on the wall, a bunch of black-framed photos of–*where*? Was it France?–were closely hung together. It felt like a fancy *tavern*, like the old Chapala places his grandad had taken his family in Mexico when Maximus was still a little boy. But there had been no white tablecloths back there.

Maximus stared at them, the bright smoothness covering his own table, then at each one in the room, at the whiteness. There was something *American* about it. Clean tablecloths. Clean floors. Clean sidewalks. No *dust*. It seemed silly, but it moved him.

Herb plunked himself down next to Maximus and waved Dickey, the maitre d' over. "Get my friend Maximus here a shrimp cocktail and a bowl of French Onion, will ya, Dickey? I'll have the same–a bourbon, too, and…" he looked at Maximus, "a coke, I'm guessing."

Maximus smiled. The busboy–not a *boy*, a man, Maximus noted, by now he knew what the job was–plunked a bowl full of sourdough down on the table with a side of thick butter slices in a ceramic dish, then reached around his back to a side counter and grabbed a couple of glasses of water.

"So we're gonna have to do something about that name, my friend. I'm gonna call you Maxy–okay by you?"

"My brother calls me that. But I like my–"

"Nah, nah, nah. Here in this city, you gotta have a nickname. If your brother calls you Maxy, then Maxy it is. But I know you've got a damned good tale about how you got that name. And I'm a *story* kind of guy. So tell it to me."

Maximus took a breath, then ran his hand atop his head, smoothing his straight brown hair. "It was great-granddad's name–in Chapala. That's outside Guadalajara, in Mexico."

"Yeah, kid. I know where it is."

A guy in a white linen suit with a pale blue tie waved wildly from across the room at Herb. Herb smiled a kind of fake smile and nodded his head at the guy. While white-linen-guy was waving, another man, two tables away leaned out of his chair and hollered sarcastically, "Herby! Well, I never!" then leaned back.

"Who's that?" Maximus whispered.

"The loudmouth?" Herb dropped his white napkin in his lap with a snap of his wrist.

"No, the waving guy." Maximus nodded his head in the man's direction.

"That's Mel Wasserstein. Wrote a book called *How to Be a Dentist without*

Taking it in the Teeth. Every friggin' dentist in America reads the thing when they're setting up their practice. Guy made a fortune."

"The other guy?"

"Lawyer. *Attorney*, they all want to be called now. He's *huge*."

"What about the woman with the...the big...you know..." Maximus curved his shoulders toward his lap, trying to hide his hands, quickly miming big bosoms.

"Hey, hey, now!" Herb laughed when he said it. "Gallery owner. Top of the line. Sells Picassos."

"And they all hang out here? *Why?*"

Herb laughed again, this time a huge bellow. "Did ya hear that Dickey?" Herb yelled across the floor. "Maxy here wants to know why all these muck-ety-mucks hang out in your little *shack*."

He guffawed again, and Maximus turned bright red.

"Aw, don't worry about it, Maxy," Herb cooed. "It's all in good fun here. Hey now, I write for the *Chron*, and I need a good story–a hook, they call it– every damned day. So you tell me, and if it's any good, I buy you a plate of sole after the soup and shrimp. Now, *spill*." Herb shoved a mouthful of bread into his mouth with two whole chunks of butter on it and chewed. His fingers were short and the skin was wrinkled, like a working man's hands.

"You're *Herb Caen?*" Maximus's brother read the column to him every afternoon. Manuel loved the guy. "You're really *him?*" Maximus said, wide-eyed, his eyelashes blinking very quickly.

"Yeah, yeah, but who cares about all that rot." The waiter dropped the bourbon and the Coke on the table and Herb took a gulp of the alcohol. "I wanna hear about you."

Maximus spoke, but he stared, too. "My great-granddad was in a gunfight, middle of a dirt-road town near Chapala, dropped his pants to the ankles–"

"No shit!" Herb stopped chewing.

"Naked to the shins..."

"To stun the guy?"

"Yeah. That's what they say. And a pretty woman came out of the hotel and said, 'You've got a *maximus* appendage there, Carino.' "

"*Carino* is 'darling' or something?"

Maximus nodded. "And they got married. Eight kids. My papa's father's one of them."

"So, how'd you get here?"

Maximus froze up a bit. His father had told him to never tell the details of how they'd arrived–not *ever*. Not even to the woman he would someday marry.

Herb watched Maximus's face. "Hey, you ain't the only one in this room who got here however you could get here. Your parents?"

"My Dad's about to be a *Beefeater* at the Sir Francis Drake down the street." He said nothing about his mother. She was getting thinner and was continually exhausted.

"Well, that's a good beat. *Beefeater*. He'll do well."

"Your mom?" Herb picked a small ice cube out of his drink with his fingers and popped it in his mouth.

"She's–not–I…I think she's *sick*…" Maximus's voice came out haltingly. He was shocked he had said this out loud, having not yet uttered it to anyone. He dropped his head and stared at the tablecloth.

"Say no more, kid," Herb said quietly. "Charlie!" he yelled to a waiter. "Get this boy a plate of Sole, will you now? *Meuniere sauce*! I'll have one, too!"

Herb was charming, Maximus had to admit, and by the end of the meal he started liking the way his nickname sounded coming out of Herb's mouth and vowed to try it out at school. Maxy. It had a nice ring to it.

"Now, give a listen, Maxy. How 'bout we work together a bit, you and me?" Herb said after they ate, picking at his teeth with a wooden toothpick.

"Whaddya mean?" Maximus said, forking the last of the pan-fried fish.

"I grew up in Sacramento–28th and Q Street. Humid enough to make you sweat in the shower in summer and freezing as an ice-fisherman's ass in winter, and the place was bland as milk toast. I was always looking for an angle, like you must be. And angles aren't easy to come by in this city. So, you're, what? Seventeen?"

"Yeah…"

"So, you give me tips from the neighborhood, from the hotel, from the Mission District, from the immigrants trying to make it here first-generation. You tell me tales. Family stuff. Local heroes. Funny stuff you hear or see. I buy you lunch and pay you something. That sound okay?"

"But what if these people don't want anyone knowing how they got here or who they are?"

"Naw. It'll all be first names. *Anonymous*. You get it? Or we can change names or details if it's…you know…*delicate*. You want to? I think you'd be good, kid. You've got *sensitivity*."

"And you'd pay me?"

"Yep."

Maximus reached out and shook Herb's hand. "Okay."

Herb slammed his palm on the table, making Maximus jump. "Alright then! I'll see you here next Tuesday. Four-thirty. Don't be late."

Herb got up, pulled at the edges of his suit jacket, and yelled across the room. "Charlie, put the damned bill on my tab, will you? *This* lunch was worth it!" Then he winked at Maximus and walked out.

———

A day later, Maximus came home to their Mission District apartment to find his father crying into his hands at the kitchen table. It was exactly five in the afternoon, and he had trudged up the stairs with the thick weight of his schoolbooks in his arms, listening to the bells ringing in the Mission's bell tower a few blocks away. He'd expected to open the door to another round of Manuel lobbying his father to move the family to Wisconsin, which is what his brother had been doing every night for weeks until his mother arrived at home. Manuel had got it in his head that a place called Wisconsin Dells was the *proper* place to have a dairy farm, where a family could buy up serious rural acreage, and there were lakes nearby, too.

"Why *not,* papa? Why can't we go?"

"Manuel, *por favor.* Enough! You can go when you're grown. But now, we live *here.*"

"But it's cheaper there."

"There are jobs in the farmland that pay a *Beefeater* like me at a fancy hotel?" my papa would say, exasperated. "You know where these jobs are?"

"No," Manuel would pout.

"I didn't think so."

But when Maximus opened the door and saw his father this night, his feet froze themselves to the kitchen floor and he dropped his books, as if he had turned from flesh to stone. There were tears pouring down his father's face.

"Papa...*what?*" he choked out, rushing to the edge of the table.

His father kept sobbing and did not look up. Manuel stepped in from one of the bedrooms, and said simply, "Mama's going to die. She's at San Francisco General. They can't make her breathe."

Maximus knew, from the neighborhood tales, that General was not the place you wanted to go if you were really sick. People died there—or so the neighbor kids said. But it was where everyone without insurance went; it was the place you went if you weren't rich or employed by some big company.

"She's got lung cancer, that's why she's been so tired," his brother said dourly.

"But she never smoked—*ever!*" Maximus shouted.

His papa winced at the table.

"Maxy...*shhhh!*" Manuel hissed. "They said you can get it like any other thing...it's just where she got it...in her lungs..."

"She can't! She can't just *die!*" Maximus whimpered.

Manuel stepped across the room and grabbed Maximus by the arm. "She's going to, *hermano*, you can see it in her eyes. Now, we're all going to go down there tonight and stand by her bed, and we're going to *be there* with her until it's over, you understand me? So you gotta be strong."

Maximus began to cry, and his father got up from the table and put his arms around him, the two of them dripping tears onto each other's T-shirts. Manuel moved close and wrapped his arms around both of them, and all three stood still, weeping in the middle of the tiny kitchen until the light moved through the window across the pale, linoleum floor and died out above the neighborhood rooflines.

—⁓—

Maximus went to see Herb the next Tuesday. The columnist was sitting with his back to the room in a bright blue suit next to four other middle-aged and heavy-set men, all of them drinking and guffawing. Maximus walked slowly toward him and caught the end of a story—a joke, surely. "...And her dress caught in her heel and ripped from the waist, and she was bare as a jaybird. The preacher said, 'Whoever looks upon that woman will be struck blind!' And the old guy in the front pew said, '*I'll take a chance with my left eye!*' "

The men laughed uproariously, one of them saying, "Herb, you're the only guy I know who can tell a goddamned *clean* joke that's any good..."

Maximus stood behind Herb, silent tears brimming in his lower lids.

Herb turned around, his massive grin melting into limpness as his eyes met Maximus's.

"Whoa, kid. Maxy. What's wrong?" Herb said with genuine concern.

Maximus started to cry. "*Mi madre*...she is in the hospital." He knew he was not "keeping it together" as his brother Manuel told him he must do, but he could not help himself.

The men at the table looked at him solemnly, the laughter caught in their throats. Herb got up, scraping his wooden chair on the tiled floor. He spoke softly. "Okay. It's gonna be okay. Let's you and I take a walk, Maxy, waddayousay?"

The afternoon light was dim, a kind of barely-there sun behind the fog with low gray clouds overhead, and it was chilly and windy—a late April day. Herb pushed Maximus along on the sidewalk with his strong, short-fingered hand centered in the middle of Maximus's back, and it felt comforting walking down Bush Street together, the same way it had felt comforting when his brother Manuel had blown breath on his forehead when they were stuffed in Rocky's car all those years ago.

Funny how things come back to you in a flash. Kind-heartedness.

"Look, kid, I know this seems awful right now—and it *is*—but you're going to be alright, you hear me? You *will* be."

Herb walked them around like that for a good hour, wandering the streets, both of them moving their feet and not talking. Maximus did not know where they were walking—"Union Square," he heard Herb say to him—but all Maximus noticed was the crusted-and-dried chewing gum ground into the dirty sidewalks, the black tar from workmen, the stains from spilled coffee and sodas sticky on the cement. *Funny, I always thought the sidewalks were clean here.* He longed for dust, for dirty, flat stones: to be a boy again, at home outside of Chapala. His mother had been well there.

Finally, Herb hailed a cab, paid the driver, and put Maximus in it.

"Take this kid to General, okay? And take it easy on him with the bat-out-of-hell driving, okay? His mother's in there." He slid Maximus onto the cab's back seat and closed the door, handed the cabbie some bills, then stuck his head into the open window. "You come any day you want, you hear me? I'll buy you lunch, and you talk if you want to." He reached a hand in and patted Maximus's shoulder. "Don't be a stranger."

———

Maximus took to wandering the city after school, first taking the bus to General to see his mother, then afterward, walking and more walking. Something about Herb ambulating him around Bush Street and Union Square that day had wired itself into his legs. He couldn't stop himself. He needed to *move.*

The days when his mother was in better shape—the doctor had given her a month, at the longest, to live—he'd sit with her and hold her hand, let her tell him of her childhood in Chapala, of how she'd met his father, how they fell in love.

"There will be a woman for you, now," she breathed into his ear when he'd arrived the first Tuesday after she'd been admitted. He leaned into her to kiss her cheek. She hissed now more than spoke, her voice trailing faintly in the air, abandoning her with the disease. Maximus pulled a chair close to her bed and pressed his ear near her face to hear her.

"No, Mama. I am too shy," he said back.

"You will s–ss–see, my s–ss–son." Her S's had become difficult for her to pronounce, as if they were vanishing from her mouth before she could form them. "Love is–s–s waiting for you. Like Papa's–ss and mine."

Holding his mother's overly thin hand in the hospital, he remembered accidentally walking in on his parents in bed once, when he was eight years old, in Mexico. He had been sent home early from school because a pipe had flooded the classroom, and he stood, stunned, in the tiny hallway looking at his mother astride his father's body. They were naked–there was no sheet–and she was rocking on him and moaning. He moved from view, around the wall, and then stood for a long time and listened to their love sounds, their words. "Oh, oh, *mi vida*–oh, oh, oh…" his mother moaned. Later, when he told his father what he heard–he did not tell him he *saw*–his father said, "Do not be sorry, *ever*, my son, for making a woman happy. It is a great gift."

It pained him that she would go, would *die*, that his father would not have her that way; that his father's love, his life, *su vida*, would disappear. That they would all lose her, never hearing her soft voice again, waking up one morning to an empty place at the kitchen table.

She'd begun to cough then in her hospital bed, badly, looking at him as if she could read Maximus's thoughts. "Ah, *mi tesoro, agua por favor*."

The coughing didn't stop after she drank, she wasn't able to catch her breath, and Maximus ran to the nurses' station. One large, broad-faced nurse stood up, facing him, and said, "Son, this is how it happens. It's just part of the end." By the time his mother had stopped coughing, Maximus was a wreck.

So, he walked. Simply and purposelessly, he ambled around the city, landing in one dense neighborhood or another, staring and walking and searching, barely registering what passed by his eyes. He felt the cold, the fog misty in its creeping afternoon blanketing of the city, but he saw nothing.

He walked the Avenues, North Beach, Bernal Heights, the whole corridor of neighborhoods along California Street, and then all the way past Glen Park one day with no coat, shivering the entire way in the fog. He did not want views–no sweeping landscapes or splendid city vistas. He wanted people, packed-in with families, yelling across verandas and shouting in tiny neighborhood markets. He wanted women scolding sons, pushing baby carriages, scuttling children from parks. He wanted mothers.

—⁓—

When it seemed his mother had only a few days left, Maximus headed into Japantown, an old neighborhood near the Fillmore District. The hills of Pacific Heights rose to the north, and the fog almost always rested in the valley's chilly streets.

He wandered in and out of all the Japanese shops he could find looking for something–anything–that might cheer his mother, but he found nothing. He walked there every day for hours, finding comfort in the strangeness of the neighborhood: the rice-paper walls of the interior shops; the foreign shapes of the foods–was it *fish?*–often on display in fake-colored orange and yellow plastic in the windows; the unknown and seemingly unknowable language of sharp sounds he heard there. The strangeness made him feel alone, barren, outside of love, and he wanted that feeling.

For several days he had felt like someone was following him, but when he turned to look, no one was there. Once, he noticed a Japanese girl with long black hair falling to her waist, carrying her books twenty steps behind him, but when he turned sharply to catch her gaze, she simply stared at the ground.

Then, on a Monday, he'd gone to see his mother after school, and she'd hoarsely whispered the same thing to him. "Your *carino* is coming…*tu proprio amor*…your own love, my boy…"

As he left, she lifted her hand–a huge effort by then–and waved to him. An hour later, walking the same Japantown block for the sixth time, he felt an icy bolt rush through his whole body, his limbs shot through with it, and he knew she had died.

After the funeral, after the friends and neighbors had gone home–Alejandro from *El Contadore* had brought Peruvian lamb shank for the whole neighborhood and refused to take a dime–Maximus spent some of his money getting a ferocious massage in the Kabuki bathhouse in Japantown. He let a withered Japanese man beat on his back while he cried into a metal bowl that was dropped, clanging, onto the cement floor, three feet under his nose in the face cradle. The man was nonplussed by his sobbing, and Maximus wept bitterly, dripping tears and snot into the bowl from the face cradle above, heaving from his midsection, while the man pounded his grieving musculature.

When he left Japantown that day, he heard, in his head, a whisper as clear as if his mother herself had whispered it in his ear. *An angel comes for you.*

———

Mauricio, his father, had kept working, had not taken time off at all. "We need the money," his papa had insisted. His father had also refused to talk about his mother's death, and it had left a hole—a torn spot in Maximus's heart.

His brother kept up his rat-a-tat, constant conversation about buying a farm in Wisconsin, but with a softer tone. "Now that Mama's gone, we should go, Papa; we should buy *land*, Papa, it's time. It's out there *waiting* for us…"

His father would simply nod, not actually acknowledging him, but moving his head just the same.

The next Tuesday, Maximus skipped work at the hotel and went right to Le Central. It was misting on Bush Street and Maximus leaned into the outside wall of the restaurant's brick, a few steps from the plate glass windows in front of the place, waiting for Herb to arrive.

When Herb showed about fifteen minutes later, Maximus was damp and rumpled, his straight brown hair flattened to his forehead. Herb got out of a cab in a navy blue pinstripe with a yellow handkerchief in his suit pocket, and another tall but disheveled-looking man with a loose tie at his neck and an ill-fitting brown suit trailed him as they got out of the taxi. Herb turned and took a single, laser-beam look at Maximus, wet and leaning against the wall, then said to the man, "Oh, shit, Carl. This is *not* gonna be good. You go on in. I'll catch you another day."

Herb walked to Maximus and pulled him off the brick with one of his strong hands, wrapped an arm around his shoulder and said, "Walk with me, son. I'm taking you to Sam's today."

"She…she…" Maximus began to tear up. "She *died.*"

"Yeah, I guessed as much. At home?"

"At General." Tears came down Maximus's cheeks against his will. He fought them.

They walked a few blocks in silence, the clop-clop of their shoes slapping the wet and drizzled-on pavement.

"Alright now," Herb said. "We're gonna go in here, and you're gonna tell me anything you feel like tellin' me…alright with you?" Herb guided him inside the place—a carved wooden bar, lacquered booths, and again, white tablecloths on all the tables. People shouted out to Herb as they entered, but he hollered, "None of that today, you idiots! We're in *mourning.*"

The place went solemn as a cathedral in an instant, and Maximus felt naked, as if everyone could read his face and see his ripped-open heart, his shaky vulnerability.

"Billy—a couple of bourbons over here quick and two bowls of New England, okay?"

"He's a kid, Herb—" Billy said staidly from across the room, a grim look on his face. Billy wore a long white apron over white pants, and his thinning hair was swept over his pate with something that set it in place.

"I don't care. He just lost his mother. Call it two for me, you got me?"

When they sat, and the bourbon came, Maximus stared at it.

"A strong sip'll do you good," Herb said. "Drink a little."

The alcohol found its way into Maximus's brain quickly, and in a second or two he found he could breathe easier. The soup was better, thick and creamy, and full of tender little clams. And he talked. Just spilled it—the hurt, the loss, the fact that his mother had got him here but was never coming back.

Maximus leaned over the table and whispered. "They put us in a car, in secret compartments, and this guy, Rocky, got us across the border. I'm sure *mi madre y mi padre* paid him nothing, *nada*—it was all they had—but he got us here. And they did it for us. For me and my brother. So we'd have a *chance.*"

"Listen," Herb said after a while. "There's nothing worse than losing someone you love, especially someone who made a huge sacrifice for you."

That week in his column, Herb wrote about Maximus's mother. Not by name, and not with details of their border crossing, but about what it is to sacrifice, to work hard for your kid, to give something meaningful to those you love, and then to die. Maximus was touched.

Every week after that, Maximus walked the neighborhoods looking for stories for Herb. It amazed him how many people had a tale: some story of overcoming, of hardship, of loss or heroism, of inspiration. Their stories helped spread out his grief across the faces of the city, made him feel as if he was not alone anymore.

There was the veteran who came home from Vietnam to find out the house he had built with his father had burned to the ground, with his whole family in it, and then the man rebuilt the house, plank by plank and brick by brick. There was the Polish immigrant family in the Castro who had lost seven babies before their first birthday, and then later adopted triplets. Hopeful stories. A woman who had had a hard time of it as a child—no money, nearly starving—who had built her own business and now had a kitchen-supply store in Chinatown that made a tidy profit each year. The crab fisherman ("Crabber," they called him), who found first love at the age of fifty; the Palestinian and Jewish couple who danced every weekend to Big Band music at Earthquake McGoon's under the Bay Bridge stanchions.

Maximus and Herb took to walking after their weekly meal, Maximus telling Herb about all the people he had met; their stories, their inspirations, losses and loves.

"There's *hope* in your stories, Maxy, I'll give you that," Herb said one sunny Tuesday in October. "You ought to think about writing—you'd be good."

"I never knew how much *hard* stuff people were holding inside…"

"Yep. It's astounding when you add it up."

"I can't figure out how we stand up…how we keep walking."

"Ordinary bravery, Maxy." Herb patted Maximus on the shoulder. "Just ordinary bravery. That's what it takes to keep on living."

—⁓—

Walking in Japantown became Maximus's *in memoriam* to his mother: a living version of a tribute to her, learning about a different culture, the way his mother had taught him about America, the way his brother ensconced himself in books about Wisconsin and farming.

He would see the same Japanese girl walking sometimes, but perhaps she lived in one of the blocks he liked to walk.

A month after Magaly's death, Maximus walked for two hours, in and out of several rice-paper walled shops that sold herbs and dark gnarled roots in wooden bins, then gift shops with lacquered black boxes and Japanese Geisha dolls set on stands, food stores with dozens of incredible-looking items he did not recognize.

He sat down on a bench on the street, and the Japanese girl came and sat next to him. She said nothing, just sat. Maximus said nothing, either. She was lovely—straight black hair to the middle of her back, flat bangs that grazed her delicate eyelashes, eyes that darted quickly away from his, and hands that seemed to flutter around her body as if they were birds longing to alight on a perch.

She leaned in and said, "I'm Nori. I've been walking with you."

Maximus startled. "*Walking* with me? What do you mean?"

"I walk, too," she said simply. "I see you. I walk in front of you, around you, behind you. *You* don't walk just to walk," she said smiling.

He turned to her. He felt as if someone had sliced into his solitary thoughts and looted them. "You've been *following* me?"

"Well, you don't *own* the street, you know." She crossed her arms over her body and looked boldly into his eyes. "I thought you would be nicer."

"I *am* nice. It's…today is…is…it's a month since…" his eyes teared up.

"Aha. You lost someone. That is why you walk." She looked pleased with herself.

"My mother," Maximus said.

"I'm sorry for you." Nori dropped her head. "I lost my brother. I loved him." Her voice wavered.

Maximus spun his head towards her and took her in. *You will meet an angel,* he heard in his head again. His mother inside him, speaking.

—⁓—

It took three months of walking neighborhoods together after school before Maximus was ready to call Nori his girlfriend, a month more before he knew he loved her.

Herb would ask him each Tuesday, "How's it going with your girl?"

"I don't want to talk about it," Maximus would say, reaching for a hunk of sourdough.

"Kiss her already, will you? You gotta let her know how you feel…"

"I'm *seventeen,*" Maxy said.

"All the better," Herb said, winking at him.

One Tuesday afternoon, Herb had taken both Maximus and Nori to lunch at Jackson-Fillmore Trattoria and then left to let the young couple be alone. The two hiked through Pacific Heights (block after block of steep view-vistas overlooking Alcatraz and the Bay) as the sun was setting. They stopped in the Park up from Steiner Street and sat on a green bench with peeling paint. Maximus gently reached over and put his arm around Nori, pulling her near him.

She tilted her head sideways and looked at him, her face close. "Nori means *tradition*…did you know that Maxy? My name?" she whispered. "And I will break all of mine to be with you, Maximus Avila. I already love you."

He kissed her then, leaned in and pressed his soft brown lips to her delicate pink ones. She lifted her face up and opened her mouth to him, and he felt a rush of fullness in his heart like a river, like an *ocean,* welling up inside him as if he had been swept up into a whirlpool of twirling and floating currents. He was not afraid. It was a sweetness he knew, somehow, not from himself, but from watching his mother and father.

"*Mi corazon…mi tesoro…*" he said to her in Spanish, kissing her. *My heart. My treasure.*

—⁓—

When they made love for the first time, Maximus felt as if his mother was floating in the doorway, smiling. It was an odd sensation: *I am touching a naked woman and my mother is here.* But somehow it felt right, as if Magaly were blessing them.

He had brought Nori to the fourth floor, the two of them alone in his family's apartment, then led her by her tender fingertips to his single bed in the room he shared with Manuel.

She pointed to a bed. "This is your bed? We wouldn't want to *do it* on Manuel's bed, now would we?" She winked at him, smiling with a wicked little grin, and laughed lightly.

She peeled her clothes off piece by piece, standing, while he sat on the edge of his bed watching–removing her flat cream-colored shoes, her tan sweater, her white knee-length dress, a wine-colored lace bra and matching panties.

She had asked him the day before. "Red, black or white? What do you like? Maybe something else?"

"What are we talking about?"

"*Underwear*, Maxy. What do you like?" She was older than him–eighteen.

He'd gone red in the face, and she had laughed at him.

"I like you," he said, "in anything."

"Watch out for shy girls," Manuel had told him. "There's a fire pit inside them." His brother had taught Maximus how to use a condom, how to slow down for Nori, how to practice beforehand.

When he touched her naked body, bright sparks went off in his brain. The softness of her skin was like lying down in a field of velvet-leaved flowers. His heart raced, his need pulsed. When she sat astride him and pressed against him unapologetically, he lay back, surrendering to the bed, and to her, his arms over his head and staring into her eyes.

She was framed by the brown tones of the wooden-knobbed dresser behind his sightline across the room, and it touched him–the gorgeous languidness of her form set off by the rudimentary wooden object.

"There will be no one else for me, Nori," Maximus whispered, staring at her delicate and undulating body. "There will be you and me, only. Like my mother and father. *Mi vida.*"

—⁂—

Nori's family had not approved; they bullied her about falling in love with a young man who was not Japanese, shamed her. In the end, they tried to bar her from leaving the house. Maximus's father said she could live with them, and she moved in on a foggy, gray-and-drizzling February morning. His father's progressiveness, letting Nori stay with them, surprised him–Mauricio had been raised Catholic, after all–and Maximus was grateful to him, loved him more for it.

Manuel, of course, said it was the perfect time to buy a farm, to move to the Midwest, all of them. It was like a drum he beat, over and over again. *Relentless,* was all Maximus could think, but he knew, too, that another loss was coming, tick-tick-tocking in his direction: the day his beautiful brother would pack up and move to Wisconsin, away from him.

While Maximus and Nori were both at San Francisco State, they married. A simple affair at Alejandro's Peruvian place, and a ceremony by a Unitarian minister. His father loved Nori, grieved heavily when they moved into their own apartment, and his brother Manuel, with his string of *want-me, want-me* girlfriends, loved her too. Herb became a regular in their new kitchen, and a fine friendship blossomed between Herb and Maximus's father. A comfort, Maximus knew, to his papa, and a thrill for his brother Manuel.

Just after Maximus and Nori married, Manuel got a small scholarship from the Caterpillar Company to attend University of Wisconsin, River Falls, off I-94, to study agriculture. By autumn he was gone. He got what he wanted, was living in farm country and on his way. The hurt of him gone stuck like needles poked in Maximus's head which twisted and stung each time his brother called long distance.

At Herb's insistence, Maximus studied Journalism and Creative Writing and got his degree. Nori got hers in Fine Art and planned to teach. He worked at the Tadich Grill on California Street as a waiter for the years that he studied–an old-time seafood house with high ceilings, polished wood booths, an endlessly long counter and black-and-white chicken wire tile on the floor. When he worked, he wore big black work shoes and a long white apron tied in front of his pants–the very vision of himself he'd had when he was sixteen, leaning against the bricks across from Le Central. He would love the old, downtown eateries of his youth, the places that Herb had introduced him to, all his life–Le Central, Sam's, Tadich's–and would always hold them dear. They were the unlikely places where he had discovered that no matter where he had been born, he could find new places where he was befriended, where he *belonged.*

When his brother graduated UW, their father left the Mission District apartment in San Francisco and went to live in Wisconsin, where Manuel was starting his own dairy. They pooled their saved cash and bought a beat-up place outside Mayville, in Dodge County, east of the Horicon Wildlife Refuge. Then Maximus got invited to do his Master's in Literature at UW Madison, among other places, but the choice made him waver. He loved San Francisco. It felt like home.

"What do you *want?*" Herb said over glasses of bourbon in Maximus' and Nori's kitchen. The fog had rolled in, it was late afternoon, and a slice of mist was seeping through the cracked-open Victorian window.

Maximus leaned in, his elbow sliding off the kitchen table. "I want to feel like we're in the right place, like we're home. And San Francisco–"

"So you'll make a new home, in Wisconsin," Herb said, winking at him.

Maximus's brow furrowed. "Yes, but–"

"Don't worry so much, Maxy. C'mon! You've got an adoring wife who wants to go, a brother and a father who are already there. For Christ's sake, you know you're going!"

"I just–" Maximus waved his hand, letting it trail off to the right of his newly broadening body.

"If you hate it, you can come back. There's no law that says–"

"I'm gonna miss you, Herb. That's all."

They clinked glasses, toasted each other in the air.

"Well, hell, Maxy," Herb said, his eyes misting up a bit. "That goes without saying."

—◦◦◦—

He and Nori did go, buying a tidy house for next to nothing in Monona, across the lake from the University, then fixed it up into a lovely family home. Nori finished her Master's, and Maximus became a professor of literature at UW. They had two beautiful girls by the time he was thirty-one, and he came to love the Wisconsin landscape, the way it supported and held his family; the way the land seemed to fill itself with the smells of the soil as it grew things, regenerating itself each year into another new season.

He had a good friend, too, an anthropology professor at UW named James Krawitsky, whose parents, Asa and Josie, lived up near Wild Rose. James' wife Ellie got close with Nori, and the two families took summer vacations together in rented cottages on the lakes near James' parents' house. It was a good life.

On weekends, unless there was a blizzard, they often made the drive up to Mayville to see his father and his brother's new family. Manuel's wife, Astoria, was a warm and funny woman who'd come from the Netherlands, and Maximus adored their little boy, Paolo. His brother's farm–no surprise–was successful, but Manuel ended up hiring a manager to work it and instead sold heavy equipment for John Deere, making a killing and travelling all over the state. His brother made friends easily, like when they were kids, often smoking cigars on his porch with a guy named Ponty Bayswater who insured his farm, or going out riding with a client or his farm hands. He was as happy as Maximus had ever seen him.

Herb wrote letters, and so did Maximus. Every once in a while Herb would call long-distance.

"How's it hangin', Maxy? You President of the university yet?"

Herb's voice was full of mirth, and the sound of it brought tears to Maximus's eyes. "No, no, Herb. Just a lowly Lit professor."

Then, after all the news was shared, "You sound good, Maxy. You sound *happy.*"

"Only thing that's missing is you, Herb. Walking around San Francisco, sitting down over a bowl of New England with a bourbon."

"Amen, my friend. Nobody found heartstring stories like you, Maxy. Miss you every day."

Nori and Maximus stayed close to Herb until he died on a gray day in early February in 1997. When they flew to San Francisco for the funeral, Maximus decided to try to find Rocky, the guy who had gotten his family across the border. He knew his life was good: he was full-time at UW, he'd finished his third book of poetry, he had a loving wife in Nori and beautiful kids. He wanted the man to know.

Rocky DiRetzo, it turned out, was alive and well and living in a little working-class town near Monterey, a couple of hours by car from San Francisco.

On the day they were to meet, Maximus gathered photographs he had brought from home–Magaly and Mauricio, his parents, at a birthday party in the trailer in San Francisco when they had first arrived; one from the day his parents married at City Hall as the "Avilas." He brought photos of Nori, and their children; of Manuel as a boy, and as a man, on his farm; a good handful of himself seated at Le Central or Sam's or Tadich's with Herb. He had stuffed them all into a large envelope, along with the *Chronicle* columns of Herb's for which he had contributed a line or two, a story or a reference.

Rocky was waiting at a tiny table in the little café on the water's edge in Monterey, where they had agreed to meet. The wind was blowing outside, whipping in gusts. It was gray and moist, and Maximus–fuller around the waist now, the way Rocky had been when he had stuffed Maximus's family into the back of his Pontiac–smiled as he made eye contact with the man. Maximus would have known him anywhere: the gruff voice gruffer now, his arms spindly, but the same honest face. *El unico bandido honesto.*

"Well, *motherfucker,*" Rocky said. "Look at you, all goddamned *respectable.* You were just a scared, whiny kid when I met you." He laughed robustly.

They sat for a long time, talking over the years of their lives, Maximus's family's years in San Francisco, and now Wisconsin.

"They put me in for three years, I got out in two," Rocky said about his jail time. "My café got bought by some woman, turned it into a black-and-white jukebox joint, failed in a year. I got set-up here in food distribution afterward, and I hire every Mexican I can, just to spite them." He grinned. "*Legal,* though. I knew, after that, I wasn't ever going back to the *joint.*"

Maximus sighed. "I wanted you to know what you gave to us, to my family. You helped us. I wouldn't have my life, my wife, my family…would've never had my education."

"And you would've never hung out with friggin' Herb Caen, for God's sake! That's *too much!*" Rocky picked up a couple of photos of Herb and Maximus and chuckled, shaking his head. "You do stuff for whatever-the-hell reason at the time, and it changes things…who the hell knew?"

"I want to thank you," Maximus said, tearing up and reaching to pat Rocky on the arm. "What you did was brave. If you ever need anything, you call me and my wife. I'm at the University, in Madison. Find me if ever…" He passed Rocky a card with his name and number on it.

"Aw, that's not necessary…*really.* I'm alright. I'm not anything special."

"You *are.* We all are. Herb used to say it."

"What'd he say?"

"We've all got to stand up for each other. He had a phrase—"

"What was that?"

Maximus thought for a moment, trying to recall. "*Ordinary bravery*—that was it. We've all gotta have it to live."

"Well, then," Rocky said, and Maximus saw that his eyes were misting.

When they parted, Maximus hugged Rocky, and then went over and stood by the cement pier on the backside of the café and stared at the sea. He called out the names of the people he loved, one by one—the people who had changed him for the better, who had led him to his rich and contented life, at home on the shores of Lake Monona. His mother, Magaly. His father, and brother Manuel. His friend from the Peruvian restaurant, Alejandro. Nori, his beloved; his children; his little nephew. Herb. Rocky.

The sunlight was breaking through the clouds at the water's horizon line, and it suddenly blazed into a brilliant pink and gold band, ravishing the sky with brilliance.

"*Mi corazon, mi vida, mi Tesoro.* To you—to each one of you," he said out loud into the wind. "My heart. My life. My treasure."

White Bass are runnin', Bill.
That's the good word!

Fishing

At four a.m. I rise and put the coffee on. I don't drink coffee, but it doesn't matter. The electrical currents in my brain that cause me to move habitually, mesmerizing me with automatic movement, are embedded so strongly in place that the pot is two-thirds full before I remember: the coffee drinker is gone.

I set the pot on the stove, turn it up, then pad through the house barefoot on the wood-planked floors, letting the stuff cook until it burns. The kitchen and living room fill with the rubbery, metallic odor of it–some sort of justice in the vengeance of it. Then I remember my brother's commentary on being rejected and left: "Jillian, resentment is a poison you swallow hoping the other person will die." Barclay. He'd said it gently, calling from La Crosse, trying to be helpful.

"You want me to come down? I can. I'll just get in the car." I heard his dogs Shep and Grover barking in the background; he was rarely apart from his canines. *Best friends,* I thought bitterly. I had thought mine was my husband.

My brother, at thirty-nine, had been divorced three times. If I let him come, he'd be pragmatic and seasoned at the arc of marital loss, up in my grief. I couldn't stomach it.

"No, Barclay. I'm muddling through," I'd said, lying.

In my kitchen, the blackness of the still-night sky weights the windows as if they're covered by heavy woolen blankets. I grab the coffee pot from the stove and lift the coffee maker from the counter–plastic chassis warm and the overcooked liquid sloshing–and carry them, barefooted, across the gravel driveway to the trash can. The icy, late-autumn Wisconsin morning pierces me, my feet sharply needled by tiny, chewed-up rocks. The sky is blacker than I remember it being at this hour, my small northern lake town covered by a pall of darkness.

I inherited this house outside of King, sitting right on Dake Lake–my parents' place, buying out my brother–and my husband and I had kept it because we said we liked being out from town, alone together, a tiny little house on the edge of the water. Now, just the thought, *alone, together,* sends stinging flashes of pain into my brain, and I shake my head sharply to free myself of it as if there are bees landing on my face.

I nurse a secret truth as I walk, coffee machine in hand–a dreadful and appalling one, and not just in this moment, either, but each night as I pull back the weathered, linen bedspread and lie alone in our bed. *I hope it's me who dies.* Not to spite him, not to hurt him or make him pay, and not even with any sordid want of doing harm to myself, but because I've had *enough.* I'm worn thin, wrung out by months and months of yearning for things to somehow right themselves, pretending that they will. I'm limp and exhausted and feel no shame in admitting that I don't care anymore.

I have refused to cry, the weight of holding in my grief like walking with huge stones strapped to my body.

The uneven glass of the toolshed's battered, wood-framed window mirrors my reflection as I pass, coffee maker and pot in hand. My brown hair is unwashed and matted, thrown to one side; my face looks drawn and pulled downward as if gravity had grown weightier overnight. My clothes hang limply from my limbs, having not been changed in days.

The siding where the garbage can rests is battered: old, chipped-paint wooden planks that my father had once nailed to the shed when this place was my girlhood home. There is a pile of light blue, fiber-cement siding next to the garbage can that we had planned to install months ago–an abandoned job, and my ex's idea: the rotted and pitted wood of the shed a precious memory to me, but to him, "an eyesore."

I approach our giant, empty black trash bin (which I grudgingly admit I have never been able to move to the curb without his help), open it and let it fall: pot, hot coffee, electrical wiring and apparatus. It's self-pity at its finest.

I stand and stare at the morass of mess in the can, now below my reach, the broken glass shattered over cord, plastic, and burnt coffee, then consider the lazy-Susan sampler plate of what I could use today to absent my head from my own unraveling self. I ponder the options: alcohol (I can't keep it down); food (I'm already nauseous); drugs (I don't have any); shopping (I hate it); or sex (*hardly*).

I sniff the icy air meanly. I have no choice but to feel every ounce of my own sinewy pain today.

My bare toes are frozen to the gravel, and as I begin to step, little pieces of rock prick at my skin and lacerate the bottom of my feet in staccato, pin-sharp stabs of pain. A glint of bare street light streaks into the shed as I pass, the door ajar where I left it five days ago when he emptied out the last of his tools and junk. All at once, I want to throw up, and I steady myself on the door jamb.

The wave of nausea passes, and as I turn to go my eyes settle upon my father's thirty-year-old fishing gear stashed in a dusty corner of the shed. I stare momentarily.

"I will go fishing then," I say out loud to no one.

In the freezing cold pre-dawn, it feels like a century since I fished (I remember it's literally been a quarter-century), and I find I do not remember how to begin.

I move towards my father's gear, and like spying a pinhole of light in a pitch-black room, the fog that has been clogging my brain is pinpricked a bit–a tiny pressure release in the balloon of my loss–and as I reach for his ancient, closeted rods, there, before me, is a broad, handsome man with a shock of black and gray-streaked hair standing over my ten-year-old self, teaching me how to push a night crawler through a fishhook.

"It wasn't called a *fishhook*," I say as I finger the rod. My left temple throbs. I have forgotten the language of this. I know worms and hooks and fishing line, but I have lost the delicate finesse of the detailed vocabulary my father taught me. The words fall flat–"rod," "line," "hook"–my generic knowledge leaving me bereft, as if in my adult life I should have tried harder to love what he loved and learn what he knew.

My brother Barclay hated fishing, couldn't sit still in a rowboat or by a streambed, preferred trekking through the woods with his dogs. When we fished, I got my father all to myself. It was my favorite time.

I want to be near him now, the father who truly loved me and would not have sought his own escape from me under any earthly circumstance, yet died and left me anyway. I pick up a flashlight from the floor, balancing it and shining it upwards, and begin gathering all that I can of his fishing gear.

There are three poles–a shiny black one which appears gray at first, covered with dust and cobwebs; a severely cracked blond wooden relic; and a polished burnt orange one which was once the exact metallic hue of my first Stingray bicycle.

My father bought the pole the same day he bought my bike, coordinating the colors so that they would match.

"Jillie! Jillie! Close your eyes!" he'd said to me. "Come on now. Close 'em! Okay, okay. Now, *look!*" He pulled the orange Stingray from around our paneled Ford Station wagon and lifted it upright with his left hand, holding the fishing rod up in his right like the torch on the Statue of Liberty.

"Look what I found! A matching pole and bicycle! Our favorite things, Jillie—yours and mine!"

Tears sting my eyes as I stand in the shed, remembering him, and I pull the orange rod to my chest—a sharp and withered replacement for the father who would have held me on this day, would have let me bury my grief against his thickening belly and shoulders.

I force myself to move and reach—to try at least—and I beat back spider webs and falling pieces of cracked ceiling tile to free the rest of the gear. There are the other two rods, a tackle box, some buckets, a couple of nets, some waders, and a knife for filleting. I am amazed to find that much of the stuff still looks functional.

I have no recollection of lines or how they work or what one must do to prepare them. I figure I'll take all the rods as they are and hope against reason that one of them will still work, reeling itself out into the stream as if it knows what it's doing.

I stare at the gear. Suddenly, I have no faith whatsoever that I can do this. I feel *called,* that's all: as if some invisible force could lift me from the desperation of my self-neglect with a thin thread of hope held together with fishing line.

In my kitchen, I make myself a breakfast of whole-wheat rolls and cheese, apples and tea, and wrap it all into a basket. I know it is wishful thinking to assume that I will eat, but I take it anyway. I pack the gear and the food in the car, start the engine and steer towards the highway.

On the mornings we fished, heading for the Wolf River out near Fremont, my father would have stopped for doughnuts and coffee in Waupaca at a little café called Gert's which opened at five a.m. and served only homemade pastries.

"Wanna little something?" Gert would say to me with a warm, yellow-toothed smile. She wore a fishnet atop wound-up gray hair that pulled into a peak over her forehead, and a white apron stained with frosting.

I would point to a giant tray of huge, glaze-covered cinnamon rolls, warm from the oven and dripping with sugary frosting, and she'd pop one onto a paper plate and wrap it in tin foil. The cinnamon roll was as big as the plate and three inches high, and it would take me all morning on the riverbed to eat it, my father smiling at me each time I took a bite, his warm brown eyes crinkling at the corners, as if his little treat to me was all I would ever need to find happiness.

Gert's—now a second-hand store with a crumbling exterior—flies by on the left side of my driving sightline, and the ratty Goodwill fare in the window snaps my heart into broken, dry reeds.

A little farther on, I pass Shadow Lake heading out of town—one main street of wood-paneled and weathered-brick storefronts: hardware, diner, gift store, farm supplies and two taverns—and veer into US-10. Twenty minutes later, I make a sharp, severe turn onto a one-lane county road, taking the steeply banked turn quickly, the way my father used to—a crack-the-whip-in-the-car effect that used to always make me laugh out loud.

I swerve a little and check my face in the rear-view mirror: loose-skinned, mouth tightly pressed at the lips. No laughing today.

The next few miles to the river pass by in near darkness, my headlights not nearly enough to lift the weighing blackness of the sky.

At the junction of a sandy, dirt road, I pull over to a little battered shack on the downside of a rural intersection. No one is around, but as I open the door, I see a white plastic pail with a tight, sealed cover, and inside it, several Styrofoam containers of night crawlers. I open one of the Styrofoam cups to check—wet dirt and crawling things—and I notice I'm surprised to find them alive. I leave five dollars in an empty pail and take my cargo back to the car.

Twenty years ago, old Alfred Nebus would have been here at this hour, shaking my father's hand and talking over the floating abilities of various kinds of bait.

"Alfred! What's the good word?" my father would say to him.

Alfred was over eighty, a retired farmer, and had spent a lifetime fishing the streams and lakes in our county.

"White Bass are runnin', Bill. That's the good word!" He'd bend down creakily, the dome of his bald head shining towards me and his skinny arms reaching into a pail, saying something sweet like, "You're gonna be a *fisherwoman* when you grow up, and a damned *good* one, now aintcha?"

I'd nod, and he'd pull a handful of lollypops out of his pocket for me and let me choose my color. I chose green every time—my father's favorite. He and Alfred would laugh, and Alfred would say, "She loves you somethin' terrible, Bill. You know that, don'tcha?"

"Sure do, Alfred. Love her more, though."

Every once in a while, there'd be an older guy out there, too, who sold farm insurance, sitting in a collapsible fishing chair next to Alfred, the two of them "chewing the cud," as Alfred liked to say. The guy was a jokester named

Ponty, always making me and my dad laugh. Once, on my eleventh birthday, he helped me do a handstand in the grass, holding my feet in the air, then made me stay upside down while my father and Alfred sang the whole happy birthday song.

Today, it's a miracle to me that the little shack still stands, and I bless the son or niece or grandchild of Alfred's who leaves me these night crawlers, these gifts.

On the road, the darkness has broken into a pink and windy dawn, and I breathe a little lighter now. I hate the dark. As a child, I had terrible nightmares for a time after my mother died, which resurfaced so vehemently in the three months prior to my husband's leaving that I awoke screaming several nights a week. Yet my eyes would blink awake in the morning, wide open and full of the denial of another nebulous day.

"He's told you he's in love with someone else, so you know what's coming, don't you?" my therapist had said to me.

"So what?" I had retorted, rebelliously pushing back. "Knowing doesn't help a damn thing. It just makes the inevitable leaving more drawn out." I had been right.

The day he left–he had marked the day on the calendar clipped to the refrigerator, as if it was a concert or a dinner date–I had pressed him for 'goodbye sex.' Stupid. He was loading boxes out of the spare bedroom where he'd been sleeping, back and forth into his pickup truck. I stood in the oak-framed doorway watching, and once, as he passed, I reached out and grabbed his biceps and pulled myself into his body, pushing my hips into his. I held on and pressed hard.

"This is what you *want?*" he'd said incredulously, his large hands pressing me away at the shoulders. "Really?"

"To say goodbye. Do it. *For me.* Please." The back of my T-shirt was damp from sweat, though it was a windy, forty degrees outside, my body going hot and cold all day long as he packed.

"Jillian–*don't*–" He grabbed me strongly by the chin with his left hand and stared at me, holding my body back with his right.

"Just get inside me! *Do it!*"

I yanked at his belt buckle and unzipped him, slid my hand into his boxers.

He hesitated, writhing away from my grasp, and I held on harder. Then I saw him relent, and he pressed me fast and hard down on the carpet. He pulled at my jeans and then his, yanked off my underwear, left my T-shirt and bra on but wrenched them up, then entered me–no tenderness, no foreplay. I wanted it like that, ground against him hard, flipped myself over on top, groaning. My unshed tears burned behind my eyelids, and I was pounding against him, a ridiculously unlikely excitement pulsing up between my thighs. When I got to the edge, I shouted, "Make it *hurt!*"

He shoved me off him, almost jumping out from under me, then went immediately limp.

"You're a mess!" he said, scrambling on his knees for his jeans. "Shit, Jillian. *Jesus!*"

"And whose fault is that?" I said, deadened.

I pushed my naked body back against the open bedroom door, my T-shirt and bra still balled up against my upper chest, staring at him as he stumbled out, tripping over my feet. Two tears dropped, against my will, from my face onto my bare breasts.

—⁓—

On the road, three minutes later, my car pulls up to the edge of the Wolf River, the water moving in scalloped wakes and delicate sheets across its blue-green surface. There are clouds, close-in and soot-colored, threatening to storm, the sun thickly buried behind them. I am shaking out my father's waders, fearing tarantulas and black widows (though I know this is not their latitude), or giant June bugs, though it's late fall, almost winter. My throat tightens at the vision of dead and dying June beetles, their scaly brown backs and bellies floating toward me in the water. Nothing seems logical to me anymore. Nothing adds up. I fear things that don't exist. I pretend that what's happening isn't. I refuse to see what's right in front of me.

The water at the river oscillates in my sightline, and I stand, momentarily frozen. "Huh," I say to no one, "I have no idea what I'm fishing for."

I set up the orange pole first, hook a nightcrawler, reel out the line. It creaks, but miraculously it works. The wooden pole sticks and jams, nothing doing. But the shiny black pole lets out its line effortlessly, as if it had been waiting for my unsteady hands to give it another chance to reach into the purplish-green, rushing water. I stick the butts of both poles into the edge of the soft streambed and reach for my thermos.

November, I think to myself. *What runs in winter?* This spot on the Wolf was my father's favorite when the White Bass were running. *Was that spring or autumn?* I am struck by how grief has obliterated my memory. My reference points have faded and jumbled, and I feel awash with no firm ground to stand upon. *Was it Spring?*

"It's the best time ever, Jillie—you put your line in, and you pull out a fish! It'll give you *fishing fever*." My father had flashed me his favorite grin, the one he knew lit up the room and weakened me to do whatever he wanted me to do. It was our secret joy: me holding out on some pleasure of his, and him slowly convincing me, his exuberance in swaying me over drawing him out in loud, boisterous assertions of "fevers" and "the greatests" and "best evers."

Suddenly I am stricken, bent over with the sharp pointedness of agony stuck in my chest, the places my father enlivened in me ravaged and on fire with my need for him. That someone should *care* that I have the "best time ever" knocks me to my knees and I am weeping on the cold earth.

"Come *back!*" I yell out loud, pounding the ground with my fists, face-down in the weeds and mud. "*Goddamn* it—come back!!"

I cry in heavy sobs, my shoulders collapsed around my heart like a fallen deer with an arrow in its flank. My muscles give way to the frozen ground, and my hands reach for the dirt. I cannot hold myself up any longer. Rivulets pour from my face and wet the soil, snot and gasps caught in the icy grass. I rise momentarily to vomit in the weeds, and then fall again, giving up.

I find it shocking that the break in the dam of my grief should be borne alone, that the pouring out of its depths are plummeted by this wholly solitary moment, and while I know no one will be coming from out of the underbrush to hold me or save me, the child in me still wants it. *Please! Where is my father when I need him?* I cry. *I want him to come back!*

After a long time, I rise and wipe my face, not knowing what force will help me stand again.

Something is different. The light has changed, the stream has colored into a bright blue-green in the early morning sun, and my lines—both of them—have bites. My heart beats quickly; I am not sure which line to reel in first. I reach for the orange one, and in two seconds I am fighting with the line—more from the wake of the stream's current than the weight of the fish—and as I draw it out of the water, I see what it is: a White Bass.

A large school of them writhes below my feet, and for a moment my breath goes out of me. I reel in the second line, re-bait, cast, pull in another. I spend all morning baiting and catching, a rhythm of completeness that overtakes my grief and blots out my numbness. I fill my buckets, my plastic bags, my break-fast basket. There are more bass than I can count.

"I'm sure there's a limit on the lot of you," I say to a particular fish, "but I don't care."

It must have been spring when we fished, my father and me. It seems like that should have been when it was, when fish would school towards the surface, mate, and begin again.

I feel a thin thread of certainty returning to my limbs as I pack the car with my loot: these fish, all of these White Bass that should not be running in November. My face in the car window looks different. Piqued with what?

Interest. My face looks *interested.*

The engine hesitates, sputters, then starts, and I sense a movement in my heart, a mysterious beating. My father is near. In the car, the smell of fish is suddenly everywhere.

As I drive my face creases into the first small smile I have smiled in months. I will eat the fish all winter and spring will come. 🖋

You like every man that smells good!
What—he licked your hand and you
knew it was love?

Doggie Stay

Shelby Barkingham was a dog trainer. She was a groomer first, a business she started in La Crosse, Wisconsin at the age of twenty-three with a broken-down orange and white VW van her father had left her in his will, and six thousand dollars she'd saved from waitressing at a local bar called The Cap Gun. The place was an annoying hell-hole–battered clapboard, peanuts in barrels with piles of shells all over the floor, the constant stench of stale beer and bleach–where customers got cap-guns and a roll of red, textured cap tape at their tables, then blasted the firecracker sounds at incessant intervals from their fake firearms. Shelby hated it.

When she hit her longed-for savings mark of six thousand, she moved out of her mother's tiny two-bedroom house, got herself a single basement apartment off Fifth and Winnebago in the Washburn neighborhood, and set up shop. The place was walking distance from Houska Park on the Mississippi and the "World's Largest Six-Pack," a giant replica of beer cans which reached a height of eight-times a human being's stature and whose sign boasted, "Would provide one person a six-pack a day for 3,351 years."

She named her first business *Pretty Dog*, and after getting the van painted a bright turquoise blue, she hand-stenciled letters in a vibrant red on the side of it:

PRETTY DOG
Mobile Dog Grooming Studio

And, in smaller letters, just below:

Shelby Barkingham, owner
(Yeah, I get it)

Shelby's best friend Kelsie, a six-foot, curvaceous production assistant on the local *News 8 Morning Show* and an occasional weekend waitress at The Cap Gun—always acerbic and edgy—burst out laughing the day Shelby drove up in her newly hand-lettered canine-washing van.

"*Bark*ingham? *Bark, bark*—you're a dog groomer? That's fucking *hilarious!*"

"Hey! It'll get me outa that scum-bag bar," Shelby said.

Kelsie screwed up her face and squinted at Shelby. "I thought you liked it in there," she said with delighted facetiousness. "Career path and all that."

"Shit, yeah," Shelby said, playing along. "See myself at fifty with some drunk asshole reaching his hand around my back to grab my ass. Can't wait."

"Keeps a girl young." Kelsie laughed loudly—a big guffaw.

"It's not *that* funny."

"Funny is funny, baby," Kelsie chortled. Then she looked at Shelby, smiling. "Your own business at the age of twenty-three?"

"Fuck, yeah," Shelby said and patted the side of her van. "I'm gonna be stellar at this."

Within six months Shelby had married Judd—'Judd the dud' her mother called him—a stunningly good-looking six-foot-four ex-basketball player from UW Madison with a shock of shoulder-length blond hair who never held a job longer than five weeks. He could palm a basketball, and his huge hands were a marvel to Shelby in bed.

He mostly sat around in Shelby's single apartment reading sci-fi novels while she hustled all over town washing grime and dirt off the pelts of slithering and lurching canines.

"Why you ever married that man is beyond me," Shelby's mother Evvy (short for Evelyn) snorted one day when she came by to wash Ruff, her mom's fifty-pound Shepherd-and-Labrador mutt. Ruff had been Shelby's dog, but when she moved out, her mother had badly needed the company, so she let Evvy keep him.

"Mom, give me a break, okay?" Shelby was in the van with the back and side door open, elbow deep in dirty water, hovering over Ruff in the specialty tub she used for bathing dogs. It was hot, humid, and she was sweating. "It's not like the string of schmucks you date is any better."

"Hey! At least I don't *marry* them!" her mother huffed. "And I haven't had good luck since your father died. Not my fault."

Her mother, at fifty-five, was still beautiful—tall and curvaceous and olive-skinned with thick black-brown hair that cascaded down to her waist, and a perfect set of thick bangs that grazed her lashes and made men stare into her eyes when they met her. Shelby felt plain and ordinary next to her mother, having inherited her father's thin face and watery blue eyes, her own long limbs appearing *useful,* while her mother's looked graceful.

Ruff lurched, and Shelby caught him quickly by the waterproof collar she always used when bathing dogs–a skill she'd pretty much mastered in the first few months of washing and grooming.

"Judd's looking for a job, okay?" Shelby said, scrubbing Ruff's flanks.

"No, he's not! He's a *moocher!*" Evvy said. "All he does is lay around while *you* work–"

"Mom, *please*–"

Ruff leaped and Shelby leaped with him, throwing her five-foot-seven thin frame on top of the dog, hunkering him back into the tub. In an instant she was sopped with dirty dog water and suds.

"*Jesus!* I don't know how you do this all day long!" Evvy said, jumping back from the splashing water. "I really *don't.*"

Shelby drained the tub into the street gutter and began brushing Ruff's matted brown-and-white-spotted coat. "You're a mutt," she said into the dog's eyes, smiling. "Plain and brown-haired, just like me. But you're lovable."

The dog licked her face–a big, sloppy slap with his tongue across the front of her mouth, nose and forehead.

"Ugh! *Seriously,* Ruff?" Evvy exclaimed to her dog.

"*That's* how I do this all day long," Shelby said to her mother. "I love dogs." She kissed Ruff on the nose.

"Yes, you do," Evvy said, reaching up into the van for Shelby's leg, patting it.

Ruff shook his damp coat in one electric shake, sending a fine spray of water into Shelby's face.

"Oh, Ruff!" she said and pressed her cheek to the top of his wet head.

―⁓―

Two years later Judd was gone. Shelby had finally kicked him out. More than his joblessness, she'd caught him having phone sex with an old girlfriend in the middle of the afternoon on their bed.

"Good riddance," her mom said when she and Shelby went to the county clerk together to file the papers. They walked over to a little Mexican cantina afterward and gulped down three oversized shots each of good tequila, getting a little teary-eyed from the booze.

"Where am I gonna find another guy as handsome as him?" Shelby moaned into her mother's shoulder. A man on Evvy's right kept trying to lean in and catch her mother's eye, and Shelby gave him a dirty look.

"Any day of the week," Evvy said with a bite in her tone. "Seventeen of 'em sitting around The Cap Gun waitin' for a sucker like you to let 'em loaf on your couch while you sweat bullets trying to make rent."

"I mean it!" Shelby cried, and tears began to roll down her cheeks.

Her mother hugged her. "You're just bemoaning not having sex with him."

"His hands–"

"You've told me," Evvy said, patting her drunken daughter's head.

"I'm plain."

"You're not."

"I look like Dad."

Evvy sighed, then took Shelby's face in her hands. "Listen to me. Your father was good and kind and he was beautiful to me every single day of our life together. You understand me?"

———

Four months later, Shelby met Lance at a friend's birthday party–a big beer garden scene with lots of people she didn't know dressed in upscale clothing and shiny, expensive shoes. She had been leaning against a wall–hiding, really–in a space between four giant ferns with a 3 Sheeps IPA in her hand, texting her cousin in Kewaskum.

She had let Kelsie cut and shape her hair with long bangs that morning, and she was self-consciously pulling and twirling a piece of her hair across her forehead when Lance sauntered over and tried to strike up a conversation.

Once, when Shelby was fifteen, Evvy had cut Shelby's flat and shoulder-length hair into a kind of longish pageboy, and instead of being cute–her mother's intention–her hair had lain flat and plastered to her head and had made her look ridiculous. She had grown it all out as fast as possible and had never bothered with hairstyling again. But Kelsie had come over that morning and feathered bits of Shelby's hair into place for the party, and she had to admit it looked pretty good. Lance stared at her.

"I hear you've got a dog training business," he said, trying hard. He was cradling a Heineken, turning it around in his hands.

"Who told you that?" Shelby said.

Lance pointed to Kelsie, who was dancing across the room with a thick-bodied man a whole head shorter than her. Kelsie waved, smiling wickedly.

"Well, okay, maybe I do," Shelby said defensively. *I suck at this,* she thought. *I'm a friggin' train wreck.*

"I'm Lance." He stuck out his hand and shook hers, very intently, like he was on a job interview.

Shelby laughed. "Shelby."

"So?" Lance said.

"What?"

"Dog training?"

"Oh. Right. I used to have a dog grooming business, but I kicked my husband out and I got a *training* certificate, too. I do both now."

"You're married? You don't look old enough–"

"*Was* married. Deadbeat husband. Gone–thank fucking *God,*" Shelby spit out. She said it with just enough venom to remember that she wasn't quite over her breakup, figuring, after a crack like that, Lance would beat a path across the room from her in less than ten seconds. But he stayed put.

Shelby was wearing tight black bell bottoms, boots and a lightweight print blouse, while every other woman in the place was in an expensive dress and high heels. She felt outclassed, but Lance didn't move.

She looked at him, took him in. He was genuinely good-looking, in a sort of geeky way–little wire-rimmed glasses, shaggy black hair falling over his ears, slim but with pouty red lips. Ridiculously soft brown eyes. He smiled, and those pouty lips turned up sweetly. She was immediately smitten.

"Wanna dance?" he said, reaching out a long-fingered hand.

"Yes I *do,*" Shelby said.

—⁓—

Lance had a great job as an engineer for a local industrial supplier–he was in charge of hydraulics; *impressive*–with a weird techie name that Shelby could never pronounce correctly. Within six weeks, he'd moved in with her. Two months later, Lance proposed.

"You're like a goddamned *Labrador,*" her mother said when Shelby told her about getting married. They were having lunch at the Dipsy Diner, Ruff at their feet at an outside table, the sixties tune *Don't Let Me Down* blaring on the outside speaker. The early autumn heat was winding down, just-turning leaves on the trees above them wavering and threatening to drop.

"I mean, for God's sake!" Evvy shoved French fries into her mouth while she spoke, ramping up her volume. "You like every man that smells good! What–he licked your hand and you knew it was *love?* Why can't you just *wait?*"

Shelby dropped her burger onto her plate, the tomato and lettuce sliding out the side of the bun. "What's so great about waiting, mother? I mean, any one of us could drop dead tomorrow..." She sucked hard on the straw in her chocolate milkshake, taking a huge gulp.

"So this is about your father dying?" Evvy leaned forward off her red plastic chair. "Shelby, *marrying* a man is not supposed to be a reaction to–"

"He's beautiful! He's sweet! And he *wants* me!" Shelby said, stomping her long feet under the table.

"You can't marry every man you have a crush on! I swear to God, you *sniff* every man who's good-looking!"

"Mom–"

"You just met him–"

"Be happy for me, will you please?"

Evvy sighed loudly, flipping her lustrous hair over one shoulder. "How can I be happy when you have no *filter?*"

—⁓—

Evvy had been right. Lance lasted all of eighteen months. He left on the day of Shelby's twenty-seventh birthday. He became depressed–about what Shelby could not figure out–within three months of their tiny, backyard wedding in the green space behind her mother's house. By their six-month anniversary he'd stopped having sex with her altogether, just wouldn't respond. Shelby tried, but he got worse in winter when it was snowy and gray; refused to take meds, refused to get help. He was like a *cat*, she decided–withdrawn, never initiating, isolated–staring out the window when he was home, never speaking. She needed a *dog* kind of man, that much she knew: warm, enthusiastic, lapping her face. Lance wasn't it.

During Lance's bouts with depression, she'd gone back to school to get a veterinary technician certificate, so once she was on her own again–"Strike two," Evvy had said, "and time to get a grip"–she thought she'd better get her act together and stop spending her energy on lethargic men.

"I'm not marrying anyone for a long time, okay? You happy?" Shelby said sitting across from her mother at their favorite little gyros place. They were perched under a bright red umbrella on the sidewalk, a metal sampler of six different sauces plopped between them. Ruff sat at their feet, having just been walked at Houska Park on the river's edge, and Shelby slipped her foot out of her flip flop, rubbing his coat.

Her mother sucked the ice cubes out of her iced tea and chewed, sopping up some spilled sauce with a rust-colored paper napkin. "Thank god for *that*," she said under her breath, crunching ice. Evvy pulled a piece of lamb out of her Gyro and dangled it above Shelby's mouth, then popped it in. "Taste this!"

"I'm turning over a new leaf. A new *paw*, as it were," Shelby said, chewing the lamb and forking a green pepper.

Evvy laughed, then turned serious. "But what's that really *mean*, Shelby?"

"It means I'm starting a new business. I found a cheap piece of land with some old farm buildings up near Rice Lake. I'm going to take people's dogs to–I don't know what you call it–but, like, a doggie camp. On weekends. Let them run."

Her mother dropped her gyro and sat back in her plastic chair, looking Shelby straight in the eyes. "That's a dead-to-rights, *fabulous* idea! Bingo!" she said, clapping her hands.

Shelby smiled. She truly loved her mother. All her life, they had palled around together–she and her mom; her dad and mom together with her–as if they were all friends. And though that brought some weirdo issues ("Who's the parent, anyway?!!" she'd once screamed at her mother when Evvy befriended one of Shelby's friends), she largely felt blessed that she'd gotten to have a genuine and human relationship with both of her parents. They were honest, too. "Oh, come on, mother!" Shelby had once hollered at Evvy. "I don't get to see my cousin Dory because Dad didn't become an attorney? Isn't that a bit *stupid?*" "It's not *my* fault!" Evvy yelled back. "It's them! They act like he betrayed them by becoming a teacher and your father can't stand all those snide comments every time we're over there!"

She had watched her parents' marriage with fascination: goof-ball pranks on each other, witty barbs and jabs, boisterous laughter and open affection, and, Shelby suspected, lots of good, healthy sex. It pained her that she couldn't find the same thing for herself.

Ruff licked Shelby's hand under the table, sniffing for food, but Shelby was glad for his touch. "You know what? Ruff is like Dad was. Loyal and true."

Her mom leaned over the table and patted her hand, reading the arc of her thoughts. "You'll find someone nice. I swear to God, you will." She said it intently, her eyes wide open and glistening.

Shelby teared up. "Mom, I'm not *looking*, okay?" she whispered. "After all the *shit* you've given me about marrying loser men–"

Her mother's eyes caught someone's behind Shelby.

"*Shhh!* There he is. Be *nice*, okay? I like him." Evvy had begun seeing a dentist named Avery–kind of lackluster and solid, Shelby thought, like a lapdog that never wants to move from the space on top of your thighs. But her mother found him comforting, she could tell.

Avery sat and joined them, "Hi, hi, all around," he said nodding at Shelby, then leaned in to kiss her mother. "Evvy. What's the good news?"

It made Shelby bristle to hear him speak her father's nickname for her mother. Not Evelyn. *Evvy.*

Shelby got up. "Well, I should go…"

"No, no, *stay!*" her mother exclaimed. She reached for Avery's hand. "She's starting a doggie camp up in Rice Lake! Isn't that a great idea?" Her mom clapped her hands together again.

"That's just *fine,*" Avery said, the timbre of a grandfather's approval in his voice. He was older.

Shelby leaned over and kissed her mom. "See you next week. Ruff's bath week."

"You don't have to–" Evvy said.

"But I *do,*" Shelby smiled. "See ya, Avery." She forced a smile then turned to go.

⁓

When she arrived at her client's house to bathe and train Argo, one of her favorite little lap dogs, Shelby's head was spinning, and she was chewing on her lip–a newly acquired tic in which she sucked in the right side of her mouth and gnawed on it like a chew toy. The client's house was a huge five-bedroom down WI-35 sitting right on the Mississippi.

"Sorry I'm late," she said to Felicity, Argo's owner. "I was at lunch with my mom. And her *boyfriend.*"

Felicity's peroxided hair was cut short in two-inch bleached blond spikes that were sculpted into place with a seriously strong hair gel, framing the tiny, delicate features of her face. It never ceased to amaze Shelby how people chose dogs who resembled them. Felicity looked just like her Pomeranian.

Felicity wrinkled her little nose, and said, "No worries. Just so everybody's happy." She laughed, *ha, ha, ha, ha, ha,* like short, staccato Pomeranian barks. "You're happy for her?"

"Sure–I guess…Maybe not. We'll see."

"Have a little *faith* in people, Shelby," Felicity chirped, tilting her pert, white-blond head to the side. Argo stood behind his owner and tilted his little head exactly the same way, staring in Shelby's direction. It took all her effort to not burst out laughing.

In the van, she plopped Argo into the tub, filling it with warm water from her mobile tank, and in two seconds he went from a white fluff ball to a drowned rat. She scrubbed him a bit too vigorously as she thought about her mother, and Argo yipped.

Yip, yip! Stop it! He was saying. *Too hard!*

"Oh, Argo!" Shelby said, patting the dog's matted little head. "Sorry! I'll ease up."

Argo stuck his wet nose on Shelby's, and she laughed, softening her scrubbing motion.

It wasn't that she didn't like her mother's boyfriend, and if he made her mom happy, then all the better. Her father's death had been grueling for Evvy–a drunk driver, on the way to Goose Island to fish–and she wanted her mom to be easy in her heart, the way she once was with her dad. She didn't know if Avery could muster the same kind of partnered enthusiasm.

Argo looked up at Shelby sheepishly and forlornly, as if being wet somehow took away all of his doggie-charm.

"Don't worry, Argo," she said to him, leaning over the tub with her eyes very close to his. "I promise you'll be fluffier than a puff ball when I'm through with you."

Argo nipped her nose lightly and barked–a sing-song sound–and Shelby stared at him, amazed. *I want my poof back!* Argo seemed to be saying. Dogs *did* talk, she was certain; you just had to learn to hear their language.

On the back lawn of Felicity's grand five-bedroom, Shelby put Argo through his training paces. Sit, heel, sit-then-heel-then-sit-then-heel. And though Felicity didn't like Argo to be trained for party tricks, Shelby couldn't resist. He was smart, so she taught him to roll over, walk on hind legs while she held his paws, do a somersault on the grass, do a little dance to Michael Jackson's old classic, *Thriller*.

She gnawed the side of her right lip, mulling over Evvy. *What if my mother marries that guy?*

For months she'd harbored a ridiculous and self-serving fantasy that her mom would hook up with a woman–some iconoclastic, artist-type who would meld right in with the two of them, an extension of mother and daughter, a bridge. She knew the fantasy was born of her need to make her father irreplaceable, or maybe it was her own sublimated desire, that old bantering that always crept into conversations with girlfriends after a bad breakup.

"Maybe I should try women," Shelby had said to Kelsie after Lance finally left, "since I sure-as-shit am failing at men."

"But then you'd have no *unh, unh, uh,"* Kelsie said with a rhythmic grind of her hips.

"I think you can *simulate,* Kelsie–"

"Oh, Shel, you're just bummed out. Two down, and all that. Go sleep with some hot, young thing and you'll feel better. Don't you dog trainers have some meetups or something? There's gotta be at least one do-able guy in that crowd, right?"

She *had* slept with someone. A romp with the guy who worked at the doggie supply store. It hadn't helped.

"*Lonely* is the word for this," she said to Argo on Felicity's back steps. "I'm better off with your kind."

Argo stood on his hind legs and balanced for a quick second before Shelby caught his paws. When she kneeled down, he licked her right ear, then her left.

"That does it," Shelby said to Argo. "Next time, I'm marrying a dog."

—⁓—

Leaps and Bounds, Shelby's day camp for dogs, was a robust success, almost right from the start. No one was more surprised than Shelby. She was used to living on very little, had kept her tiny single basement apartment on Fifth Street through both marriages–she'd never bothered to put either husband on the lease. The mortgage on her piece of property in Rice Lake was small, and as the business grew, she built out the land with new, dog-friendly barns for her weekend canine visitors, and remodeled a couple of chicken coops for herself and Idella, a twenty-two-year-old Honduran worker she had hired who was ridiculously strong and terrific with dogs. Her cousin Dory came up from Kewaskum a handful of times with her boyfriend Cord and helped, too.

She passed her business card out wherever she went. It read:

LEAPS AND BOUNDS
Doggie Day Camp
Shelby Barkingham
Certified Trainer and Vet Technician

And, on the back side:

Bark, bark.
The pun is not lost on me.

On weekdays, she trained and groomed in town, and on weekends, she took her canine charges up to Rice Lake, letting them do what dogs do best: run and play. Her mom dubbed Shelby, "Dog Trainer to the Stars," since word of mouth had gotten out at City Hall and at the UW Campus in La Crosse, and she now had a cadre of City Council members' and Professors' dogs on her roster. Many had become weekly regulars—a little grooming or training during the week, and then a piling into the van for a yipping and bark-friendly excursion up to *Leaps and Bounds* camp.

Shelby had a method, too, proven over months and months of hard work. Clients had to pay for four weeks of bi-weekly training in town, then three sessions of "socialization" (essentially a haul-ass trek to the dog park with four, then ten dogs), and if the new canine did not try to bite or tear into another dog, only then was the pet allowed to attend *Leaps and Bounds*.

She had thought putting restrictions on her doggie camp would deter; instead, it had heightened her cachet.

"Shit, yeah!" Kelsie said to her over dinner. "They think you're exclusive. That's so take-no-prisoners!"

They were having gin martinis and steaks, celebrating at Digger's Sting, a steakhouse downtown, for Shelby's twenty-eighth birthday and Kelsie's recent engagement. The place was dark and oak-planked, a dropped ceiling with yellow and white stained-glass lamps overhead and beer taps poking out of antique barrels on top of the bar. Kelsie was beaming brightly, lit from the inside like a hot fire in a brick oven, gazing every sixteen seconds or so at the one-and-a-half carat on her left finger.

"Now all you need is a good *guy* in the picture!" Kelsie lifted up her left hand and wiggled her fingers, flashing the ring.

"Fuck, Kelsie! Would you *stop it?!*" Shelby said, pulling a face. She gulped her gin.

"Sorry!" Kelsie said, flushing, quickly putting her left hand in her lap. "I just never thought I'd—"

"Okay, I get it. But could you just—"

"—*Tamp it down* a little? Sure." Kelsie reached between the martini glasses and grabbed Shelby's hands. "Sorry."

Shelby's eyes went wet, and she wrapped her fingers around her friend's hands. She opened her eyes very wide, arching her eyebrows and then pulled in her lips, tight, inverting them, chewing on her right side.

"What?" Kelsie said, looking intently at her.

"That guy from last month—the one with the huge Great Dane? Said he wanted to see me, slept with me, disappeared."

"Not again…" Kelsie groaned, rolling her eyes.

"You *said* sleep with some hot guy—" Shelby said, tilting her head sideways.

"I meant *for fun.*"

"I tried that! It didn't work!"

"*Who?*" Kelsie said with deep-throated authority, leaning in.

"Aaron Beekham." Shelby grinned, a bit mischievously.

"Really! You slept with the Beek-Man? The guy who works at the doggie supply store? And you didn't tell me?"

"He's fucking *gorgeous.*" Shelby drew lines in the air with both hands, delineating a set of broad shoulders and a tiny waist.

"Intellectual as a box of nails, though," Kelsie said, chewing a large piece of her rare steak. "Was he any good?"

Shelby laughed. "*Terrible!* Scuttled out the door at three a.m. with his tail between his legs. Barely even said goodbye. But, *oh my god,* what a *body*–"

"Couldn't use his equipment, right?" Kelsie snorted, rolling her fork in her mashed potatoes. "And not a 'let's-have-breakfast,' morning-after sort of guy, I'm guessing."

"How come you always know this stuff beforehand, and I never do?"

"Because you're a *magnet* for beautiful men without a decent set of brain cells or an ounce of grown-up, adult character."

"*Ouch!* Fucking *hell,* Kelsie! That's harsh!" Shelby pointed her fork across the table.

"Sorry! But, c'mon! You know that's what you do, right? You choose these guys who–"

"Why do they like me? I'm hardly a knock-out–"

Kelsie popped another bite of meat into her mouth. "They smell *sex* on you, you idiot! You like the sack, they smell it and they wanna rub up against you. They sniff you out like a border collie sniffing urine on a lamp post."

"*Nice.* Thanks, Kelsie,*"* Shelby snorted.

"Men have a high-strung nose for women who want to *bed* them. That's all I'm sayin'."

A tiny little tear rolled down Shelby's cheek. She stared down at her uneaten steak, knife poised in the center of the meat.

"Look," Kelsie said, sincerely. "There's nothing wrong with you. You've just gotta stop saddling up for the beauty pageant and find a *nice* guy who'll just love you. That's all."

"He doesn't fucking exist," Shelby snapped and downed her drink. "Only dogs love me."

"That's the whole goddamned point, Shelby! Get your head outa your own ass and find yourself a good, loyal mutt to settle down with!"

— ᴍ —

Six weeks later, her mother's boyfriend Avery did Shelby a huge favor. The owners of the house that topped her basement apartment decided to sell and move to Maine, and Shelby wanted to buy the place–a classic, old, two-story house with a darling front porch twelve steps up from the sidewalk. It had a big backyard with a handful of fruit trees, a wide sundeck with a viny bunch of morning glory growing over it, as well as a terrific kitchen. She had the down payment and could show barely enough income, but since she never used credit cards (she always bought used vans for her business with cash), she had almost no credit history. Avery stepped in and co-signed her loan. She was touched.

"It's nothing, nothing…" he'd said, standing over the desk at the bank with a pen in his hand, Evvy behind him, beaming. "It's just a little *help*. Everybody needs that once in a while, right Evvy?" He smiled broadly, his white and gray hair lit up from behind by a bit of sunlight angling in through the bank's window.

Shelby nervously pushed and pulled her hands in and out of her jeans' pockets. She kept looking at her mom's face, then back at Avery's. "I mean…just so you're *sure…* "

"You're a responsible business-woman," Avery said levelly, bending over and signing his name. "Why wouldn't I do it?"

Shelby chewed her right lip. "It's just that I could get hit by a *bus* or something, and then where would you be?" She saw her mother flinch and watched Evvy's face go instantly white–she hadn't meant to say that; she knew her mom couldn't stand the thought of losing her, in a car accident no less, but it had just popped out.

"Oh–*God,* Mom! I only meant–"

Avery dropped the pen and turned and wrapped his arms around Evvy. "Don't worry, sweetheart," he purred into her ear. "She's going to be fine. I promise. Just *fine.*" He patted her back, an older man's assurance in his velvety tone.

Shelby dropped her arms to her side, sighed, then smiled at her mom in Avery's arms. She had got her house, yes, and she knew–it wouldn't be long–a stepdad, too.

— ᴍ —

It was the fall of Shelby's thirtieth year when she met Barclay. She'd taken to volunteering at the Coulee Region Humane Society, out past Onalaska, on weeknights–at Kelsie's insistence.

"*Do something* that eats up some nighttime hours so you don't end up shacking up with guys who are shitheads, will you please?" Kelsie was pregnant, four months, and the pregnancy had made her both more insistent and more edgy.

"Like what?" Shelby had said.

"Oh, come on! Volunteer or something. Do something with dogs. Maybe you'll even meet a *nice* guy instead of another slam-and-jam *jerk* who's going to screw you and then walk out on you!"

They had hired her on the spot at the Humane Society, and Shelby found she enjoyed it. Each Monday, Wednesday, and Thursday night, she walked the insanely bark-filled corridors of the dozens of dog kennels, talking to each canine in turn…and, when no one was looking, slipping small chunks of Swiss cheese into their mouths from her pocket. She had a gray shirt they'd given her to wear that read *Shelby Barkingham* in bright blue embroidery on her chest.

She had favorites: Fife, the high-strung Samoyed, whom she had trained to calm down with the silky tone of her dog-training voice; Bella, the blue nose Pitbull who had once been abused, who was slowly, under her tutelage, becoming sweet and docile; Axel, a roguish reddish-brown mutt of indeterminate parentage (probably Setter and Shepherd) who liked to chew shoelaces and the hem of her jeans; and Rory, a yippy unlikely mix of Dachshund and Lab.

She was squatting, leaning over Rory, had him out of his kennel and was petting him on the flanks of his hot-dog-shaped brown body, yapping back at him as he yipped.

Rory wriggled. *Yap, yap! Yap-yap-yap-yap!*

"Yes, yes, Rory," Shelby purred. "*Good dog.* You're a perfect ball of joy, you know that?"

Yap-yap-yappity-yap! He licked her neck.

"Yes, yes, you good little thing!" Shelby held him up off the cement floor with both hands, still squatting, and Rory immediately nuzzled into her chest and quieted, a low, contented growl coming from his mouth.

"You're goddamned good with him, aren't you?" a voice said from behind her.

Shelby jumped. She hadn't heard anyone enter the kennels, and she hopped on her haunches then leapt up quickly, Rory still in her arms.

Barclay stood in front of her, not two feet away, a short, compact man with warm brown eyes and a receding blond hairline, the gray Humane Society shirt stretched over his belly and broad chest.

Rory went crazy, *Yapppp, yapppp, yapppp, yap-yap-yap-yap-yaaaaaapppp!*

Shelby turned away, but Rory wriggled in her arms, ready to pounce.

"Hey! What the *fuck?* You scared the living daylights outa me!"

"And poor little Rory here, too," Barclay said calmly, pointing to Rory's stick-on nametag over his kennel. "Let me have him." He stood behind Shelby's back and cooed at Rory, then gently guided him over her shoulder into his own arms. "That's it, little guy. You're okay! You just didn't hear me come in, that's all!"

Rory went calm in an instant, whimpering softly.

Shelby knew a dog person when she saw one. Everyone in her trade did. Dogs knew instantly when a human being was kind or warm, when they were not afraid, and when they *listened.*

"So, you're a canine-lover–I get it," Shelby said with a bite in her tone, still annoyed over being startled. "You wanted to prove that to me or something? Who *are* you?"

Barclay held and patted Rory, the dog gently licking the back of his neck. "They say you're the *best…*"

"Who says that?" Shelby crossed her arms over her chest, kicking the toe of her battered brown suede boot on the cement floor.

"Front desk, volunteer coordinator, board members–everyone." He put out his hand. "I'm Barclay Snahrall."

Shelby stood back, grabbing the chain link kennel door with one hand. "No way. Your name is *not* Barclay *Snarl.* As in, *bark, snarl?* Nobody would name their kid that."

Barclay put Rory down on the floor and gestured to his embroidered name on his shirt. "*Snah-RALL.* In the flesh. Witness the idiot parents' idea of a good pun."

Shelby's eyes softened. "You must've gotten massacred in elementary school."

"Had three dogs. Big ones, and nobody messed with me. Came to love dogs, though. Saved my ass."

Shelby put out her hand and he shook it. "Shelby Barkingham."

"So, if we ever got married, we'd be *Bark-Bark-Snarl!*" He let out a huge guffaw–a truly warm laugh. Rory ran circles around his ankles.

"*Ha, ha,*" Shelby said sarcastically. "You thought that up just now?"

Barclay grinned. "Pretty proud of myself, actually."

Shelby stepped sideways and took him in. He was built a bit like a compact car: wide-set, strong and full through the middle but not fat, thick arms and short fingers. Shelby gazed at his feet, fleshy and thick in black canvas lace-ups. Not her type, she knew, but for ten years, her *type* had only gotten her into more and more trouble. She looked up and Barclay was smiling–a full, warm grin, with a dimple in his left cheek that softened his face into pure, boyish charm. The dimple was, Shelby had to admit, adorable.

Barclay chuckled. "What? You like my *shoes?* Or you're checking out the girth of my–"

"Hey! Don't get any ideas, *Barclay,"* Shelby said, purposely over-enunciating his name. "I'm not getting married ever again anyway. Two ex-husbands and I'm only thirty. So *there.*"

"Three ex-wives, thirty-nine, no kids, two dogs. We're more than even." Then, off Shelby's stunned look, "I was *young.* So, do you date?"

"Jesus! You think you can just walk in here and–"

"If I like you, and I can *tell* that I do."

Shelby picked up Rory and put him back in his kennel. "Yeah, well, I don't date. I *marry.* And I screw that up, so I'm not doing anything. Got it?"

She turned sharply and walked down the corridor, with a chorus of attendant canine barks shooing her out the door.

—∾∾—

Barclay was nothing if not insistent, but respectfully so. He worked his board contacts at the Coulee Humane Society to get himself assigned to all three nights that Shelby worked, which meant that for months they took their breaks together in the linoleum-tiled, gray break room, a situation Shelby at first resented.

"Hey, I told you I don't date," she said two months into his shadowing of her weeknight volunteering. "So why the hell are you following me around like a twelve-week-old Beagle? You're always *here.* Don't you work?"

Barclay was leaning over the microwave in the break room, staring through the glass oven window at a something he had spinning inside it. "My folks died, left me and my sister a small chunk of change, and I make it last. *Okay,* Barkingham? That alright with you?"

"Sorry," Shelby said sincerely. "You have a sister?"

"Yeah, Jillian. On the Chain of Lakes over in King. Turned out her husband was cheating, got the woman pregnant. She didn't know."

"Ouch."

"She'll be okay. Just needs some time."

"I wouldn't be."

"Yes, you would, Barkingham. You're *formidable.* A force of nature."

She stared at him, stunned. *A force of nature?*

He took the top off his dinner, something in a glass container with a Tupperware top, then smiled his dimpled smile, flashing his warm brown eyes at her.

Shelby was eating a burrito out of a yellow paper wrapper that she'd brought from home—cold beans and cheese in a flour tortilla—and he was feeding himself some kind of rice dish, warm from the microwave, that smelled rich and wonderful.

"What *is* that?" Shelby said, leaning in.

"Risotto. Seafood with white wine, broth and butter."

"Where the hell did you get *that* on a Wednesday night in the lost dog club where we're babysitting?"

"I made it, Barkingham. I like to cook." He opened his eyes at her surprise and tilted his head. "What—you think guys can't cook?"

"I…uh, most guys, in my experience…" She screwed up her face, considering him, chewing on her burrito.

"Most guys have no *finesse*. They can't romance for *shit*. They pull away before the kiss is done, they leave before the night is over, they snuff the candle before they even light the fire. *I'm* not most guys."

Shelby stared at him. His confidence bowled her over. *Who the hell feels that sure about themselves?*

"Wanna taste it?" He offered her a forkful from his own fork. Shelby stared at it: the intimacy of it struck her, his mouth having been on the tines, and she took in a sharp breath.

"I don't have *fleas,* Barkingham. Taste it!"

Shelby leaned in and slipped the risotto into her mouth. The rice was perfect—*al dente*, buttery, shrimp and baby scallops with…*what?* Tiny bits of lemon rind? It melted in wine-infused perfection in her mouth.

"Damn, this is good," she said.

"It is, *right?*" he said, sure of himself. "Food is romance, Barkingham, plain and simple. Any idiot with a sensual bone in his body knows that."

———

When Kelsie and Shelby's mom got wind of Barclay, they couldn't resist harassing her. Shelby now had a *tell:* she was being charmed, and she couldn't stop talking about him.

"Barclay *this,* Barclay *that,* " Evvy said to her one night over dinner with Avery. Her mom and Avery had married, moved into his beautiful house up in Brice Prairie off Lake Onalaska, and her mom was happy. "When are we meeting this guy?"

"We're just *friends*, mom," Shelby said, embarrassed.

"Like *hell* you are!" Evvy exclaimed. "You're intrigued!" Her eyes went wide. Shelby turned and tossed the salad, avoiding.

"Give her some room, Ev," Avery said evenly. "It's good to start as friends– we did. But you've still got to find the attraction, right Shelby?" He smiled and winked at her, delivering pork chops to a platter.

At the park, Kelsie was edgier. "Fuck yeah, *try* him, Shel," she said pushing her toddler, Jasper, in a baby swing. "C'mon! This guy has *chops*. He's waiting. Any man that can wait can…*uhn, uhn, uhn*." She ground her hips in the air.

"You still gonna talk like that when Jasper's chatting away in full sentences?"

Kelsie grimaced. "I have to clean up my mouth–I know it," she said, pulling a face. She gave the baby swing a good shove, and Jasper let out a loud and delighted shout that sounded like, *Gaaaaaawd!*

"And how's that working out for you?" Shelby said, bursting into laughter.

"Oh shit," Kelsie said, chuckling. "Hey. Seriously. Just don't let the good one get away, alright? You're more than due."

Shelby found, after a time, that she couldn't keep her hands off Barclay. She'd pick at some piece of lint on his sweater or nudge him in the ribs when he made a joke (usually at her expense) or touch him on the forearm when she asked him something, staring into his warm brown eyes when she did it. She liked his *smell*, too. When she got up near him she'd take a deep breath, taking in his earthy scent. *You're sniffing the man–get a grip already!* But she couldn't stop. She wasn't attracted to him, she was certain, but then, why couldn't she keep her hands and her nose to herself?

Barclay received these gestures calmly, evenly, it seemed to Shelby. He would stop, standing very still–eerily still, like the first time he had snuck up behind her in the kennels, seeming, to Shelby, as if the world had stopped spinning for him or the air had stopped circulating. He didn't move and he didn't try for her: he simply stood stock-still and let her come closer. It mesmerized her.

He teased her one day when they were standing in the light-blue hallway to the kennels about her dog-training voice. "You *coo*, Barkingham. Like you're talking to a baby."

"I do *not*," Shelby said, squinting her eyes at him.

"You do. You're a dog *coo-er!* You want everyone to think you're so tough, but you're a big ball of jello inside for anything that loves you."

"Maybe I am," she said, dropping her guard. She reached up to tussle the hair on the back of his head. *What had made her do that?*

Barclay froze, breathing evenly and staring at her, and she retracted her hand, looking down at it as if it wasn't attached to her body.

Then, Barclay kissed her. Just up and did it. If Shelby was honest about it, she knew he had been waiting for a moment of encouragement from her. She had given it to him.

It was a Wednesday, after they had cleaned kennels and visited with each canine, and she had stepped in close to him after their dinner break and whispered, "Come here."

He moved in and stood a few inches from her face–he was exactly her height–and she had breathed on him. Stared into his eyes, inches away, and stood there.

"Here? This close?" he said, letting his eyes lock with hers.

"Yes," she said. "Right here."

It was what she did when she was training her most resistant canines, staring down, close-in, seeing who would flinch first. But it was more than that, she knew. She was allowing herself to get near him. Very near.

The next night she was excited and giddy–she was adopting Rory at the end of the week, the little Lab and Dachshund mix, bringing him home to her own house–and as she put him back into his kennel and stood up to attach the clasp, Barclay turned her around and pressed her up against the chain-link fencing, leaning into her, slowly.

He slipped one strong arm around her back, protecting her from the press of the metal fencing, kept his face back from hers, and looked at her. "You're beautiful," he said, with a purr in his voice.

"No, I'm not," Shelby said quietly, staring back.

"You're beautiful *to me,*" he said, and then pressed his lips to hers. His mouth was like melting butter on hers–warm, not overly pressing, but firm and, of course, because it was Barclay, confident. *What was it about confidence that was so compelling in a man?*

He smelled like fresh linen and clean-scented bar soap. His lips were full as she kissed him, and as she felt the sensual press of them on hers, she opened her mouth to him and pulled him closer.

Shelby was used to men who moved their arousal up against her in three seconds or less–thickening in jeans pressed up against her legs or pelvis–but

Barclay didn't. He held his hips back, keeping his strong arm around the small of her back, and made her *wait for it.* She arched her lower body toward him, lifting herself away from the chain-link, but he pulled his hips back farther, still kissing, not letting her connect.

"Not yet," he breathed into her ear. "You'll have to *wait.*"

—⁓—

On the night they went to bed together for the first time, Barclay cooked for her. Nobody Shelby had ever dated had cared to draw her out, not by cooking for her, certainly, and not sensually either. Her dating was all "slam-and-jam," as Kelsie dubbed it, fast and visceral, and her marriages had happened so quickly that she'd hardly gotten to know her husbands before she was living with them. Barclay–the 'not-her-type,' shorter-than-her-preference, receding hairline and thick-bodied man she thought she could never warm to, had aroused her. And he had done it by waiting for her. Like a good dog trainer, he had done it by listening. By learning about her. By *liking* her.

"You don't go to a man's house for dinner unless you're ready to have sex with him," her mother had said gently the week before, her eyes trained on Shelby's. "Are you ready?"

Shelby smiled. "I am," she said.

"Okay then!" Evvy said and hugged her daughter.

Barclay made her a seared scallop appetizer, then beef bourguignon, and for dessert, a home-made preserved-lemon ice cream topped with crème fraiche that he had made by hand. She was touched. He had flowers as a centerpiece, a good wine, and checkered cloth napkins on the hardwood table.

"You've entranced me," he said at dinner, lifting his wine glass and looking at her through the rounded lens of the reflection in it.

"I have *not.* That's just sex-talk," Shelby said, looking down at her napkin in her lap. But she said it softly.

"You *have,*" he said, reaching for her hand, "and you always will." With her fingers in his palm, locking eyes with her, he led her to his bedroom, laying her back on the bed. Then he balanced himself over her on his elbows, kissing her.

Shelby wanted to rip her clothes off and get naked next to him as fast as she could, and she reached for the buttons on her shirt, unbuttoning quickly, but Barclay stopped her. "Let me," he said, and proceeded to take his time undressing her.

He unwrapped her like a longed-for birthday present, kissing each bare space the unbuttoning revealed, pressing his hips to her through their jeans for a second or two between each button, then pulling back. By the time he got them both naked, she was arching her whole lower body toward him, aching for pressure.

He lifted her on top of him, and said, "Where I can see your eyes..." then gently guided her down on top of his arousal.

She rocked, and he slowed her several times–"Go *slow;* I don't want to miss one second of this"–easing her back from the rise in her excitement. Then, after a heated bit of making her hang on a ledge, he grabbed her hips and pressed, a rush of bright flashes exploding in her brain and groin, and she cried out, closing her eyes tightly.

She caught her breath and began moving on top of him again, slowly. "Now, you..." she whispered.

But he stilled her, pulling her into his chest. "Just for you, tonight...I'll wait."

"No! I want to–I mean, for *you*–"

"It's a gift. So you know I mean it, Shelby," Barclay said, reaching up and stroking her cheek.

She slipped him out of her and curled into his chest, then put her hand on his belly, patting him. "Stay with me?"

He lifted her head with both of his hands and looked at her solemnly. "You really want me to?"

She gazed longingly into his warm brown eyes. "*Stay*, doggie. Please? I want you to."

"And be your loyal hound?" Barclay teared up.

"Yes, please?" Shelby asked plaintively, kissing his dimple.

"Already am," he said, and pulled her to his chest.

––––

Their wedding invitation read:

Bark, Bark, Snarl:

You are Cordially Invited to the Canine Lovers' Wedding Celebration

Shelby wore a simple sheath dress in ivory, with a long veil that, up-close, had lace dogs woven into the sheer tulle. Their cake was in the shape of an over-sized dog bone–chocolate with fudge frosting with a handful of dogs drawn in blue and pink frosting on top of it.

Kelsie was her maid of honor, and at the reception she stood, a little tipsy on Prosecco, and said, "It's been a decade-long quest, but, thank *fucking* God, Shelby finally found her mutt and it turns out he's a *prince!*"

Her mom and Avery stood up and sang the Beatles' tune *All You Need is Love,* all in dog-barks, which brought the house down.

Shelby's favorite cousins showed, Dory with her wrangler boyfriend Cord, and Will Henry with his redheaded girlfriend Alisa, and they'd all danced until midnight. It was a true celebration.

After the wedding, Shelby and Barclay moved into her little house on Fifth and Winnebago, and Barclay brought his two hefty dogs, Shep and Grover, and along with Rory, her adopted little Dachshund and Lab mix from the Humane Society, the five of them settled in to a domesticated contentment. A hand-painted wooden sign over their front door read, "Snarl all you want, but love rules here."

Five months into their marriage, Shelby ran into both of her ex-husbands in one week. She hadn't seen either of them since her divorces.

She walked into Vinyl House on a Monday afternoon—a retro record store near UW that she and her first husband Judd used to frequent when they were getting along—and there he was, standing in the eighties section as if he'd materialized out of thin air, a *Tears for Fears* album propped under his right arm.

"I wanted to say I'm sorry, Shel," he said to her when they sat down on a bench outside the store. He looked down at his massive hands in his lap and wrung them. "I fucked up. You were good to me and I screwed it up."

His jaw had gotten harder, his mouth a little thinner—he looked more like a man—and though she knew he was probably just as good-looking as when she had been with him, something had changed. She felt no *pull.*

When they parted Shelby shook his hand. Though it seemed strange not to hug him, she felt no need.

Two days later, her second ex-, Lance, walked up behind her in the grocery store checkout line and tapped her on the shoulder. She had heard he'd gone to South Carolina for a job, but he stood in front of her, his black hair still shaggy and his pouty red lips still full. Funnily enough though, when Shelby looked at him, she didn't find anything compelling about him.

They stood outside the grocery store for a few minutes, Shelby shifting her paper bag full of food from arm to arm, and Lance said, "You're happy. I can tell."

"I am," she said, dipping her head and smiling. "Things are good."

When he left, he kissed her on the cheek, and there was no charge in it, the old electricity of him tamped down to the level of an acquaintance's greeting.

When she got home from the store, she could hear Barclay cooking something in the kitchen, and the smell of sweetly herbed meat sautéing made her smile. Shep, Grover, and Rory yapped and licked her hands.

"I'm home!"

"Hey, Barkingham! Get in here! I'm making you meatballs–by hand!" He came down the hall and handed her a glass of red wine.

"Missed you," he said, and nuzzled her neck, the dogs running circles around their legs underfoot.

She put her wine glass down on a side table and took Barclay's face in her hands, suddenly serious.

"What?" he said.

"Nothing," Shelby said, her eyes filling. "It's...you're the most gorgeous thing I see all day."

"Naw..." he said, shaking his head and smiling. "Not me. I'm just a *mutt*." He brushed a tear off her cheek and reached both of his arms around her.

"You're so *beautiful* to me," Shelby said, holding him and setting her face down on his shoulder. "You always will be."

He pulled her back from his chest.

"Always? For all our dog years together?" Barclay's dimple creased his face, and his eyes glistened.

Shelby smiled. "Always," she said.

I mean—good God!—who in the world could possibly need to spend twenty thousand a year on eyebrow shaping?

Leaving Lefty

Lefty, my boyfriend, did eyebrows. Not hair. Not make-up. Just eyebrows. Seven-hundred big ones a year, a swanky co-op in Soho and a tiled-roof Spanish in the Hollywood hills. All on the dubious merits of whimsically placed (or not placed) eyebrow hairs.

My best friend Jorge, who called himself "A Hefty Hunk of Latin Love"—or HELL, for short—slid slightly off his heavily lacquered barstool and leaned in toward my ear. It was two days after Lefty's unceremonious and temporary exit with another man, and Jorge pursed his lips, then hissed at me with venomous inflection, "Lefty is *fey.*"

I leaned over the bar—Midtown, minimalist, over-the-top New York City chic—and ordered two more ridiculously priced martinis. I needed gin.

"I'm telling you, Gil—he's trite, he's insignificant, *and* he's fey," Jorge snipped.

"What do you want from me?" I badgered back at him, waving down the muscled-and-pectoral-flexed bartender who appeared to be sneaking a hit off a joint at the end of the bar. The room was dark, black and tan and leather-themed, and heavy on the black. The place was about as far from the Rhinelander, Wisconsin farm country I grew up in that I could fathom going, but I suddenly had a ridiculous urge to go back—to disappear into the clandestine corn fields where I used to fool around with high school boys who, by their own assertions, weren't *gay*—no, God help them—but just *experimenting.* I wanted to be invisible again, like that.

Jorge sucked the pimento from his remaining olive in one deep-throaty breath. "The eyebrow, my ass!" he snorted. "It's the *mouth* that really matters, flyboy, and you know it." He kissed his pillow-soft Peruvian lips together with a *smack*, the wide-set pools of his chocolate eyes electrified with pique.

"I'm perfume!" I said, irritated. "I know not a goddamned thing about the eyebrow!" It was three in the afternoon, and the gin was going to my head.

"Ha!" Jorge huffed. "And neither does *he!*" His black-brown curls—a full mop of them, goddamn him—bobbed as he spoke, perfectly offsetting the coffee-and-cream tinge of his face in the half-light.

I was, for better or worse, the perfume editor ("scents," we called them) for a not-so-insignificant New York publication; it was perfume that had made my career. I'd gotten off the bus from Rhinelander at age eighteen, and I'd stayed for decades. And yes, I had made something of myself, had climbed a gay-themed ladder of success, in New York City, no less; had escaped a rural, upstate-Wisconsin closeted life.

Just then, however, I had been humbled—oh, so publicly—by the pomp and circumstance of one very fortunate and fornicating eyebrow stylist. Lefty had taken off in the middle of a lavish East Side dinner party with a couture cashmere designer with nary a nod my way—gone for two days without a word. And though I wanted to believe that when he sauntered back into town (and into my bed), self-satisfied and blasé about it all (with a perfect little lie about where he'd been and why he hadn't called) that I would throw him out, I knew—in truth—that I would not.

He promised to be faithful—that's all I could muster in my heart.

I smoothed my gel-sculpted, thinning hair with one swipe and then gave up. I was sure I looked like hell. A long, thin, horizontal strip of mirror hung behind the liquor bottles on the bar's wall at eye-level, and I stupidly caught my reflection. I looked how I felt—sallow-cheeked and small, distorted in that awful fun-house sort of way: pale and stretched out at unflattering angles.

I asked Bartender-Boy for matches—"Give him whatever he *wants*," Jorge insisted emphatically when I asked—though I couldn't smoke in the place, and I had quit the nasty habit years before anyway. Officially, I was nicotine-free. Unofficially, I smoked when I was stressed, and at that moment, I needed something to do with my hands. I did not wish to revert to my fifteen-year-old nail-biting and fiercely insecure farm-boy gay self, but I was precariously on the verge.

Bartender-Boy handed the matches over—a black and khaki-green, oblong-shaped book of them—stupid, garish design—batting his lashes at me as he let his fingers linger in my palm.

"No, no, *no*," I said sharply, catching his eyes with a razor-gaze and drawing my hand back, quickly firing up a matchstick. "I'm rebounding…"

"And you're old enough to be his *father*," Jorge quipped out of the side of his mouth. "In case that *matters*."

I shut Jorge up with a narrow-eyed glare, then waved the match-stick out with a flick of my wrist, sulphur catching in my throat. I looked down at the slight paunch forming around my fifty-two-year-old self and grimaced. Bartender moved his sculpted, twenty-something face into a sultry smile, chuckled, then placed our drinks, winking at me.

"And it doesn't count as *rebounding*, Gil," Jorge snorted, "if you won't break up with the jerk." He turned his face away with a dramatic toss of his head and soldiered on. "I mean—good God!—who in the world could *possibly* need to spend twenty thousand a year on eyebrow shaping? He's a *thief,* that's what he is! A spoiled-rotten-brat-*diva* and I'm glad he's gone!"

Jorge was doing his best to make me feel better, and though it was a catty and theatrical attempt, I was not biting. I had been humped and bumped right off the stage—"Give him the hook!" I heard in my head, my farmer father's old joke: aping the jostle of a Vaudevillian being snagged around the neck with a cane, then dragged off-stage behind the curtain to be cursed and shamed. That's how I felt: hooked and slammed to the ground. Stepped on. Seven years of my life with Lefty—a man who was once wickedly funny and affectionate, but who had become meaner and meaner the more successful he became.

I gulped four huge sips of my martini, downing it. "Another!" I cried dramatically, as if I was in a *Bond* movie.

I turned to Jorge. Jorge was makeup—a "*-stylist,*" not an "*-artist,*" he would emphatically enunciate when some backwoods innocent made the land-mine-erupting mistake of calling him the latter—and just then, two rungs down from Lefty on the *Who's-Who-in-Ultra-Glam* insider call list. Truth be told, Jorge would have loved to be in Lefty's shoes. Still, he made a damned good living painting famous faces in the coveted castles of the print-model world. And he *was* on his way up, no matter what Lefty said.

"In six months' time every catwalk model you live to hate will be endorsing your makeup line…" I raised my empty glass and pressed the chill to my cheek, blowing my words out with breathy commercialism. "*Jorge Herrera. Stark-Naked Makeup.* You'll be huge."

"As will *you*," Jorge said, leaning in closer toward my face, a bit bug-eyed.

"No, not me," I said, looking down into my depleted drink. "All that I will be is *alone*."

—⁓—

Jorge wasn't just blowing smoke. I did have my own little entrepreneurial venture—if I could keep my head out of my debilitating relationship with Lefty long enough to focus on it. A perfume line called *Stripped.* Serious interest, so said my attorney.

Neither Jorge nor I were responsible for coming up with the nudity angle—God knows it's been done and done, but good ideas work for a reason, so there you are.

At a Tea Dance in the Meat District—retro-leather vibe, big barn of a dance floor—Jorge had jumped up on a platform and began gyrating next to a slim, black-and-wavy-haired god-like creature who was giving him the eye. The man was a dark-haired Jesus look-alike with close-cropped Javier Bardem facial hair.

"I'm Jason," he yelled over the din. "I'm a meat purveyor!"

"Really?" Jorge yelled back, pulling me up on the platform by one arm. "What *is* that?"

Lefty was with me, already dancing with another man and smiling from twenty feet away. Young, blond and handsome—that was Lefty—in a wide-set, full-bodied way; not tall, but meticulous about "lean fashion," as he dubbed it, body-hugging clothing that clung to his sculpted biceps and thirty-inch waist. I watched him as he pressed his slim hips up against his dance partner's thigh, eroticizing the movement of it, eyeing me. A tease. Not so fun after a second or two, I found, and I turned away to look at Jorge and his new friend.

"What's a *meat purveyor?*" I heard Jorge over-enunciate loudly over the vibrating and pulsing bass.

"Classy meat cuts," Jason hollered, lighting a half-smoked joint. "Chefs. Nightmare customers and a warehouse full of pigs and cows. This is my place! No cows tonight!" Jason spun around long enough for me to look up and catch a glimpse of the prongs and clamping objects hanging high above the floor. He passed me the joint, the burning scent rich and pungent.

I shook my head. "No, thanks."

"You cut up cows on this floor?" Jorge hollered back. Jason smiled and shimmied his Greek-god shoulders. The backbeat rattled underneath me, and I suddenly felt nauseous. I reached for my tequila shot and downed it, then swilled and back-pocketed my bottle of beer and grabbed onto a nearby rail.

Animal slaughters. I had grown up on a cattle farm. My father raised beef, grew alfalfa and corn—Rhinelander, Wisconsin was *ultra*-rural—and as soon as I graduated high school, I caught the first bus off it. Gay, fey, and all things fashion. That was me. Not such a great match for a teenage boy in corn country. My older sister Daniella used to drag me to the old brick library in town, to a dank little room in the basement to get me away from the farm when my father was slaughtering. Even the smell of newly cut meat fifty paces away in the barn, pungent and bitter, could make me throw up. Now, the thought of standing on a meat-threshing floor (for lack of a better phrase) flipped my stomach in a cruel way.

"This is Gil!" Jorge shouted, still dancing, nodding at me and thrusting my hand out by the wrist to shake Jason's. "I'm Makeup! He's Perfume!"

Jason twirled and tipped his wavy locks to look at us. "*Jorge's Stark Naked Makeup* and *Gil's Stripped-Down Perfume*. There you go. Fifty-mil a piece I'm betting!"

I looked at Jorge and Jorge looked at me–Lefty long gone, out the door with his dance partner, I was guessing–and with wide eyes and plots hatching, off we went.

———

"Specialized styling, *darl*, and Jorge just *doesn't* have it!" That was Lefty–smug–standing in my Upper East Side apartment after he'd returned from his gallivant with the cashmere designer, his pet name for "darling" rolling off his lips with a drawl. He liked to play at being Southern, as if pretending could blot out the fact that he grew up rural and working-poor, with an unemployed father and next to nothing in a tiny little place outside Chippewa Falls called Thorp. We had that in common, our Wisconsin roots.

It had been ten days since I'd been drinking twenty-seven-dollar martinis with Jorge in that dark, Midtown bar, and the thought made tears prick and sting at the corners of my eyes. But just then Lefty and I were on our way to dinner with Jorge, an event I had had to lobby for relentlessly and with excru-ciating diligence. I needed to level myself.

"Gil, come on! Jorge is *invisible!*" Lefty said to me, gazing into my gilt-framed hall mirror and adjusting a hair or two of his own prima-donna placed eyebrows with a dab from the tiny tube of structural gel he always kept in one pocket. "Why you want us to *dine* with the man–"

"Why do you always have to trash Jorge?" I said, cautiously, but with more whine in my voice than I intended. "He happens to be a good fr–"

"Doll, doll, *doll!*" Lefty screeched, much higher-pitched than necessary for my close-range ear. "Jorge is not coming up! I'm up, you're coming up, and Jorge will not climb this ladder any more than my two-hundred-and-eighty-pound *father* will ever become Calvin's underwear model! So let it go, Gil!"

I stared at him. *He wasn't always like this*, I thought. *He used to be sweet.*

Lefty turned and kissed me, libidinously and deliciously. I succumbed, in spite of myself, finishing the embrace with his hands wrapped around my ass and a press of his hips cemented in, hard and close. "Just for you, Baby," he whispered in my ear, then pulled away.

But I knew it then. Unkindness never helps a relationship; it always comes back to slap you in the face. *Unkind to my friend, sometime soon you'll be unkind to me.* The cheating–yes, yes; on some level I suppose I knew it–was a species of cruelty which I had allowed but not tolerated well. Outright meanness was something else. Bright red flags. Thirty minutes later, that not-a-welcome-parade, fabulous flag-waving of character flaws would come back to bite me in the ass, sure as sugar that burns on a high flame.

We were seated at a table at Café des Artistes on 67th and Central Park West–Lefty, Jorge and me. Lefty wouldn't deign to utter the new name of the place–*The Leopard*–wouldn't allow *me* to utter it–claiming loyalty to its old owner, whose hand he used to try to kiss if George would let him (the guy filed bankruptcy on the place in '09.) But I suspected it was territorialism: Lefty staked out much of his early, recognizable fame at the *des Artistes* bar.

The place had been a power-broker's room for years, and though I had always felt ill-at-ease inside it, I found the new, sleek, light and airy version of it cold. *Colder.* I missed the tempering that the dark wood walls and hunter-green upholstered booths gave to overly ambitious conversations; the softening the dim light and heavily polished oak bar brought to power-hungry lunches. Now it felt vaporous. I yearned for the old menu, too–the comfort of too much cream and butter in every contentment-inspiring entrée, throwbacks for me to my mother's heavy-cream macaroni and cheese with farm-raised bacon in coarse chunks.

I'd thought that leaving a place–farm country; that small-minded northern Wisconsin prejudice against *my kind*–would make me never want to go back. But it wasn't so. Three decades later, whenever I was in over my head, I'd long for the simplicity of the place, for the unpretentiousness of people who looked you in the eye and said their piece.

The evening at *des Artistes* was supposed to be Lefty's attempt at condescension to what he clearly believed was my now-beneath-me (and beneath *him*, certainly) friendship with Jorge. An unspoken offering, I had hoped, of amends for taking off with the cashmere designer. He was supposed to make an *effort*, for my sake.

I was lingering over the haddock-and-potato gratin–a nod to George Lang's menu, the old owner, and an appetizer special for the evening–smearing too much of the stuff on artisan bread. Jorge was doing his best, too, so I thought.

Friendly. Chatty. He was *trying*. Then, all at once, to the chase:

"So, Lefty," Jorge said, looking him straight in the eye. I saw the call to duel in the gaze, and pushed one more piece of bread with haddock into my mouth. Lefty had, of late, been unable to stand human eye contact. His eyes would flit left and right with a flicking of his head, an affectation he had developed with the mega-sale of some gold-dust-infused eyebrow gel which he hocked on major cable stations. He broke Jorge's gaze in a split-second, lifting his drink aloft as if he was in a Tennessee Williams play.

"I understand the price of *gold* is just *skyrocketing*–" Jorge said, his eyes twinkling.

"I don't think that's *true*, but it's *so* nice of you to point that out, Jorge–" Lefty sneered, waving over the waiter for another bourbon.

"So what happens to your *price point* if those little gold *vapors* go ratcheting themselves up through the stratosphere?" Jorge brought his martini up to his lips and sipped delicately, feigning concern.

I shot Jorge a mean, *stop-it-right-now* glare. He smiled back at me with as much innocence as he could muster.

Lefty not only did not answer, but turned to stare–*hard*–at two young, hard-body suits who hovered near our table dressed in expensive blue and gray cashmere–Tom Ford made-to-measure couture, surely, and Christian Louboutin shoes.

"I believe I was asking you a question," Jorge said, very nicely, actually, but firmly.

Lefty's eyes refused to budge.

I am horrible at trying to save the moment when the train begins veering off the track, my Midwestern confrontation-avoidance showing itself like a skittish farm dog who's supposed to bark at intruders but stands stock-still and impotently staring instead.

The place was packed that night, the bar crowd backing up into the tables, and Lefty looked the blue-suited hard-body up and down again, staring straight-eye-line from our table into the man's beautifully-clad cashmere ass, lasciviously making a point of it.

Lefty reached for blue-suit and touched the man at the small of his back. Suddenly he was standing, chatting up both men. It was the tone of his charm I remembered, not hearing the words over the restaurant's din, and I was instantly saddened.

"Alright, that's it!" Jorge said, hissing across the table at me.

"Oh Jorge. For God's sake," I said, rolling my eyes. "He's just *looking*."

"And you can stomach this? This, this–*whoring?*" Jorge's nostrils flared, dilating enough so I could see the hairs in his nose standing on end.

"Stop being so goddamned dramatic," I hissed back at him, staring into my gin. "We have our arrangement."

"No, you don't!" Jorge said, too loudly. "He has *his* arrangement and you get screwed!"

"It's me. It's my fault. I'm not exciting enough."

"Jesus, Gil. *Fucking hell.*"

"He said he would stop–"

"And you call this *stopping?* The man screws around the way you and I drink Martinis! *When*, Gil? When are you going to wake up?" Jorge's big brown eyes bulged out towards me, his head of curly hair bobbing with emphatic insistence.

"I can't..." I muttered.

Jorge looked at me solemnly, and then stood, throwing his napkin to the floor, poised for an exit. "Gil, I can't stand here and watch this kill you." He stormed out of the restaurant's entrance door, turning once before he exited to glare at me, then disappeared.

I looked down at the napkin in my lap, then at my hands. My skin was dry–or drying, surely–crinkles of flesh making the space between my forefinger and thumb papery and old-man-looking. My nostrils began to sting: a sure sign of tears.

It was a ridiculous injustice that Jorge should plainly witness my denial–my refusal then to see what was barreling down at gunpoint on my heart bright and blazing to him, but to me, a mere blip on the screen of "having it all." I suppose my fear of being alone (and aging alone) was just that strong: "trying" with Lefty had become an addictive tell, like a man who can't admit that his life is tanking on a dozen daily doses of cocaine.

Lefty went home with blue-suit. I went back to an empty house, a wake-up call and an impending breakup.

—⁂—

The day Lefty came to gather up the last of his things from my apartment, I stood stock-still in front of the mirror in my master bathroom, staring at myself. We had not talked or fought; I had not spoken up for myself. I had simply told him I wanted to be alone. It was a lie.

My sister had called from Lake Geneva, happy. She had met someone. A much-younger man named Delbert. Her ill husband had died over a year ago, effervescing into skin and bones in a hospital bed for months and months in her dining room. She deserved to be happy now. I said all the right things—I loved Daniella—but what I felt was, *Why can't I find that? What is so wrong with me?*

I heard Lefty let himself in with his keys, and the *click-click-click* of the tiny, grinding sounds of the metal objects in the keyholes sent my left eye twitching, and though I held my hand over the left side of my face and willed it to, I could not make it stop. He did not come to greet me, and as I heard him rumbling around in the hall walk-in closet that had long been his, I beheld my own face in the mirror: left eye convulsing, eye sockets sagging, dark bluish-black circles beneath them. I had not slept in days. My eyebrows were wiry and graying, winding hairs poking out in unflattering directions, and tears burned under my lids as I scrutinized them.

I could smell him, just steps away. The brassy scent of his hair gel stung in my nostrils.

Lefty was rustling about, humming in the hallway. *Humming.*

Doing my eyebrows had always been an event between us: one of the first things he had done when we met was to style them for me—a loving act which, I had to admit, instantly made me look younger and more put together—and he had made me laugh uproariously through the first styling, goading me to get over my aversion to what I thought would be the pretentiousness of the act. He had won me over then, me sitting on a low stool and him badgering me to sit still while he plucked, shaped and dyed (covering my gray), and then used his famous (now patented) miniature trimmers to cut each individual eyebrow hair at a unique angle—the blunt cut of regular scissors much too gauche and pedantic for his taste.

Lefty dropped something in the other room, a box perhaps, and I startled. *What is it,* I thought as I beheld my aging face in the mirror, *that has a man hold on by his fingernails to a relationship which long ago has ceased to be kind? That has turned sour, even hateful? Why did I stay with him?*

Suddenly, I had tweezers in my hands. I began to tear at my eyebrow hairs, first on my left side, then my right, pulling them in bunches, ripping at the hairs like I was rooting out a poison, the twitching spreading ferociously to both sides of my face.

Lefty furtively appeared in the doorway of the bathroom, I turned to him, the left side of my face marred now by completely razed hair, the bareness of my eyebrow bone dotted with tiny spots of blood. A tear rolled down my cheek, but I wiped it away with some vehemence.

"Oh, Gil–Baby, *no!*" Lefty said, reaching out towards me. There was horror on his face, and as I flinched and retreated back from his reach, a look of genuine remorse flashed through his eyes, and then, a split-second later, they went blank. Cold. Empty.

I knew in that moment that the truth of why I had stayed with him was ridiculously, embarrassingly terrible: I had kept hoping. I had wanted him to stop being unkind; to be the man I thought he was when I first met him.

"Just go," I said.

A year-and-a-half later, Jorge and I stood in film producer Barry Bettenberg's Hancock Park mansion in L.A.–a huge old-world Spanish, one of ten of various architectural styles, we were told ás we entered–and on this night, decked out in a gaudy and gay-themed Christmas extravaganza. I loved Los Angeles: it was wicked, lawless, garish. And it reminded me how far I'd come from Rhinelander.

At the door, we had been "invited" to sign a release by a burly bouncer which read, "Repeat what happens at Barry's and you're toast. We've got more lawyers than you do for damn-sure." Another bouncer patted us down and collected our cell phones. "No photos, big boy," he said to Jorge, filing them coat-check-style in mesh bags looped on hangers and hung on portable closet rods.

We entered and strolled, taking the place in.

Gargantuan garlands were strung from every surface with tiny red-and-green lights in the shape of penises. Silver-rimmed tables loaded with sculpted canapés sat on glitter-tiered trays, a life-sized sculpture in pate of a body builder's chest and biceps at the center. Outside the wall of open French doors, an outdoor "meat garden" with carving table after carving table of prime rib, ginger-roasted pork, candied and smoked hams, and whole barbequed turkeys served by gorgeous men in tiny black briefs with gold spray tans. A chocolate bar with chocolate waterfalls, then plates of carved and sculpted male members–solid, not hollow–sat under a huge gazebo.

"Jesus," I said, letting my eyes run the length of the penis-lights winding up the oak-carved banister where two naked Santas (the waiters, as promised in the invitation, in furry red G-strings and nothing else), were deep-throat kissing on the stair landing.

"*He-Soos!*" Jorge replied, pronouncing 'Jesus' in the proper Spanish, his voice an octave higher than usual. "Gil, get me a *drink,* will you please?"

Then I saw him. Lefty. Perfect Prada suit, white-collared open-necked shirt, hair coiffed and gelled. Holding court by the champagne waterfall–and not just any wedding-gauche, three-tiered silver-plated number. This alcoholic spectacle could hold whole human bodies in its statuesque carved-cement glory–our host's exact end of the night intention, I was sure.

Lefty leaned back, pontificating on some subject or other and filled his flute with a ballerina-type float of his arm trained under the flow of champagne. I knew that look–the waving of one hand with flair, a cocktail held aloft in the other for emphasis.

I overheard the words, *Krug Clos d'Ambonnay* behind me, and if that truly was the case, the amount of champagne in that vinous waterfall could have paid off my New York apartment at $3,500 a bottle. I was instantly on edge. I watched him.

Two naked Santas stood nearby laughing, attendant to him, pursed lips then flamboyant guffaws. A joke. Not so funny by the looks of it, but he had always known how to hold an audience. The help, making nice.

Lefty had fallen from grace. Some club or other, over dinner. Someone's iPhone turned toward him in video mode, and Lefty spewing catty misogynist crap about a famous actress's ass: the body double, the real ass's size, blah, blah, blah. Twenty-four hours afterward, he was a dark star on every social media site complete with video clips of his foul-mouthed *faux pas*.

I could see, across that huge room, near the patio doors where he stood, that he was nervous. First big social event after the fall, I was guessing. Loss of income these last months. I heard my mother, standing at her farm stove, in my ear: *All that goes up, must come down, Gil. Stay humble.*

Jorge was being chatted up at the indoor bar by a Major Movie Mogul and a gorgeous woman–one of maybe three women present in a body-to-body sea of men–she in a tailored short black dress and shiny patent leather stilettos; all class, friend, no beard, since Movie Mogul was all the way *out*–but "arrival in high places" being announced to the room just the same. Three hundred men in a house and Mogul had chosen Jorge. *Bravo.*

My perfume, "Stripped," had done modestly well. Nothing huge, but enough to buy a tiny summer cottage in Sag Harbor and put something away for when the silly show of my career was all over. Jorge had done a thousand times better, seven lines of products and a national marketing campaign, and I was proud of him.

I hovered near the prime rib carving table–God knows why, since the smell of meat had always been a precarious thing for me, especially when I'm upset–and seeing Lefty had rattled my poise.

I stared. I could see that it had begun to show on him: the meanness around the mouth; the tight little lines above the lip; a bit of sagging in the cheek. It was more than eight years ago I had let him into my life. He had been ambitious, proud, hilariously witty in a way I could never pull off, hungry for the success I had and more. Young enough so he could lean on me, profess love, promise me things that I believed in. He *had* been enamored with me at our beginnings, or so I needed to assure myself, for I did not want to believe that I could have been blind enough to choose body-sculpted magnificence, youth and pretentious ambition over genuine love.

Across the room, Lefty touched the earlobe of one of the naked Santas, then leaned in and kissed it. He had done that to me, many times–a flirt and a tease when he wanted something–the first time, the night he proposed he move into my Upper East Side apartment, a conversation that had not gone well. I had been seeing him "exclusively" (that was our deal; no tricks) for three months.

"Think of what we can *be* together, Gil," he cooed in my ear. "The kind of life we could have."

He was lying on my chest after sex, and I was stroking his hair. His bicep–fine and muscular–was pressed against me, his arm draped over my softening belly. I said nothing.

"Kiss me," he said, and then leaned in to place his mouth over mine. He knew how to rouse me with a kiss; how to make me believe that he meant it.

He shifted his hand down to my navel, placing the flat of his palm over it. "Don't you want to love someone?" he intoned, his face very close to mine.

"I do, but–"

"Gil, don't you want to love *me?*"

I hesitated just long enough to anger him.

He got up quickly and faced me, picking up his pants from the floor, pulling them on with particular vehemence.

"Where are you going?" I sat up. "Lefty–*don't*–"

He grabbed his shirt and shoes and stomped toward the door, his socks and briefs still in a pile on the gold plush area rug under my oak four-poster. He turned to face me, his blond hair flattened from my hands and the bed, his azure eyes narrowed. "Gil, whatever it is you think we're doing here–whoever you think you *are*–well, you're not as important as you think. So if I'm not *front page* enough for you–"

"I didn't say that," I said.

"Yes you did. Right there, in that bed."

"Lefty–"

"Don't *bother*, Gil. Call me when you've grown a *heart*."

A week later, I let him move in. I helped him, introduced him as "a bold new style-maker"–hard to believe I actually uttered those words–brought him in under my wing. Made his career, you could say, though I don't like to claim that.

—⁓—

At Barry's party, I was still staring in Lefty's direction, standing alone and pressed against a broad and heavily polished oak-framed entryway for support opening into a huge room with black velvet furniture. Jorge had sent two of the naked Santas my way–twenty-year-old body builders in furry red thongs, Santa hats, and black work boots; nothing else–who began to salaciously dance with me. House music had been turned up, rattling the floorboards. I was an unwilling partner.

Lefty caught my eye.

I held a Sake-tini–a ridiculous drink made of chilled sake, cucumber juice and vodka with a cucumber garnish–horrible, really–and boy Santa number one was pulling up my shirt to bare my belly. I played along, for spite, I suppose, but my heart was not in it.

Jorge to the rescue. He grabbed me by the arm and steered me to the bar. "What the *hell* are you drinking?"

"Sake-tini," I said, stoic as all get-out.

"Where's the olive?" he hissed.

"No olive," I said into my drink, "just cucumber." I laughed sardonically.

"Let me have that," Jorge said, grabbing my glass. "Hey Santa! Yes, yes–*you!* We need help over here! Serious timing issue! Gin martini, olives, as fast as you can!" He threw a twenty to the naked Santa behind the bar, tipping him.

"Now you listen here," Jorge said with mother-hen resoluteness and concern. "There is nothing worse than you pining for some asshole on his way *down*, for God's sake–" of course, I had long ago made the sad mistake of telling Jorge what Lefty said about him, that Jorge was not *coming up*–"so suck it up and be a *man*, Gil. Enough of this whining over a jerk."

"Look, it's my life–" I muttered.

"No it's not!" Jorge said, replacing my drink. "It's mine, too! I have to listen to it after he uses you again. I swear to God, Gil. You want to go off and pull another *Palm Springs*–"

I had slipped and slept with Lefty. Months before; big Palm Springs Styles Section event. Stupid. Woke up the next morning, and two sugar-coated sentences later Lefty was gone.

"I won't. I just want to talk to him–" I snapped.

"I swear on my mother's grave, Gil, if you *bed* that man–"

I waved Jorge off and headed towards Lefty. Lefty's eyes caught mine in a tractor beam–instantaneous terror, masked in split-second cover by an I-won't-ever-care-and-who-do-you-think-you-are stare, then a toss of the gaze back to hold court.

I approached and the Santas fell quickly back–"Thank God!" their eyes read, retreating briskly with quick turns of the back and trays held high. Lefty's scent, his expensive-but-brassy aroma, permeated my nose and throat.

"Well, well, well–*Gil*," Lefty drawled. "Darl, I see you've become one of us."

"*Us?*" I said, straining to make a point.

"*Stripped.* Your perfume. Outdid yourself. Never thought you could. How about I buy you a drink to celebrate?"

"Drinks are free," I muttered. I was not drinking, my martini full, spilling slightly.

"Yes, yes, Gil," Lefty said in a biting tone, reaching for a cigarette. "I believe that's the point."

"And that's the difference between you and me," I spit out, not knowing where the words were coming from. "You'll offer when it costs you nothing. But when you've got to give something, forget it."

"Now, now, don't be *bitter*," Lefty uttered dryly. "It looks ugly on you." His eyes darted around quickly, screening for an exit strategy, then dropped to his champagne flute. "Well, I think I need something stronger than this. If you don't mind–"

I grabbed him by the arm. Firm. Not aggressive. "It hurt, Lefty. You used me. And I'll never fall for another *you* again, do you understand me? You're unkind and *awful*."

He threw his head back to make some crack or other, but the directness of my honest outburst landed on him–God knows how. He stopped to stare at me, deer-in-headlights. I still had hold of his arm and was gripping strongly, holding his elbow out at a sharp angle from his ribs. I looked down at my hand, clamping his still-shapely bicep.

"Enough!" I hissed, dropping his arm as I turned to go.

Halfway across the room, I looked back over my shoulder. The small circle around Lefty had gone suddenly quiet, and he was standing there, abandoned by all–instantaneous, hushed silence–the center of not-so-gracious attention. It was the briefest moment in time, a public recognition that something cruel had passed between us, the perpetrator outed.

Jorge was on the far side of the room with a straight visual shot to my little scene, and I saw the worry in his eyes drop away and replace itself with something like pride as I trudged back in his direction. "*Bravo*," he mouthed to me, Movie Mogul whispering in his ear over the din.

I turned down a hall and found a quiet room. The library, it seemed. I sat down quickly, having left my drink somewhere along the way, then took a huge breath and hissed it out as slowly as I could.

"He's not even *remotely* worth it," I heard from a cushy, green-velvet corner chair right behind me.

The man was dark, slim-to-almost-skinny, fortyish, with kind eyes. And he was knitting.

"I'm Jack," he said, a warm lilt in his voice.

———

Almost a full year after the Bettenberg party, I stood with Jack, the knitter, at the corner of 13th and Broadway, heading for Union Square—Jack's new neighborhood, having moved from L.A. to be near me. It would also be, in a moment, the first time I knew I was truly in love with him.

I had not thought I could love after Lefty; I had decided my heart was inept, that I was better off alone. But Jorge had encouraged me to try with Jack, and so I had.

We were heading to some shoe store or other, a basement sale that Jack had an enthralling need to attend. There was a dead-sounding *thump* in the middle of the street—that horrible, dull *thud* of metal hitting flesh—and in an instant Jack was crying, his head angling at a severe angle with tears dripping down his face.

A Labrador-mutt had run headlong into traffic and gotten hit by a produce truck, the driver less than sympathetic, jumping out his driver's-side and bellowing at the bleeding and wounded animal.

It happened in two seconds the way awful things do: one moment I was annoyed with the way my new parka tag was rubbing through my T-shirt onto the skin of my upper back, and the next, something terrible had happened within spitting distance of my body and I feared I was watching something die. I stood stock-still—that yelping, pain-filled dog cry like nails on a chalkboard—no breath in my chest.

A small crowd had gathered in seconds on two corners, gawking, confusion and concern in each stare as blood pooled on the asphalt.

Before I could connect thought to action or distress to movement, Jack had run into the street, leaping through taxi cabs and oncoming traffic, and took the animal in his arms.

Jack shouted, "Animal hospital—goddamn it! *Somebody!!* Where the *hell* is the nearest vet?!!"

"30th and Park!" someone yelled from the sidewalk.

Blood spilled onto his shirt and jeans, but he did not look back. He ran, the dog bouncing against his chest, his thin arms wrapped tightly against its flailing body.

Jack would tell me later that he ran the seventeen blocks to 30th and Park with the dog in his arms because no one else would, or because *someone* had to, but I will know (and maybe it is only me who will ever know) that he could not stand by and watch another creature writhing in pain. That his compassion overtook him the way it always does when a person is genuinely kind to the core.

The dog, Esther, named after Jack's favorite deceased Aunt, survived with only a slight limp, and moved in with him.

—···—

As the months passed, the things I found I loved best about Jack were simple. He liked to stand naked in his living room and adjust the angle of the television (which he kept on a rolling stand in his tiny apartment), queuing up a movie while he ran the bath, then he'd position the set so he could see it from the tub, and slide in and watch. "Come join me!" he'd holler, and so I would, the two of us lying close and splashing water across the old chicken-wire-styled tile on his bathroom floor. It was something Lefty and I never would have done; it would never have occurred to him to ask me.

Jack liked to read lying flat on the looped blue-and-gray wool area rug in the middle of his room (the place was barely more than that; a minuscule single of an apartment), his dog Esther splayed out on his belly. He'd prop his head up with two bed pillows and turn the pages of complicated historical novels, his free hand stroking Esther's head. He could lie like that for hours, content, looking up every now and then to grin at me when he felt me watching him. I found it serene, doing nothing, really: napping or reading or listening to music, being together.

On weekends, he would make me stay out of his closet-sized kitchen to cook something special for us—lamb roasted in pomegranate juice and port, or some other thing he had dreamed up. (His Sunday morning peach-and-walnut waffles were a miraculous event.) I'd sit at his tiny table with a white cloth draped over it and wait. He'd appear with the dish in his hands, placing it in front of me with a bit of pomp and pageantry, singing out, "Ta-dah!" It touched me, his need to please me, and I was moved that he liked to have Jorge over for dinner, too—the three of us crammed around the barely-there, tiny table, bumping elbows as we ate, laughing.

In bed, he was tender, giving. Intimately, I was a man who'd been trying to breathe with my mouth open in a sandstorm—I was dying for air. Jack gave it to me. It was devotion, plain and simple, and I breathed it in.

⸺ᨓ⸺

In early May, after Jack's and my second winter together, I sat in my friend Carolyn's kitchen in the Village, the room a gourmet extravaganza of catering glory. She and Jack were cooking, stirring chocolate ganache in a double boiler, layering a fig crostata.

Jack, the knitter, the dog-rescuer, would become my husband. We would marry in a week, and the two of them were taste-testing for the wedding. Daniella, my sister, would come from Wisconsin from her Lake Geneva house. My parents, at Daniella's urging, have sent cards—one a piece—they don't fly anymore—with best wishes and a little money for a gift.

Two weeks before, Jack and I had flown to Rhinelander where I introduced him to my mother and father, a trip that had gone surprisingly well. Jack had spent at least half the time over the stove with my mother, the two of them frying and baking and sharing recipes like they were long lost friends; he'd made my father laugh and they'd parted with a warm handshake, my father's best effort at affection. I was pleased.

In the kitchen, Carolyn pulled a *Clafoutis* in a cast-iron skillet from the oven (port and quince), thick mitts covering her hands, and I smiled at Jack as she placed the pan on a metal cooling rack. Carolyn turned and winked at me, grinning. Her seventeen-year-old, Denton, bounded through the door, hugged me, Jack, and then his mom.

"Taste this, Denton," Jack said, offering him a bit of the fig filling on a wooden spoon.

"Wedding stuff, Gil?" Denton asked me, sticking his fingers in the copper-bottomed chocolate pot.

"Fingers out!" Carolyn quipped, tease-slapping his hand. "Homework!" she said, smiling, as he headed into the hallway and ran up the stairs.

Denton was gay. Carolyn and her husband never blinked once over it. Denton's boyfriend was welcome in the house, allowed to sleep over, allowed to stay in his bedroom. Kindness. Acceptance. At seventeen. I was bowled over by it.

"You're a lucky mother," Jack said to Carolyn. "He's a good person."

"I *am* lucky," Carolyn said, tearing up, and Jack leaned in and wrapped his arms around her, hugging her.

With Jack, my life had grown simpler, less heavy. I no longer moved in the circles of the fey and the fickle, the places in which I was made to feel less-than, where ambition pained my heart. I gave up perfume, makeup, *eyebrows*. I had come back to a truth I learned in Rhinelander, at home, without ever realizing I had absorbed it. That a person's worth is based on how they share their heart, and nothing else.

Jack and I sold my place in Sag Harbor and bought a quaint little cottage on Lake Mohawksin with a huge deck, near my parents' farm in Rhinelander. We moved, just up and did it. Jack and my mother became especially close.

Jorge retired on the success of his makeup line, then fell in love with a goat-cheese farmer from Upstate New York and bought them a huge farm. He called me constantly, we laughed over our new rural lives: no specialties for either of us anymore. I had become a generalist—a lover of the simple, the ordinary, and the true. I wrote: unpretentious novels for young gay kids, hopefully sharing something worthwhile about character, benevolence, finding love.

I had never noticed, in the days when I was with Lefty, how kindness was a barometer for everything I would choose to live for in my life, but now I know it is so. What I might earn, or be famous for, or even look like as I age couldn't matter less to me in the end. How I might fall from grace, or make mistakes is not the thing either. It's how I get up again, who supports me, who is there to love me and let me love them back. To have genuine friends, to have found acceptance with my parents, to be lifted up by a man I'm devoted to who is kind to me and wants me for my heart: this will sustain me.

—⁓—

Last month, on a trip to visit Carolyn in New York, I ran into Lefty. Jack was with me, and so was Denton, Carolyn's son, and we were coming out of the subway at 53rd and Fifth. Lefty was getting out of a black town car in a pricey gray and charcoal pinstripe, a full-length camel-hair overcoat thrown over his shoulders.

I knew what Lefty thought as he spied us coming up from the subway stairs to the sidewalk—us in jeans, sneakers, parkas—the corners of his mouth turned up into a sarcastic sneer. We were ten feet away, and he threw his head to the side, about to speak, and without a thought, I turned Jack and Denton by the elbows and steered them quickly away up the street.

"*Kindness*, Denton," I said. "Run from everything else."

Jack smiled at me, twined his fingers around mine, and I looked up at the open city sky, grateful. 🐦

Her long and lean arm draped elegantly toward the ground—it was elegant, wasn't it?—as she pulled a green leaf from the space between her sandal and her toes.

Green Leaf

The radio hissed a blast of scratchy, abrasive static–louder than usual this time, for some ungodly reason–and I jumped six inches, banging my head on the squad car's ceiling. "How's your *stake-out*, Delbert?" Colleen, our dispatcher, shouted over the air. She let out a loud cackle, cutting it off in mid-air, halfway out of her mouth.

"Colleen,"–I was annoyed–"for God's-friggin' sake, do you have to shout? I can hear you just fine if you open your mouth like a normal person and *speak.*"

She ignored me.

"You catch any bad guys? Heist-meisters? Jewel-thieves? Or some prissy Lake Geneva *doyenne* hauling ass downtown with the family credit cards?" She guffawed at her own joke, loudly and full-on this time. She liked to play at being hard-boiled, as if we weren't holed up in this miniscule, overly-wealthy, nothing-going-on Wisconsin lake town, but it just made me feel like I wasn't cut out for being a cop.

"Just doing my job, Colleen," I said, drily.

I had been hiding on a side street off Lake Shore Drive on Maytag Road, west of Highway 120, waiting to pick up speeders breaking the thirty-five-mile-per-hour limit–an easy afternoon of fish-in-a-barrel, since no one ever obeyed the law unless there was some event in town, weekenders clogging the roadway and dragging traffic to a mind-numbing crawl. Lake Shore was the main route in and around the south side of the lake–tree-lined, high-end properties with a stream of wealthy Chicagoans trafficking in each Friday afternoon.

"Oh, for fuck's sake, Delbert, nothin's happening in this damned town! Laugh a little! It makes the day go faster."

"Yeah, yeah. Ha, ha," I said, with no particular emphasis. "You happy now?"

"Whatever," she said, sighing into her mouthpiece. "Captain wants you in here today at four, okay? Some shit at Fontana beach. Really, he wants to take you out for a beer. He thinks you're not happy here." I could hear her clipping her cuticles with the little pair of stainless steel manicure scissors she kept propped in an antique can on her desk.

I didn't say anything.

Clip, clip.

"Kimmel, you heard me, right? Four o-clock."

"I don't need…look, I'm *fine!* Just leave me alone!" I said.

"Yeah, well…Captain thinks–"

"I got it. We done?" I picked up my speed gun and held it up with one hand. Three cars blazed by at 46, 52, 60 m.p.h. I groaned.

"You're killing me with joy, here, Kimmel. Look, you're not going to get any action in this town without some *juice* and a little attitude. Women here need a *pulse,* if you know what I'm saying…" she trailed off, and I heard the *clink* of her cuticle scissors dropping into the can.

"I do fine," I snapped.

"Yeah, not really though," she said before I clicked off, so kindly that it hit me in the chest, like a basketball slamming into my ribs and knocking the wind out of me.

She was right. I wasn't fine. I was dried up.

I stared straight ahead across South Street at a bush–a hedge, really–two hundred feet long and twelve feet high, perfectly manicured. Lake Geneva.

It was my thing lately, staring. A little over a year into this job, and nothing going on but the occasional break-in on a fancy summer rental, some farm kid running off with a flat-screen or smoking dope in the owner's living room with six of his deadbeat friends.

How I had gotten here? I'd been in San Diego–not my hometown, Milwaukee was, but where I worked a suburban beat for eight years. Sixteen months ago, I'd put in for a couple of East Coast posts, and this one, too, and then Lake Geneva Police Department interviewed me (on video, which was a little weird), and two weeks later I was here in a squad car, sitting by the side of Lake Shore Drive.

I'm a decent cop. I know the law, and I don't panic in an emergency–at least, that used to be true–but I never wanted to be anywhere near the inner city action. I never had the stomach for it. But why, at thirty-nine, I needed to flip everything upside down, I don't know.

Well, that's bullshit. I know. I just don't like to fess up, because the weight of it knocks me flat on the cement and I can't cope.

So that's where I was the morning I saw her. Sitting in my Lake Geneva-issue squad car, staring at the almost unreal green-green of the hedge across Maytag, listening for the hum of the gardener's mowers on pricey outdoor square footage–the grating of gears and the smell of cut grass and gasoline–watching them sweat it out over turf, then three-in-a-truck hauling ass to the next property. I envied them their camaraderie.

She was walking. Alone–no dog, no friend, not running or jogging. I caught her in my rear view at about a hundred yards, and like a reflex, started pretending I was doing something important in the car, shuffling some papers and checking my screen. At 6'3", I'm tall and big for a squad car, and I always feel uncomfortable inside the thing. I shifted my body, feigning competence.

I looked up again, caught a glimpse of the driveways to the brown-and-gray-shingled, three and four million dollar lake houses before I saw her. She hadn't seen me at all, but something–*something*–made me want to stop and look at her. Stop and watch. So, I did.

She was wearing a white and gray floral print skirt, halfway up the thigh, lightweight with one of those wrap-around ties, with just enough lift in it that when she walked the fabric floated left and right over her upper legs, as if the wind had caught it. But there was no wind. Sheer white blouse, sleeveless, made of the same lightweight stuff. Long, wavy brown hair, lanky limbs, and the whole effect was as if she was drifting down a river, not walking. I stared.

It was an athletic and delicate walk, unhurried, like a lean animal patiently taking in the scents and sounds of a known scenery.

Then, as she came upon the car, something sad. I couldn't see her face yet, not clearly, but I could feel it in the movements of her body–the slightly dropped shoulders, the eyes down, the weightiness of some kind of sorrow, some kind of loss.

I shook my head. "You're losing it, Kimmel," I said to myself. Some crazy projection of grief I had foisted upon a stranger. And *why?*

"A sublimation," a therapist had said to me, before I had left my old life in San Diego.

"What do you want now, Delbert?" the shrink had asked.

"For it to have never happened," I had said without thinking.

I started tapping the gearshift quickly in the car–a tic I had acquired in the last year–and in a second, she was outside my open window, passing, and she looked in and said, "Hi there." A kind voice. Yes. Kindness. That's what it was.

I had become an observer: of people, of moods, of the tone of a room. Stuff

I never cared about or noticed before. I wrote now–sketches and phrases, pieces of verse. It had been suggested to me that it might help me. It did. A verse-writing police officer. *Yep. That'll get you far.*

I looked into her face and said, "Hi," back to her. She was older than her body movements; older than her shape suggested or than I had placed her at a distance. But she was beautiful.

She paused for the slightest, imperceptible moment, and I smiled at her. Really smiled. What made me do that?

She smiled back and kept walking, waving an angled peace-sign with two fingers off her right hip, her skirt floating lightly across the backs of her legs as she moved.

I knew I was looking for details–another tic, now–every day staring, sitting almost stoically still in this untroubled, quaint lake town, far away from anything impoverished or dangerous. A place with enough outward tranquility that I could sit and think and gather up the moments of what it meant to be alive; a place I could be untroubled by duty, and not crave or want or need anything from anyone; to simply notice.

Seeing her was a moment of noticing, nothing more. And in a second I would have given her up to my own mental prose, my own verse-hunting musings and memory, but then something happened.

She stepped through the wet grass that bordered the one-lane road along the giant green hedge, and I watched her stop and look down at her own foot. She reached for it–one long and lingering sweep of her well-shaped arm–then delicately drew a leaf or a piece of plant out from in-between her toes (it had caught there), and she swept up the green thing to her face so she could look at it; consider it. It was glorious: the arc of her arm downward, the graceful bend, the languishing moment of nothing but a dance of her hand to the grass and then gently called back to her face. The delicacy of it aroused me with a rush as strong as if she had run her fingernails up my inner thigh.

It was a second in time. Nothing. Everything. I had felt a moment of something pulsing in me. Something that had not rushed through my body for so many months. Years, if I was counting.

In a few minutes I would have usually headed over toward Buttons Bay beach, or driven the length of Linn Road to mix up the landscape. But I didn't.

Instead, I pulled the notebook from my back pocket–the therapist's idea, writing "as it arises in you," she had said, and I had looked at her blankly, then incredulously, at the time–and I wrote: *The need you've never known might save you. Or, it might not.*

It was a weekday, so the drive back to the station was easy–not the weekend snail's pace from Chicago's escapees flooding into Geneva–and I parked and locked up when I got there, trying to put on a good face. For all of her pain-in-the-ass qualities, Colleen was usually right, and she had her finger on everything that was happening with Geneva Village's police force. She knew before all of us that Jeff Felton's wife was leaving him; that Claire Heine was getting a serious growth taken out of her intestines; that the Captain's daughter was pregnant by her boyfriend's best friend. (The daughter ended up marrying the guy.) She knew that the former state trooper who badly wanted on our force last January was getting charged with sexual harassment on his last job. God knows how she got it, but she had the dirt on all of us.

So when she said the Captain was worried about me, I knew she wasn't bluffing. She mostly used her information to give those of us who needed to know a heads-up. I had to give her that.

"Hey, Cap!" Colleen yelled when I came into the station. "Kimmel's here!"

She was thirty-ish, full-bodied and big-boned–beefy, really; a loud dresser in flowered and bright prints, and, oddly, it gave her knowingness weight. "He's got a string of perps so you better get out here!" She cackled and winked at me, and then went back to her post, picking up her cuticle trimmers.

"Very funny," I said sarcastically. Colleen watched me closely while she trimmed. *Clip, clip.*

The Captain came out of his office. "Grab your keys, Kimmel. You're driving." He patted me on the back.

We drove to the other side of the lake to Gordy's Boat House near Fontana Beach, the Captain directing me through the backroads past huge estate front lawns and high-end summer houses with tennis courts to the lower-priced, middle class neighborhood. I tried to keep a conversation going as best I could. Beaches, tourists, fishing, weather.

Eric Fiori, the Captain, was salt of the earth. Family man, good guy, easy-on-the-soul. The kind of guy you wanted to have a beer with. But not that day. Not for me.

On the bar's outdoor deck, with a couple of Pabsts, Eric leaned over and slapped my shoulder. "Look at that, Delbert," he said, pointing at a fisherman across the channel who was pulling some sizable catch into a net.

I squinted to see what the guy got but couldn't make it out. Instead, I noticed the water–blue-black with reflected streaks of orange from the sun filtering through the shadows of the buildings and the boats; the gray-white of the dock's weathered wood. I stared at the broken-down boards.

I was hard on people once, I thought. *People I loved. I weathered them.* I winced.

"You okay?" Eric said.

"Yeah, sure–just got bit by something, I think." I reached down for my right calf, feigning, and as I reached, in a split-second the moment came back to me: her, today, reaching for her foot with a sweeping arm, long and lean and draping elegantly toward the ground–it *was* elegant, wasn't it?–as she pulled a green leaf from the space between her sandal and her toes. The rush of watching her filled me again, and this time the arousal made my face flush. I crossed my legs quickly and reached for my beer, feeling the Captain's eyes on me.

"Listen, Kimmel." Eric was talking low, in a conspiratorial tone. "I want to make sure you're alright here. It seems–"

"Fine, captain," I interrupted emphatically.

"Look, I'm gonna lay it out." He took a breath. "Colleen did a little digging–"

"Jesus!" I said under my breath.

"Yeah, well, I didn't authorize it, if that's what you're thinking, and I sure as hell didn't look you up, but you know she's got the goods on half the town, right? It's not just you."

Eric took a big gulp of his beer, then looked out over the water. "Meg and I lost a child, a boy, when he was three years old. I know this might just be me, Delbert, but I wanted to be *off the planet*–I wanted to be dead for a good, long time after that."

I said nothing. I stared. I saw the rippling of the water at our feet–tiny wakes floating in scallop-shaped lines across this captured bit of lake. I saw the shine on my shoe, the reflection wobbly as if it had merged with the water.

The Captain followed my eyes from the channel, and down, and back up again. "Your wife–your daughter–"

I tightened up as he spoke, felt my body ice up and go cold, right through the sweat on my collar.

He leaned in and put his hand lightly on my back. "I think you know what I'm sayin'. Watch the current here. It can pull you down. If you ever need to talk…"

Tears stung at my inner eyes; like needles, they pin-pricked the underside of my lids. I fought them. "Thanks," I said, when I had got my voice, looking straight ahead.

He got up. "I'll catch a ride back. You finish your beer."

I stood to shake his hand, and he clapped me on the back in a sort of half-hug. I stayed standing for a moment, watching him go.

Then, out of the corner of my eye: a long, flared, golden-colored skirt. Cascading brown hair. Those arms.

It was her. She slipped into a small economy car, silver–nothing special–and, alone, put the thing in gear. I startled, walking quickly, but in ten seconds she was gone.

A sign. An illusion or a crazy-making hope. *How is it that an apparition can wake me?* I'd felt nothing for two full years–it had all gone dead–and then the movement of a single arm through space reaching, could suddenly, and this time, even fiercely, press on my insides and make me *want?*

—⁓—

That night I couldn't sleep. I had rented a small single apartment over a garage on Dodge Street–plain and bare, a brown-carpeted room with a tiny kitchen and an old gas oven, and I hadn't bothered with much more than a bed and a secondhand, rickety table and chair I'd picked up at a Goodwill-type store. The place was too close to the station for my comfort, but everything else around the lake was outrageously priced (way out of my ballpark on a cop's salary), and the plainness of the neighborhood had suited me, to be on the outer edge of a commonplace little street smack dab in the middle of Lake Geneva and Lake Como, facing what I was sure would be harsh, even virulent winters when they came. It was the middle of the heartland, but to me, it felt like the end of the world. A bare apartment I was dropped into, alone.

It had taken me months and months to bury the daily grief, the complete immobilization of numbness (for a while before I had come here I couldn't even work.) Though Eric had done a kind thing, trying to reach out to me, all it had done was start the cycle of images all over again. I lay on my flat little bed in my apartment and tried to will the visuals out of my head. I couldn't.

Burning. Lungs filled with it, slammed with smoke. Getting thrown to the ground by two firefighters who had dragged me out and tried to keep me from running back into the disintegrating house to get them.

I got up and went down to my car. I drove, up and down Highway 120, then all around the lake off side roads into neighborhoods with giant, darkened houses–some with those automatic security lights that popped on if I pulled into a gated driveway to turn around–not knowing or recognizing where I was; just needing the automatic motion of something, anything. The spin of the steering wheel through my hands on a too-sharp turn in the blackness, the kicking-in of the engine barreling with my foot heavy on the gas pedal.

I knew I needed to go home and try to sleep if I was going to be any use at all the next morning on duty, but I knew, too, what sleeping meant: it meant dreams. Bad–no, that was a euphemism–*awful*–dreams. Eric's little pep-talk had kicked in the door on months and months of keeping them at bay. To-night, I knew, they would be back.

At 2:45 a.m. I finally gave up and pulled my car into my driveway, a little dirt and tire-tracked area on the side of the garage that housed my apartment. I went upstairs–*why not that night? Why didn't I go upstairs? Why had I slept down-stairs on the couch?* I lay down on the bed, fully clothed, and though I fought sleep, it caught and leveled me anyway.

The heat–a singeing of the boards under me, and I feel it burning my bare feet and skin. There's fire, a sickening, electric-orange hue with white-hot and yellow flickering around the edges of the flames, and I study it, as if I am awake. The hot-ness is like a wall, like steel, but I push my body through it with all the will I have in me and climb the stairs, the steps disappearing one at a time underneath me, as I mount them. I turn from the hallway and they are burning: my wife, my daughter, burning in our bed. Why wasn't I here, in the bedroom with them?

A sharp-pitched sound–a screaming siren–startled me and I jumped awake, falling halfway off the bed. No: not a siren. The barking of a yipping neigh-borhood dog. *Every piercing sound.* That's how it was in the beginning. I heard sirens in car horns, screeching brakes, dogs barking.

I was covered in slick sweat, and immediately angry–so fiercely pissed off that…*what? That life is so fucked in the head.* The gripping of my jaw and gut made me feel like throwing up, and then, as I slid off the bed onto the floor, suddenly: her face. Not my wife's, not my daughter's, but the graceful, walking woman.

—⁓—

There was the issue of finding her, which could, I knew, be ridiculous. She could be a weekender from Chicago or Milwaukee who occasionally stayed on for a few days, randomly appearing in town. Worse, someone who lived very far away, here on a lark–a rental car, a room; nothing more–who I could lose forever.

Lose forever. Yes. That was the pinpoint of it. The thing I could not talk about or even have mentioned to me; the numbing seasons lost to loss, like an alcoholic's black-out years.

I vowed to patrol the neighborhood where I first found her. The thought made me laugh. "Found her," loosely translated, meant that I had already attached myself to a fantasy of her help, maybe even salvation. To a person I did not know. *A sinking man,* I thought. I got out my notebook and wrote: *Drowning in numbness and clinging to anything I can get my hands on.*

I decided she was a float sent to me in the midst of a rip-tide–no, not a rip-tide: a shock. She was a float in my drowning stillness, the aftermath, the utter unbelievable truth of my rescue and not theirs. Not my wife's. Not my child's. The guilt of being the sole survivor; the stunning boomerang of an accident, of harm, and then being left standing when those I loved were not.

Waking up in the morning and remembering that they were never coming back.

The next afternoon I sat in the same spot off Maytag Road, staring at the overarching trees, hoping she might be a regular walker, out at more or less the same hour of the day, but I did not believe this. Something in her movements told me that she was freer than that.

We'd gotten a new recruit at the station just out of law enforcement academy, and the captain was angling for me to take him out in my patrol car. Paolo Avila, a charmer, good-looking, twenty-ish. Chatted up a storm about his dad's dairy farm out in Mayville the first day I met him. I'd convinced Eric that I needed to be on my own a while longer, for emotional reasons. But it was really about *her.*

It took three days before I found her. I covered all of the small lanes around the lake, six, eight times a day, circling back to neighborhoods like a homing pigeon after fielding the day's calls–lost key lock-outs, car break-ins, 911-ambulance back-ups.

She was walking down Sue Ann Drive toward Rushwood Park when I spotted her–all of the streets nearby named for children a long time ago, I suddenly realized, and it grieved me and struck a pinpricked blow to the barely inflated air-balloon of my courage. *Laurie Street, Connie Circle, Bonnie Brae Lane.* But she was coming towards me!

I was out of my car and walking–not my official, all-business, police officer walk, but a stroll. I was wearing my uniform, blues with shoes shined (not my doing, but the local shoe guy in town.)

"Hello!" she called out, about twenty feet away from me, her voice kind again. I smiled. "Is there some trouble?" she asked. "I saw you out here a few days ago. Has something happened?" She was wearing a pale blue dress, a summery and flowing thing that made her body look lean, and her hair was pulled to one side.

I wanted to shout, *Yes! Something has happened!* But I didn't. It strained me to make small talk. It always had before, but now I had been emptied out. I wasn't close to having the light touch or the happy interest that's required for it. But I didn't want her to leave. The moment mattered.

"I'm on a break," I said, as breezily as I could muster. "I like to walk these neighborhoods."

She laughed a robust laugh. "I do, too. It's a solitary person's labyrinth."

How had she done that? Shown me a piece of her loss, and laughed, open-heartedly, at the same time? I felt myself being pulled: two sentences, and already drawn in to her. How was that possible?

Wanting is a trap, I heard in my head, *it only leads to pain.* The fight to stay numb.

My therapist had said, "People will show you who they are in less than five minutes. All you have to do is listen, watch and *feel.*" She had said it in response to my "fear of moving on"–a death-sentence therapeutic label of emotional immobility and ineptness, and I had resented it. Now I wanted to trust that adage, that supposed truth.

She looked up and angled her face into the sun. "It's something about the fact that there are still some of the old, shingled houses left here. History. Something good."

"You have one? A house?" I asked, genuinely interested.

"I do," she said, smiling at me broadly. "Off Knoll. Down there, across Lake Shore." She reached and pointed. That arm, lifted, graceful, like a piece of sculpture.

"Oh, *across* Lake Shore," I said, "*closer* to the lake.*"

She chuckled. "Oh, don't be too impressed. Mine's one of the old ones. Brown shingles."

"How is it, living here?" I was sincere. Something I had not been for–what?– months, certainly. Two years or more, easily.

"Empty, if you want the truth." She turned her eyes to mine, watching how her difficulty landed on me, and I stopped walking and locked my eyes on hers.

Her face–was she forty? Fifty?–flushed, and I saw tears begin to form in the corners of her eyelids. I knew it wasn't divorce. It was death.

She looked down at the asphalt and said, "I should go."

"Don't," I said, and lightly touched her forearm with my fingers.

She looked up at me, startled, and said, "Really?"

I nodded.

She paused, shook her head as if to shake out something that was clouding her vision, then with a tinkling bit of laughter in her voice, asked, "Would you like to walk with me?"

—⁓—

Her name was Daniella. *Something lovely,* I thought, when I heard her say it out loud. I didn't care about much anymore. I could walk through my daily life like a puppet, like an imposter, even. I could pretend as much as I needed to, to get by, but I cared about being near her. Why? And why all of a sudden?

I came to walk with her every day, and we strolled the lanes of her home: Eugene Drive, Marianne Terrace, Sue Ann Drive–streets that had been named for someone else's child, someone's family. It seemed dark, and yet somehow right, that even the streets called up our grief–that though we had barely outlined our stories of it, told our names and our simple histories, our personal facts (always the facts) of terminal disease (her husband), the fire (my wife and daughter)–it was watching us, following us.

I had not been able to speak about it at all, to anyone, the words like knives in my chest, barely piecing it out to the therapist I saw after it happened. But to her, I could say it and not collapse or fall down. I was astounded.

She carried her loss like a weight she was constantly pushing to the side with a heave and a shove; then, on some days, a sloughing off or a shedding of a skin. Her grief was visible on her, like a layer of sticky stuff membraned between her and the world, but it had wisdom in it, too, and humility. The ability to pause and notice.

"You know, I think losing him changed my personality," she said one cloudy afternoon, the two of us sitting on her wide front steps. Her house was simple, two stories with white shutters, down a long driveway and set on a grassy plot with a broad front porch.

"It seems to me you've probably always been a good person. Awake and kind. Just my opinion," I said.

My "breaks" had been growing longer. I was stealing an hour or more a day to be next to her, driving back to her between car accidents, break-ins, some stolen equipment out of the back-end of Pier 290 Restaurant, then a couple of runs around the lake with that new kid, Avila. Already, she and I had created a habit. I would park four or five houses down, a different spot every day, and then show up at her door. We'd sit and talk for a few minutes, and then we'd walk.

"Well, that's perfectly nice of you to say, Delbert—" she said, wriggling her bare toes on her porch steps.

"I wasn't trying to be nice. I was trying to be *accurate*. It's less taxing for me. I don't have the capacity for bullshit anymore."

She laughed her robust laugh, throwing her head back freely. "Well, all the same, I've become something I never thought I'd become."

"What's that?"

"You really want to know?"

"Yes."

"*Isolated*," she said levelly.

She lifted her arm—that delicate, well-formed limb—and put her hand over her eyes in embarrassment. "Oh, God...I'm sorry. I'm not fit for anything." She moved her hand from her face, and her eyes lit up from behind—a kind of glittering in the center of the irises—and she smiled at me as if her own humanity amused her.

"You're perfect," I said.

—⁓—

I watched her move on these walks, each day; watched the form of her body—athletic, mature, yet still girlish. How was it that she had preserved her girlishness, even in grief? She had to be older than me, maybe by a lot, but I had come nowhere near preserving my humor or my lightness in my loss, and certainly not my youth; yet she had. I was gray and heavy-bodied at thirty-nine, half in my skin and half out. Deadened. Until now.

Sometimes I stared. She would catch me and laugh—a warm laugh, a recalling of a humor that was once, I was guessing, more full; that hinted it might be able to find a richness like its predecessor again.

The push of my heart toward her made me feel wide awake, and I couldn't help it. I wanted to touch her.

Her neighbors began to notice us. *What's that cop doing over at your house every day? Always the same guy, isn't it?* She began to sense things; rumors. She brushed them off.

"Oh, good God," she said to me one Tuesday morning as we headed down Garrison Drive. "You'd think I was seventeen and my twenty-three-year-old high school track coach was sneaking into my basement." She threw her hair back. "I'm a more than grown woman."

"Does it bother you?" I said, looking ahead. My throat had caught in the saying of it.

"No, it doesn't," she said emphatically. "It's none of their damned business who I make friends with."

"Did that really happen?"

"What?" she ran her long fingers through her hair and then tied it up in a tucked coil in one smooth motion. The sight of her neck, long and naked, instantly aroused me, and I dug my hands deep into my pockets.

"The teacher?" I said, needing something to say to cover the sudden heat in between my legs. "The coach, when you were seventeen?"

"It did," she said, smiling wickedly at me.

I laughed–*really* laughed–the rareness of it like cracking open a crate that has been sealed for years and then gives up its dust when pried open.

She got quiet all of a sudden, mentally floating someplace far from me, her attention vaporizing. I wanted her back.

"What're you thinking?" I asked with a sharp enough intent to make her startle.

She looked down at her hands, then skyward, as if some untethered answer lay up there. I watched her eyes as they searched. "I was thinking about how old I am."

"You've never told me–"

"How old were you when you were your adult height?"

"Does it make you uncomfortable? How tall I am?" The thought made me instantly nervous. I quickened my pace, walking faster.

"Delbert. That's ridiculous." She chuckled at me. "Why should it? I'm just trying to get a picture of you when you were younger."

"I guess I was seventeen or so. Tall enough to make my old man back away from me when he was pissed, if that's what you're after."

"Right," she said, drifting into thoughtfulness again.

I modified my gait. It was a hazard of long legs and tallness: sometimes I walked too fast for her and had to remember to pace myself.

"I used to have growing pains day and night," she said, looking down at her body. "I was five-foot-seven when I was twelve. I tripped on things." She laughed broadly.

"I'm sure you were a sight to see then." I imagined her at eighteen, twenty, twenty-five. Long, delicate, lean. An erotic, young animal moving into the world.

"*Gangly* is the right word, I think," she said. "I get them now. All over again."

"What?"

"Growing pains. In the middle of the night, my shins ache like they did when I was a teenager." She looked up at the sky again, fathoming.

"I didn't know you could–"

"Psychosomatic, I'm guessing. Just grief in another form." She pulled at her blouse, untucked it from her jeans, let the lightweight hem float as we walked. "I used to take my brother Gil to the library in town, to protect him. He was gay, and in Rhinelander back then you might as well have been painted orange."

"Did he stay there? In Rhinelander?"

"New York City. As far away as he could get. Then he married a wonderful man named Jack and they moved back. They live on Lake Mohawksin now." She looked ahead, walking faster.

"Must've been hard on him. Back then."

"It was. The library was this old, brick, Carnegie building, and I'd drag him to the basement, into this little room with rolling carts and no chairs. We'd hide out there, my brother in a corner reading, me with my back up against the wall and my aching legs stretched out on the floor."

"What made you think of that?" I was straining my neck to read her face.

"Reworking pieces of my history, I guess…trying to make them fit." She looked at me, taking me in. "It's *you*, Delbert. My tall, tall friend, walking next to me, both of us with our growing pains. I don't know–it just struck me. Does that sound trite?"

"It feels heavier to me than that," I said.

"You are my *friend*, aren't you, Delbert?" She said it tenderly, both yearning and sadness in her voice.

I wanted to take her in my arms, pull her into my chest in a sweeping up of limbs. All it would have taken was one strong lunge of my body for hers, a pull of my hands around her upper arms and my rush of longing indulged, her breasts pressed up against me, nothing withheld or paced anymore. But it was too soon.

"I am," was all I said.

—⁂—

How does a man know a woman isn't yet aware of his yearning? I don't know, but I could tell. *Maybe she never will be*, I thought. But I didn't have the luxury of believing that. I knew she was older than me. By now, I knew. Her references, her timelines. I didn't care.

I had needs again. My body pulsed and welled with them and my insides filled with images of her. I dreamed–scenes of boats, for some reason, and her in them, taking me someplace. An island, a cove, a grotto of rock in the sea where the sun would angle in and light up the water next to us. Rowboats, sailboats, canoes. Her, me, rowing or drifting, always precariously rocking in the water, but thrilled–both of us–by the movement. Then, on the shore, the sand, naked.

I would wake in my dire little Dodge Street apartment, a remnant of the kind of life I used to have, now ablaze in my body with need. A need I had not felt then, before, or possibly ever. The kind of wanting that had me grab on to my own flesh, fervently pulse my hips, and breathe out her name at the moment of climax.

Her husband had died over a year ago: colon cancer. Three rounds of chemo, radiation, drugs, a trip to Mexico to a last-chance, alternative clinic, and at the end, a hospital bed in the dining room on the ground floor of her house. His name had been Samuel. *Sam.*

A few weeks into our walks, I asked. I was off-duty, and we had walked all the way into town from her house, passing the over-priced shops–organic coffee store, European pastry shop, two-hundred-dollar upscale shirt and skirt storefronts.

"Have you tried to see anybody? Since Sam…" I couldn't say the word 'died.'

"Oh, God, no…" she said. "Have you?" She paused in front of a real estate office with photos of five-million-dollar homes in the window, then strolled ahead.

"Once," I said sadly, turning away. "Didn't go well."

"Ah," she said kindly, then stopped at a floral shop staring at a display of some kind of lilies, big white petals with dramatic stripes of pink threaded through them. "I put all of Sam's clothes in a pile on the bed in the guest room. I was going to give them away, and then I fell apart. I can't go in there now. I keep the door shut and walk by as if there isn't a room there."

"That's the thing about fire," I said glibly. "Poof! There's not a thing to throw away." I was trying to be brave–a new tactic–but it was astounding how the loss could well up and level me in a split-second. My eyes burned.

"I shouldn't have said that," I mumbled, stopping and staring at the cement. She gazed into my face. "You okay?"

"My daughter had these flowered-print shoes–they were sitting on the front steps outside…" I choked on my own words and squeezed my eyes shut hard, bending forward at my waist, trying to hold the tears inside me by sheer will.

"Delbert," she said, almost a whisper.

I stood up and looked at her. "I didn't do enough...didn't give them enough–" I hissed under my breath.

She eyed me, then after a few beats, leaned in near me and said softly, "I can't speak for you, but I'm not really fit for anyone. Probably not ever."

"Don't say that," I said, putting my fingers lightly on her forearm.

She looked at me curiously, platonically.

She was innocent.

How incredible, I thought.

———

My wife had known things about me without being told. She knew the hurt places–my difficult, disapproving father; my mother's premature death. She didn't press, and it made things easier on me, but it distanced me just the same. She had wanted me to cook with her, to be in the kitchen in the evenings when she was making dinner with our daughter. A simple request. I refused.

"C'mon, it'll be fun!" she said, "We'll all be in here together." She turned up *Creedence* on the old retro boom box that sat on our kitchen counter–a tease; my go-to music when I needed to blow off steam–and looked at me pleadingly. She reached into the refrigerator and grabbed a bag of green beans and tossed them to me, her eyebrows arched, throwing them like a football, inviting me. I caught the bag, then walked over and put the beans back in the refrigerator, and half-slammed the door closed.

My wife sighed.

I had just got off the phone with my father. Never a good thing.

"He doesn't want to play with us," my wife said to my daughter, and then stuck out her lower lip.

"Oh, well," my six-year-old said. "His loss."

I spun my head around to look at her, this child of mine, and she simply shrugged and went back to her coloring book.

I caught my wife's eye, her face red with fury.

A waste. A ridiculous waste. To not be a part of love. To not care to. For what? What did that get me now except regret?

———

My mother used to teach me to bake when my father was on duty late at night—he was a detective in Milwaukee, where I'm from. She always worried about him, especially when he was working undercover, and she was angry about it, so she baked to have something to do when he was out at night. She needed the company, and I was an only child, so there you go. I got good at it.

My father used to argue with my mother when he got home and found me still awake. "For Christ's sake, Joyce—he's thirteen and it's eleven-thirty at night! And you're teaching him to *bake?*"

"Oh, shut up, Dan!" my mother would say. "It's not my damned fault that you're out in the middle of some hell-fire half the night, and we're here all by ourselves with our stomachs in knots, worrying about you!"

He'd grab a beer from the refrigerator and slam the door shut—there was always somebody slamming a door in our house; a trait I'm ashamed to say I carried over—but that was the extent of the physical stuff. Some sharp words, a slam, and then a quiet sulk, the two of them. They never laid a hand on me, or each other, but the yelling didn't help.

My father would sit down across from me at the oak Ethan-Allen table that sat in the middle of our kitchen—almost midnight now, or even later—and say, "Jesus, Delbert. *Baking*. Not football. Not baseball. Not woodshop. *Baking!*"

I'd shove the cake I was eating at him—a huge piece of peach or plum or apple or fig (my mother loved fruit cakes)—and storm up the staircase, then slam the door. In the morning, half the cake would be·gone. Never a "Thank you," or, "Hey, Delbert, you're awfully good at that, after all." Just the cake—gone.

It had started then, the baking, when I began to notice that my parents were angry at each other. Why? What for? There was never a clue specific enough to get at what was underneath the fury, just a string of tiny irritations that got blown up into something stupid. They erupted, fizzled out, silenced themselves within ten minutes, but it kept happening, three, sometimes four times a day. It rattled me. No. It *hurt*.

I baked through it, hanging out with my mother late at night. I did other things, too: wrestled in high school, played the drums for a while (my father hated that; the noise), and was a decent enough student. But when things got rough—when my dad had his first heart attack, when my mother started having anxiety attacks and wouldn't quit smoking—I baked.

My mother died from the smoking three days after my eighteenth birthday (lung cancer, a pack-and-a-half a day), and I couldn't get out of the house fast enough. I became a cop. I suppose it's what I knew, that's all. I never could go back into the kitchen. It pained me.

—*m*—

It was a Sunday with her, with Daniella, a couple of stolen hours when I should have been patrolling, when I should have been on top of the traffic at the very least. There was a big art show in town–giant white tents, more-clogged-than-usual side streets, jaywalkers and crazy drivers pulling U-turns in the middle of the road–and I should have been out there in it, but I wasn't. I was with her.

We'd gotten more courageous, more willing to talk about the stuff we weren't talking about anyplace else. Death. What it meant. What it left for those of us still living.

"I figure the whole thing is rigged. Life, I mean," I said with an edge. "You just get over the crap you were raised with, and then–*bam!*–something hits you that you can't possibly ever get over, and what's the goddamned point?"

"I think God's an asshole, generally, and specifically, too," she said, "If there's such a thing as a God…"

We were walking down Cisco Road, on the other side of the lake. She want-ed a respite from her neighbors' prying eyes, so we had met there, parking up near the Community Church. It was gray, mid-morning, and it was muggy.

"Because of your husband's cancer? Or because he's gone?" My shirt was already sticking to my back.

"Both." She squinted and looked up at the clouds, then flipped off the sky with her middle finger. "Fuck you, God," she said, a bit of a sob caught in her throat. "Just *fuck off*, will you?" Then she quickly laughed at herself and looked over at me. "That's a giant help, don't you think?"

"At least it's honest."

She snorted. "Yeah, that and twenty-five cents will get me…" She trailed off.

Then, without warning, her tears began falling. No sound coming out of her mouth, no body convulsions or squinting of the eyes. Just dripping water, falling from her eyelids.

I was surprised, stunned for a moment. I'd never been good at comforting a person who's upset; not for myself, or anyone else. It was hard for me, even with my daughter, to stop and put my arms around her when she cried. It strained me to offer warmth because someone needed it. But I made myself.

I took her by the shoulders and leaned in and kissed her face, in the mid-dle of the street, pressed my lips against her cheeks and forehead and tasted her: the falling, salty-bitter tears, the faint smell of mint on the edges of her lips from her toothpaste.

I held her, pressed my chest into her, calmed her. I felt her heartbeat through my shirt, against my skin; felt arousal pulse through my veins.

Then she murmured into the front of my shirt. "What if it doesn't matter what we did or didn't do? What if it's enough to have gotten through it and still be here?"

I was feeling better. It had been weeks walking with her—the platonic openness at first, the sexual charges under the surface and my own obvious need, the genuine connection with another human being—a woman; and an older woman, I was guessing. All of it was making me feel less heavy. I knew her by her body, her movements, her insides. I could sense her and smell her, could comfortably walk next to her with no pressure, no effort, just ease. Where had that come from?

There were days I couldn't get there—a flood when the bathroom pipes exploded at Button's Bay Beach and they needed extra hands; the day a drunk SUV owner crashed his rig right into the ice cream truck at Williams Bay (no one was hurt, no thanks to the drunk idiot.) Those days were darker for me. I'd slip back a bit, mood-wise, but all in all, hanging out with her was a lift, an opening in the dark cave I'd crawled into.

At the station one day, I brought a plum cake. Homemade. I baked it. It's ridiculous, I know—a verse-writing cop who can bake. I get it. But there it is.

"Jesus Christ, Captain—you gotta see this! Kimmel's got a friggin' secret life!" Colleen shouted when she saw the cake.

The Captain came out of his office and looked at the plate I was holding. The cake looked good. I hate frosting, so I had glazed it, and the thing looked like it could be in a bakery window. Eric looked confused, scrunching up his eyebrows, surprised; and then, recovering, he said, "Well, damn, Delbert. Look at that, will you? What did I tell you, Colleen? You just never know about a person."

"Hey, man. That looks really good," said Avila, our new recruit, his eyes big as saucers. He took two big pieces and headed out the door, grinning.

I'd been passing out slices on paper plates, and I started cleaning up a bit, Colleen leaning on one side of the huge, old, school-issue wooden desk we kept in the front office, the cake on the other end. She was staring at me.

The Captain went back into his office with a third piece of the plum. "Hey, Delbert! Thanks, man. You sure you don't want to open up a bakery?" He smiled warmly. Something had shifted. I could see it. He was less worried about me.

Colleen was still staring. She was flicking her perfectly manicured middle fingernail against her thumbnail, making a *click, click, click* sound.

"What?" I said.

"Something, Kimmel. *Something.*" She eyed me. "You've got a friend. Someone to go have a beer with." She was testing me. Digging.

"Don't know what you're talking about, Colleen." I kept my head down, scooping cake crumbs into my hand with a knife. "I'm just the same." I smiled though, and then she saw it in me.

"Oh, God *damn*, Delbert! A woman! Thank the fuckin' godforsaken angels!"

I stood up. "I didn't say—"

"Jesus Christ! It's about holy-hell time!" She clapped her hands and guffawed loudly, then slapped me on the back—hard. "Captain!"

Eric yelled from his office. "Give the man some dignity, Colleen! And stop saying 'fuck' in the office, will you?"

She ignored him. "Delbert here has a woman!"

I flushed—I couldn't help it. "She's just a friend," I said, low and pointedly.

"Bull*shit!*" Colleen said to my flushed face.

"Colleen!" the captain shouted.

But I smiled. And so did she. And I heard the Captain chuckle.

Since I'd been walking with her, I could do it again. I would wake up in the morning needing to bake something, anything. A cake. Scones. Biscuits. I baked every day in the tiny little oven in my apartment for two weeks. I didn't know what to do with all the stuff I was making, so I baked, and whatever I couldn't eat in a day or two or didn't want to bring in to the station, I threw away.

There were other things, too. I was humming again. Something I used to do when I felt good, working and humming to myself, walking and hearing a tune in my head. I swam some days. Took off out to Fontana or drove to a private spot I could sneak into near Cedar Point, and jumped in. That was new.

She called me; we talked on the phone. She'd taken to calling me 'Del.' The week after the plum cake, she asked me to come by her place and walk.

We had come upon the small hidden park at the end of a cul-de-sac around the block from her house, a postage-stamp sized children's playground with a fenced swing set and a grassy area to sit in the shade. We sat on a small bench with peeling green paint and splinters threading out on each end.

She reached down into the grass and picked three dandelion flowers, her arm lovely and delicate, the way I had seen it on that first day as I watched her cross the road, and a rush of blood filled me below the waist. She popped the tops off the flowers, then held the heads in her palm and began pulling each tiny yellow-orange petal out, one by one.

"May I ask you something?" she said.

"Of course you can," I said gently. A shiver ran through me. She had courage.

She sighed. "If you could change anything at all, besides the fact of your family's deaths, what would you change?"

It was the question I could not ask myself; the break in my heart that would not heal over, which would not mend without its unveiling and unraveling.

The stinging in my eyes—wakes of watery pain, pricking at my eyelids—came in a split-second, and then: a flood.

Tears spilled heavily and so excruciating to bear that my stomach convulsed, and I bent over, hiding my face, slumped and sobbing. It was as if she had pulled a stopper out in one fell swoop, had yanked at the cap of my numbness and it all erupted, the rank and unspeakable awfulness of what had been held in now dumped out on the ground below my feet.

She placed a single hand on the middle of my back—a willfully strong touch, enough to soothe yet still make room for my grief.

I wept for some time, anguish rolling over me in waves, and I could not stop it. She sat, then wrapped those graceful arms around me, until I emptied out, until I could breathe again without convulsing.

I pulled at my shirttail and wiped my eyes and nose on it and looked at her. I felt I was pleading.

"I was *h-h-hard* on them," I stuttered. "Not g-g-gentle enough. Not enough." I cried again.

She moved her hands to either side of my face and turned me to her. "They're not here to forgive you," she said. "So I will."

She kissed my cheek, close and hard, and held my head in her hands, then wrapped her long, sculpted arms more tightly around me.

—⁓—

There was a day when it shifted. There always is. I knew that the recognition of what we were moving towards had struck her, unavoidably and pointedly, and it hadn't dawned with ease. This–*us*–whatever we were doing, seemed to suddenly pain her.

She called to ask if we could go over to Lake Como on my day off. But she was edgy. Unusually so.

"My neighbor asked me this morning if I was seeing my *'inappropriate friend'* again today," she said to me on the phone. "Can you believe that crap? I need to get out of this godforsaken place. I'll pick you up."

She was coming over.

I knew enough not to try to spiff up my apartment; there was no doing that. I thought for a moment of meeting her someplace in town, but I wasn't cagey enough to pull that off. She had asked to drive over and see me, and I had simply said yes.

I suppose I was hoping. I knew we were at the place that two people come to when intimacy presses on the heart and skin and body parts to *act*; to move inside each other, to feel what had been building over the past months of our private camaraderie and closeness, our time building a mutual need–I was sure now–for each other. I had kept it at bay, let her pretend she didn't know where this was going; had let her, and me, both unravel our pain, loss and numbness, sidestepping the issue of desire. But now the jig was up.

I was in the driveway when she pulled up, and I helped her out of the car.

She looked around. The front house, my landlord's, was plain enough. Not battered, but not well-kept or brown-shingled like hers; the old yellow paint cracked and beginning to peel. The yard was mostly hard-packed dirt, with a little summer grass, and though it wasn't overgrown, it wasn't much to look at. We went up the stairs over the garage to my apartment, and I let her go first. She peered inside, then turned on the landing and faced me.

"Did you just move in?" she said with a bite in her tone.

I winced. I had not felt her judgment yet–not directed at me, anyway–and it was like a hard, twisting pinch in my stomach.

"Delbert–God," she said directly and solemnly, stepping into the middle of the apartment. "It looks like you've made no effort at all." There was anger in her voice. Punishment. I didn't know why.

Suddenly the room looked half as big as it usually did, miniature and diminutive.

"It wasn't important," I muttered, looking up at the ceiling.

"Yes, well, *that's* evident," she spit out with ire.

"What's going on?" I said, genuinely confused. "Am I missing something here?"

She snapped her head and turned away from me.

I changed the subject. "Do you want to go for a—"

"I don't!" she interrupted, spinning towards me, her pitch sharp and piercing. "I want to know what you want from me!" Her eyes were burning, full of indignation.

I stepped back quickly, stunned, banging the back of my thighs against the pointed edge of the handle on my small oven. I stared at her, hard.

"I want you to answer me!" she demanded, her lower lip trembling.

I spoke softly. "Daniella…"

I moved in to try to kiss her, tried to slide my arms around her waist, but she grabbed them at the wrist and pushed them away with some vehemence.

"I'm not letting you do this to me. I *can't!*" She pushed by me and ran down the stairs.

I went after her, the engine of her car already rumbling by the time I got down the stairs. I shouted, "Come back, God damn it! Come *back!*"

———

It was twelve miserable hours later when she called and asked me to come over. It was night, after ten. I had been staring blankly at the television screen in my place, not focusing. I hadn't moved since she left.

"I'll be there in ten minutes," I said into the phone.

I drove too fast down Lake Shore—certainly too fast for a cop—and had to keep calming myself on the way there, taking the vehicle down to a steady speed. *Just get there in one piece, Delbert.*

I had no idea how this might go, what she would say, how or if it might end. I rehearsed scenes in my head, trying to prepare myself.

In her house, she passed me a glass of something herbal and alcoholic.

"I make it myself. It's from an old family recipe. It's strong." She was apologetic, humble.

I gulped a bit, then sipped. The drink had a kick. She held her own glass in her hand, watching the dark brown liquid move as she shifted it, and then rolled her head and sighed a huge, relinquishing sigh. She was going to tell me something.

"Delbert, I am older than you think. And I could let you think otherwise, it happens to me sometimes, but…"

"How old?" I said, sounding sharper than I had intended.

She sighed again. "Fifty-seven. To your—I'm guessing—what? Forty?" She said it deliberately, watching it land on me.

"Thirty-nine." I looked into her face. Studied her.

"Ah. Okay, then." She calculated in her head. "So I'll be sixty-eight when you're fifty."

A groan escaped from my lips. "We should be so lucky," I muttered.

Her eyelashes fluttered up toward the ceiling and her lids filled to the brim, wet and full, a small sound escaping from her throat. She looked at me with *what?* Relief? Gratefulness? Sorrow and delight at once?

She stood up then, and took me in–full-on, unashamed, looking up and down my body. Then she touched me, setting her glass on the counter and running her fingers over my arms, my thighs, my belly; the thickening beginning between my legs underneath my pants. With her hands, she took mine and turned them over in her own, touching the lines and the joints, the veins and the flesh. Then she leaned back, gently pulling me through the house to her bedroom, her eyes trained on mine.

At the edge of her bed, she leaned in and kissed me, and I found I could kiss her back. (The one time I had tried since my wife died, I could not.) The taste of her was herbal–the alcohol–and musky. I did not stop her, so she kissed me again, deeply into my mouth, tasteless this time but for the flavor of intimacy– wet and dark, sour and sweet all at once.

Stepping back from me, she lifted my arms into a dance step. I slipped one hand around her waist, moving in close, and with the other I caught her palm and fingers and lifted her arm, dancing to no music, to the air, to the breeze, to the aliveness of touching another human being. I watched that arm that had so simply captivated me in a moment of numbness and noticing; the arm that had led me here.

I unbuttoned her blouse, resting my hand upon her side waist. She pulled at her skirt zipper, eased my belt out from its moorings, peeled back the layers of my shirts–button-down, T-shirt–then tugged at my jeans.

It pained me to stand naked in front of her, it stung and burned another, deeper layer off the protective coating of numbness I had cultivated for so long, the only protection I could muster to keep myself from having to feel. I winced, and she saw me do it, but she didn't move. She looked at me and took me in.

I had done that: gone numb. I hadn't known any other way. And now I did not care to stay numb. It did not matter if I was burned in this, if I was harmed or hurt; just that I had fire enough to care, to want, to need and desire her.

She took a step back from me and gently unhooked her bra, dropping it, her breasts fleshy and draping.

I fell to the floor, on my knees, and drew her legs out of her panties, staring at her feet—those feet that had first had me notice her, long and delicate like the rest of her; toes with a green leaf caught in them—and I kissed them. My head rested against her belly, holding her there, on my knees, both of us naked and unwound from grief, from loss, from accidents and diseases and unplanned acts of neglect and pain. *This time, I will not hold back. Not for a dead mother or a difficult father. Not for a wife or a daughter who's gone now.*

On her back, on the bed, I caressed and moved my mouth with intention and kindness, meaning to please her. I gave her all that I had: drawing her to me, using my fingers and belly and hands, making her want. Not letting her have me until she needed as much as I did, as much as we each should need each other in love, all of us.

Here was another soul I could hold and know, want and love, and who would love me back. It was more than love; it was a calling. And I would go this time, willingly, fully, blindly and full of ardor, knowing that the moment—noticing it, feeling it, needing it—was all I would ever own, all I could ever have. If it should be taken from me again, in a half-second, in the tiny burst when a star I had always believed would be skyward burns out and then suddenly, almost abstractly, falls from the sky—well, I would not miss this part of love again.

There, as I entered her and rocked her beautiful, human, alive body upon my own—one bare, graceful arm resting upon my shoulder, the other held aloft in my hand as she pleasured herself astride me—I saw the shape of her delicacy, the litheness and fleshiness all at once; the maturity in her; the kindness and willingness to love. The movement of a moment noticed, paid attention to, and held inside me. A moment held dear.

—∿—

There were eyebrows raised in town, I knew. A thirty-nine-year-old man marrying a fifty-seven-year-old-woman; a local cop and a longtime homeowner (who's shingled lake house was worth a couple of million now.) There was gossip, stories of our families' deaths bandied about as if it were dinner theater; 'gold-digger' accusations (me), sex-starved widow stories (her). Store clerks who I'd never seen before recognized me when I went to the hardware store or the dry cleaners; I'd see it in their faces.

I couldn't have cared less. I had friendship—the captain and his wife Meg, the new kid Paolo and his dad Manuel who came down from his Mayville farm for lunch once in a while, or to go fishing.

More than that, I'd found something private in this tiny lake town, something secret and full of wonder, and it had helped me to heal. I'd stumbled upon more than love: I'd found the *willingness* to love. To be in it, all the way; to revel in every touch, every day I had with her. And if that was death's legacy to me, well, so be it.

I'll still flout surrender to a God, still stand with her and flip off the higher power in the sky that kills off some of us before our time; that allows for unexplained pain and distance in relationships and the inability to find a road to overcome them. I'll still curse loss, and the numbness that strikes the heart because of it.

But I'll also bless love, and kindness, and the need and ache of devoted bodies for each other. The grace of a single arm, moving delicately, as I watched, reaching for a simple, green leaf stuck between sandal and toes. A miracle in a tiny moment of noticing. ❧

You heave the boot with some force, a good-sized two-and-a-half inch chunky heel at its base, and glass shatters everywhere…

Atotoniclo

You are just fine–you *know* you are; you're just friggin' *fine,* for God's sake–managing, bearing up–you're absolutely *handling* it. And then one day, you abruptly realize, you most certainly are *not.*

It is the day your husband dies, and you are standing next to his bed–home now, nothing they can do, the two of you in this box of a Milwaukee apartment (not your *real* home; that was Janesville, a life before this *wasting.*) He is disconnected from all of the tubes and beeping objects and screens he has been wired to–screens you watched for months on end, like a mesmerizing but over-dramatized Thursday night movie-of-the-week (red, digital numbers declining or rising; alerts and alarms going off so often that you came to think they were part of the clatter of your own brain)–and then, all at once, you throw your heavy-heeled boot through the apartment window.

You heave the boot with some force, a good-sized two-and-a-half inch chunky heel at its base, and glass shatters everywhere (it is an old window; you are not really sure if you will ever get the shards out of the cracks in the wood floor) and three hours later, you are still there, picking tiny sharpened pieces of shredded glass out of the area rug under your husband's bed. He barely rec-ognized the upset when it happened–the sharp smashing crash of the window shattering–and as you crawl around, hours later, next to his box spring (what used to be the box spring of *your* bed, together), picking up minuscule pieces of ragged glass with your fingernails and hypnotically focused two inches off the plush of the rug, he opens his eyes, your husband–just once–then looks at you and says, "Feel me when I'm gone, will you?"

When you moved to this place eight months before, he was already weak, not yet the skeletal shell of himself that he'd become, but pale and thin and wan-looking just the same. He couldn't help move your weathered green corduroy couch or the weighty headboard for the bed—no boxes full of heavy pans or books or junk—and the minute you and the hired guy got the bed onto its metal frame, he'd fallen on to it, breathing way too hard and then wheezing repeatedly. His eyes opened wide when he saw your face—the panic in it—and in a split-second, you sensed he knew that you hated this place, this empty rented apartment and what it would come to mean for the two of you.

He had smiled then, with his mouth soft in the parting of his full lips, and his whole face and body seemed to come back to himself, warm and quirkily charming and needing you. He'd pulled you down on the bed, guiding you on top of his body, and as he kissed you, he whispered in your ear, "Seeing you is living."

—∿—

Two days later (you sat with his body, no breath, for a full forty-eight hours, not calling anyone), you lift your laptop into the air—something about the emails pouring in with chirpy messages like, "We know Denny will get better soon!" and "Denny will be up and around in no time!"—and you lift the thing six-and-a-half feet in the air (your arms reaching with all of your lean height) and drop it onto the hardwood floor, just to see it crash. To be honest, you do more than drop it. You hurl it.

You are not, by nature, volatile. You are patient, so you are told; not easily aroused to anger, ever. But this—this vanishing experience, this ghosting of the man you have loved with all of your might—is not bearable. And, you determine in your heart, *it is not natural.* It is wrong. It lights a match inside you, the robbery and condemnation of it a prison sentence of violation that cannot be requited, and it incites you inside like an erupting wildfire.

You are certain that you *hate* whatever fucked up God there is, whatever deity is responsible for this heinous theft.

He was a junior high school teacher—the "was" you are immediately using to think of him two days after his death, the past tense of the man you loved so fiercely for eighteen years of your life, rattles you enough that you take a hammer to the bedroom mirror—dangerous; the thing is an antique and it shatters into some wickedly obscure shapes, things you should never pick up with bare hands—but you do it anyway, not giving a shit and cutting three fingers in one swipe (nothing serious, but enough to bleed well for sure, and drip all over your shirt.) As you rise from the floor and look into the newly kaleidoscoped mirror–eyes flat, long brown hair matted to the sides of your long face–you realize: *I am absolutely not okay.*

The thought sends you over the edge–a meltdown coming right up under your skin, like an explosion that bursts through the floorboards then catches the gas lines, blowing everything up. You lose it. The hammer is now in both of your hands, and you beat the bedroom door, smash all the glass out of the framed photos in the hallway–wedding; sailing together on Lake Michigan when you had that old, rickety sailboat; barbeques in your old backyard; trips to Alaska and New Zealand, holding up beers in a pub in Sydney. Photos of you, caught by surprise in your vegetable garden in Janesville, before you lost the house and moved to this bland little apartment in Milwaukee to get closer to the hospital.

Hospital. The word explodes in your heart, and you are at it again with an incensed fervor: you hammer the kitchen cupboards, pound the sheet-rocked walls, beat and slash the canvas paintings (your very own, painted with your own hands and favorites of his), and pummel the front door.

You try your luck on the front window, but it is solid; nothing doing. You try again with a weighty metal desk chair and all of your body weight behind it, and still: no crash. Finally, you take a heavier, thick-legged, wooden bar stool (the chair you sat in at your kitchen counter, sipping wine when he was strong enough to cook dinner), and you send it sailing through the plate glass into the tiny square of snow that is your front yard.

You instantly remember a solid wooden bat he kept, his father's; a slugger of an old baseball relic trapped in some back corner of the hall closet. You go to the closet door–the rattling, wobbly handle slipping in your hands and the smell of stale vacuum cleaner bags and dust wafting up at you from the darkness–and you dive right in there on your knees, digging with your hands through folding chairs, mops, vacuum cleaner parts, stuff tipping left and right and banging against the closet walls as you scour the baseboards with your arms.

You grab the bat and pull–all of the stacked junk falls on top of you, beating your limbs and back–and you grasp the weathered wood of it to you like a child, and collapse on top of his running shoes (four pair in wild color schemes–he had a thing for them), and you lay there on the floor of the closet, gasping.

When the tears come, you are unprepared for the way they rip you from the inside, and you stay there for hours, hunched into a ball on the closet floor, clutching the bat, weeping into his shoes.

———

It is the neighbor who finds you, the newest one from across the street who you have barely said hello to. She is kind, and you are grateful because there is nothing else to be: you are swollen-eyed and–let's just say it–hysterically beside yourself; your hands bloodied from the mirror shards and your clothes spotted with big, red splotches. You have the baseball bat in your hands when you come to the door, the big wooden barstool is tipped over in the tiny square of snow-covered grass in the front yard, the window's plate glass splintered all around it, and the inside of your place is completely trashed.

And, of course, there is his body.

Your neighbor is gentle–she must've lost somebody she loved fiercely, too, once; she isn't horrified, she doesn't judge–Laurel by name, and she gets you into the shower, makes some calls, gets you dressed, and finally takes you across the street to her house to sleep in her guest bed.

When you look at yourself in the mirror of Laurel's lavender and floral bathroom, you think, *Of course I saw this coming. But it didn't make a damn bit of difference.* It hit you like a tidal wave anyway, an ear-splitting rage erupting in your head and a disemboweling routing out your heart.

Somehow, days later, when you walk back into your place, it has gotten cleaned up, the glass man has been called for the front window (you later discover that Laurel paid for the cleaners to come in, coordinated the window repair with your building manager–how *kind* people can be, really), but your paintings are gone, the evidence taken out; and now, all that is left of the mess is some photographs left on the kitchen counter, the frames gone, the handful you haven't completely ruined sitting there in tattered-edged pile.

———

You don't want a memorial for Denny, you don't think you can bear it. All of that reminiscing about him poised to send you over the edge again (I mean–*come on!*–you have to face the fact that your husband is dead when a hundred people, including dozens of his junior high school students, are all standing there saying so.) But your mother comes from Boston where she has moved from Stevens Point to be with her new husband Warren, and arranges one anyway.

Your handful of friends and work acquaintances show up from your office and politely and overly-gently pay their respects–they've heard you'd gone ballistic–in the receiving line that your mother insists upon having at the funeral home. They stare at you with bewildered and widened eyes–you had been well-liked; a receptionist with a ready laugh at a farm insurance agency–an over-fascination transparently readable on their faces at your slip off the edge of normalcy. The agency had been run by an old guy named Ponty, before he retired, who had offices in Green Bay and Janesville–a warm and funny person who was always nice to you. You had not told his son Terence, who runs the place now, or his wife Claire Rose, about Denny's illness (not able to talk about it without imploding), calling in sick too often with no good excuse.

Claire Rose leans in to you as she passes through the receiving line, whispering in your ear kindly, "Elise, dear. Why didn't you tell us?"

You have no response. Later, you will find that the envelope she presses into your hands has a check for one thousand dollars in it.

You miss your brother David, who would have pass-blocked for you today with your mother, would have stood next to you and shuffled people away neatly and quickly. He called from the road, filming for *National Geographic* on Everest or Kilimanjaro, you can't keep track. He avoids your mother like the plague, anyway; her controlling bursts, telling everyone what they should think and feel. Why he ended up being able to *run,* to get away, and you stuck close, you don't know.

Without David, your mother stands next to you while you grit your teeth and shake hands as more mourners approach, and when you begin to drift and glaze over, she grabs you by the elbow and says, in an utterly rational tone, "Pay attention, Elise! *This!* This right *here!* This will help you to accept that he's gone!"

Your mother handles the dinner that is hosted for Denny after the service at his once-favorite restaurant, a fish place on the water in Milwaukee, a place the two of you used to drive to from Janesville when you still had your little clapboard house there.

You avoid your mother at the dinner, but take greater pains to dodge Denny's mother, Edwina, hovering on the opposite side of the room from her, staying as far away as you can manage. She has come down from Oconto Falls, complaining about her trip (the snowy roads and the traffic in Milwaukee); the memorial service (it was not in a church); the food at the restaurant (too rich, too expensive; it should've been a potluck at your apartment.)

After the dinner is served, people begin to get up and say things about him, about Denny, about this man you had adored and lived with and needed for more than eighteen years, and once you realize that this will go on for a while–people standing up, saying what a *friend* he had been; his students crying, saying how much he had *given*–you walk outside and throw up over the deck railing.

—⁓—

The first counselor you're sent to is cold and belligerent, short-tempered, clearly a mismatch for her job–it's the county health system, you have no money–and five minutes into your first session she has not looked at you at all, her rigid and pruned face buried in a file instead, her voice a muttering pedantic tone of demographic-detail as she scribbles notes.

She has been told (you are sure), about your destruction escapades, and you can feel the judgment in her tone and even seeping out of her pores without ever meeting her eyes. She finally looks up at you, twelve minutes in (you are watching the clock) with dead eyes and a freeze-you-to-your-chair stare, and says blandly, "Let me guess. You want *drugs*–anti-anxiety–that's what you *all* want."

You stand and scream, "My husband just *died,* you fucking idiot!" Then you pluck her Master's Degree diploma off the wall from whatever school had the audacity to matriculate her, and you smash the thing on the gray linoleum floor where the frame breaks into a satisfying multiplicity of pieces, glass glittering at your feet.

She screams back, "What the hell do you think you're doing?!"

But you simply clap your hands together like a child who has found the exact right button to push with a nasty parent, and then you spit on her shoes and leave.

The second therapist is a Buddhist, a man, and God knows how he ever came to be in the county health system in Milwaukee, but there he is, sitting across from you, kind and humble and generous of spirit, with not a disapproving bone in his body. His name is Barry, and he is sixty-ish with bright, blue-green eyes and gray, tightly curly hair. He sits, each week, shoeless and cross-legged in his chair, psychedelic socks on his feet. In your first session, he holds a blue rope in his hands and asks you to hold the other end, then tells you to pull on it, feeling the tension.

He says, "Tension is a normal part of life, Elise. Notice how you can feel it and not be done in by it, just like pulling on the rope."

It sounds utterly ridiculous to you when you hear it, but somehow, when you leave, you are comforted by the thought, and you go away that day feeling more peaceful than you have felt in months–certainly in all the months since your husband was dying (because that's what it *really* was, a truth the Buddhist helped you to tell in the first few minutes; that it wasn't only *an illness,* it was Denny fading away and getting ready to leave you for good.)

"It's an unraveling, watching someone you love die…" your Buddhist said gently.

"Well it worked," you gasped, unable to breathe and talk about Denny's death at the same time, "because I've undeniably unraveled."

—⁓—

A handful of sessions later, your Buddhist closes his kind, wrinkled eyelids, breathes, then opens them again and asks you a question that knocks you over. He says, "Can you see things from where you're standing now and *live* at all?"

You are stymied.

You had tromped through the dirty snow for twenty-seven blocks, in the cold, to get to his office. The car was sitting there on the street outside your bleak apartment, but you didn't take it.

Wet from the knees down even after your session, you walk out into the gray-brown slush of the half-frozen street and admit to yourself that you are *not* living. At least not in the way your Buddhist means it.

Ten pounds have vaporized off your body, and you throw up anything you eat that's more complex than oatmeal. You have lost six temp jobs since Denny has died. Six jobs in fourteen weeks. You cannot go back to your office; you have been told by the HR woman that you are "too volatile." (You could go to Terence, the owner; he would let you come back, but you agree with yourself to let sleeping dogs lie.) You have not erupted at any of these temps jobs–well, maybe a bit at the first one when the owner of the *In-A-Minute Print and Copy Spot* asked you to make coffee for him and you told him to *shove it*–you have simply walked out onto the sidewalk from offices or stores or counters and then walked home in the cold without a word.

But that's progress. I didn't break anything, you think.

When you see your Buddhist again, you say to him, "Ask me that question again. The hard one."

He rephrases. "Can you *live* from where you're standing? Can you regroup and create a life here–here, where you loved your husband before he died?"

It is an honest question, and it slices through you. Your eyes well.

"No," you say, sure that the roof will cave in at such a heart-baring retort. "I can't. I cannot stay here."

"Good," he says. "It's good to know that."

—⁓—

Your husband's name had been Elden–it was a laborious name, old-world, the name his mother always used when she spoke to him, but you called him Denny, the name his friends had given him. When you were both out of college at UW Madison, he had given you an eighteen-carat gold necklace with a small, inch-wide "Denny" stamped out in the pendant in cursive, attached to a chain, and you have worn it always, fading styles be damned. You have not had it off your body in twenty years. Now you cannot wear it–it feels as though it's burning the skin of your throat–and so it sits on the dresser next to the shattered mirror like a totem.

If you think about it, your necklace is the only thing of value you have left from the marriage–house, sailboat, second car, all gone–besides your small diamond engagement ring, your battered, paid-off Honda four-door, and a small teacher's pension Denny has left you. There's no life insurance, nothing but nine hundred dollars left of your savings and the thousand dollar check from your boss, Terence, and his wife Claire Rose. Since Denny had only been a teacher for eleven years, the pension will probably amount to just five hundred a month and change. Not enough to live on. Not in Milwaukee, surely.

You are not fit to work, you know that. You cannot even stand to converse with people now, let alone do a series of *tasks* with them.

In your next session with your Buddhist (you are at it two times a week with him now, the copays dwindling your savings by the day), you say, "I've been thinking about what you said about me not being able to stay here." You smooth your straight brown hair firmly with both hands, pulling it down with a torque of force–a tic you have acquired in the last several weeks.

"Was it me who said that?" he asks pointedly. "Or was it *you?*"

"Right," you say, curling one lean leg underneath you in your chair. "I think it was me."

"Yes." He smiles.

"So, if that's true–"

"Is it?" he queries, intent. "I mean, for *you?* Is it true you can't live here? If it is, it's better to say it as a *statement*–something you've decided for yourself, as opposed to an 'if-then.' "

Your chest tightens; a gripping begins in your throat; a burning sensation fires behind your eyes.

"*Tension?*" your Buddhist says, watching you.

"Yes," you croak out. He hands you one end of the blue rope, and you both pull on it. Then you pause, and breathe, just as he has taught you to do.

"If I can't stay here, where can I *go?*" Your voice instantly rises–too high–the pitch toward frenzy in it already caught in your throat, ready to pop. You coil your end of the blue rope around your palm, pulling. "I can't *work* for God's sake–I can't even stand to *talk* to anyone."

"What if you don't have to?" Barry says with a velvet tone, calming you.

"Have to *what?*"

"*Work.* What if you don't need to? You have a little money–"

"Where in hell am I going to *live* for five hundred goddamned bucks a month?"

"There are places…" he says evenly, pausing to let the thought sink in. "Depends on where you go."

"Not in *America*–"

"No."

Tears spring immediately under your eyelids. You shout, "But I'd be alone!!"

"Yes," he says softly.

You stare at him; he waits patiently. "Oh, I get it. I'm alone now anyway. So it wouldn't make any fucking difference."

"Aha." Barry pauses, then says, "If you could see it–the place–"

"I can't–"

"But if you *could,* in a flash, without editing yourself–just an image–if you close your eyes right now and *see it,* what would it look like? A town? A farm–what?"

You close your eyes. You *do* see it. You *do.* Battered stone and dirt streets. Cement and rock houses. Dry ranch land. The light cresting over an old colonial city made of stucco and stone. A white-washed church on a dusty road.

Your Buddhist says, "You see it, don't you?"

"Yes," you say, opening your eyes. "It's Mexico."

"Ah," he says, smiling at you.

—⁓—

You are already packing when you phone Denny's mother, Edwina, in Oconto Falls to tell her you're leaving.

"Where will you *go?*" she says, the short-tempered judgment in her voice palpable in a split-second.

"I don't know yet, not *exactly,*" you say quietly. She has never been particularly kind to you, only tolerant. Denny had said that was because she needed to one-up you, wanting to let you know that her mother-son relationship came first, before you. It was mean-spirited, and it had not been true.

His mother assumes, of course, you'll leave the apartment in Milwaukee, go back to Janesville, or move to Oconto Falls, where she lives. Denny's hometown.

"You'll come *here*, then," Denny's mother says with emphasis. "Or Janesville. Which one?"

"No," you say, levelly. "I'm leaving the country."

You know the punch is coming.

"You're *what?*" she yells into the phone receiver.

"I'm leaving the country."

She gasps. "*That's* how you're going to treat his memory?!"

"This doesn't have anything to do with–"

"You're his *wife!*" she bellows, amping up. "And you should get yourself *straight* and come back here and do what's right! All of this *nonsense* you've perpetuated! Smashing and beating things!"

"You don't have any say about what I–"

"I most certainly do! I'm his *mother!* And I'd think that a woman your age would know better than to go around *destroying* things and gallivanting around in some *foreign* place after her husband's death!"

She has behaved this way each time she has not gotten her own way–all eighteen years of your marriage–but you have largely walked out of rooms or placidly handed the phone to your husband. You have never stood up to her, and suddenly now you realize you should have long ago.

"Edwina! Knock it off!" you say with as firm and bold a tone as you can muster.

"I will *not!* You're not some freewheeling, twenty-year-old *loose* thing who doesn't know where she belongs! You're not *young* anymore, either–you're forty-two! So if you think you're going to catch some younger man–who wants you for your *body…*"

You erupt at this–almost shriek, really; the match to the gasoline fire–and then you bellow so loudly that you cannot believe it is your own voice bellowing.

"*SHUT UP!*" you scream into the phone, stopping her abruptly. "You know what, Edwina? YOU'RE A WITCH!!"

"How *dare* you!" she snorts. "You spoiled, selfish–"

"I never liked you, Edwina, and neither did your son!!!" Then you slam the cordless on the wood floor as hard as you can, shattering it to bits of wire and plastic, a satisfying one-hurl demise.

It is mean, what you have said to her. It is not like you. But it is true, too, and freezing her in the tracks of her spewing has been two decades overdue.

You know at once that you will never speak to the woman again.

———⁓———

The question, after the fiasco phone call with Edwina, is where to go. Which town? You have barely any money. All of the cash from your Janesville house– what there was of it–went to medical bills. You have paid for specialists, a ridiculous amount of care outside your plan, alternative stuff, even a hospital stay in Germany for infusions that ate up thousands.

Your mother cannot help you; she is deep in her new husband's armpit in Boston, and has no interest in your travails.

"Figure it out!" she says to you in a chipper tone when the two of you speak on the phone. "You're smart and you can do it!" As if her need for you to be self-sufficient is weighty enough to make it so, absolving her of any responsibility to help.

"Mom, *please*…I've got nothing left. I'm broke–" You're begging.

Warren, her husband, mutters something in the background.

"Warren says it's all about *character development,* Elise. You know how smart he is. You'll be *fine* on your own! You'll see!" she says brightly, and then hangs up.

She *could* help you financially, that's the knife in your side. She has been well able to ever since your father died seven years ago but she has refused on numerous occasions, most notably for Denny's medical bills, and then, when the two of you lost the Janesville house. You are hardly surprised now.

You spend the next hour of your afternoon dropping all of your aunt Loretta's china (you inherited it from your mother's sister, but never liked it) into the giant black garbage bin out the backside of the apartment complex. You figure out quickly that if you wheel the open bin about four feet out from its usual cage, tip the lid back–the smell of raw garbage wafting up into your nostrils–then stand on the second floor of the building's service stairs and drop the plates, they'll crash with just enough velocity to make an amazing echo as they shatter into bits.

A neighbor sticks her head out of her small square of a bathroom window and hollers, "What the *hell?*"

When she sees you perched over the wooden stair railing, plates in hand, she says, "Oh, Jesus, it's *you.* Go ahead!" then slams the window shut.

You smash each one, the whole set: dinner plates, salad, soup bowls, coffee cups, and saucers for twelve.

On a Tuesday, your landlady shows up at your door and hands you a letter from her attorney which says that she is suing you for twenty-odd thousand for trashing her apartment. Her name is Mrs. Bleak–a hilarious moniker that you think is exactly apt: she has ratted, jet-black dyed hair with one severe white streak hair-sprayed across the top of her beehive. Since you are guilty (you did smash up the place, after all), you are humble and take the letter in hand with no push-back.

You find out that you are not really legally liable for anything yet, that she'd have to take you to court, and given your circumstances would not get much for the effort–but you think *fair is fair*, and you tell her you will sell your Honda sedan and give her the money. She agrees.

After that, here is what you've got: five hundred and fifty-six dollars and sixty-seven cents a month from Denny's pension. Nothing from the car. Seven hundred and sixteen dollars left in a savings account and the thousand dollar check your boss and his wife gave you. Enough to get you someplace, one-way.

While you decide on a town in Mexico, you throw everything out of the apartment that it is possible to throw out, and you take carloads to the second-hand store near you, so much so that you hear the guys at Basic Thrift (your neighborhood, the bulk of the bounty left there) say as you pull up, "Oh my God, there she is again! She's having a fit or something!"

You laugh at this, since you owned so little, stuff that piled up in closets and some weathered furniture–a teacher and a receptionist who came from a small town and lived simply enough to get through Denny's dying–everything gone now; just a stupid, vapid, empty, rented few rooms that you cannot afford.

On the fifth drive back from Basic Thrift, it hits you: Guanajuato. A place you went with Denny once, a place you spent a month of your life, years ago. Probably not inexpensive enough now, but it is the only place you really know in Mexico, and you're bound to find a little outpost nearby that's cheap enough for you to live until you figure out what to do.

You drive to the library, research it and decide *yes*, then book a plane ticket. You will be gone in four days.

—⁓—

On the plane you have two gin-and-tonics. You usually never drink anything but half a glass of wine; your long-limbed and slender form does not hold liquor well–but today you hold it fine, and you watch the landscape below you from the plane's altitude, not buzzed at all.

I am completely alone, you think, staring at the checkerboard of geography miles below you. But the thought doesn't scare you this time, and it doesn't make you angry, either. *Hmmm,* you think, *I am not angry today.*

You feel lighter, as if you had climbed out of a black and dank cave and fresh air had suddenly rushed into your lungs.

—⁓—

The town you remember is San Miguel de Allende–a romantic, picturesque mix of stone streets and multi-colored houses with an exquisite, peach-colored, gothic church at its center called the Parroquia. You remember Mayan farmers selling home-made beaded objects; fruits and smoked meats on sticks and exotic ice creams sold from rolling stands; Mexican ranchers in cowboy boots and random mariachi musicians strolling and playing music through the tree-covered square.

When you land in San Miguel's *centro,* shuttled into the town from the airport in Leon, it is still the same as you remember it–lovely–and you are instantly comforted. You do not feel like smashing anything. You think, *I have swum across the river.*

There is no river–it's high-altitude chaparral land here; no water–but that's what you feel. As if you have swum upstream across the current of your grief, and then crawled up along the rock bed on the opposite side of it.

You are armed with a six-year-old travel guide (lifted from your neighborhood library in Milwaukee) and five suitcases (you bought four of them at Basic Thrift for twenty bucks; junky old things, but they got you here.)

Everything you own is in the cases–every coat, every shoe, every sweater, a handful of pans, some silverware and plates, a pile of books, some sheets and blankets, and toiletries. Standing in the square with your appallingly meager haul of possessions, a terrible wave of fright comes up from your stomach into your throat, and you think you may be sick, but then something makes you look up.

Birds. White, gray, black, mottled–whatever they are–it's five o'clock in the evening, they are diving and rolling, filling the air like a sky full of falling and streaking stars above the exquisite peach-colored gothic church, which you stand at the foot of with your cases and nothing else.

As you look up, the early spring evening light is lavender and gold behind the old gothic spires. You smile, feeling–the first time in over a year–delighted.

Your first act (you have planned it), is to walk over to a small tourist cart ten feet away, keeping an eye on your cases, to buy a postcard of the church, the Parroquia, the photo framed with poinsettias on the edges of the snapshot.

You sit on top of one of your cases, take out a pen, and write to your Buddhist.

"Dear Barry: Just here. I can see the light from where I'm standing, and it's really something." You will mail it tomorrow. You write one to your brother, David, though he won't be home in Wautoma to get it for months, and one to your old boss and his wife.

It costs three dollars to get across town in a cab, and you have to lobby the guy to find you an inexpensive place to stay.

"Un hotel, por favor," you say sounding ridiculously American. "Dirt cheap, please. *Suciedad barata.*"

"No señora," he says, "no *barata*. No cheap. Rosewood! Is nice for you, no?" he smiles, his bright white teeth reflecting light. He is short and stocky, and his face is kind.

"No Rosewood!" you say, remembering the pink luxury hotel from your travel guide research. "No dinero!"

He looks at you helplessly, throwing up his hands. "*No dinero?*" Then he pulls over, ready to throw you out.

"No, no!" you say, laughing, handing him five dollars. "I can pay *you*. Just no Rosewood."

—⁓—

You spend five days in San Miguel in a forty-dollar a night hotel out on the edge of town out past the *Instituto*–the art school–walking the streets for hours by day, looking for a place to live. You must find something fast.

The hotel is a tiny box of a place and has peeling turquoise paint both inside and out. Your room is no bigger than a walk-in closet with a falling-apart sink and a shower down the hall, but the bedding is clean, and Lupita, at the front desk, is sweet to you.

"Tourista, no?" she says after she opens the door to your room for the first time.

"No," you say, smiling at her. "Mi vida." You know the words mean *my life*– hardly an exact answer–but you have no more accurate Spanish to explain, and the translation pleases you. *My life*–here. The thought makes you calm, calmer than you have felt since Denny began to waste away in front of your eyes.

Amazing, you think. *I have nothing to show for my life but I feel calm.*

A guy named Francesco who has his own shoe design place around the corner from your hotel (lots of multi-colored leather boots with thick heels for walking the stone streets) sees you trudging back and forth each day, looking for a place to rent, and after a few "hola's" and "buenos tardes's", he invites you in for a coffee, then takes pity on you when he hears your story and tries to help you.

"I have only five hundred American a month," you say, slightly ashamed. "That's for *everything*."

Francesco laughs robustly. "That's more than many Mexicans!" he says, "and they have *ninos*. Babies. "

"I have Mexican residency to pay for, I'll need a lawyer, and if I stay, I want a house," you say boldly, having not even registered the thought before you say it out loud.

"Okey-dokey," Francesco says, smiling at his American slang. "Then you don't pay more than nineteen hundred pesos for a room, no?"

"How much is that in dollars?"

"About a hundred, I think."

The next time you have coffee with him he writes down a few friends' names and addresses for you, potential rooms to rent. You immediately go knocking on doors (no phone; you ditched that with the rest of your American crap), and finally, one guy says he's got a cousin in Atotonilco—the next little town over and a fifteen minute bus ride—who's got a place by the river.

You have no reference point for 'the river'—you don't remember one—but it sounds nice.

"Solo," he says, smiling. A single.

You rush to the end of the street you've been directed to, Calzada de la Luz, and catch the bus marked "Sanctuaria," the bus line named for the bright white, starkly pristine church and attached yellow compound that sits at the center of the one-road dusty town of Atotonilco. You vaguely remember seeing the diminutive village as a tourist with Denny years ago and making some crack about it.

"How do people *live* here?" you had said to him. "It's all dust."

"Well, it's better than some inner-city neighborhood in Milwaukee, all crimed-out and druggie. It's charmingly ragged, I think." He had grinned at you. "Let's buy a house, here, Elise!" he teased. "I'll retire, and you can paint, and we'll eat corn porridge and be happy as ducks in a mud puddle!"

You had turned up your nose, and he had laughed out loud at you, and then slipped his arm around your waist and guided you up the stairs into the lovely white church—cool inside—shaded from the July Mexico heat and filled with religious sculptures hanging from the open beams. The two of you had been instantly reverent, touched by the simple beauty of the place, and he had pulled you into an alcove, kissing you deeply.

It astounds you how close to living like that you are now. How being here makes you feel him, but not in a sad way. Here, you are not furious. Here, you can take deep breaths.

You say to the driver when you get on the bus, "Atotonilco, si?"

"Si, señora," he says, eyeing you. It costs you nothing to ride the bus, a smattering of pesos in coins, the equivalent of about twenty cents U.S., and you sit close to the front and try to make conversation.

"Caliente–no? It's *hot.*"

"Si, si," he says loudly, wielding the bouncing bus in a big wide turn from the stone streets onto a half dirt, half paved road. He is short and strong-looking, built tightly and compactly with a round belly, about fifty, and he has to slip part-way off the huge driver's seat to fully depress the pedals.

Dust spews up from the road into the open windows, and you cough once, covering your mouth.

He laughs at you, and you immediately recognize him from your cab ride a few days before.

"Cabbie?" you say, not knowing the Spanish. You mime driving with your hands on an ethereal steering wheel.

"Si! Si!" he smiles at you and points, the bus veering slightly with his one-handed holding of the wheel. "No Rosewood!"

"Elise," you say, leaning toward him, pointing at yourself. "Si!"

"Eduardo," he says nodding, swerving to avoid several huge potholes in the road.

You would stick out your hand to shake Eduardo's, but he grips the oversized bus wheel with gusto and then laughs as you jump when he hits a pothole the size of a bathroom sink.

"Es *Mexico!!*" he shouts, laughing at you. "America, *no!*" He guffaws very distinctively: *ha-ha, ha-ha, ha-ha,* as if he's playing a child's game.

"Eduardo, do you know–*donde*–how to find Miguel Angel in Atotonilco?" You pull the note out of your pocket which Francesco's friend has written for you. "Miguel Angel *Acosta?*"

His eyebrows raise. "*Vecino!* Next door!" he says and points to himself. "You *prima?*"

"No se," you say, not understanding.

"Familia?" Eduardo says.

"Ah, no!" You smile at him. "*Alquilar*–I want to rent a room from him."

His eyes grow wider, as he bumps the bus from the paved road to packed dirt.

A few minutes later, Eduardo drops his passengers at the *Sanctuaria* and plops a cardboard sign in the window with magic-markered letters on it that reads *fuera de servicio*–out of service, you are guessing–and he jumps out of the bus behind you.

"Eduardo will show you," he says. "Miguel Angel. *Aqui.*"

It is an odd thing. In Milwaukee, in America, you would never let a man you did not know lead you down a dirt path, descending down a dusty rural stretch toward a dried-up riverbed. But here it seems fine. Eduardo is earnest and kind, and says, "Practica English. *Yo.*" He points to himself. *"I* will practice."

You don't know how to ask Eduardo how he can leave his bus and show you around, but he seems completely unconcerned, strolling and taking his time.

"The bus?" you say pointing behind you.

"No problema! Es *Mexico!*" he says, and attempts to ask you in English if you have ever met Clint Eastwood.

"Make my day!" he says, faking a gun shot with his right hand. He smiles, his face as bright as a ten-year-old's.

You laugh–out loud and noisily; your face breaking into the shapes of a guffaw–and the feel of it, after not laughing for so very long, is like glass breaking across the surface of your skin: a crackling, but with no smashing required.

When the two of you find Miguel Angel, he is standing outside a battered white stucco structure, his house, hammering together what looks like a small, rudimentary table. He is sixty-ish, with a flat belly and a shock of slick gray-and-jet-black hair that needs cutting, an overgrown clump of it falling into his eyes each time he turns his head.

Eduardo explains why you are here, but Miguel Angel is suspicious, and he eyes you up and down.

You say, "Amigo–my friend is Francesco. *Zapatos.* Makes *shoes.*"

His face brightens, and he says, "Francesco!"

"Si! Francesco!" you repeat.

You both repeat this a number of times–"Francesco! Francesco!"–until, finally, you ask, *"Alquilar?* A room for rent?"

"Si, si, alquilar!" he says, smiling.

He shows you to an attached room on the back side of his house. There is a wooden door with a rusty iron pull on it the circumference of a softball. The door is heavy, Miguel Angel kicks it open, and you step into a musty stone room–as big as your old living room in Janesville–with coarse fieldstone as walls and floor, and a blackened stove pushed to one side. On the opposite side is a toilet and a claw foot tub (clearly, by the scraped sides of the thing, dragged here years ago) with a single metal pipe over it, coming out from the wall.

You smile, delighted. You have always wanted to live in a stone house. You had imagined it quaint and green and full of pink bougainvillea, next to a pool, and this is hardly that, but you want it instantly.

"*Cuanto cuesta?* How much?" you say, staring at a coiled metal bed frame. "Is there a bed?"

"Solo? No esposa?" he says, pressing you, his eyes wide.

"My husband died," you say, and Miguel Angel looks at Eduardo, confused.

"*Muerto,*" Eduardo says, and both men look at you compassionately.

"Si, si," Miguel Angel says sadly. Then, "Mil seiscientos cincuenta pesos."

You have no idea what that means, but Eduardo writes it down on a scrap of paper, pulling a pen from his pocket–sixteen-hundred and fifty pesos–and you are instantly grateful: less than eighty-five dollars a month.

—∿∿—

You used to think you were struggling, back in Janesville, when you had ridiculous medical bills that you could not pay and were losing your house. Then, you had thought you were "scraping by" to pay the heating bill.

Now, after two full months in Mexico, you know that in order to make this work, you will have to save like a miser, and live on nothing. You do not want to work; you want time to simply *rest*–something your Buddhist said might be worthwhile, "taking time to contemplate the healing of your heart."

You will need a chunk of change if something happens. More than that, you have a plan: if you live on one-hundred-or-so dollars a month and save a few thousand a year, within a few, you'll be able to buy some beat-up stone structure, live in it, fix it up slowly. Maybe rent a room.

It's funny to you now, in your instant state of Mexican paucity, that sense of struggle you had in Milwaukee. You still had things then. You spent fifty dollars a month on vitamins and your shopping list had lots of things on it: plain Greek yogurt, olive oil, butter, feta cheese, salami, fettucine, chicken thighs, whole wheat bread, frozen pineapple, broccoli.

Now you eat only oatmeal, lettuce, and eggs. You trek all the way to San Miguel on the bus to buy the oatmeal in a tiny neighborhood store that has "American" things, and you buy the lettuce and eggs at a miniscule market in Atotonilco for about three dollars a week. There is a lemon tree near Miguel Angel's place, and you routinely steal the fruit (Eduardo tells you to take it–he says the woman who owns the tree is old and cannot leave her house), making tea from boiled lemons, and sometimes dousing your scrambled eggs with them. You are amazed at your diet: oatmeal for breakfast, a lettuce salad for lunch, fried eggs for dinner. Every day, the same things. Sometimes, you buy tortillas, a hundred for three dollars, from a young girl who sells them from her family's side window: you can see the mounds of ground corn and mashed up limes behind her in huge piles on top of a coarse wooden table.

You feel that the oatmeal-lettuce-eggs regimen could have been some new slimming diet posted in *Women's Health* or on some stupid blog, but for you it's survival.

You have bought two gallons of castile soap and you use it for everything–washing face and hair, hand washing clothes and towels in the bathtub, even brushing your teeth.

After a few weeks, you ask your landlord, Miguel Angel, if you can have chickens. You have calculated the cost of feed. Having your own chickens would save you money for sure. Miguel just laughs at you.

"Pinche!" he says, snorting in the saying of it. "Crazy! You cannot have chickens without a chicken house! The cucarachas will get them!" He is teasing you. He mimes a fox or a coyote then pulls a blue bandana out of his jeans pocket and wipes his nose, laughing at you.

"Oh," you say, embarrassed. "A chicken coop. Stupid! Of course!"

"Pinche–Elise!" You know the slang now for *pinche*. It means dumb-ass.

Francesco comes out every couple of days in his battered, open Jeep (he can't drive it in the rain as the convertible flaps are long gone) and sits with you and Miguel Angel and brings beer. Eduardo comes over, too, when he sees the dust of the Jeep from his house a half a mile up the road, and the four of you sit on Miguel Angel's front porch–a tilted wooden-slatted thing that catches the legs of the ripped, naugahyde-covered chairs that Miguel has absconded with from some junk heap. It always takes a few tries each to get all the legs of the chairs steady on the slats, to not have one of them fall into the spaces between the boards, and there's much laughing and cursing in the process.

"Fucking *gringo* chairs!" Eduardo says laughing and winking at you, falling off the thing as the left back leg drops through a hole.

Francesco has brought tequila–good stuff–because he sold five pair of boots to wealthy *touristas* from Mexico City.

"White-boy chairs! *Estupido!*" Miguel Angel says. You are teaching him American slang, and he likes to say "white-boy."

"Here. Elise. You–the first shot," Francesco says and pours tequila into an old coffee cup. *"Primero."*

Francesco is tall and somewhat bulky—strong arms, thick legs, with a ruddy face that seems to always have a half a day's growth on it. He is friendly and kind, and he translates well, and you find you like him.

"Ah…princesa!" Eduardo laughs.

"Princess?" you say, smiling. "Hardly. I'm as far from *princesa* as any American woman can be."

"No, no! Princesa, I think yes!" Miguel Angel says, waggling his finger at you.

This scene, you sitting on a rattletrap porch, perched on the backside of a nothing town, overlooking a nearly evaporated river with three Mexican men whom you have come to like immensely, amuses you. You do not know why they like you, but they seem to, and they laugh uproariously whenever you tell them about life in America.

"There are no cracks in the roads in America. No giant potholes. Not like here. *Freeways*. All smooth."

Francesco translates, and they all yuck it up.

"Pinche! Americanos!"

"No chickens in the yard in America," you say pointedly.

"No huevos? *Estupido!*"

You say to Francesco, when the tequila has kicked in, "No wife for you? No *ninos?*"

You know that Miguel Angel, your landlord, never married, but he had a girlfriend in Guajanuato who he saw every few weeks until she left him two months ago and didn't tell him why. Eduardo's family—his wife and two daughters—are in Mexico City for his daughters' school, while he stays and drives busses and taxis to support them. They are supposed to come back in the summer. But Francesco has a good business and a house above it, and you wonder.

Eduardo and Miguel Angel stop laughing when you ask and stare at you. Clearly, this is not a happy subject.

"Never mind," you say quickly, sensing your error, "I'm sorry."

"It is nothing," Francesco sighs. "She is in America with another man. And my daughter."

You stare at Francesco. You have felt light here the past month, but these men's losses suddenly bring your pain up into your throat, burning like it used to.

"*Solo*," you say gently. "Me too."

—⁓—

A month later you ask Eduardo when his family is coming–it is almost summer, and you are standing in his yard up the road from Miguel Angel's, helping him feed his chickens. You think of David, your brother, on the edge of a mountain somewhere, your only genuinely loving family member.

"Your *familia* is coming? *El mes de junio.*" Almost June. Your Spanish is getting better.

He is bent over, tossing feed toward some of the birds, and when you speak he sharply turns to you, the look on his face like a twelve-year-old boy who has lost his mother.

You know instantly that they will never come.

Eduardo tears up and without thinking you drop your basket of feed and go and put your long arms around him–you, half a head taller than he is, his round, pouchy, belly pressing into your body as he weeps.

He does not apologize, he simply cries bitterly until he is done, then pulls a bandana from his back pocket, wipes his face, looks up at you, and says, "*Angel.*"

———

On the fourth of July, a holiday you have had a terrible time trying to explain to Francesco and Miguel Angel the historical meaning of (a *Tea Party?* In a *harbor? Explosions?)*, Eduardo bags one of his chickens in a potato sack and brings it to Miguel's porch to butcher for dinner. There is a case of beer, some potatoes, tortillas, and some tomatoes from Eduardo's garden. A feast.

You have scared up some sparklers–it took you hours of rummaging through stands and corner stores in San Miguel to find the kind you wanted, old-fashioned ones that look like they are from the 1970s, and probably are. The men think you cannot cook (your diet of eggs, lettuce and oatmeal has not impressed them), and you beg Miguel Angel to let you dress the bird before he roasts it.

"First, we must *ach-ach-ach!*" Eduardo says, making a cutting motion with his palm at his throat.

Animal butchering, though not pleasant, is not shocking to you. Outside Janesville, Denny had friends–Jude and Penelope–who you visited often, who milked their own cows and butchered their own chickens and raised rabbits for meat.

"Can't we just get chickens from the store?" you had said sarcastically on one visit there when charged with the task of pulling feathers off the dead bird.

"Where do you think the store gets them?" Denny had laughed. "And don't let Jude and Penny hear you say that. I'll never hear the end of it." He leaned over and kissed you then, wet and full, his eyes full of mirth.

At Miguel Angel's giant iron stove, Eduardo boils a huge pot of water, then sharpens a knife.

Francesco says, "You sure this is good to watch for you Elise?"

"*Granja*–she comes from a farm place," Miguel Angel says, confident.

"Si, si, but…" Francesco shakes his head. He is sensitive where women are concerned, protective; he will stop in the street to help a woman with a heavy bag or a wobbling cart.

"I'm okay," you say. The last few weeks you've been teaching abstract painting for six dollars a day to Mexican and ex-pat kids in the tiny studio above the *biblioteca,* the library, taking Eduardo's bus into San Miguel three weekdays. Francesco, and sometimes Miguel Angel, too, have been checking up on you, popping their heads into the art room every few days to make sure you're okay. You appreciate the kindness.

"I'll be fine," you say now.

Eduardo takes the sharp knife, grabs the chicken, and gently slices it at the neck, letting its head plop onto the ground. He lets the bird run and fly in wobbly circles until the muscle-memory of its movement dies away and it melts into a heap.

He grabs it by the feet, holding it upside down, draining its blood, and then says, "Elise. Come and we will pluck."

You dip the bird upside down in the boiling water, the way Eduardo tells you to, the way Denny's friends used to–the completeness of the act so elemental: living, befriending, helping, eating, dying–so simple here that you well up with tears and feel your husband next to you, close. It as if he is breathing on you, on your neck, the way he used to before he wrapped his arms around you from behind.

It is the first time since he has died that you have had this experience (Miguel Angel has told you over and over again that a day will come when you will be spiritually *visited*)–a feeling that Denny is hovering behind you, his warm exhales in your hair, laughing at you, with you. You wonder if you will ever return to Wisconsin or walk the lanes of Janesville, the town you chose together; the place you loved when you were in love with him.

These past months you've covered paths the two of you walked when you visited San Miguel de Allende years ago, trying to feel him, remembering him. And now, standing next to Eduardo, the sensation of Denny simply electrifies itself on your skin, familiar and tactile, as if you could lean back and he would catch you, his arms pulling you in.

Eduardo sees you crying; he seems to know what it is that's passing through your heart. His own eyes well, rimmed with tears, and the two of you pull at the dead chicken's feathers, cleaning the bird to a puckered and bare nakedness. He laughs through his tears, and then so do you, the two of you chortling and crying and smoothing the dead bird's mottled skin.

—⁓—

Later, at dinner, the four of you sit on your ratty chairs, balanced on the rickety, falling down porch with plates in your laps, beers in bottles and coffee mugs full of tequila balanced on porch slats at your feet. You spiced the bird with wild sage from the side of the road, butter (a luxury), lemon rind, apples from a stand in town, and salt. The potatoes you seared on top of the iron stove and fried the tomatoes in oil.

Francesco licks his fingers, plopping the meat from a chicken leg into a tortilla and says, "Ah. A talent we did not know about. You will cook again for us?"

"I will," you say.

You stand and ask Eduardo to put down his plate, handing him a sparkler. He pulls a lighter from his pocket and lights it. You light yours end-to-end from his and begin to move, drawing lines of fallen starlight into the air in front of the porch.

Francesco puts down his plate and takes two sparklers in his hands, lights them, and dances with his arms moving straight up and down in the air, lines of beautiful fire framing his rugged form.

Miguel Angel is up with you too, now, and the light from his hands dribbles and sparks like snowflakes lit in kaleidoscopes from a midnight full moon.

Your sparkler dies, and you light two more, and fly with them this time, leaping–your heart full from this sketching on the sky, knowing, just now, that you are *alive;* you are truly living.

You think of Denny, the husband you loved; of your brother David; of Barry, your Buddhist therapist. You watch these Mexican men with their fire-lit sparklers who have befriended you–Eduardo, Francesco, Miguel Angel–who have helped you to come back to yourself.

Eduardo sidles up next to you and whispers, "We are four alone–*cuatro, solo*–but we are *afortunado.*"

Fortunate.

You breathe and dance, and wave your arms with shimmering light. *Yes*, you think, *I am fortunate.* It is all you can ask for.

So I suppose you and I are going up these mountains together, is that it, David Traxler?

The Trek

I met her in the Himalayas, trekking up the Everest Valley in Nepal. I was on a *National Geo* film shoot–video, actually–climbing with the latest excuse for a Summit Expedition: this time an "Everest Environmental Project." Supposedly, we were there to clean up the bright yellow oxygen containers trashed by hundreds of climbers on their way down from trying to ascend the peak. In truth, we were going up to climb the summit–to photograph and film it–and on the way down we would pay the Sherpas twenty dollars apiece for each empty O2 canister they could carry off the mountain and out of the valley. The *Nat Geo* angle was simple: it was so entirely rare to actually *reach* the twenty-nine-thousand-foot summit–through ice storms and crevasses and avalanches and quirky fall-outs–and even though a posse of climbers would try every late spring, more than half would fail. *Geo* had paid me to film several years in a row for the chance moment of glory when, and *if,* our climbing team did hit the jackpot.

I saw Anna on the first day. Our crew had been dropped by a series of battered, sixteen-seater, tin-can planes into the tiny, nine-thousand-foot town of Lukla that morning–a hair-raising, nose-dive landing experience between peaks, precipitously dropping the rattling aircrafts onto a five-hundred-foot gravel field (if you could call it that) no wider than two driveways, which pulled up short before a massive pile of rocks. It was a stomach in the throat experience for all of us, even the seasoned Sherpas, and though a handful of us had done it before (some of us many times), we cheered and cursed when the thing safely came to a lurching stop.

Three hours into the trek, I was still trying to get my breathing and stepping rhythm, shifting my pack around on my shoulders, and I was wondering, now at forty-seven, how much longer I could stand to do this work. A month of shooting at Everest, two more in Pakistan climbing and filming K-2, and probably another trip back to Kilimanjaro in the fall. I knew I'd be skinny and wiped out by mid-summer after months of climber's food (the grainy stew called 'dahl bat' cooked at trailside teahouses not nearly enough protein for the physical exertion), I'd have new injuries in my knees and hips and more gray hair, and my marriage would be an even bigger disaster.

I hadn't seen my wife for four months. We'd been on the outs for at least two years, probably more. She'd gotten sick of me being off someplace shooting for months at a time, started sleeping with someone else, left enough bread crumbs for me to figure it out. We hadn't ended it, just went on with each other, pretending. I'd already been to Patagonia, Burma, Annapurna, and Kili in the last year and it was only the end of April. *When was I going to get a life?*

The last argument we'd had about it hadn't ended well.

"I'm your *wife!*" Camille had yelled at me, throwing a saucepan lid clattering to the tile floor in our cottage's kitchen. "You think I *like* being the one to tell you that you're tanking our marriage? You can't be *gone* seven months of the year and–"

"Shit, Camille! This is what I *do!*" I sounded self-righteous and I knew it. "How do you think we pay for all this–" I gestured to the house: quaint, lived-in, enveloping. It was perched right on Silver Lake, outside of Wautoma, a lovely Wisconsin setting.

"So it's about the *house?* That's what you care about?"

"Camille. *Jesus!* What do you want from me?"

She stood very still and stared. Then, quietly: "It's not the treks, David, and you know it. Are we going to be honest with each other, or not?" She opened her eyes especially wide.

I pressed my lips together–hard–and didn't speak.

The tension in her eyes dropped away and she said, "That's what I thought."

It wasn't only the travelling that had unraveled our marriage. Neither Camille nor I had known what to do with the distances, so when she started hooking up a couple years back–only when I was gone, I thought, but I didn't know–I'd started indulging, too. What I called "on-the-road experiences." I liked to pretend sometimes that it was just me, *roaming*–a trite and awful euphemism for dismantling a marriage, and not nearly enough of a compelling explanation for why I strayed–but the truth was, it had undone me, her sleeping with someone else, and my own affairs afterward hadn't helped. I felt like nothing stuck, like closeness rolled off of me–oil and water.

Then, Camille began a serious thing with one of the guys she hired for the camp she ran in the summer months–upstate near Minocqua, so potentially not a threat to our 'reputation'; a conversation we'd actually had, I'm embarrassed to admit–but then the guy followed her and started shacking up at our place when I left for Patagonia in January. That was a first. It screwed me up. The guy was quite a bit younger than Camille, and it cut me like crazy sometimes–*our house, our bed*–but when I really spent time thinking about it, my honest reaction was, *Good for her. She should have somebody who can be there.* Terrible, I know, but there you go.

Eddie Simonson, my oldest friend in our tiny lake town (when I was home, rarer and rarer these days) had said to me a full year before, "You know, the two of you *act* like you're divorced, so maybe you should just *get* one."

—⁓—

I was huffing that first day, breathing hard, heading up the trail from Lukla. Three hours in, I hit a level space where a stone teahouse popped into view, and I dumped my pack against a large flat rock and leaned against it. The place was a one-room, stone cabin on the side of the trail, with a couple of Nepalese women running it who fed the trekkers.

The easy trek up had taxed me already, not fully recovered from my last gig in South America, or the two before that. My knees were feeling it–sharp little needlings with the weight of my gear on my back–and I had been chewing on my failing marriage for the entire morning trek.

Trekking was what we called the hike up to Base Camp at seventeen thousand feet with our team of volunteers. There'd be seventy of us and it would take us nine days to get there. Once we set up camp we'd prep for the actual snow-and-ice mountain climb, when the team of twelve climbers and Sherpas would head up with cramp-ons and gear and rope lines to try to take the summit, and I'd do my best to film it.

Though trekking was much easier than the snow-and-ice climbing we'd face in a couple of weeks, I still had only a day or two on the hard-packed dirt trails to let my mind wander before I had to dial myself in and concentrate. Once we got to day three and moved above the tree-line, the traverses would become ridiculously steep, cut sharply into the sides of snowy mountains and filled with large stones–an ankle-twisting hazard with every damned step–it was dangerous–and, carrying my heavy pack and gear, I couldn't let my mind drift. But it was that first day.

I'd been sitting on the ground against my pack for a good twenty minutes, the smell of some kind of stew from the teahouse drifting out from the open doorway, and I was turning things over inside my altitude-altered, headachy brain. *What the hell did I want, anyway? If I wanted someone to care for, someone to actually dig-in with me, then why the fuck didn't I stop this crazy-assed globe-hopping and offer myself to a woman?* I knew it was my fault, avoiding and letting things unravel—my own antics and issues—not who I chose or who I slept with. I was tired of myself; disgusted, really. Now, I just wanted to *stop*. I wanted the stupid, wild ride of my pretending to stop spinning so I could step off.

Camille and I had been friends once—I had loved her—and I thought that was enough seven years before when I married her. But then it wasn't. I felt like a shit, but I loved my work, too, and it had cost me. She had drifted away, and I had gone searching for something to deaden my loss, to fill the empty places. A kind of excitement I'd gotten hooked on but couldn't maintain. Did I want something true? I thought I did. *How,* though?

You are such a friggin' mess, Traxler, I thought.

Something sharp in my pack poked me and I shifted, then lay back, trying to calm myself. I closed my eyes. *Breathe in deeply, hold for one, two, three.* It's was a therapist's strategy. *Relax your chest, breathe out.*

One of the teahouse women walked out and nudged my thigh with a steaming bowl of food, and I opened my eyes, grabbed it.

"Hey—thanks," I said. She nodded and went back inside.

The accepted drill at Everest Valley teahouses—the battered, stone cabins that fed and overnighted trekkers on random stops along the trails going up—was that you ordered some *dahl bat*, a grainy lentil dish, or a spicy soup with carrots and potatoes, and then sat outside on the stones or the ground, or a table if the place was big enough. Then you waited an interminably long time while the teahouse women prepared the dishes (they made them one at a time.) The women's faces were a deep brown, like barely creamed coffee, and speckled from the high-altitude sun. They wore weathered climber's clothes (North Face zip-ups that were gifted or left behind by trekkers and climbers) with hand-made red-patterned Nepalese aprons over them, green or red kerchiefs on their heads. Each sported at least one pure gold crown as a front tooth and wore strands of gold chains about the neck. There were never any men running the houses—the women's husbands were trekking guides, and during the season, they'd be off with some climb or other making their money for the year in a few short months.

My team was sitting on a make-shift stone deck overlooking the gorge, but I sat alone, a few feet away, on the ground. I ate, spooning the *dahl bat* into my mouth with some vehemence, hungry. The dish was usually spicy, but this was plain, bland, just boiled lentils and onions in broth. Didn't matter. I finished it, sat back and closed my eyes again.

When I opened them, there she was: Anna. Dressed in a pink, V-neck T-shirt cut off at the waist, tight blue jeans, standard-issue Patagonia brown hiking boots and carrying one of those custom-made packs bulging at the pockets with gear dangling all over it. She had shoulder-length black hair which was falling out of a single band, and she wore no hat.

She walked up–was she trekking alone? *She couldn't be*, I thought–and dropped her pack on one of the steps of the teahouse. Two young Sherpas came up behind her, dropping their gear next to hers. They were both dark-skinned with ropey muscles. I scanned the trail, but no one was following.

Alone. Trekking with two Sherpas. Daring. It suddenly thrilled me.

She was medium height–which meant that she was strong, carrying a weighty pack like that–and after dumping it on the ground, she moved her shoulders, stretching them by drawing her hands together behind her back, bending over slightly. As she stood back up I saw a gold navel ring above the line of her jeans.

Her gear was blocking the two steps into the teahouse on one end, and though my climbing team would know exactly what I was up to (there was another door to the tiny place fifteen feet away, wide open), I went and stood before her with my bowl in my hand, pretending I needed her to move so I could get inside. I figured I'd force a few words at least.

Evans–Tuff, we called him, because he could scale anything, the tougher and more precipitous the better–saw me step up and stand in front of Anna and he shook his head in my direction, then gave me a scowl. He'd watched me in action with women before–the last two Everest climbs and two K-2's, too; and though he didn't know how bad it had gotten with my wife, he knew I was married and didn't approve.

Anna's legs were stretched out on the dirt, her Sherpa guides sitting nearby, and my presence was a bit of silent insistence that she get out of my way.

She leaned forward and looked at the other door on the opposite side of the tiny stone teahouse–ten steps away, literally–and she glared up at me with a look on her face that read, *You can't use the other door?* She was annoyed, clearly, and her fire-lit black-brown eyes nailed me to my spot in front of the step.

"Hey–sorry. Just trying to, you know–get in here…" I said sheepishly. I wanted to appear humble.

"You're kidding, right?" she said, and then she laughed–a resonant and re-verberating laugh that sounded almost musical, harmonic. "It couldn't be that you came over here because you wanted to say *hello*, could it?" She eyed me. "I mean, *Jesus*. Be a man about it, will you?" She said it with a bite, but kindly, too, lightly chuckling.

How had she done that? She had scolded me, but it was salty and sweet at the same time, full of delicious bravado. I felt an electrified bit of arousal travel up my inner thighs.

She began to stand, and I helped her up, easing her to her feet with my hand on her upper arm. Firm. Athletic. She was shapely–not thin, but fit and full and womanly. Her scent was musky and sweet from sweating.

Her Sherpas (twenty years old at best, I was guessing) watched with big, open eyes, rapt. I saw a flash of territorialism in one of the young men's glances up at me: *Beware, American. She's in my charge,* it read.

On her feet, she faced me. At five-foot-ten, I'm strong and fit at the beginning of a trek (thinner afterward, when I have to eat six meals a day to gain back my body weight from all of the exertion), and I felt her physical presence instantly in relation to mine–how she would fit in the crook of my arm with her cheek pressed up against my chest, what it would feel like to lie face-to-face and slide my hands down her backside onto the roundness of her ass and pull her body into me.

I dug my nails into my palms to get the images out of my head. I was experienced enough at this to know that I had to slow my impulses way, way down, then woo and draw and play at being casual about whether I wanted her. Truth be told, this was the part I loved: the fire-to-a-match burst of desire kick-started on my skin and flesh; the sweet and pressing anticipation of touching, fondling. The excitement that let me *forget*. Imagining the steps, one at time, of undressing her before I did; the delicate dance of drawing desire from nowhere, from nothing, into *want*. I had gotten good at it.

She spoke. "Anna Ocursia. Don't even ask where that name comes from." She stuck out her palm and shook my hand strongly, confidently, as if she were on a job interview.

I laughed. "David Traxler. So, Anna, *what the hell*–where's your last name come from?" A tiny rebellion.

"I thought I told you not to ask me that."

"I don't do everything I'm told to do." I gazed hard at her.

She let loose a loud laugh. "Well, *that's* hardly a surprise."

"So, your name? Where it's from?"

"You really want to know?"

"Sure." I said.

"Latvian. Years ago, of course. Via Spain. Then America. Bastardized some-where along the way–have no idea what the original was." She eyed the ground. "Would you like to have a seat in my living room?" She gestured grandly to the dirt, and sat back down on it.

I joined her.

"This is Dawa," she introduced one of her Sherpas, "and this is Tashi." Nei-ther man reached out his hand, so she said, "You can shake his hand. He only *thinks* he bites."

I guffawed, probably too loudly.

Dawa's eyes softened and he shook my hand, delicately. Tashi saluted me from his left eyebrow with two fingers, something I was guessing he picked up from a left-handed climber. Both wore beat-up North Face parkas with thick zippers, weathered boots, and brightly colored hand-knit caps.

There was a moment of awkwardness after that. Anna sat silent, looking out over the gorge before us. It was an almost vaporous look–a simple stare–and I wondered if maybe she wasn't the bright flash of heat and intensity she had first appeared to be. Sometimes, that happened with a woman. You'd move in thinking there was something there–something intelligent, provocative and bold–and instead it would all be show, a momentary effervescence. Like a scent that gets sprayed into the air and then dissipates before you can catch what you had hoped would be a heady and enveloping aroma.

I needed that draw: the challenge of a woman with bravery and spark, a full and heady hit of my drug of choice. A sexual mountain to climb that would, at least momentarily, fill the growing hole of my emotional and geographic wandering.

She stared hard, taking in the landscape. It was not unimpressive. I knew it by heart now; had trekked it eight times up and down–this was my ninth–and I was not blasé about its gifts. Even at just over nine-thousand feet, the scen-ery was stunning: in the distance, rolling green hills with centuries old decon-structing stone walls mapping out the agricultural boundaries of each ancient farmer's land, and at close range, gorges of peaks beginning to jut upward, the Dudh Kosi river below us down strikingly steep trails (which the teahouse women climbed each day to carry water back up to their houses, God knows how.) The sky was already whitening, an effect of being at higher altitude, and it would color in more obscure and vivid ways the more we ascended. Within a few miles the trees would thin into a rock-only landscape and everything green would be gone. Scents would sharpen, the icy air like freezing crystals in the nose and lungs.

Possibly her sudden blandness was wonder. I watched her.

"No more green after today. No trees," I said. "It's all rock from here on up. A ridiculous *rush of up*." I tried to catch her eye.

"It's a *thrill*, isn't it?" she said, softly and almost under her breath. There it was. The spark.

"It is." I matched her soft tone.

Tuff got up with several members of our team and pointed up the trail. "Hey Traxler," he said with a grim look on his face. "Time to hit it."

"Anna, this is Tuff—our crazy-assed climber. The man can scale anything." I grinned up at him.

Anna smiled. "Hi."

I spoke quickly. "I'm gonna hang back with Grolsh and Weimer. I'll catch up with you, Tuff," I said, ducking my head and dodging his gaze.

Tuff nodded at Anna, heaving his heavy pack on his back. "Yep. Thought so. See ya, Trax." He headed up the trail, not looking back.

I leaned against the two big rocks behind me and put my hands behind my head, elbows out.

"What was *that?*" Anna said, watching my face.

"Nothing," I said. "Just guys being guys." I started re-lacing my boots, consuming myself with the effort.

She looked over and I caught her scan for my left ring finger. No ring. I had not worn mine for so long that there were no tan lines, no weathered piece of skin where a slice of gold might have worn it band-shaped and smooth. She saw me catch her looking, and she smiled at me, a little wickedly.

I watched her take in a big gulp of air, then she shook her head, laughing lightly at me, as if it had already been decided what would happen between us.

"So I suppose you and I are going up these mountains *together*, is that it, David Traxler?" Her eyes flickered, and she turned up the corners of her mouth in an impish grin.

She would *have* me. Her confidence sent a shiver of thrill between my legs and I flushed with it.

———

We were still on packed-dirt trail and not very high, Anna and I. It was day two of the trek, early, and we were heading up to Namche Bazaar, a tiny cluster of about sixty dwellings and buildings perched on the side of a sharp mountainside at just over eleven-thousand feet. We had a good five hundred feet more to go before we hit the rock-filled paths heading sharply up. The view was already incredible, with dramatic drops down to the Dudh Kosi river and the Everest peaks beginning to jut up in our sightlines.

I had a few young Base Camp volunteers with me helping to carry my gear who were up ahead, and Anna and I were trekking with her two Sherpa guides, Tashi and Dawa. The four of us had gone quiet crossing the third swinging suspension bridge over the river, breathing and stepping.

The bridge, made of thick metal wire and thin planks, was swaying with the movements of our body weight, a sharp two-hundred-foot drop to the rushing water below us. I was enjoying the thrill, feeling the mist from the gushing rapids in the sheer gorge under us, our bodies undulating back and forth precipitously as we stepped. I thought of Wautoma: the lake, the insulated small town I lived in, the stuff I was running from. My marriage falling apart. A sister I loved, Elise, having taken off to a nowhere town in Mexico after her husband died of brain cancer. My mother, dismissive and controlling with my sister, suffocating and cloying with me, off in Boston with her wealthy new husband, refusing to help my sister hang on to her Janesville house.

Away. That's what I had wanted. To be gone, away from all of it.

On the bridge, Anna came to a full stop on her last handful of steps and looked down through the slats at the gorge below us. It made me flinch.

"Look ahead, not back, Anna!" I called out. It was the simple mantra that had kept me untouched by serious injury for multiple trips.

She cleared the bridge, heading up-trail on the packed dirt, then turned and laughed at me. "David, I'm *fine.*"

I knew this trail like the back of my hand after eight years of ascending it every spring, so I ought to have been able to come up with some bit of small talk once we got back on the rock paths and over the bridges, but I was watching her instead, and she was letting me watch. I could feel her stand up straighter with my attention, as if she were a flower or a plant that was turning and reaching its leaves and petals toward the sun. She was unapologetic about it, and it excited me.

"Dawa is from Kathmandu—his brother's going to law school there," she said. She was breathing out with each step, the way I had taught her to do that morning. "I met him. He and his wife, their baby, Dawa and his ten-year-old brother live together in a five-hundred square foot room, including the kitchen. And you know what? They all seem happy. How is that?"

Dawa turned to her.

"You don't mind me saying that, do you Dawa?" she said to him kindly. "It's just that Americans have so much more comparatively, and it's such a shame that we don't have what you and your family have." She turned to me. "It's palpable, their happiness."

"So it is," Dawa said, evenly. His face was a dark almond-brown; his eyes calm as a saint's. He was not tall, probably five-foot-six tops, but his lean and long-muscled limbs made him appear so. "But we want big houses, too."

He smiled at Anna, and she burst out laughing.

"Of course you do! I didn't mean to be condescending. Forgive me." She spoke to him with respect, even reverence.

"Nothing to forgive," Dawa replied, again with exquisite evenness. "Happiness is a gift of the heart-gods. Nothing to do with houses."

Anna chuckled. "You're, what? Half my age?" She turned and looked me in the eyes. "If we could bottle that kind of wisdom for our twenty-year olds–"

"Twenty-two," Dawa interrupted, shifting the pack on his back. "Tashi is twenty. We are cousins," he said seriously, pushing upward on the trail.

"Yes. Well. You're both astounding, in my opinion," Anna said, breathing out as she stepped.

Tashi saluted me with two fingers again–he had been the one to shoot me the warning look when I approached Anna–and in his not-as-proficient English said, "Look like you man married." He tapped his left ring finger with his right index.

Anna laughed and looked from Tashi to me. "Wow! No screwing around, David Traxler. Are you?"

"No," I lied. "I'm divorced."

The lie hurt, like an esophagus-sized stone being dropped down my throat into my stomach, pressing at my insides.

For God's sake, I thought, *are you that desperate?* But I didn't correct the falsehood.

Tashi looked me over and I read his face: he didn't believe me. Or maybe it was my guilt, my own lie twisting my instincts into beguiling knots. I had had my time here in this Nepalese and Tibetan high country–eight years in a row climbing here, yearning and efforting for the summit, and I knew something of these people. I found them intuitive, attuned to stuff Americans weren't attuned to, calm in spirit and ethical. I did not want to anger Tashi or Dawa before I could get to Anna, nor did I want to spar with Tashi's protectiveness.

It was a lie of convenience, a lie of need. An empty place I had been trying to fill by means other than anything honorable. But I still believed that I would–*soon*–find the will to finish my marriage and set myself on a path of something genuine with a woman. *How,* I didn't have any idea. But if I was truly honest with myself, I didn't know what the hell I was doing. I just wanted her.

—⁂—

By the middle of day two, the trek would get precipitously harder. We would stop and sleep at the end of the day at Namche, at eleven thousand feet, for two days, and for everyone on the trail (except for the Sherpas and some of the regular climbers), the daytime hours getting there would be an exercise in re-learning how to take in air. I had ditched my team that morning before falling in with Tashi and Dawa and Anna, exiting with the excuse that she needed the help.

"She's got two Sherpas, for God's sake. She hardly needs *you*," Tuff had said to me as I packed up my gear, my back to him. "And you've got a *job* to do."

I heaved my pack on my back and adjusted it, pulling the clasp of the hip support tight. "Yeah, well, her Sherpas are friggin' twenty years old, and she's forty, so she's gonna need my help. And I'm not supposed to be shooting until Base Camp and you *goddamned well* know it Tuff, so step aside." I pulled my trekking hat down low over my forehead, set my sunglasses on the bridge of my nose and stepped in front of him, heading towards Anna.

I wasn't wrong. Anna *would* need help pacing; she'd need advice. But that wasn't Tuff's point.

He wasn't the only one who'd tried to stop me or set me straight. At home, in Wautoma, I'd inevitably find myself wasted on a bar stool a few nights after I'd landed back in town after a trek, sitting with my best friend Eddie at Grimm's Tavern—a little hole of a place that smelled like stale beer and stewing bratwurst. I'd tell him about the last woman I had fallen for and bedded on the trail, the infatuation still high in me, and the yearning, now that she was gone, fresh and body-rending.

"You don't really want anyone you're sleeping with, Traxler," he'd said to me the last time I was home. "You just want the *hit.*"

"Eddie, you've got to get this—she was really *something.*" That was Marina. In Burma, a travel writer. Funny, witty. Good in bed. Six feet tall, tiny and lovely breasts, red-headed, all limbs. That's what I could remember about her.

"Like the last one? Or the one before that? C'mon man, there's a word for what you're becoming."

"Forlorn," I said, smiling into my whiskey. If I was asked what color Marina's eyes were, I wouldn't have known—that was the truth. And we had only finished the thing months beforehand.

"*Addicted* was what I was thinking." Eddie said it soberly, and it landed on me like a short punch to the gut.

"C'mon, Eddie. That's hardly fair. I just haven't found the woman who will—"

"You don't *want* to find her. You want the chase. And that's fine when you're not married—well, hell, it's not fine even then. You're *forty*-fuckin' *what?*"

"Forty-seven. What the hell's that got to do with—"

"Look, you tell them it's only for the trek—whatever. But it's not about whether you're being *honest*, Traxler. It's whether or not you're being *selfish*. And I think you are."

He tipped his shot glass, drank, then stood to go. "Trax. Finish your goddamned marriage and get on with it, or you're gonna be old and alone. And I ain't gonna be wiping your ninety-year-old ass, you get me?"

He was right. Completely right. My marriage faltering had wounded me and I hadn't been dealing with it. I'd been filling the empty space, that's all. But I still needed it—the hit, the elation, the fast pursuit for the *feeling* of love—the mystical thing that would happen when Anna and I took off our clothes, pressed up against each other, and for a few intent moments, let go of everything except each other's skin. We would need each other with *angst*—so I hoped—tormenting ourselves with pleasure, knowing we might literally fall off a cliff or disappear down a crevasse, or simply walk away after making love and never see each other again. *That* was the hit. The heightened potion of in-the-moment need that regular life couldn't get near.

I had hiked quickly to the edge of the trail outside Anna's teahouse where she and her Sherpas were waiting for me. She had her hands on a set of prayer wheels built into the side of the trail, spinning them. Prayer wheels lined the entire trek all the way up to Everest Base Camp—big, gallon-sized cylindrical cans that had been painted with bright, textured Tibetan letters on red and gold and bright blue backgrounds. They were set on metal spikes in a wooden frame at elbow level, meant to bless the trek you were on if you wheeled them with your hands as you passed by. I came up behind her and spun a few myself, smiling.

"Listen," I said, when she and I stepped over to a rock-perch, swallowing some water before we headed up. "Don't take the drugs." Altitude drugs were popular. Every doctor prescribed them, and Anna had them, too.

"Why not?" she said.

Dawa was within earshot and looked up at me, assessing my intentions, I was guessing.

I looked back at him, giving him my most serious stare. I turned to her.

"Because the damned stuff is going to make your vision go blurry and your hands and feet feel like they're being pricked with pins. You'll also have to pee every half-hour–at least that's true for some people."

She looked over at Dawa. "You take them, Dawa?"

"We do not need them. We are acclimatized all the time," he said.

I laughed, loudly, the icy morning air catching in my nose and throat. "Anna. Dawa and Tashi go up ten or twelve times a year. They could stand on Sagarmatha and sing an aria and never need a puff of oxygen."

"That is true, David," Dawa said evenly.

"What's Sagarmatha?" Anna said, squinting her eyes and looking up at the rock-edge of the cliff we were standing next to.

"Sagarmatha–*Everest*," Tashi said, and saluted her with his left fingers.

"I don't understand–" She was sweet to him. Tender.

"It's the Nepalese name for the mountain," I said. "Or, Chomolungma for the Tibetans. They believe that these peaks are kings and queens that they can call on to help them when they're in need." I wanted to say, *I'm in need. Need for you, Anna.* But I kept my eyes trained on Tashi, smiling at him.

"So what am I supposed to do if I don't take the meds?" She was genuinely concerned.

I pulled my water bottle out of my pack and held it up. "You drink three or four liters of water a day. You *look ahead* with every step, and you stop every time you feel light-headed and breathe until it passes. You stay off the white-flour carbs as much as you can, and you acclimatize *two full days* at Namche. That's what you do."

I was right, but I had an agenda, too. It would not hurt her to skip the drugs. But more importantly, I wanted her to feel every single sensation when I finally got her into bed. I had long ditched the altitude drugs on the trail for exactly this reason.

She looked at Dawa. "Is he right? I mean–God–he does this for a living. He should know, right?"

"I think you are very healthy," Dawa said, "and I think he is right."

She threw her head back and laughed, and I wanted to slide my arms around her and press my body up against her right there, on the trailside. To drown in that laughter, that glorious willingness of hers to just *go* and be led.

—⁂—

To woo another human being in a day or two–to make her *want*–seems ridiculous by regular, daylight-hour standards, but trekking is another world.

To trek with a woman is to come to know her. I learned, that second day, that Anna lived in New York and she was a technical writer; that her father was a doctor, her mother a violinist who left her dad for another man when Anna was fourteen; that she was an only child. She'd been divorced for five years. But trekking made her say more: what she *felt* about her mother leaving, how it had wounded her. How her father didn't recover well. How it had left them both scarred. That her ex- was still her best friend, how she wondered sometimes why she divorced him. The trail tended to do that. The exertion made you talk from your heart, without noticing you were doing it.

I spoke about everything but my wife. I told her about Wautoma, Silver Lake, my best friend Eddie; my sister Elise, her husband Denny wasting away in a Milwaukee apartment, my mother refusing to help. My treks, shooting Everest, Kili, Burma. The upcoming climb on K-2.

We talked through eight full hours of trekking and rest points, all the way up to Namche. We were quiet, too, for long stretches of the trail–walking and breathing, taking in glorious sightlines and inhaling the crisp, thinning air filled with the aromatic scents of another, snowy land–things most trekkers, like Anna, would probably never experience again in a lifetime. It was an intimate act, and I knew how it played out with a woman–the intense exertion and the rare, peak-seeking moments, so gorgeous and passing so quickly, so effervescently–and that, all by itself, could make her want to mark it with desire.

We sexualize what we love, what we're fascinated by, a lover had once said to me, and it felt true. I had watched it happen with several women: the wonder filling them up; my days-long, hour after hour focus on them kick-starting the *want* I so needed.

"What do you do–I mean, for a living?" I had asked that morning. I had my water bottle in my hand as we trekked and I passed it to her. *Her lips where mine had been.*

"I write essays, articles. Engineering stuff, from all over the world. Medicine, new technology, that kind of thing. Three on wind-power this year. *That* was a trip."

"Why?"

She downed a bit more of my water and passed me the bottle. "Had to get to Berlin, Sao Paolo, and Britain in one month, then got to see a demo in the desert in North Africa."

"That sounds…" I pressed my lips to where hers had been on the bottle, tasting her.

"*What?*" She was sweating, and she unzipped her jacket under her pack's harness.

"It sounds *difficult.* Hard. Impressive, actually. Are you *difficult*, Anna? *Impressive?*" It was a cheesy joke, but I laughed anyway.

"I'm a rock-climb, baby," she said, grinning. She flashed her eyes at me. "You sure you want that?"

I glanced her way. "Yep, I do." I had the instinct to touch her arm, but I didn't. I wanted to wait.

"Listen," she said intently. "Let's not *pretend*, okay? You and I are going to do what we're going to do with each other up here in this thinning air, and then we'll leave each other be. That's what you want, right?"

It stunned me. "Uh, yeah. I…"

"You're not looking for more?"

"I guess I want to find someone as much as–I mean, *sometime*–"

"But that's not what *this* is about, is it?" She said it calmly, no edge.

"I don't know–*hell.* I guess not."

"Good," she said. "Then we'll be fine." She stepped ahead.

Tables turned, Traxler. It shut me up for a while.

We trekked into Namche about three in the afternoon, wandering through the sixty-or-so dwellings and small Nepalese stores, looking for a teahouse to stay in. The town was situated on the side of a terraced and steep mountain up from the Dudh Kosi. The first time I stood in Namche, I could see all the way across the lower Everest Valley below, the sightlines sweeping over a vast landscape down–green-green fields cut out among centuries-old rock fences, rolling hills set against the ridges of mountainsides, then thinning out to mountain rock as the elevation rose into the town. It was, even after all of my treks, like viewing evolution itself–like seeing the gods of geography at work, as if creation was being formed before my eyes. That first time, I had sat on a rock for four hours watching the light change across the landscape.

Anna paused with me on a rock jetty, staring out. There was a pale pink band of sky behind the peaks framing them in a horizontal bank of mist, then a distinct line of light blue fading into white as we looked up, the mountains a purplish brown in the foreground and the green-green below us.

"*Jesus.* It's fucking *gorgeous,*" she said.

"It is," I said, reaching for her hand. It was the first time I had touched her intimately.

We dumped our gear at a funky teahouse lodge (the place smelled of boiling potatoes), larger than most and made of wood and stone, cut in on three levels of the hillside with a string of tiny rooms on each floor. We both went off with a teahouse woman to find a room. I got my own, just in case Anna changed her mind. Then I walked her to the small hillside bakery in the town.

Off a bite-full of coarse pastry, I said it: "I'd like to spend the night with you."

She threw her head back and laughed, that warm laugh of hers, full of delight. There was a rough-hewn cup of grainy-smelling herbal tea in front of her.

"I thought that was already decided." She drew my hand near her face and licked the spice-and-sugar pastry filling off my fingers, taking my skin into her mouth, watching my eyes.

The sensation prickled up fast and sweetly along my inner thighs. "I thought I should at least *ask*," I said, a bit sheepishly.

She didn't answer me for a long time, just dipped her head down toward her tea cup, sipping, her loose black hair falling forward. I suddenly panicked, afraid she was going to say no, absolutely *not;* or worse, tell me I was an asshole for assuming, that she'd changed her mind. But she didn't. She took both of my hands in hers, leaned in to kiss my neck, and whispered to me, "What's it like at eleven-thousand feet? Is it a rush?"

We had dinner in our teahouse with twenty or so people from that day's trail elevation, all gathered in a wood-planked room on the top floor of the place. It was a slow, drawn-out, gregarious event with gamey aromas filling the room from chili-pepper spiced potatoes and seared meat. We shared a yak steak, the best protein we'd get for days. Sitting near each other, a bit apart from the group, playing cards–no reception for devices, just being *still* and focusing on each other–created a calm; a closeness. The black cast-iron stove was burning yak dung for heat, giving off a burnt grassy smell, and the snow on the mountains outside the steamy windows was a lavender color in the waning light.

We waited until it was late, until everyone in our lodge was settled. Then she led me to her room, in a corner of the teahouse down a dim hallway under the kitchen, far away from everyone else.

"You chose this room?" I said.

She smiled a sultry smile and pressed me through the doorway.

I couldn't get my clothes off fast enough.

She let me watch as she took her time, baring down to a bra and sky-blue panties. I lay down on the wooden cot built into the wall and tried to beckon her into the open sleeping bag. It was freezing, and bits of snowy air whipped through the wood-slatted walls patched into the stone. She shivered, but still waited. There was only a candle for light, stuck into a half-cut-out tin can lined with tin foil which reflected wobbly lines onto the bare stone walls and across her body. I shivered on the hard bed bunk and gazed at her. Her eyes flickered and she pulled her hair loose. Her breasts were not large but they were lovely, draping beautifully and exquisitely round. She had rounds of softness at her inner thighs; her legs were fit and fleshy.

"Come to bed," I breathed, reaching for the rough Nepalese blanket piled at the end of the bunk. "I want you."

She moved to me and lowered her body on top of mine, and as our skin met, she said, "David…let me feel you…" I drew her whole form in against my chest, my thighs, my arousal. She smelled of sweet, dried sweat, something aromatic in her hair.

When she slipped me inside of her, we stayed still, pressing against each other, not moving, her sitting astride and me holding her by the hips. Our eyes locked together in the wavering light from the candle. It was courageous, staring like that—most women closed their eyes or looked away—and it sent a sensation into my arousal that felt, in a split-second, riveting. Then she lay her upper body against my chest, still straddling me. I felt something in her drop away—the bravado gone, softened. She was *with* me.

I had thought she would be immediately athletic in bed, eager and physical, but this was more: a yielding, as if she had agreed with herself to trust me, if only for the moment. She spoke in a deep whisper, lightly running the tips of her fingertips along my side waist and along the edges of my armpits. "You're a good thing, David. You're perfect now, no matter what…"

Her head tilted back, and she closed her eyes as her breathing quickened. Slowly and deliberately, then more fiercely, she rocked herself on me, each rhythm changing and shifting like waves disappearing into each other on a shore, breaking from different angles—rhythmically rising, then tender, then escalating.

I kissed her, and there was no emptiness in it, no sexual urge without feeling or vigorous attempt at feigning passion. She was not holding back, and it moved me. I turned her over, slowly pressed against her face to face, stroking her slowly and pulling back enough to tease. I wanted, in that moment, for her to *need* me. *Where had that come from?* No press for her quick pleasure followed by my own intense release—none of that. I wanted her to *need.* I wanted it now, and I wanted it for afterwards.

Why now, with Anna?

When she climaxed she was loud and uninhibited, and though by then I couldn't have cared less who heard us, I was thankful she had chosen this room deep in the basement corner of the lodge. She turned me over on my belly then, surprising me–not done with me–and pressed her still-aroused self against the small of my back and began to rock again, the wet of her slipping across my skin in the fleshy curve below my lower spine, her breath heightening. I had never had a woman do this to me–pulse against my neutral body parts for her own pleasure–and the passivity of the pose thrilled me, being *taken*, the *want* in her climbing with heat between her legs all over again.

I was moved by sex, I knew it. Electric and uninhibited sex, certainly, and this was that. It was what I angled for first, my barometer of what was possible, as if it could kick-start by itself what I'd been missing and unable to sustain: closeness, devotion, intimacy. Maybe it was just the weariness of my unravelling life choices catching up with me, but without warning, in the middle of making love to her, I wanted a woman who would care about me. Who I could stay with. *Her.*

Afterwards, as her breathing calmed, she kissed my back, the sides of my face. I turned and held her. The light from the tin-can candle was dwindling.

"Listen, Anna…"

"Yes?"

I spoke into her hair. "After this? I mean, can we–"

She ran the fingers of her left hand down the mid-line of my belly hair. "David, let's just…"

"It's too soon, I know. Way too soon. We hardly know each other…"

"You're right."

In my head I calculated the hours we'd talked the past few days, how long it would have taken to get to know her like that on regular dates. I felt emboldened. "But I'll come to New York. I *will*…"

She breathed out hard. "Oh, can we not–"

"No, Anna. I mean it," I said intensely. "Can't we *try?*"

She lifted herself up on her elbow and looked into my eyes. "It's just for now–that's what you said," she intoned gently, "You and I will go back to our–"

"No! I can't let you leave. That's *ridiculous.*" I pulled her tight to my stomach. Tears stung my nostrils. *What the hell was I saying?*

"You're serious?" She lifted her head and took me in.

"Anna, please," I said, yearning in my voice. It shocked me.

"David, we're both moving targets. We're both gone half the year–"

"*Look ahead, not back,* Anna." I intertwined my hand with hers. "I don't want to be a moving target anymore. I want *you.*"

She started to speak, but I stopped her, reaching for the sides of her face and closing my mouth over hers, kissing her. Refusal was not an option. I would have her. I had to. I kept her up until five in the morning; it was light before she made me let her sleep.

—⁓—

The next morning I was high and giddy from no sleep, still smelling Anna on my hands and my unshaven face. Tuff caught me out on the packed dirt street and gripped me by the arm.

"What the *hell?*" I said, shaking him off.

"Traxler, it's none of my goddamned business, but I've watched you do this too many times, and I swear to God if you haven't told her that you're married, I'm going to."

I pulled my lips into a thin smile, calmly. "She knows, okay? It's her choice." Another lie.

"Fucking *fine,* then," he said, grimacing. "You're a goddamned *hazard,* you know that? I hope you fall face-first for her and she dumps you on your cheating ass." He stormed away from me, down the dirt and snow-packed street. It rattled me. But I hoped against hope that he wasn't right, that beyond my dwindling ability to *partner,* I might find something with Anna that I'd be willing to fight for.

Anna had gone off with Tashi on an acclimatizing hike–a big one, up to the Thami Monastery, a red, gold and orange temple perched on the side of a snowy peak. It had rows of vibrant-hued prayer tapestries inside called *Thangkas* hanging from the rafters, and wooden chests along the walls with tiny half-opened drawers overflowing with scrolled prayers. I'd done the trek at least six times, and I knew they wouldn't be back for eight or nine hours. How she would pull off the exertion after being up all night with me, I didn't know. My plan was to *sleep,* then go up a much milder trail and come back. Each of us had to go up in elevation that day, as well as the next, at least a thousand feet, then come back down and sleep at Namche to let our brains and lungs adjust for the higher altitudes coming up. There was always some idiot–usually a guy–who thought himself invincible and went up without the up-and-down altitude adjustment. The previous year, a nineteen year old track star went up without acclimatizing, and the kid died in his sleep at sixteen thousand feet. Acclimatizing was serious business.

Anna was wiped out when she got back at the end of the day, but I tried to get her to take a walk with me anyway. The sun had already dipped behind the peaks.

"Anna–come on! Take a walk with me around the town."

"A *walk?*" she said incredulously. "David–babe–I barely made it back here."

That word, *babe* sent a shiver of shock into me, fear shooting through my heart at what I had to tell her.

She crawled into bed immediately. I let her sleep for a while, then went up to the kitchen and got a bowl of *dahl bat* and some tea for her and brought it downstairs. I woke her with my kiss, and she got up slowly and pressed her body up against me. I pulled back.

"Oh…" she said, taunting me. "Had all you can take last night, huh…?" Her voice was throaty and soft.

"Anna…I have to–"

She pressed me. "No, David. You *promised…*" She slipped cold fingers under my layers of sweaters, smiling.

I took her by the shoulders. "I have to tell you something!" I said, almost yelling. The room went instantly icy with my seriousness.

She sat back and looked at me hard: a dead-on, take-no-prisoners stare. "What?"

I choked up, straining to get the words out. My eyes began to burn. "I–I…"

She looked into my face, and her voice went thin and small. "You're *married,* aren't you?"

My heart sank, and I looked at her imploringly. The air in my lungs felt hot, burning, though it was freezing in the room. I didn't speak.

"Are you?" She opened her eyes wide.

"Yes." I dropped my head. "I should've told you…I'm sorr–"

"David, *don't.*"

"Anna, I should have–I mean, before we–"

She was irritated. "Look, I guessed, alright?"

"You guessed?"

"It was the way you flinched when Tashi asked you on the trail. And the fact that you never brought up a woman's name in two days of trekking together."

"But you slept with me anyway."

"Maybe I didn't want to know." She looked straight at me, unapologetic.

"My wife and I–Camille–we've barely seen each other for the last two years. It's my fault. Now she's got some guy–in our *house*–that she hired for this camp she runs–"

"Stop, David. I really don't need to know the details. It's *fine.*"

"I'm going to ask her for a divorce."

Anna laughed, a small eruption of it.

"That sounded pathetic, didn't it?" I said, meeting her eyes. "It's just that–I don't know. I *felt* something with you that–"

"Look, David…" She trailed off.

"I'm sorry, Anna. Truly." I was sincere. "I thought that…" I stopped myself. "Yeah, honestly, I don't know what I thought."

She stared at me for a long time, and then breathed out lightly. "You know what? It doesn't matter. Everybody I know is in some sort of relationship *limbo*. I don't think I have a friend in the world who has anything traditional. I've been divorced from my ex- for five years and we still sleep together when we're single. Who am I to judge?"

I put my head in my hands. "I just can't seem to make anything match what's up here." I nodded toward the mountains. "That sounds lame, I suppose."

"The thrill of never seeing a woman again…how *telling*, David." She said it with a bite.

"It's more than that…" I looked down at my hands. I was wringing them.

"Really. How so?" She wasn't pleased.

I couldn't answer.

She took in a sharp breath, drawing her legs into her chest, then pressed her back against the wall of the bunk. "God. I'm so stupid. You weren't looking for a good *romp*." A sarcastic edge entered her voice. "You want a woman who's compelling enough to make you leap. If she's enough then maybe you'll want her after the trek? Then you'll leave your wife? That's it, right?"

I flared a bit. "And what about you? You suspect I'm married and you slept with me anyway?"

"Hey, I didn't lie! I'm single. You *told* me you're divorced–"

We both went quiet.

"So, Anna…are we just selfish people?" I said with a dour tone.

She made a guttural sound in her throat. "This is what it is to use people for fun, wouldn't you say? Amazing in the moment, regretful in the *denouement*. That is, if we have any conscience at all."

"I don't regret a single second, Anna," I said breathily. Then, off her surprised look, "I *don't*. There was something there–in that bed, and trekking with you–"

Her eyes flashed at me. "So you want me to *hope*? With a man who, I'm guessing, hasn't been true for–*what*–how many years?" She threw her head back with the emphasis and accidentally banged it on the wood plank fitted into the stone wall behind her. The board rattled.

"Damn it!" she said, rubbing her head.

I did want her to hope. That's all I wanted. "Please, Anna. I'm going to call Camille and end it. I will."

"What, from up here on your climbing team's satellite phone? That'll be a pleasant experience for her. *Jesus,* David."

Little tears formed at the corner of her eyes and she stood up, sliding off the bunk, and I watched her set her jaw, steeling herself. Then she gathered up my clothes and pushed me out into the hallway with them, closing the wood-plank door and locking it without a word.

———

My team was set to leave from Namche at seven the next morning. I hadn't slept, and the strong tea I was swallowing in the teahouse's kitchen was burning my stomach lining. The milk in it smelled sour, but I drank it anyway. I wouldn't run into Anna again for days–or ever, if she changed her mind about climbing Kala Patthar, her last and highest-point destination above Base Camp, or if she took another trail with her Sherpas to avoid seeing me again. I banged on her door before I left.

"Anna, please! Let me in for a minute!"

She didn't respond. I knocked for a long time, bruising my knuckles on the hard wood planks, saying her name over and over again, until finally, I stopped and stood there outside her door, listening to her move around her room.

I said, loudly enough for her to hear, "I'll see you at the bottom of Kala Patthar. I'll wait for you." My gut twisted, but I left.

I had blown it. And it wasn't like I could just call her on a cell phone and say, "Hey, where are you now?" There was no reception, save for our team's generator-powered uplink, and that was spotty at best and only accessible to the team once a week. I couldn't call my sister Elise, she'd dumped her phone when she took off for Mexico, and Eddie, back in Wautoma, would hardly sympathize.

If our team was lucky, once we got to Base Camp–and so often a climbing team was *not* lucky–the weather would stay clear during daylight hours for at least three days, and we'd get a go-ahead to go up-summit from the satellite service via our funky generator-powered communication set-up. If they couldn't get through to us, which often happened, we'd have to make the decision ourselves, taking the risk. After eight years of trying to summit, I knew that the weather systems on *Sagarmatha,* on Everest, were so varied and volatile that you could watch them push up through the Valley and descend from the sky, dumping storms or rain or wind or freezing sleet in a matter of minutes, from out of nowhere. The avalanches were even more unpredictable.

Anna and her two Sherpas were splitting off from our route, going up another peak called Gokyo Ri at seventeen-five. For days she'd be trekking treacherous, thin trails cut into the precipice side of mountains filled with sharp and slippery stones, then attempting to sleep at sixteen-thousand feet, which was ridiculously difficult. I worried for her.

If they made it, they'd come down a bit in altitude, then trek back up the Everest Valley trail to a little group of teahouses above Base Camp. Then they'd go up Kala Patthar at nineteen thousand–a hand-to-foot, vaporous-air climb up a mountain that looked like God had dumped a sky-full of gigantic rocks on it. From its peak, Kala Patthar looked directly into the side of Everest, with a clear drop off its backside to the valley two thousand feet below. It was stunning.

It was a crapshoot what day, or whether or not, they'd arrive at the little village near Base Camp, and a crapshoot whether I'd still be there. It was anyone's guess–the weather, the satellite guys, the climbing team, the Sherpas, *her.*

———

Days later, exhausted from six more days of trekking up to Base Camp and acclimatizing, I finally got my five minutes on the satellite phone. I called Camille. I knew I should wait until I got off the mountain, but I couldn't. I wanted to tell Anna the next time I saw her–*if* I saw her–that I had ended my marriage, that I was serious.

"Camille, I have to tell you something!" I shouted into the receiver. The connection was shit, and though I knew the handful of my mates milling outside the tent would hear me, I didn't care. "I've only got a couple of minutes on this damned thing…"

"David–" She came across with a static-y echo.

"I want a *divorce,* Camille." I said it as levelly as I could.

"You *what?* I can't hear you!"

"A *divorce!*" I yelled. I heard the talking outside the tent stop dead.

"What, now? Right now? In the middle of your–"

"It's just–*yes!* I want it out in the open, Camille! Enough already with us having separate lives!"

"You met someone, on the mountain, didn't you?"

"Yes."

"What? I didn't hear you."

"*Yes!*" I shouted.

The line went dead.

—〜—

The summit never happened. Two ice storms in a row, a freezing gale nearly blowing us off our twenty-one-thousand foot camp. Then again, at twenty-six thousand at the Lhotse Wall, the same thing. After five days up there, we turned back. Tuff sprained his ankle badly nearly falling off a rope line–the thing was swollen all to hell and it took two of us to get him down the mountain to camp.

"Good of you, Traxler," he said when we finally got him settled in the medic's tent.

"Hey, you'd do the same for me, right?" I said.

Tuff nodded, though I wasn't so sure.

I was waiting for Anna the afternoon she came down from Kala Patthar. I had paid six Nepalese kids ten dollars apiece to run into Camp and tell me if they saw anyone matching Anna's description. That morning, three of them showed up to say they saw her and two Sherpas heading up Kala. Kala was a hard climb–hand to foot all the way up and down over gargantuan rocks with thinner and thinner air each handful of ascending feet. It was slow going. I spotted her about two hundred feet up with my trekking binoculars, and I watched her descend for a good half-hour. She was climbing down over the last of the moon-scape rock piles, about to jump off into the hard-pack, when she finally saw me.

She laughed out loud.

"How was it?" I said, breaking the ice.

"*You* know!" Her eyes were flashing and she breathed her words out hard. "Fucking amazing! Everest. That other peak, Ama Dablum. The view–*God!* Even an avalanche across the valley when we were on top!"

She jumped from the rocks onto the flat trekking path and hugged me. She played at slapping me on the face, and then, catching her breath said, "Okay, David. I said *no*, and you're still here. Are you going to follow me all the way back to New York?"

"If I have to," I said, pulling my sunglasses off my face. "I told Camille," I spit out. "I'm getting a divorce. Anna–it's done." I had to be direct. Our climbing team was heading down-mountain very early the next morning and I had gear to pack.

"What? You two decided that how? Over email?" Her tone was accusing.

I spoke quickly. "Look, I think you and I can–I at least want to try. She and I have been..."

"How did you tell her?"

"The satellite phone."

She shook her head, looking down at her boots, now coated with dirt and trail dust, white scalloped lines streaking across them from where the snow had wet them, then dried. She shuffled one boot against another, tilting her head to look at my face.

"I don't know what to tell you, David. I don't think–"

"We *can*," I said. "Look, we've all stayed longer than we should have in relationships that were tanking…I mean, haven't you?"

Tashi and Dawa came down behind her, and Tashi's open face shifted into a scowl.

"You *lie*, David Traxler. Not good."

My throat closed up. "You told them?" I said to Anna.

"I did," she said, blank-faced.

I pulled her to me and held her, and she didn't resist. "I have to go. We're heading out tomorrow morning. I'll be shooting on K-2 for two months–it'll depend on the weather. But I'm coming back. Wait for me. *Please.*"

———

The day we got back from K-2 I called Anna on her on cell. We had gotten up on the top of the mountain on the Pakistani side–no little deal since the stats are pretty grim: one in four climbers dies making the attempt. We were two weeks late getting out, stuck up above a flooded and raucous river with all of our gear and no satellite reception. I was still giddy from the triumph when I finally spoke to her.

"Anna, we did it! It was *fucking* incredible!" I shouted into the phone. "I'm coming to New York to see you–"

"No, David, *don't*–I'm in Portugal. I've got a week before an assignment in Spain."

"You're in Lisbon?"

"No, the Azores. I found this old hotel here. All stone, the *Pousada* something or other…"

"Which one?" I was instantly anxious.

"David, I'm leaving in two days. I rented a sailboat for a week."

"No. Which *island?*"

"Faial."

I sighed. "So you're in Horta then." I knew my geography. Horta was where you stayed on Faial. "I'd offer to come with you, but I know you like to travel alone."

She didn't speak.

"You're still blaming me?" I said, huffing a bit.

"Not at all," she replied evenly. "It's just what happened."

Her coolness cut me, ripped a hole in my insides as if someone had walked up and pierced me with my own trekking knife and pulled it downward to make a ragged gash. I wanted her to touch me again–to feel the sensations I'd been living with in my imagination for weeks trekking down from Everest, and for two solid months climbing K-2, day in and day out, imagining her on top of me, breathless. But I wanted more than that, too: to hear her laugh, to hold her, to have her need me. To talk to her. Something had flipped in my insides–the casual ability I'd cultivated with other women to bed-and-leave without consequence was now burning inside me in places I didn't know could ache. *Anna.*

A few hours later, I paid nineteen hundred dollars for a ticket to the Azores, arriving unannounced at her hotel door cradling an armful of flowers. She stepped back against the carved wooden door of her room, staring at me. When she laughed, my knees turned to soft glue.

"Oh, God, David. What're you doing here?"

"I'm...I don't *know*–" I said honestly, pushing the flowers into her hands. They were lilies, and two or three of them had browned and wilted a bit. "Here. For *you*," I said with too much emphasis.

She shook her head, then hugged me, mashing the flowers between us. "What the hell. Come in."

We had dinner in her room–an old stone space with narrow, floor-to-ceiling French doors with waffling antique glass in them, which opened out onto a view of a rough-hewn barn and the sea golden and pink-skied below it. The salt air scented the entire room.

After dinner she beat me at Scrabble, making a complex word from the four letters of "site" on the board.

" '*Exquisite.*' I'm spelling that right, aren't I?" She winked at me.

"*You* are," I said, sounding ridiculous even to myself.

"Yeah, yeah–don't think you're gonna get me to give up beating you with that *wooing* crap. I'm going to beat your ass at this game and enjoy every second of it."

She laughed uproariously at the look on my face–defiant, challenging–and I felt the push of my jeans against my flesh again; the instant sensation of need.

Her fingers reached across the table and grasped mine, and she led me to her bed. I had reveled in her presence for so many days–alone, yearning–and from so many imaginary angles other than being inside her, that now I was afraid.

She saw the fear flash in my eyes, and she whispered, "It's okay, David." Her simple, kind thought for me aroused me fiercely.

She trained her eyes on mine, boldly and calmly, unabashed, like she had in the Himalayas. It was a powerful opiate, looking at her, touching her, running my fingers along the newly tanned lines from her bathing suit bottoms. I felt like I was finally tired of playing at love, tired of my vaporous wandering. Her stare made me want to be with someone who I could want for years, who could trust me. I laughed at the thought. *Trust. Surely not, with me.*

"What, David?" she said, smiling. "What's funny?"

"You're here, and you want me–"

"I *do*," she said, catching the sexual innuendo in the back of her throat.

I had meant it tenderly–a truth I was trying to tell–but she was playing with me.

Afterward, as we lay spent on her bed, she started to sing.

"Please don't," I said. "It'll break my heart."

She lifted up and looked at me to see if I was kidding, and saw that I wasn't. Then she fell back into my arms, and lightly stroked my chest with her finger-nails.

"Anna, can I come with you on the sailboat?" She was leaving the next day.

She spoke gently. "David. If you come with me you have to know what this is. It isn't forever."

—*w*—

I would lose. For two years–more–I had used the trek, the room, or the circumstance to have the woman I wanted, to *win,* and then I had left. It had been easy. A kind of *taking,* without consequence; a way to feel love, or some version of it, leaving long before I could get hurt again.

And now Anna had me. On a boat. In the middle of the Portuguese sea. Seven days of sailing and a crash course in learning how to man the schooner (I had been on one a couple of times as a teenager, but I hadn't known what I was doing), and I had argued my way into a corner with her.

It had started the first day. She had brought nothing with her–bikini, T-shirt, shorts, sweatshirt, toothbrush; all of it stuffed into a slim, string-tied bag slung across her back, checking the rest of her stuff at the hotel. She had laughed at me when I hauled my heavy pack on board.

"What?" I said, off her sarcastic look.

"You're going to be naked or in your trunks most of this trip, David. Where do you think you're going to wear all of that stuff?"

It was nothing, but it irked me. *Her*, light and unaffected; *me*, needy and baggage-laden.

We'd gone to five islands, from Faial to Pico and Sao George, then Terceira and Graciosa–gorgeous, vividly-hued ocean sunsets and quaint little villages. But the tension had grown between us the closer we came to the end of our week.

"*No*, David! Tie it like a figure-eight! Back and forth–the way I showed you!" she snapped at me on our last afternoon. I was fumbling on purpose, not paying attention.

"So, let me guess," I snapped back, snubbing out the joint I had been smoking. I sat beside her, crouched and pulling my cotton shirt over my shoulders, the sun biting into my red-tinged skin. "You won't stay with *me*, so you're going back to your ex-husband, is that it? Or is it some other guy?" I said bitterly.

We had sailed back in the direction of Faial and were floating about a half-mile offshore, where, in another few hours, we would moor the schooner and my time would be up. I could see the shoreline, the rocky edge of it a craggy blue-black line in the distance.

Anna reached for the joint I had just put out. "I don't know, David. We talked. That's all." She lay face-down on her stomach, pressed against the bright white deck of the sailboat with nothing on but bikini bottoms. Her bright blue and yellow bathing suit top was rolled up in a ball next to her.

"Be fucking *honest*, Anna. Christ!"

"Honest? You're kidding, right?" Her head lifted from the deck and she opened her eyes extremely wide.

"So, your ex- will take you back, after everything got fucked up?" I sniffed the air: bitter with salt and blasting hot like an oven.

"Don't say it like I was unfaithful to him. I wasn't." She was up on her elbows now, her bare breasts draping toward the deck.

"You mean, 'Not like *you*, David.' " I mimicked her and she grimaced.

"You did whatever you did in your marriage. That's between you and–"

I flared. "Why the hell did you invite me on this goddamned island-hopping trip?"

"I didn't invite you. You invited yourself." She relit the joint, inhaled, then blew smoke through her teeth, chuckling lightly.

"*Jesus*, Anna!" I bellowed. "What the *fuck* are we doing here?"

She sighed. "I don't know, David," she said evenly, watching my face as she spoke. "Having a little fun. That's what *you* said, as I recall."

The boat swayed, and Anna rolled over on her back, baring her fleshy, tanned breasts. She reached with her leg and wrapped her foot around my ankle, smiling at me with a wicked grin.

I felt a quick and prickling press in my trunks–the against-my-will arousal of seeing her bare-breasted–and it irritated me. I forced myself to look out at the waves, which were gaining a little clip with the afternoon wind. She flipped over and slid forward on her stomach, kissing the tops of my sunburned feet.

I winced. "Anna–for God's sake–" I shook my feet out from under her face. I sounded petulant and I knew it.

She sat up, crossing her legs, nearly naked in front of me. "We've got a few more hours, David. Don't ruin it."

"Screw it," I said under my breath, and went below deck.

I mixed myself a drink–canned coconut juice and rum without ice and downed it, then sat down on the schooner's unmade bed. It had not been made all week, the light blue cotton sheets strewn and tangled at the foot. She would laugh if she saw my cocktail and say, "God, David, you can't mix a drink to save your life." I loved that laugh, though it could make me feel small and diminished.

Ten minutes later she dangled her feet into the hatch, her perfect, bright-red toenails shining, then leaned her head in. "Don't get drunk," she teased. "I'm going to want you in twenty minutes."

Too late, I thought. I'd had three by the time she came down, the sugar and alcohol mix already giving me a splitting headache, and she crawled in next to me in the bunk, pressing up against my back.

"Let's not fight, David, okay?" She stroked my face.

I felt an irritation ignite instantly in my belly. I turned and held her by the shoulders. "Look, I can't just *lose* myself in you and then–".

"*Shhhhh…*" she purred, then slid her fingertips down my bare sides, her hands slithering into my trunks. I pushed back against her and then away, resisting, but she rolled over on top of me and pressed. *I can't,* I thought. But two minutes later, she eased my trunks off and I let her do it. She wriggled out of her bathing suit bottoms and I pulled her in and held her tightly. Then she touched me, played with me, pressed, but I rose and fell, going soft. Hands, mouth, pressure–no arousal. Nothing. I writhed, ground against her pelvis– sure-fire for me, every time–but I stayed wilted, drained. It stunned me.

"This never fucking happens to me–" I said, red in the face and furious.

"David, it's not a big deal. It's time for us to go, that's all." She kissed my cheek, got up off me and headed up the ladder to the deck, leaving me naked on the narrow, foam mattress.

I looked at my flaccid flesh. "Jesus fucking *Christ.*"

When I stood up in the galley, the schooner took a slam off a huge wake and I bashed my forehead against an open cabinet. My liquor stash. A good-sized bruise would form above my right eyebrow. *Perfect,* I thought sarcastically.

A minute later, I climbed up on deck where she was standing in her full blue and yellow bathing suit, the yellow ties of her crisscrossed top strung over her strong back. She moved in and held my face, then kissed me.

"Anna, I wanted to say I'm—"

"No, don't. *Really.*" She pulled her lightweight string-tied bag over her shoulders, backpack-style, then stepped over the corded railing of the schooner, curling her toes over the edge of the boat.

"What're you doing?"

She dove then, a clean arc off the side of the sailboat, coming up for air thirty feet away, the blue water parting for her water-slicked, black-haired head.

Her legs and arms pumped as she turned, athletically swimming toward shore.

"Anna!" I yelled. "Where are you going? You can't *leave* me on this thing—"

She treaded water and shouted, "You're going to be fine on your own! You'll see!"

A sizable wave came up under the sailboat, and I quickly and clumsily grasped on to the boom, but then the boat settled easily over the wave and evened out.

"See, David!" Anna called from the sea, her head bobbing above the water-line. "No crash! You're going to be just fine!"

"Anna! *Jesus!* Come on!"

She turned away from the schooner and swam vigorously, farther and farther toward the harbor, ignoring me.

As I looked around at the endlessness of the seawater around me, the port a good half-mile away, I felt it: how alone I was. Unaided, abandoned. A person moored in the middle of the ocean and inept, with the barest of skill in navigating back to a safe shore. It was the entirety of my adult loving laid before me, and it was my own damned fault.

I had thought I was coming half-way around the world to woo her—a kind of Hail-Mary pass or a shot in the dark that she'd want me; that alone in Portugal, she'd come to *need* me. But I knew, just then, watching her—stroke after stroke as she swam away from me—that she had let me come to say good bye.

She had *planned* to make me find my way back by myself.

Anna, who I wanted with all my heart, would return to her life, and I would return to my divorce papers in Wisconsin, my empty house. Alone.

I stood on the deck, staring into the blue-green sea, the bright Portuguese sun glittering off the swaying water, knowing I'd be altered by this, by her, and that I would want to be.

The hot air burned my throat, and I breathed it out with force, gazing at her now-distant form.

"So long, Anna," I whispered, then whispered it again.

I shifted the rudder, my sun-singed face turning into the crisp early-evening wind, and with an unsteady hand, steered for shore. ꙮ

These people! Do they not understand that there are options for being an adult? Good God almighty!

Kewaskum

Dory was twenty-four years old when she left her family and her Milwaukee County home for the town of Kewaskum, Wisconsin, population four thousand, two hundred and twenty-one. Her full name was Dorothea Browne Fathom, and her entire family clan had become lawyers. In fact, she and her three older brothers had been carefully named for their expected eminent careers.

"We are *attorneys*, Dorothea," her father had said to her every year since she was six. "We do *not* call ourselves lawyers." Dory called them lawyers anyway.

Each child in her family, it was assumed, would eventually land at their parents' firm of Fathom, Fischer, Blume & Browne–a stuffy, high-priced group of estate planning attorneys in Milwaukee that her mother, Eleanor Josephine Browne, and her father, Willis Bertram Fathom, had founded in the mid-1980's with her mother's two brothers.

To say the place was inbred with Fathoms and Brownes was a ridiculous understatement. There were uncles, two cousins, an aunt on her father's side, two of the cousins' daughters, and her grandfather Browne, still hanging on to his office at age eighty-six.

Dory's father and mother had both gone to law school at Michigan, and each of her older brothers–Jonathan, Jefferson, and Will Henry–had gone to the University of Chicago, then joined the firm. Grandfathers on both sides had been estate planning attorneys, and grandmothers had been estate planning attorneys' wives.

"There's a *career* in being a useful attorney's wife," her grandmother Lillian had said to Dory when she was twelve. "And *you* have a choice. Estate attorney or attorney's wife. That's more of a choice than I had."

When Dory graduated from Colby College in Portland, Maine with a degree in Liberal Arts–her mother had called it an *I-don't-know-what-I'm-doing* degree–she did not apply to law school. She did not *try* to apply to law school. What did she want to do? She had no idea. But she knew, for certain, that she did *not* want to be an attorney.

It was anathema.

"You're *ungrateful,* that's what you are, Dorothea!" her mother Eleanor huffed in dramatic courtroom decibels when she had gotten up the courage to tell her parents.

"It's *Dory,* mother. I don't go by Dorothea anymore." It was an old argument.

"I named you for a *reason,*" her mother said. "And you will not be undermined in your *career* by some idiot bastardization of your name!"

Dory stammered. "Look, I'm not cut out for…I mean, I *can't.* I'm not like you…both of you are–"

"What! What are we?" Eleanor shouted. Her mother was standing in the living room of their polished wood-and-plank, Cream City brick Fox Point home with a scotch in her right hand, waving her left for emphasis, her father seated primly on a newly-acquired, handmade brown leather chair with thick wood trim that matched the wainscoting in the room. He still had his dark gray business suit on at eight o'clock–light-blue shirt and robin's-egg-blue tie–a drink in his hand and the tie still knotted tightly. In fact, Dory could rarely remember seeing him out of a suit.

She was four weeks back from college–five years, including a couple of study semesters in Eastern Europe and part of the summer in Maine–standing in front of her parents in droopy, bell-bottomed sweat pants and a T-shirt with hand-drawn mountain peaks printed on it which read, "Women on Top. Annapurna. 2020."

Two workers with leaf blowers were wending their way across her parents' tennis court outside the living room window, the high-pitched whine of the machines stinging in Dory's head.

Willis, her father, was level, never raising his voice, but he used his tone for emphasis. "You're not *thinking,* now, are you, Dorothea? We raised you to *think.*" He knitted his fingers together, leaning forward so his elbows rested on his knees and his crossed middle fingers touched his nose. "You'll think this through, and you'll *see* that–"

"Dad, I can't. I'm not wired that way." There was only one Fathom, her father's youngest brother, who had gotten his law degree, dumped it, taught developmentally disabled kids, and then died in a car accident up in La Crosse. His wife and daughter had been kept at arm's length by her parents (they were decidedly *not* in the attorney clan), and Dory had hardly ever gotten to see her cousin Shelby or her Aunt Evvy. It was a cautionary tale.

"*Wired that way?* What's that supposed to mean?" Her mother was ramping up—the scotch kicking in. "*Really,* Dorothea! If you can't tell us what it is that's so important to veer off for, from the *family*—you don't even *know!*—then you'll give us your stiff upper lip, do what's right, and go to law school! There! It's settled!"

Her mother was not unattractive. She kept her hair in a neat page boy, had it colored and highlighted in rich brown tones—"brown for a Browne," she always said when she came back from the hairdresser—and wore Gabriela Hearst and Bottega Veneta suits that flattered her fleshy, imposing figure. Her parents were exactly the same height, five-foot-ten, a stately and commanding presence made together when entering any room.

Dory's flat brown hair fell past her shoulders, un-styled, and her body was thin and petite, just five-foot-four. She had always felt diminutive in the presence of her parents, and particularly with her older brothers, all broad-shouldered and six-feet-plus.

Her mother paced, the condensation from her drink dripping in tiny droplets onto the white, hand-woven wool rug under her feet, long fingers gripping and re-gripping her glass. "Your grades were not stellar, darling. We all know that. But you can get into someplace decent—Minnesota, Virginia—Christ, maybe even Michigan—on our family name. You can do it! We'll help you get there." Her mother's expression turned sympathetic, and Dory began to crumble.

She teared up. "I can't…"

"You *will,* darling," her father said, rising and putting an arm around her shoulder.

Her mother bristled at her father's affectionate gesture, then softened again and smiled at her. "Dorothea. Put on some nice clothes and we'll take you to the club for dinner. Day boats scallops tonight—your favorite. It's going to be *fine.* You'll see."

Dory looked up into her father's slightly lined face, his arm still around her upper shoulder. A crisp-looking haircut of short, styled, silvery hair. Blue eyes. He was handsome.

"Dad. Look at me," Dory said, wiping tears away from her face with the back of her thin hands. "I can never be what you want me to be."

—◆—

Her brother, Will Henry, closest to her in age but still five years older, winced when she told him.

"Jesus, Dory, you've *fouled out* of the family. That's kind of asinine, you know what I'm saying?" He was a basketball nut, an everything-sports fan, and Dory thought he was obsessed in the way that some people get addicted to sex or a food product, or binge-watch TV shows that they can't pry themselves away from.

They were at a hole-in-the wall bar in Whitefish Bay where Will Henry lived, drinking some local IPA. It was muggy, early August, their beer mugs sweating circles of moisture on the carved-up maple bar, peoples' initials hacked into the thick surface. Will Henry's eyes were glued to the screen behind the booze bottles. "Come on, Giannis! Don't bring us that shit!" he hollered at the Buck's forward. He had wanted to be a sports attorney, maybe even an agent, but their parents had squashed that idea, their mother threatening to cut him off financially in law school if he did.

"Will, for God's sake–it's an exhibition game–"

Will Henry ignored her, flopping the weight of his long, well-shaped, black-haired bangs to the side with his left hand. A rebellion. Long hair. "What the hell, Dory? They're going to kick you out. Mom'll make sure of it. Look what they did to me."

Dory picked up her beer glass and held it up to Will Henry's face, looking at him through the golden liquid. "If I squint through this beer…yep. *Jeez.* I swear to God, Will, you look like a sports agent."

"Not funny," he said bitterly. "And not going to happen."

"Why not? Goddamn it, Will! You could still do it. You're only twenty-nine."

"They'd never…"

"For *fuck's* sake! You're an adult. You've got some money. Do what you want."

"Don't be crass."

"I'm not…I mean, why does everyone in this family have to do what *they* did? What's so terrible about doing something different?"

"That's the *code.* You know it as well as I do. You want to be invited to Thanksgiving and Christmas? Those stupid family picnics? You want your kids to have grandparents?"

"It's not *fair–*"

He looked back at the screen, unconsciously sliding his sweating beer glass in circles on the wooden bar. "Just buck up and do the law school thing. It'll make everybody happy."

Dory reached out with her right hand and cradled his chin, then turned his face toward hers.

"Everyone except *me*," she said.

———

Her mother did, indeed, kick her out.

"You will not stay in this house and refuse to go to law school and then think we will support you," her mother said, caging her on the staircase two days after she had seen Will.

"I was planning on getting a job."

"What *kind?*"

"I really don't know, Mother. Then I'll move out." She ran her hand along the smooth brown lines of the polished wood staircase railing.

Eleanor put her hands on her substantial hips. "No. You'll move out *now.*"

"I haven't got any money. Just my summer savings—"

"Law school, you stay. No law school, you don't. Those are the terms." She had her *I'm going to win this case if it kills me* look on her face.

Dory knew the look well. She stood for a long time, staring at her mother, not speaking. Two minutes. Three. A staring contest. Her mother's left eye began to twitch.

Finally, Dory spoke. She said it softly. "Alright, Mother. I'll go pack."

Eleanor's eyes went wide with surprise.

———

For the rest of the summer, Dory camped out near Port Washington on a private piece of farm land owned by the parents of her best friend Alisa. It was balmy and sunny in the mornings, humid and hot in the afternoons, with a hint of the upcoming fall chill coming off Lake Michigan at night.

"In a month or two it's going to be cold as morning-after sin out there," Alisa said to Dory on the phone. "My parents won't show up until Thanksgiving, so you've got the run of the place. You should stay in the cabin, Dor."

But Dory preferred to sleep in her tent. It was a really good one she had gotten in her college sophomore year as a birthday present from her brothers, and it had cost over a thousand dollars, she knew.

"Holy hell! Look at you! You've left the *counselors'* roost," Alisa said to Dory when she visited the farm and saw Dory's tent. They were swilling bourbon in paper cups, sitting on tree stumps, bundled in sweatshirts and blankets in the early evening fog. "What does the *jury* have to say about that?"

Alisa was tiny. Five-foot-one, wild, bushy red hair that made her appear three inches taller, green eyes, full red lips.

"My mother's not speaking to me. My father, one text so far. 'Come home. Go to law school.' That's all he said."

"These *people!* Do they not understand that there are *options* for being an adult? Good God almighty!"

Dory enjoyed Alisa being indignant. It made her feel not crazy.

Alisa was an artist (giant, fine-lined pencil portraits of faces) and lived in the basement of her parents' brand-new ceramics workshop in Milwaukee–her father loved to throw pots–"an indulgence of too much cash," Alisa said. "But I can't really complain, now can I? It's free rent for God's sake."

The two young women had grown up next door to each other in Fox Point, a block from the Lake Michigan shoreline, same age, Dory's parents having never figured out that their neighbor's Port Washington vacation place was really a pot farm. Daniel and Jewel Bayswater, Alisa's parents, made their living, supposedly, with a "gardening company"–the ceramics studio was "a side business"–surreptitiously shipping their product in gallon-sized tomato paste cans from their farm's grow room to dispensaries in Colorado and California. Alisa's granddad, Ponty, had sold farm insurance in central Wisconsin, and her father Daniel had learned the agricultural trades well, parlaying them into an under-the-radar, high dollar marijuana business.

It had never occurred to the parental Fathoms to ask what *kind* of gardening their neighbors were engaged in. A class thing. Though the Bayswaters owned a beautiful home right next door to theirs, Dory knew the Fathoms believed that entrepreneurs were *not* in the same strata as estate planning attorneys.

—*w*—

Five weeks after she'd moved out of her parents' place, Dory got a job running a warehouse out in Kewaskum, near the unincorporated area of Farmington outside of West Bend. She'd been looking for a job in Milwaukee or Waukesha, maybe even Sheboygan, but it was too expensive to find a place to live on her own, so she'd started searching "farther afield," as Alisa dubbed it. She'd camped the whole time on Alisa's land in Port Washington, using the public library off WI-28 when she needed wifi to search for jobs.

"You're gonna end up living *way out there*, aren't you?" Alisa said on her cell when Dory told her about the job. "And, oh-my-god, a warehouse! Your parents are gonna *shit.*"

They did. There was yelling and hollering and gnashing of teeth. A threat to never be invited for the holidays. Will Henry had been right. Her mother called her a *traitor.*

She found a place in Kewaskum to live–a miniscule box of a studio apartment in the back of another, bigger house, at the corner of a four-way stop in town.

The job paid barely enough to get by–$24,000 plus health benefits–and Dory found she enjoyed tooling around on a forklift inside the warehouse, the beep-beep-beeping of the reverse gear alarm on the thing like a warning, a caution: *do not go back.*

Her cousin Shelby had called to encourage her–they'd gotten closer, adults now and no longer kept apart by the lack of closeness between Shelby's mother and Dory's folks. "You just *start,* you know?" Shelby said to her. "That's how my dog training business got going. Next-to-nothing, and suddenly it's a whole thing. You'll see. Keep stepping where you want to step, and if your shoe lands in shit once in a while, kick it off and keep walking." It was great advice.

Dory supervised ten men at the warehouse–young guys, really, most just out of high school and strong as oxen, who lifted and heaved oversized boxes of heavy stainless steel cookware into trucks for deliveries to stores across the state and the country. Her shift was three to eleven. She was small compared to the men, but smart and not shy.

"Billy G., get me four pallets of those kitchen cookware sets out front pronto, buddy!" she'd say swinging around the back end of a steel shelving structure on the forklift. She loved the spin of the big black steering wheel in her hands, the flashing yellow light atop the thing, the tight circle the machine twirled in when she torqued the wheel hard to the left. Her forklift was diminutive compared to the industrial forklifts the guys ran: more for transport around the inside of the giant place, and maybe an occasional re-shifting of small loads, but she loved it anyway.

"Gotcha, Dor!" Billy would shout back. They liked her. She was smart, a bright young woman who didn't look down on their line of work, who had chosen to show up and do it with them. She played fair as a supervisor, not prone to believing bullshit. Her first week, she'd come into the lunch room and said loudly, "Hey Abe, if you've gotta be out 'cause your wife's mother-in-law is dying, then wouldn't that be…*your mother?*"

Abe was the oldest of the lot, and the younger men in the lunch room cracked up, shoving Abe on the shoulder.

"She's no dolt, Abe!"

"Look out, buddy boy! She ain't dumb!"

Then she'd asked Abe to step outside. "Look, Abe. You want time off, you ask and I'll do my best, okay? I'll go to bat for you."

After that she'd gone in every day and brown-bagged it with them, hanging out until it was time to clock back in. That had done it. That and a few dirty jokes.

"What's the difference between a G-spot and a golf ball? A guy will actually *look* for a golf ball." "Why do vegetarians give good head? Because they're used to eating nuts." "What do you call a herd of cows masturbating? Beef strokin' off." The jokes were old, stupid, from her brothers, but the guys had guffawed all the same. In a few short weeks, she'd found a *place*.

Kewaskum was *not* Milwaukee, and not even close to the Lake Michigan shoreline estates of Fox Point.

Dory had grown up with all of the advantages of a lovely, expensive, and even elite suburban town. Tennis lessons. Private soccer coach. Math tutor. Vacations to Costa Rica and Athens and the Cayman Islands. A beautiful, green backdrop in her backyard, a six-bedroom Colonial brick house with a pool and tennis court that was now worth a fortune. Perfectly manicured lawns and flower gardens.

Kewaskum was everything *not that*.

It was plain, simple. Thick wooded glens; fields full of corn, cows, soybeans and hay. An untended, wild-looking type of farmland in spots. There was barely a "town" to speak of compared to what she'd grown up with—two main streets with a fire station, a paneled tavern with a hanging Pabst sign, a cabinet-making place, auto parts, a gift store. A Piggly Wiggly grocery on the main drag, and a battered clapboard general store which now housed only a sparsely-filled, Native American beads and gifts place.

Down the street, there was a Citgo gas and convenience store where an old, weathered wisp of an eighty-year-old man sold handmade wooden bird houses in the parking lot whenever it wasn't snowing. Dory had passed an elementary school building on her way into town, out on Boltonville Road, a boxy set of buildings smack dab in the middle of a dozen farm fields.

The town was barely a blip outside West Bend, a few-mile detour off US-45's straight trajectory to the second-home vacation cottages near Oshkosh and Fund du Lac on Lake Winnebago.

Dory loved Kewaskum the minute she saw it. There was *nothing* there. (Nothing compared to her old life, anyway.) Farms, fields, chain link fences, roving dogs, motorcycles, and big, gas-guzzling trucks. Houses with dirt driveways facing crops or fallow fields. Land. Air. No *attorneys* anywhere. Just heartland people, doing heartland things.

She'd had to buy a car with her summer savings–her mother would not let her have the new Civic they'd given her for college–so she'd bought a 1989 Jeep Wagoneer with wood paneling on the side with over 150,000 miles on it. The V8 ran like a top, and it fit right in, well-worn and a little rusty.

On her first day, lugging all of her stuff in her Jeep–books, clothes, ten-speed, camping gear, computer and a couple of bags of food; her whole life's possessions–she'd stopped at the Citgo. After getting some gas, she talked to Darrell at the counter (he had a nametag), and bought a banana.

"Hey, Darrell, I'm Dory. I'm going to be living here in Kewaskum now."

"Well, nice to meet 'cha." He was sixty-ish, chubby, wearing a worn out, yellow T-shirt that was too thin, his belly hair visible through the fabric.

"What's there to do around here?" Dory said, smiling at him.

"Absolutely *nothin'!*" Darrell said, laughing, a missing incisor showing on the right side of his upper bite. "But you should go see Chaska, guy who runs the Native American place. He'll fill you in. Down the street there…you'll see it! You can go over right now." He pointed excitedly.

Dory waited a week, though, and got settled in. Then one afternoon, she drove over to Chaska's store, parked the V8, and walked over at a clip, something excitable in her step.

She felt…*what?* In the last weeks, something had changed. She felt *free*. It was stupid, really. She had no idea what this life might mean, what it was going to cost her. But there it was: the feeling. Lightness. Airiness. An open landscape for her to fill *as she wished*. It was *hers*.

The wood on the staircase to Chaska's store was old and ratty and some of it looked like it was petrified, and Dory cautiously put one foot on the bottom stair to see if it would hold. It did. She laughed at herself, the world of privilege she'd grown up in–hip, ultra-designed buildings and solid, well-taken care of stone structures, nothing like this place. She walked across the slanted, weath-er-worn porch and creaked open the door to Chaska's store, rattling it on its hinges, a couple of thin, wavering panes of glass in its top half.

A slim man with loose, straight, black hair parted in the middle and falling past his shoulders looked up at her from behind a waist-high glass case. He was youngish, thirty or thirty-five maybe, but Dory had always been bad at guessing peoples' ages. He sat on a torn black Naugahyde stool reading a thick paperback.

"Hi," Dory said timidly. She tucked her hair behind her ears, tousling her bangs to the side.

He looked up and nodded to her. "Help you?" His skin was exquisitely smooth, and he had lovely eyelashes, long and black.

"No, thanks. Just looking around." She strained her neck to see the title of his book under his delicately long fingers, the thick tome held slightly aloft in his hands, but she couldn't read it.

The man went back to his paperback.

The floor was beaten up—years of some light-blue paint had flaked off all the way to the edges of each hardwood plank. The place had goods placed carefully on two wall shelves with large spaces in between each item, and some delicate jewelry in the glass case which the man sat behind.

Dory studied the wares. Pounded silver bracelets and earrings. Necklaces with small, brightly colored beads, woven together in mandala-type shapes, stitched together with black thread. Moccasin slippers, a few leather vests. Dream-catchers—the hanging feather, bead, net and leather art objects that she'd always loved, having sought them out at local flea markets when she was in college in Maine. The place was largely empty, and Dory liked it. There was space; only a few things to look at. It felt *easy* on her soul.

In Fox Point and Whitefish Bay and the swanky Milwaukee shops her mother took her to, there had also been space in stores: that high-concept, designed look of white-polished stone floors and five-hundred-dollar jeans hanging six on a rack. But it had always felt like...*what? Heavy,* Dory thought. It had felt weighty with the expectation of who you were supposed to be, and what you were supposed to own.

Chaska's store felt like a simple offering: *I have this. I have made some of it with my hands. Would you like to see it?*

There was a front window seat with antique-looking glass that pulled the early afternoon light, waffling it like a golden candle, wavering. The whole place touched her.

She turned. "You're Chaska?"

He looked up, startled, his eyes going instantly calm again. "I am."

"I'm Dory." She stuck out her hand. "I'm living here. Darrell, at the Citgo told me to—"

The door was briskly slammed open. "Chaska! Damn it! That door is too God-awfully delicate for the likes of me!" The woman was tall—six feet, easily–long-limbed and strong-bodied, with a full head of highlighted curly blond hair framing her face like a halo. She looked late-forty-ish to Dory–but *who knew?*–and had on fitted high-waist jeans and a yellow blouse, tied loosely under her ribs. The woman tried slamming the door a couple of times, missing the connection of the delicate *click* in the antique jamb, then laughed robustly at herself.

"My husband says, 'She's got a *master's* degree and reads everything in sight, but she can't close a door or cross a street to save her life.' I hate to admit it, but he's right." Her mouth was huge, and she laughed again at herself, then began rifling through her bulky, patchwork fabric purse for something. The door fell wide open.

Chaska came around the glass case and gently closed the door, then gave her a hug, chuckling lightly. She was a good three inches taller than him, and she bent over, holding the hug a bit longer than normal, pressing her cheek to his. "So *good*. Mmmm…yes, yes…"

Dory stood still, next to the glass case, feeling a bit invisible.

"Bertie. What've you got for me today?" Chaska said, almost whispering. He delicately removed the woman's hands from his body and held her by her wrists, smiling at her.

Bertie pulled a battered paperback out of her bag and handed it to Chaska. "I've got Faulkner. *Absalom, Absalom!* Personally, I hate this book. But you love the guy, so…"

"I love his words, how he weaves them. Not always the topics," Chaska said evenly.

"The guy can't find a *period* in his sentence structure to save his life," Bertie said, waving the book in the air as she spoke. "But it's Faulkner, so what the hell are you gonna do?"

"And the *race* stuff," Dory piped up. "It's hard to read now. Supten leaving his wife and child when he finds out she's mixed race. Taking Native American land. Slavery."

"And who might *you* be?" Bertie said. Her green eyes popped a bit, but in a friendly way. "You're passing through?"

"I moved here. A week ago. I'm Dory."

"You moved *here?* Darling, nobody *moves* here! You just end up here!" A bright laugh burst from her wide mouth.

"I wanted to meet Chaska. Darrell at the Citgo says he knows everybody."

"Not so much," Chaska said.

Bertie nudged Dory in the ribs. "Don't let him fool you. He does. It's that beautiful Sioux humility." She fluttered her lashes, winking at Chaska, then turned to Dory. "I'm Bertie. *Bertrice,* actually, but I hate that friggin' name—my parents made it up—ridiculous—so for God's sake, don't ever call me that!" She guffawed.

"Dorothea—that's mine. Same thing. *Hate* that name."

"So, you like to read?" Bertie said brightly.

"I do," Dory said levelly.

Bertie clapped her hands. "Great. Come to the school. I need a reading aide. Tutor—call it whatever you want."

Chaska laughed. "Let her catch her breath, Bertie! She just got here."

Bertie's tone turned stern. "Don't have time for that, love. These kids need help."

"You're a teacher here?"

Bertie nodded. "You've got some daytime free?"

"I go to work at three at a warehouse."

"Good. That'll do. I'll see you tomorrow, eight in the morning. You know where the school is? Farmington Elementary, out on Boltonville Road?"

"But don't I have to…I mean, like, go through a *test* or something? Doesn't the principal have to interview me?"

"Darling, this is Kewaskum. We don't stand on ceremony. You'll float around my classroom and help the kids improve their reading. That's it. We'll *pay* you. Not much, but we will."

She kissed Chaska on the cheek, lingering a bit, almost imperceptibly. "Mmmm…so good. Okay, back to work!"

The door banged closed, and Dory stared at Chaska. *Were they lovers? Didn't Bertie say something about a husband?*

"What?" Chaska said.

"Nothing," Dory said, red-faced, then turned and left.

—⁓—

At the school, she slipped into a bright and fulfilling routine working in Bertie's classroom. Eight a.m. came early after an eleven o'clock swing shift, but she found she didn't mind. Bertie was gifted at teaching, and Dory watched with fascination as the woman's enthusiasm spilled out into the third-and-fourth grade split she taught at Farmington Elementary. Bertie seemed to love fiction and poetry, and she did not believe in slowing down for kids who weren't at the top of their reading-skills level, either.

"You have to expect a lot from them, Dory. Then you watch and see how they rise to it!" Bertie said one afternoon.

Dory looked skeptical. "But you don't want to embarrass them if they can't read well, especially when they're reading out loud...I mean, if they can't pronounce—"

"You wait and see. We're doing a Studs Terkel book tomorrow. That old classic, *Working.* Watch what happens." Bertie winked at her.

"You got a copy of that book for every kid?"

"Hell, no! I bootleg-copy everything. We don't have money for new books and I don't give a shit! These kids need this." She caught Dory in a razor gaze.

The next day, when a kid got stuck on a word or a phrase, the other kids helped out—called it out like a chant four times in a row, the way Bertie had taught them, until the kid who was reading got it. It didn't feel punishing or shaming. It felt like, *we're all in this together.*

Ezra, an eight-year-old farm kid stumbled over the word "detest" in *Working.*

" 'Right now, I'm doing work that I de-, dee-, dat-...' I don't know it..."

"That's okay, Ezra!" Bertie shouted. "We're here to *learn.* Right, people? What're we here to do?"

Her class chanted, loudly. "*We're here to learn!*"

"That's right, people! So, let's say it together."

The class chimed: "De-test, de-test, de-test, de-test..." Some of the kids clapped in time.

"Yes, that's right! It means *dislike.* He dislikes it! Let's say the sentence."

" 'Right now, I'm doing work that I *detest.*' "

"And why does he detest it—this man in *Working*? Why? Ezra's going to tell us why! Go ahead Ezra! We're dying to know."

It was an art form, really, Dory thought—a sharing of literature that, once awakened in their minds, would probably never leave them. A love for words. *How magical.*

Bertie used music, recitation, play-acting, stomping and clapping, and chiming bits of poetry, making it into a kind of rap. She let the students stand on their hard plastic desk chairs when they recited poetry or read aloud. She encouraged them to dress up for any part they read from a play or short story. They came, every day, with old hats and jackets, torn bits of nightgowns, paper crowns, sticks and brooms for canes and props. Bertie taught bits of everything: Raymond Carver, Sam Shepard, Alice Walker, Auden, Dickinson, Toni Morrison, Austen, the poet Audre Lorde, and sequences of Shakespeare.

"*What* are we? *What* are we?" she would holler after a particularly good classroom session.

Her students would chant back to her. "We're happy to be here! Happy to be alive and human!"

It moved Dory to tears.

—*m*—

After two months of being a teacher's aide, two weeks before Thanksgiving, her father drove up to see her. He showed up one day at the school. She was not being invited to the family holiday, and since her dad never left his office in Milwaukee during a work day, she immediately thought someone had died. Her mother or an aunt or uncle.

An announcement came over the static-filled P.A. system: "Dory Fathom, please come to the front office immediately."

When she saw him, her father was standing outside the principal's office door under a covered walkway leaning against a rickety drain pipe that was strapped to the support post. She *never* saw him lean. It rattled her.

They had texted the briefest of information back and forth in the last weeks.
Your mother still angry. Come home.
No, Dad. Teacher's aide at Farmington Elementary now. I like it.
No more warehouse? Thank God.
Warehouse yes. Reading aide daytime.

His face, now, in front of her, was solemn. Dory prepared for the worst: to be blamed for some condition her mother had developed, her wandering away from the family the cause of some illness or downfall. The play for her to come home and go to law school. She set her jaw.

"Dad. What is it?"

His face broke into a creased half-smile. "What do you mean?" He looked a little dazed, as if he couldn't place where he was.

Dory looked at her shoes. "Dad, why are you here?"

"Can't I come and see my daughter–even in this *remotest* of places?" He shot a look down Boltonville Road.

"Something's wrong? I mean, with Mom, or–"

"No. Well, *yes*. She's fit to be tied. But that's another story–"

"Grandpa? Will Henry?"

"Everyone's alright, Dory."

Dory took a breath. "Nobody's really talked to me much since–"

"I wanted to see you, that's all."

"Oh." She looked up at her Dad. He was fidgety, a quality she could not remember ever seeing in him. "So…uh…you want to go get some lunch with me or something?"

"Ah…okay." He ducked his head back and forth, looking down the road at the farm fields, a bewildered look on his face. "Um, *where?*"

He was sincere, but his elitism struck her. She laughed loudly.

"There are places to eat here, Dad. I'll find us something."

After telling Bertie she was ducking out for a bit, she drove her father east to a little Mexican cantina near the outskirts of West Bend. There was no one in the place besides the owner, Juanita, and an older couple in the corner eating enchiladas off of oversized plates.

"Hey, Juanita. This is my dad."

"Nice to meet you, *señor,*" Juanita said. She was older and lovely, beautiful even, with dark, thick hair cascading to her waist, captured in a loose ponytail. "We love your daughter, sir! She eats with us once a week." Juanita smiled broadly.

"Fine, fine. Yes–yes–fine," her father replied. "Nice to meet you. *Fine.*" It was a tic, saying *fine* when he was out of his element.

Over big bowls of tortilla soup, she told her father about Bertie, about teaching.

"Dad, I've decided something."

"Uh-oh." He put down his spoon.

"I'm–"

"Wait. Before you say anything–"

"What?" Dory sat back and crossed her arms over her chest. The punch was coming, she knew it.

"I've been thinking about this–about what you've done–"

Dory's eyes flashed with pique. "What do you mean, *what I've done?* What I've *done* is pay my own way, got my own apartment, helped some little kids learn how to read." Her paper napkin fell off her lap, and she ducked her head under the table and picked it up, balling it up angrily inside her palm.

"I know, I know," her father said tensely. "It's just that–"

"Dad. Stop. This isn't going to work, you coming here and trying to talk me out of having my own life. Did Mom send you? Let me guess–she wanted you to–"

"No. She doesn't know I'm here." Her father stuck his spoon back into his soup and stirred it around, distractedly.

"Wait. You mean–"

Dory had never known her father to do anything her mother didn't know about. They were a team. A formidable force. A wall of resolve and unanimity and daunting drive.

"She doesn't know?" Dory was holding two tortilla chips, then dropped them into her soup, leaning toward her father.

"She thinks I'm at the dentist. That's what I mean." His voice wavered and went high up in his register, almost like a child's.

"Dad, what's going on?"

He put his spoon down and locked his eyes with hers. "You don't really *like* your mother, do you Dory?"

Dory flinched. "What?"

"You love her, I'm sure. She gave you all of these wonderful things, surely you know that. But I'm asking as a *person*, not a father. You don't really *like* her."

Dory was startled, and a masticated bit of chicken caught in her throat. She coughed.

"Answer me, please," her dad said. But it was a plea, not a demand.

"I want to teach, Dad. I'm good at it. I want to go back to school and get a credential. Maybe a master's."

"You know what your mother will say about that. No money. No *advancement.* And you didn't answer me."

"Because I don't want to." Dory looked away, tears stinging her eyes. Juanita was mashing something in a huge metal bowl behind the counter, probably the corn for her homemade tortillas.

"Dad…"

"I don't like her either, Dory. Not anymore. *There.* I said it. Now, if heaven and earth open up and swallow me whole, at least I will have been honest one damned day in my life."

—⁓—

She texted her brother, Will Henry.

Come to Kewaskum this Sat. Lake, then BBQ my place. Meet my friends.
Seriously? Out THERE?
I need to talk to you. By noon for lake. BBQ dinner. Bring chair for backyard.
Don't know. Maybe.

Dory didn't think he'd show up, but she wanted him to.

When Saturday came, she drove up to the Piggly Wiggly to get some pork chops to barbeque after the lake. Cherilynne, the checkout clerk, had been friendly to Dory since she'd first shopped there.

"I got three kids and an AWOL husband at the age of twenty-five," Cherilynne said to Dory the first time they'd met. "But I still got my sense of humor!" She had a gray front tooth, slightly pointy, which she tended to press into her tongue, and bleach-streaked black hair.

"Whatcha got today, Dory?" Cherilynne said at the counter, running the food stuffs through with one hand, speaking the prices of each item out loud. "Chili-lime chips, two-ninety-nine. Bean dip, one-fifty-nine."

Dory placed a pile of thick pork chops on the grocery conveyor belt, each plastic-wrapped over a Styrofoam bed. "I've got Bertie and Chaska coming–we're going to Mauthe Lake in canoes. Barbeque afterwards. Hoping my brother's coming from Whitefish Bay, but who knows…" She flipped her brown hair behind her shoulders. It bugged her Will hadn't said yes.

"Wheat bread, three-ninety-nine. Pabst twelve-pack, eight-ninety-nine." Cherilynne slid the pork chops through quickly, then winked at Dory. "One pork chop, three-ninety-eight."

"No, Cherilynne–I've got *four.*"

Cherilynne swept the items into a grocery bag. "Don't you be questioning me, now. I only see *one*, and I been doing this long enough to know." She looked over her shoulder.

"I don't think–"

Cherilynne leaned in, grabbing Dory by the forearm, then whispered, "You're helping those kids in Bertie's class, and my Jamie's in there next year and he's gonna need you, so let's say this is the town doing right by you, okay?" Her eyes misted over.

Dory smiled and leaned in, kissing Cherilynne on the cheek.

As she walked out, she stood outside the store with the heavy grocery bag in her hand. She knew what she wanted from her life: simple acts of heartfelt thanks, like Cherilynne's a moment before, that let her know her work had landed in people's hearts. She wondered if her mother had had a moment like that, ever.

———

Dory had been right about Chaska and Bertie. The day before they canoed on the lake, Bertie had told Dory the whole story, weeping in the telling, all of it spilling out. They were standing in the classroom–Chaska had left a moment before, having stopped by to leave a Timber rattlesnake skin for the kids for the next day's science lesson. The two had kissed lingeringly as Chaska left.

"So, Bertie," Dory said, leaning on the edge of the wooden teacher's desk. "It's been two-and-a-half months. We know each other well enough for you to tell me what's going on? You think?"

Bertie opened her eyes wide, then looked down and twirled her wedding ring on her left finger. She was sitting, wearing a full, flowered, knee-length skirt, and the thing had the look of a picnic tablecloth on her six-foot frame. She balled a piece of it in her right hand and immediately began to cry.

"I'm married."

"I guessed that, since you're wearing a ring. And you talk about your husband. So?"

"He had a motorcycle accident four years ago, got a traumatic brain injury. That's what they call it. I tried for two years to take care of him, but the brain thing—they get violent. I covered it up for a long time, then he threw a broken dinner plate at me and cut my leg. Twenty-five stitches." She lifted her skirt, revealing a long, pink scar on the top of her thigh.

Dory was gentle. "And now?"

"He's in a facility over in Fredonia. They're very good with him. Lots of meds. Hardly recognizes me when I go." She bent over and put her face into her skirt and cried, her shoulders heaving.

Dory moved to put her arms around Bertie, pulling her up to standing, Dory's head reaching only to Bertie's chest. She held on as Bertie sobbed.

When Bertie stopped crying she said, "I felt so fucking guilty at first, with Chaska. I was a mess, and God help me, I needed a friend like a starving dog needs a beef bone. But then, you know, we'd talk about books, and we'd laugh, and he kept coming around. Then one day we ended up in bed together. He saved me."

The next day, heading for the lake, Bertie's eyes were still red-rimmed from crying the afternoon before. Dory's brother Will had not shown, so she and Chaska and Bertie took Chaska's two canoes, loaded them in Dory's Jeep Wagoneer with the ends sticking out the back window and headed for Mauthe.

As they paddled the canoes across the water, Dory sat in the front of Chaska's, and Bertie manned her own.

The sun was hot, unusual for a late autumn Wisconsin day, and it was lovely. The water sparkled in soft ripples along its surface and the shoreline was filled with trees and overgrown grasses, a sunlight-catching vibrant green that shimmered against the clear blue water. No houses lined Mauthe, and there was none of the paraphernalia from her family's lakeside excursions—no jet skis, speed boats, or deck chairs propped on piers; no pontoons or water skis or tubing gear. It felt sweet to Dory, an *unadorned* place. A place to float and sway, nothing else.

Chaska spoke, dipping his oar. "Bertie told you."

"Yeah, she did." Dory turned and looked over her right shoulder to face him. "Terrible thing. *God.*"

"Maybe. Everything ends up alright, you know?" The smoothness of his paddle strokes into the water dipped with equanimity, a lush grace. *Swish, swish.* "Things fall apart and then they find another way to level out. She's the best thing that ever happened to me."

"Chaska–"

"It's the self-blame you have to get over. She bought him the motorcycle. Anniversary present."

"*Jesus.*"

"Yeah."

Dory looked over at Bertie, thirty feet away in the other canoe. "She okay?"

"She will be. Comes up for her now and then. Took a year to help her get over cutting herself up over it. The guilt."

"How'd you do it?"

"I told her that it was enough to have gone through it. It's enough to recover from it. That's all she's supposed to do. She's not supposed to do anything else except let things change and find a way to move on."

―⁓―

Back at Dory's studio apartment–a one room in-law unit behind a boxy, Kelly green house with fake French windows–Will was waiting for them, leaning against his brand-new candy-apple-red Audi. Another rebellion. Their parents and every family member at the firm drove BMW's–white, slate gray or black. The family had singlehandedly kept Jerry Gresham, the Milwaukee BMW dealer, in business.

"You *asshole!*" Dory yelled, smiling and jumping out of her Jeep. "Why didn't you tell me you were coming?"

Will grinned. "Got a surprise for you! Look who else is here!"

Alisa popped out from behind Will's car. Her red hair was bushy as usual, and she wore bell-bottoms and a faded T-shirt with black type which read: *Feminism Rules. Let Him Sleep on the Wet Spot.*

"Oh my god! You brought *Alisa?* Get over here and hug me right now, both of you!" She went around the car and pulled them together into her body, truly happy. She thought she felt something pass between Alisa and Will in her threesome hug. A look. *Naw. No way.*

Alisa stuck out her hand to Chaska and Bertie. "I'm the best friend. And you're the new GOAT people."

Chaska laughed. "*Goat...*what's that?"

"Greatest of all time." Alisa's mane of wild hair shook as she guffawed. "What'd you think I meant?"

Bertie threw her head to the side, her halo of blond curls bouncing. "We're *old,* honey! And this is farm country! We wouldn't have any idea what you city hipsters say these days." She patted Alisa on the shoulder.

"You hear that, Dory?" Alisa said, taking a bow. "I'm a *hipster.*"

Everyone laughed.

After dinner, once all the pork chops had been divvied up between the plates, grilled on Dory's makeshift barbeque (ice-block cement bricks piled up in a square with a piece of metal screen balanced on top), she cornered Will, pulling her folding chair up next to him.

"Something's up with mom and dad."

Will swigged his Pabst. "Nothing's up, Dory. Same old stone-walled story. You're the only one who's had the courage to—"

"No. I mean, *between* them."

Will laughed, a short burst. "Seriously? Come on! They're like Larry Bird and the Celtics in the 1980's. They're an *institution.*" He flipped his long black bangs away from his face.

"Yeah, well, I think Dad's tired of it. Something's wrong. He came here."

"He came *here?* Since when?"

"Since last week."

Will's eyes went wide. "No *shit.*"

"Mom's not supposed to know."

"*Of course* she's not supposed to know! He actually drove out here? He *snuck away.* Ha!" Will coughed, choking on his beer. "But that doesn't mean—"

"He said he doesn't like her anymore."

Will whipped his head around to face Dory. "*Motherfucker.* Really?"

"Yes."

"You sure? I mean, maybe he meant—"

"I didn't mis-hear him, Will. I know what I heard."

"He wouldn't say that. There's no way he says that, Dory."

"Well, he did."

Will stared at her, hard, making a grumbling noise under his breath. "Shit. Oh, man. If he's going to—I mean, holy *hell.*"

"He could've just had a bad day. Marriage—all that," Dory said.

"But if it's not that..."

"I know."

Will rolled his eyes, then pushed some air out of his lungs. "So, let's all watch as the castle comes crumbling down, is that it?"

"It could be a good thing…"

"How?"

"If the empire falls, so does its expectations." Dory reached over and put her hand on his forearm. "You could be whatever you want to be."

Will turned and looked at her, his eyes filling.

—∿—

In the next several days, Dory went out biking on the farm lanes off WI-28, ducking in and out of the town's small streets. She needed something to do to calm herself. Her father had called her twice already by Monday, guilty and needy, telling her he was getting ready to leave her mother. It was almost Thanksgiving.

Since she couldn't sleep, she cycled, very early, starting out as soon as it was light.

On Tuesday morning, she headed east on the highway, watching the traffic like crazy in her cycling mirror–it could be dangerous–then veered off onto Kettle Moraine Drive. She loved the light in the morning: the dew of late November dancing on the tiny shoots of grass in a fallow field, the sprinklers arcing water in half-moons and shot-through with sunlight on someone's property, the dense green-green of the wooded roadsides and the soft rolling landscape. The air was chilly on Dory's face, the morning bite of cold that signaled Wisconsin's late autumn mildness was about to end.

She pedaled north for a few miles, then came back and crossed the highway, riding south past the Kewaskum Town offices, then passed a couple of farms with empty rows engrained in the soil. Rows of things in her sightline had always thrilled her–the astigmatism-inducing, rapid-fire geometry of crops viewed in lines and angles, the last of an unharvested corn field with symmetrical lines of tousle-topped and sunburned stalks. Rusted metal fencing long-ago hammered into weather-beaten posts set into dirt, bales of hay tied up and dropped symmetrically in hay fields. It calmed her.

An hour later, she pulled her bike into a ditch next to a field and rested. A patch of wild sunflowers towered behind her.

Alisa had been calling and texting every day to check on her. This time Dory called her.

"I'll get blamed for this, I know it–my mother and father splitting," Dory said. She spun the foot pedal on her bike with her left hand, twirling it hard.

"That's ridiculous, Dory! How the hell is this *your* fault?" Alisa said back to her.

"I'm the domino."

"You don't really believe that, do you?"

"I don't know. Maybe. Listen, I'm gonna go. I'm on my bike. Hey, what's going on with you and Will?"

"Nothing! We drove together to see you, that's all."

Dory picked up the slightly-off tone in her friend's voice. "Alisa...I've known you since you were five. *Spill* it!" she said sternly.

"Okay, we've got a little crush. That's it."

"A we-drove-out-to-see-you-together crush, or a we-went-to-bed-together crush?"

"Hmmm..."

"You're stalling! Jesus, Alisa, tell me!"

"Bed-together crush. Slept together last Saturday after we left your place."

"Oh my god, you did not!"

"Did!" Alisa laughed over the phone line, a kind of gurgling sound in her throat. "It was great. *Hot,* actually."

Dory guffawed. "But Alisa, he–"

"I know what you're going to say. He'll never *choose* me. I'm way too Bo-ho for him, right? Your mother would have a *cow.* I think you're wrong."

"About my mother or Will?"

"Will, you idiot! I don't give a good goddamn what your mother wants."

"Watch your back, Alisa. I don't want you to get emotionally decimated because my brother can't stand up to my mother."

"Your mother's got an avalanche heading her way."

"And that's exactly the kind of thing that'll make her try to micromanage everything in sight...including who's in Will's bed."

—◦◦◦—

Over the next week, the guys at her warehouse noticed something was up. She was restless, distracted, upset.

Billy G. came up to her one evening and said, "Anybody hurts you and we get up a *posse* and beat the crap out of 'em, you got that?"

When she said she wasn't sleeping, Abe offered to have his wife come over and sleep on her couch for a night or two. "Might help you sleep with another person in the house, you know?" It was generous–hugely–and she was touched.

It had bummed her out missing Thanksgiving with her family–she'd spent it with Chaska and Bertie; she and Bertie had both been sentimental that day–and it hardly mattered anyway now. It would have been tense, even had her mother invited her, knowing what she knew about her father wanting to leave, but she still missed it. Her mother had always gone all-out on the holidays, particularly at Christmas–twenty-five family members, a gourmet spread, a gorgeous blue spruce lit up in the corner of the living room, decorated in white and gold. The last two years Eleanor had even hired a string trio which set up in the living room and played Christmas music. Dory had loved it. All of that would be gone, the minute her father stepped out the door.

On a Saturday, Bertie and Chaska dragged her to the Boltonville Fire Department's pancake supper at the station. She didn't want to go, but they insisted.

There were tables set up in rows with paper covers taped on top for tablecloths, paper plates and plastic forks in piles next to seven or eight volunteer firefighters cooking pancakes on electric griddles. Butter in large tubs rested like centerpieces on the tables, and gallon-containers of bargain syrup dripped with sticky brown liquid. A Christmas tree was blinking red and green lights in the corner of the room, paper ornaments pinned to it made by the kids in Bertie's classroom.

There was a DJ set up in the back of the place, and as soon as Dory got her plate of pancakes, Chaska and Bertie got up to dance. *Green River* by Creedence Clearwater was playing, and Dory watched as Bertie led, three inches taller than Chaska, twirling him in tight circles, the two of them laughing uproariously.

Dory wandered a bit, plate in hand and dabbing at her pancakes with her plastic fork. Chatting with Darrell from the register at the Citgo, and Mundo, the old guy who sold birdhouses outside the gas station, she had the feeling someone was watching her, but when she turned, she met no one's eyes.

Finally she sat, and a body plopped down next to her, his paper plate of pancakes slapping the makeshift tablecloth.

"Hey. You mind?" He gestured to his plate.

"Go ahead." Dory turned to look at him. Sandy brown-and-blond hair, lightened from the sun, Dory was guessing. Soft brown eyes. Big biceps peeking out from a short-sleeved blue T-shirt.

He stuck out his hand. "I'm Cord."

"*Cord?* Nickname?"

"Yep. But nobody calls me anything else."

"Dory," she said. His hand felt substantial and masculine in hers, shaking it. She tried to guess his age–*mid-twenties?* He had strong thighs, hard and muscular under his jeans, thick-soled work boots on his feet, and a little pouch–a bit of thick and fleshy belly flesh under his T-shirt, as if he'd been chubby as a kid.

"I've been watching you." He smiled.

Bertie suddenly dipped Chaska in the middle of *Rescue Me*, an old Ronstadt tune, and Dory laughed. It was the first time she'd really laughed in days.

"Yep, I have," he said.

"What?"

"Been watching you. You're new."

She turned to look at him. "So, Cord. Why do they call you that?"

"It's stupid. We had this economics teacher in high school. Was the football coach, too, and I was on his offensive line. Couldn't pronounce my last name to save his life. He'd yell at me across the field, 'Eccles–Ecklest–*Extension Cord*–whatever the hell your name is, get over here!' "

"Extension cord?"

"It stuck. Everyone calls me 'Cord' now. Can't shake it."

"What's your real name?" Dory stuffed a forkful of pancakes into her mouth, the ultra-sweet smell of the syrup tingling in her nostrils.

"Hank Ecclestone. The Hank is after Hank Aaron."

"My brother would love that."

"Baseball fan?"

"Everything-sports-fan. Wanted to be a sports agent."

"What's he now?"

"A cog in the crushing wheel of my parents' estate planning law firm."

"What about you?" he said.

Dory suddenly flared. "What *about* me?"

"Hey, hey. Easy, girl. I just met 'cha."

Dory flipped one side of her hair over her shoulder. "Sorry. I was supposed to be an attorney, too. Me and one uncle–first ones in three generations to bail on the family profession. Now my parents are separating and it's probably my fault."

"I doubt that."

She tapped her head with the butt of her right hand. "Did I say that out loud?"

"You can't make people not want to be together. That's their deal." He made a circle in the air with his plastic fork, then speared it into his pile of pancakes.

Dory stared at him, her own plastic fork poised above her plate. He'd said it so simply.

He shoveled a big forkful into his mouth, chewed, then spoke. "So, what do you do now?"

"Warehouse manager over in Kewaskum. Teacher's aide at the elementary for Bertie during the day." She pointed to the dance floor, where Bertie was elaborately twirling. "I want to go back to school and become a teacher."

"That sounds good."

"It'll go over like a lead balloon. What about *your* parents? They must have something bad to say about you," Dory said, smirking and pointing her fork at him.

"They're dead."

She flushed, turning bright red. "Oh, God, I'm sor–"

"Naw. Happened three years ago. Drunk driver. Mac at Orvis Dairy Farm down the road took me in, let me work for them and finish high school."

"You're *eighteen?*"

"Hell, no! I'm twenty. Almost."

"Jesus. Shit." Dory scraped her folding chair on the wood floor, getting up quickly. "Sorry. I should go–"

"You're sorry I'm turning twenty?"

"It's–I'm...*older.*"

"Who the hell cares? You're not thirty-eight or something, are you?"

"No. Twenty-four."

"Okay then. Nothing wrong with that. Few years–that's *nothing*. My mom was eight years older than my dad, and they had it good for a long time."

"Yeah, but you're–you're still–"

"What?"

"Jailbait. You're under twenty-one.*"

He let out a loud cackle, fluttering his eyelashes her way. "Well, when you say it like *that*..." His brown eyes softened. "Listen. I'd like to take you out.*"

"Look, I'm not–"

He put his fingers on her forearm, lightly. "You ever have anyone die on you?"

"No. Well, grandparents, sure, but–"

"People in your daily life."

"No."

"Well, I have. There's no time for fake stuff. For bullshit stuff that doesn't matter. There's only *this*. You and me and there's either something here or there's not."

"I…"

"Go out with me Saturday."

"Where?"

"Does it matter?"

"No, actually. I suppose not."

He reached out and held Dory's hand lightly then leaned over and kissed it. It sent a shiver up her arm and across the top of her breasts.

A couple of days later, she was sitting in the dirt after cycling out past the big yellow Kewaskum water tower, having dropped her bike next to an irrigation ditch. She watched as a huge tractor-trailer tried to negotiate a sharp turn into a driveway, half of a prefab house balanced on the truck bed. The house was plain on the outside, but it looked nice enough—some kind of fake wood paneling painted a bland, tan color, with heavy sheets of plastic covering the open seam of the structure. *A house. Split down the middle. Someone's life about to be lived in it, maybe split at the same seams one day.*

Will pulled up all at once in his red Audi, zoomed around the truck and veered off into a nearby dirt driveway.

"What the hell are you doing here?" Dory yelled to him. "It's two in the afternoon!"

Will swung his car door open so hard it bounded at the hinge. He ran towards her.

"It's happening!" He shouted. "They're splitting!"

"I know. I told you Dad called me."

"Yeah, but I didn't think he'd really do it. He's moving out this weekend!" Will sat right down in the dirt in his suit pants. Not like him. Things were changing faster than Dory could keep a grip on them.

He breathed out hard. "And you're never gonna believe this—"

"What?"

"As soon as he heard, Jonathan ditched his attorney girlfriend and quit the firm. Turns out he's been secretly hooking up with a food truck owner in Milwaukee named Pooja. Indian."

"Our brother?"

Will nodded. "She owns *Cu-Cu-Cay.*"

"I know that woman! She's always at Summerfest, isn't she? She's nice! *Curry, Cumin, Cayenne,* right? *Cu-Cu-Cay.*"

"The dominos are starting to fall, Dory."

Dory flared, red in the face. "Did Alisa tell you I said that? About the *dominos*? Jesus! I didn't want her to–"

"He's leaving her before Christmas. Nobody does that. This is serious."

Dory put her head in her hands and groaned.

"Look, I wanted to come out here and see you before you start blaming yourself, okay?" Will said. "You didn't cause all this. It's just what's happening, do you get that?"

Dory's eyes welled.

Will leaned in. "Listen. Mom's been controlling everybody's life for a long time, and Dad's been letting her do it. It's not *you.*"

Dory turned her head toward Will, biting her thumbnail. "What's going to happen?"

Will breathed out hard. "It's all going to fall apart. Then it'll come back together, in a better way."

She remembered what Chaska had said about Bertie's husband's accident. How it had brought him the best woman he's ever had in his life. But that was other people.

"Who says it will be better? How do you know?"

Will put his arm around her shoulder, pulling her in the way her father had when she told her parents she would not be an attorney. "It'll be messier, and maybe even harder for a while, but it'll be better. Even for Mom." He was almost giddy. "You wait and see."

—⁓—

Her date with Cord happened a few days after she saw Will. The air was crisp and cold, the bite from it sharp and moist, stars peeking out early through a barely darkening sky. Cord took her up to Fond du Lac, to an old stone hotel in town, and bought her a nice dinner. He was into poetry–an unlikely thing for an almost-twenty-year old dairy farmer and cattle wrangler. He ordered wine.

"Doesn't anybody ask you for I.D.?" Dory said, after the waiter opened the bottle and left the table.

"Naw. Everybody thinks I'm twenty-seven, twenty-eight, whatever. And these guys here know I work for Mac at Orvis–they assume I'm a working guy."

"You *are* a working guy."

"S'pose I am," he said shyly. He ran his hands through his sandy blond-ish-brown hair.

Later, after the meal, he spoke about his parents, his family.

"I was a bit of a hyper kid. I couldn't fall asleep at night. They'd feed me hot milk, keep me off sugar, turn off the TV two hours before bed and play board games with me. But the only thing that worked was when Mom read me poetry. Weird, huh?"

"Not so weird. I think it's lovely," Dory said.

"I have this favorite American poet. Charlie Smith. He has this line, '*The way out is through.*' That one line kept me from going crazy the first year after they died."

Dory murmured, then reached across the table and held his hand. "I need something like that. My dad left my mom *yesterday,* for God's sake. I can't even believe I'm saying that. He moved out in, like, *a day.* It's a mess now. And I'm the one who started it—"

"Breaking the mold?"

"Yeah."

He snorted. "Can't make your parents stay together any more than I could've stopped a drunk driver from killing mine. Funny thing is, that day, I wanted to go with them—to ditch school and go to Wausau with them."

"So you thought if you were with them—"

"For a long time, yeah. Like I could've seen the car coming before my dad did. That kind of shit."

Cord's face went soft, all of the tension draining out of it. "That poet guy has another line: '*Are you out there, just beyond me, an inch farther into the darkness than I can see?*' "

Dory decided right then that she'd sleep with him.

—⁓—

Ten days, three dates and two sweaty bike rides later—during one of which Dory had pulled Cord into a bare, harvested corn field and pressed him onto the dirt, making out with him like a hungry animal—they made love. It was after a late night at the tavern, and they had been laughing all evening, trying to teach each other how to swing dance to a local guitarist singing Al Green tunes.

"Listen, we're going to my place after this," Dory said, leaning into his shoulder.

"Or, are we?" he said. His voice became a gravelly purr when he was wooing her. "You're tellin' me what to do now?" he teased.

"I am," she said. Her legs were straddling his thigh as they swayed and she heard his heart beat, *thump-thump, thump-thump.*

At her apartment, she pulled him in through the front door and pressed him to the side wall, sliding her hands around his fleshy waist and standing on tip toes to kiss him. She felt him pull her hips in, his back pressing against the light switch as they moved, *flick-flick-flicking* the overhead lamp, flashing it on and off.

Dory laughed, the blinking light stunning her irises, then reached around to flip the light off again, and he swept her up into his arms in one incredibly quick move, his hands catching under her knees as he lifted her.

"Whoa!" she shouted. "My God!"

"Dory," he purred in her ear. "I'm a cattle wrangler."

"Not getting *this* in Fox Point..." Dory whispered.

He carried her ten steps to the bed, laying her down on the pink quilted comforter she'd brought back from college, the thing bunching up under her body as he slid her across it.

She reached for him, but he stood back and began to take off his clothes, letting her watch from the bed. He looked sheepishly vulnerable doing it, dropping shoes, shirt, pants, boxers on the floor with a wicked little grin on his face. He had a farmer tan, bronzed arms from his T-shirt sleeves down. His stomach was soft, still boyish, his thighs white and taut.

Dory stared at his hardness, then pulled her jeans and panties off in one strong pull, catching her ankle boots and wrenching them off along with the tight tapering of the denim. She threw her sweater and bra off, shoving the pillows to the floor, and lay back naked.

He leaned over her, kissed her, then gently turned her over face-down, running his hands over her skin. Starting with her neck, he moved his fingertips in languishing lines and circles over her lower back, her ass, the backs of her knees, then ran fingernails up the inside of her thighs.

"Slow and easy, girl," he whispered.

"Oh my God," she breathed.

On his knees next to her, he blew warm breath into her hair, on the nape of her neck, then down her back and body, kissing between breaths, working his fingernails down the sides of her waist. When he straddled her, she could feel his hardness pressed up against the small of her back and the flesh of her ass, and he reached around the sides of her breasts, cupping them.

Jesus Christ, she thought. *He knows what he's doing.*

It astounded Dory that some men, even boys in high school, knew how to be sensual from the get-go. As if it was wired into them. And then, like several of the guys she'd been with in college, there were men who would probably never find their way to this–this *thrill* that seemed to emanate out of Cord without effort; this barely-adult, slightly chubby cattle wrangler.

"Cord…" she purred.

Dory felt his hand slip under her belly and he rolled her over into his arms, face up, cradling her. His back was pressed up against her second-hand red cotton headboard, and as she reached her face up to kiss him, he slid his right hand out from under her knees, letting it fall between her legs. Poised like that, holding her, he rocked her with his hand–*Ohmygod, he's making me crazy*, she thought–slipping the pads of his fingers from the tuft of her sex hair into the wet inside her, and then back out again.

When he pressed harder, all four of his thick fingers against her, she came quickly–not a thing she often did; usually it took time–and then, afterward, catching her breath, she pressed him flat on the bed and lay on top of him. As she slipped him inside her she muttered, "Why in hell are you so good?"

—⁓—

"So, it's a thing, then?" Alisa said on the phone after Dory had been sleeping with Cord for a couple of weeks. It was two days before Christmas.

"Yeah. It's a thing. He reads me poetry in bed. Charlie Smith, Adrienne Rich, Terrence Hayes. I'm smitten. I've never said that about a man."

Alisa giggled. "Can we really call him that? A *man?*"

"Very funny. You can stop with the cradle-robbing jokes. He's twenty now, okay?"

"Well, I've got some news." Alisa took a big breath in. "We're moving in together. Me and Will."

"Wow! That's great, Alisa!"

Alisa went silent for a moment.

"Uh-oh, what?" Dory said.

"Will's leaving the firm. We're moving to L.A. We found Will a job."

"Yeah? You mean–"

"He's going to be a sports agent!" Alisa shouted gleefully. "Your dad's making him stay for a month to finish his client stuff, but then we're outa here. He'll have to start at the bottom, and that means no clients at first while he learns, but he's going to do it! Can you fucking believe it? We've already got an apartment lined up and everything!"

"Does my mother know?"

Alisa exhaled, a push of breath. "Not yet."

The dominoes, Dory had to admit, had indeed begun to fall.

———

Dory called her mother twice, three times, then four times in one week—not a thing she usually did—but Eleanor would not pick up.

Finally, she left a voicemail.

Her mother's authoritarian voice came booming into her ear from a recorded message. "This is Eleanor Browne Fathom, and yes, in case you haven't *realized*, you have reached me on my personal cell phone. I would *appreciate* it if you'd leave a message and *no longer* than two minutes. Have a nice day."

Her mother, demanding and indomitable, even recorded.

Dory got up her courage and spoke. "Mother, you're going to have to talk to me sometime. It's your daughter, *in case you haven't realized.*"

———

On Christmas morning, Dory went with Bertie to the nursing facility in Fredonia to see Bertie's husband. It was icy outside, ten degrees and three inches of packed snow on the ground, a close, gray cloud cover that made the sky look like a damp cattle blanket.

"You don't have to do this, you know," Bertie said when Dory opened the car door of Bertie's '64 Mustang. The thing was Bertie's prized possession: a baby-blue metallic color, black rag top, shiny rims.

"Really, all I want is a ride in your Mustang, Bertie," Dory joked, sliding in and slamming the door. "I want you to peel out and burn some rubber." The car was toasty inside, a slight heaving and groaning coming from the classic heating vents.

Bertie laughed, but the smile quickly dropped from her face. "I'm serious, Dory. It's a shit-show seeing this, and you've gotta be—"

"Look, I don't think I could've done this, all these changes in my life, without you guys. It's the least I can do."

Bertie grabbed her arm. "He's not gonna know me, I'm gonna cry, and the place is gonna depress the hell out of both of us."

"So?"

"Just so you're sure."

Dory leaned in and put her arms around Bertie. "I'm sure."

The nursing home was a squat, block building on a broad suburban street adjacent to a couple of office buildings. As they pulled open the heavy glass front door, Dory felt the sting of disinfectant rise instantly into her nose, shiny polished speckled linoleum under their feet. Three fake Christmas trees were lit up on the floor of the entryway, flashing multicolored lights.

A fleshy woman in a pink nurse's outfit and bleach-streaked hair came rushing towards them from down the hall. "Well, Bertie! So nice to see you on Christmas day!"

Bertie leaned in and gave the woman a hug. "Grace, this is my friend Dory. So, how's he doing today?"

"He's okay. Talking at least. Go on in. I'll come by in a minute." She hustled down the hallway, her stethoscope bouncing against her large chest.

Dory followed as Bertie walked into one of the rooms: two men in beds positioned within four feet of each other, a pale blue curtain half-closed between them; a television attached to the wall blaring a re-run of *Family Feud.* There was a sliding glass door on the far side of the room that led to a cement courtyard with a rusted metal umbrella and weathered metal chairs set underneath it, snow piled up atop them. The door was cracked open a tiny bit and Dory was immediately grateful for the waft of frozen fresh air.

Bertie leaned into her husband, stuck out her hand as if she was meeting him for the first time. "Hi, Gary. I'm Bertie."

"I know that!" the man said belligerently. He flipped his head sharply to the left then tipped it to look up at her. His grayish hair was wiry and stuck out, too long, over his ears.

Bertie's eyes went immediately wet and she grabbed Dory's hand. "Sometimes he—"

"I'm right here!" Gary said loudly. He began to shout. "You don't have to talk like I'm not here! I'm here!!" He waved a broad-biceped arm, nearly hitting Bertie in the head.

Bertie reached for his hand in the air and he squirmed a bit, as if he were trying to shake something out of his body, and then he calmed. He wore an old work shirt, frayed, a pale blue, the fringed edge of the collar turned up on one side. A white cotton blanket wrapped his legs on the bed.

Dory edged closer. "I'm Dory, I'm Bertie's friend."

"I know that!" he bellowed again. His eyes went fierce. "Go away! You—yeah, you! Go on, get out of here!" He pointed at Dory, shaking his finger at her, his face flushing bright red. "Out, goddamn it! Out, out, *OUT!!*"

Dory stepped back quickly through the door jamb, almost bumping into nurse Grace, who deftly slipped into the room and held Gary by the upper arm, then patted his head and slid her hand down to the middle of his back, moving it in small circles. "He doesn't like to be touched when he's agitated, but he'll let me," she said to Dory.

Bertie sat beside her husband in the only chair in the room, a rickety plastic thing, and softly wept.

Later, they had Christmas with Chaska and Cord at Bertie's house, drinking eggnog with extra bourbon. Bertie was staring at her cup.

Cord handed Bertie a glass of straight bourbon. "Here. Drink this. It'll help."

"I'll be alright. I just gotta go through this, that's all."

" 'Aint' no sin to drink when you're sufferin'…" Cord said kindly, in a kind of sing-song tone.

"What's that from?" Dory said. "A poem?" She was perched on the arm of a checkered-patterned recliner, eggnog in hand.

"Nineties band my parents listened to called Del Amitri," Cord replied.

Bertie looked up. "Title was *Some Other Sucker's Parade,* right?"

"Your parents listened to them, too?" Cord sat in the checkered chair and pulled Dory off the arm into his lap.

Bertie perked up. "I'm older than you, honey! Not my parents–*me*. I loved that song." She sang the words, loudly: *"When every heavy skyline just empties on your fate/Sometimes keepin' dry's something to celebrate…"*

"That's it!" Cord said excitedly.

Bertie's face dropped.

Dory nudged him, then whispered, "Gentler, I think…"

Chaska moved from the kitchen and held Bertie from behind her chair, pressing his cheek into hers, his long black hair spilling over onto her chest.

When Chaska went back to the stove–he was cooking stuffed chicken, green beans and roasted potatoes–Bertie stood up and said, "Alright, enough!" She batted the air as if waving off her depression. "It's Christmas for God's sake, and we're gonna celebrate the way it's supposed to be done. Cord, hand me that glass!"

He did.

"Now. A toast. Everybody over here."

Dory raised her glass with Chaska and Cord.

Bertie looked like the statue of liberty, holding her glass high in her right hand, swaying it over her six-foot frame. "I'm so friggin' glad Cord and Dory found each other. It's the sweetest thing! And Chaska–I'd be a pile of disintegrating ashes without you. Here's to life, in all of its fucked-up, unraveling glory."

"And to the ties that bind," Chaska said, raising his eyebrows, then smiling and winking at Bertie. "The new ones especially."

"To the tethers, the ties, and the *cords!*" Bertie said, her huge mouth breaking into a wide smile. She poked Cord in the ribs with her elbow.

"Very funny," he said, smirking.

Dory laughed. "To the *cords*," she said emphatically, and they all clinked glasses.

—⁓—

Over the next couple of months the ties of Dory's particular family life seemed to unravel so fast that she didn't recognize the people she grew up with.

Her father kept the firm, buying out her mother; her parents sold the Fox Point house (it sold in five days); then her dad bought a cottage on Tichigan Lake, south of Milwaukee. He sometimes rented a place on Lake Winnebago on weekends, taking Dory, Bertie and Chaska, and Cord, hanging out with her and her friends. It touched her that her father wanted to spend time with her. It was as if the courage of her life choices had created a bond between them, a rope that tied them now, more than as father and daughter, but as people who liked each other.

Her mother moved into an expensive, fifteenth floor condo in Milwaukee—all glass—with a stunning view of Lake Michigan (so Will said), then very quickly started dating a financier named Jerome Banks. Dory thought it was hilarious that the man had made a fortune in banking. Jonathan married his secret paramour, Pooja, the owner of the *Cu-Cu-Cay* food trucks, at a City Hall service, and the two of them were running her business. Will and Alisa were living together, getting ready to move to L.A.

Though Dory called her mother every week, Eleanor refused to come and see her in Kewaskum.

"The site of your betrayal. No, no, I don't think so," she said to Dory on the phone. "And then, there's that *boy* you're seeing."

Dory laughed at that, the absurdity of her mother's criticism when she herself was in the middle of a divorce.

"You're laughing? Fine, I'll hang up then," Eleanor huffed.

"No, mom. Don't hang up. It's just funny that you haven't figured out that you can't control everyone anymore with your opinions." She didn't know where her new clarity or her courage with her mother was coming from, but it was there, appearing in short bursts.

"Enough, Dorothea!" Eleanor hung up.

Still, she felt badly for her mother. She worried for her. Being left. Being at loose ends. Rebounding quickly, as if it were imperative that she settle the next chapter of her life immediately, within months. The fact that her mother had landed on her feet rapidly did not surprise Dory–Eleanor liked things nailed down, it was obvious–but she worried that her mother might crack at some point; that she wasn't telling herself the whole truth.

The worry affected her relationship with Cord.

"What if she's faking it with this guy she's with, just to have someone?" Dory said edgily to Cord in her kitchen. She was boiling water for pasta, pulling at the linguini package with wet fingers. "God damn it! What the fuck does it take to open this stupid package!"

Cord took a giant step back from her, easing across the studio apartment. "Look, I'm just sayin' let her live her life. That's what you wanted from her, right?"

"It's not the same thing. I'm not lying to myself!" She wrenched the linguini package in her teeth, twisting it.

He turned his back, crouching next to an old turntable propped on a milk crate which Dory had found at a local thrift store, busying himself with pulling an LP from its weathered jacket.

"Jesus, Cord! Could you not walk away from me when I'm trying to say something?"

He stood quickly, a stunned look on his face. "What do you want *me* to do? I don't even know your mother! And even if she *is* lying to herself, you can't–"

"God damn you!" Dory said, hurling the linguini package to the floor, where it split and cracked the dried pasta into broken bits, scattering the pieces across the marbled linoleum.

"What the *hell*, Dory?" Cord yelled.

Her eyes filled. "Can't you please come over here and put your arms around me? My mother's barely talking to me, and it *hurts*. Can't you just sympathize?"

He stood, stock-still, staring. "Well, I don't *have* a mother. There's *that*." He said it with a bite.

"I know that!"

"So what do you want me to say?"

"I don't want you to say anything! I want you to walk over here and hold me!"

"Oh. Okay."

He moved gingerly, stood next to her for a second then put his arms around her.

"Just *hold* me when I'm upset, okay?" Dory whispered. "It doesn't even matter what it's about. Hold me."

In the weeks following, her angst and irritation with her mother began to fade. It had everything to do with Cord–his parents' deaths; his ability to make her see what was important. Something about him losing his mother and father had reorganized things in Dory's heart. It had set in motion a kind of recognition of what was meaningful and what wasn't.

"You have a chance at something with your parents," Cord had said a few days after their pasta-hurling argument. "I don't."

Then, finally, Eleanor agreed to meet Dory near the Milwaukee Art Museum for lunch. At Bacchus on Wells Street, they sat in a white-tableclothed booth, a tense tone in the air.

"What'll you have?" her mother said stiffly, snapping her menu as the waiter stood by.

"The burger, rare, no sauce, French fries please," Dory said.

Her mother rolled her eyes. "They have *real* food here, you know."

"Oh, no, no, ma'am!" the waiter exclaimed. He had a very red face and was especially energetic. "We're known for our burgers. They're premium ground sirloin!"

Dory laughed, smiling broadly, and Eleanor frowned.

"I'll have the scampi with fettucine please," her mother said primly. Then, when the waiter moved away she nodded in his direction. "I don't know how anyone gets through the day being *that* sincere. It's like having a target painted on your forehead."

"You're hilarious, Mother," Dory said, reaching for the artisan bread–four pieces set neatly on a white plate with a wedge of particularly yellow butter.

Eleanor took a gulp of her iced tea. "So. Are you satisfied?"

Dory bristled. "What do you mean?"

"All *this*. Everyone upending our family life. It's what you wanted–"

Dory took a breath. "I didn't want any of this. I just wanted my own life." She dropped her eyes to the white linen napkin in her lap. Her mother was formidable, even in defeat.

"I suppose *loyalty* is passé these days?" Eleanor said sarcastically. She waved the air as if to brush off the unpleasantness, then signaled the waiter over. "Never mind. Have a drink with me. Who cares if it's noon." It was statement; a command.

Dory smiled.

"What?" her mother said.

"Nothing. It's nice to see you, that's all."

"Hmmpf." To the waiter, Eleanor said, "Two bourbons, neat, if you don't mind."

When the drinks came, they clinked glasses. Dory got up her courage and spoke. "Aren't you happy with Jerome? You seem like you are. I mean, you got on the board of the Symphony in, like, two seconds. You've always wanted that."

"Jerome is fine. He's richer than we ever were. I'm luckier than most women who get left at my age." Eleanor took another sip of her drink, distractedly looking around the room.

"You're doing all this great stuff now. Will told me you two are going sailing in St. Thomas. I mean, that's gotta be fun, right? An adventure?" Dory was sincerely interested in her mother's feelings–that was new.

"I *liked* practicing law with your father. I *liked* our life." She frowned, her lips pulling downward in a half-moon that creased the sides of her face. "And now you're dating some boy–"

"Hank, Mom. His name is Hank. He lost his parents in a car crash when he was sixteen. He's a good person."

"Yes. Well. Aren't we all."

"All *what?*"

"You know what I'm saying."

"I don't, actually."

Eleanor leaned over the table and wrapped her hand around Dory's left wrist. "I know it's not your fault, Dorothea–all of this–but I want it to be. Does that sound cruel?"

"It sounds like *you,* mother."

Eleanor kept gripping, then patted the top of Dory's hand with her free palm. "I wanted to mold everyone. To mold our life. I could see it. What our life–what you and your brothers' lives–could be. I wanted it that way."

Dory stared for a moment, looking at her mother's face, at the longing in it. Her mother's eyes filled.

"Mom," Dory said softly. "They weren't your lives to mold."

"So it seems. Well. Nothing to do about it now."

At the curb, when the valet pulled up with her mother's BMW, Dory leaned in and hugged Eleanor through their thick overcoats. Her mother resisted, then pushed out a breath and held on for a moment, her puff of breathing visible in the wintery air.

"Mother," Dory murmured in her ear. "It'll fall apart, then it'll all level out.

You'll be *happier.* You'll see."

Eleanor stood back, holding Dory by the upper arms, and said, "So much for constancy and lineage. But, I suppose you're right. We'll just have to wait and see, won't we? Goodbye darling."

Dory's relationship with Cord deepened after that. The shift with her mother was because of him; the deaths of his parents had made her realize something she found both simple and profound. That no matter what her mother expected of her, even when Eleanor bullied her, she was lucky to have a mother near to have the *chance* at an adult relationship with her. She began to see the arc of how things fell apart–that somehow, without having to drive toward it, acceptance came even if it wasn't wanted or welcomed. Dory came to understand that if *she* shifted, the people around her couldn't help but shift in relation to her. The recognition put her at ease, as if she could count on getting a second chance with her mother, another chapter.

When she looked at Cord, at the twenty-year-old innocence in him that had gotten fast-tracked into more mature manhood because of his loss, she was oddly grateful for all of it. For the hardship, the pain, for how it had unfolded and what it had brought her.

She realized, as she and Cord practically lived together in her tiny in-law apartment, that love crept up on a person. For her, it wasn't a choice; not a conscious thing at all. She had not looked at him from afar, then crept cautiously close as she once thought she should, saying, *Yeah, okay, I guess this guy fits my standards*. Instead, he had shown up one day out of the blue–all wrong for her by any measurement she was raised with–and had captured her heart with his own openness, vulnerability and hardships, and he'd done it effortlessly.

The fact that love could hit her like that, with no preparation, that she could be touched in just the right places inside herself, and at just the right moment– the split-second when her attention was turned to him at the Pancake Supper in Boltonville, a so-unlikely place for her to land or ever be–astounded her. The gamble of living and loving. Of letting things tank and fall apart, feeling the loss, then seeing the truth: that tiny bits of courage could open the gates of everything. It was grace, pure and simple, and the thought of it brought her to tears.

In the mornings, Cord rose very early, made coffee for both of them, slid back into bed with her and shared it from a bulky, ceramic mug. He'd gotten a new job working a dairy farm owned by a guy named Manuel Avila down

WI-28 in Mayville, and he talked about Manuel constantly—how much the man loved his family, his farm, the land. How he and his parents and brother had come over the Mexican border in the trunk of a Pontiac when he was a boy. Manuel's dad, Mauricio, at age seventy-five, was still out there hauling hay bales next to Cord on the flat bed. At Dory's urging, Cord started making the hour-plus drive to UW Madison to take an evening poetry class from a Professor named Maximus Avila—same last name—and in a quirky turn of fate, it turned out the two Avilas were brothers. Dory and Cord got close with the family.

Dory's father had agreed to pay for her tuition to go back to school, and she planned to start the following fall at UW. She had got her dad to say that if she and Cord were still together when he finished his lower division classes, he'd pay for his tuition, too. It was a huge gift.

Her father liked Cord, thought him smart and loved the fact that he could build things, knew about land and farming and seasons. It was as far from her father's world as anything Dory could imagine, yet Willis, Dory's dad, never tired of talking about it with Cord. He was fascinated with raising cattle, with corralling horses. The last time Dory's dad had been up to visit them, Cord had taken Willis riding on Manuel Avila's farm, rounding up cows at the far end of the place, and her dad had been thrilled.

At the end of the day, they sat on the deck of the weekend rental her father loved on Lake Winnebago, eating take-out pizza and drinking Sprecher's Root Beer floats, a stunning view of the sun in the winter sky angling over the half-frozen water, bits of early-spring grass poking out from under the snow.

"So let me get this straight, Cord," her father said, chewing his pizza. "You and Manuel and those other farm hands trained those horses to come into the corral using the sound of your voices?"

"Yep, Mister Fathom, we did."

"*Willis*, please, Cord. Isn't that kind of like horse whispering? That's an astounding thing, young man."

"Thanks, um—*Willis*." Cord grinned.

After dinner, Cord read from a favorite book of poems he'd found in the library, a piece about boldness, sunflowers having the audacity to hang their huge, brazen flowers on tender stalks.

She could tell her father was moved.

When they got home to Dory's apartment, she got Cord into the bathtub. He lay down naked on top of her, his back on her chest and her legs akimbo gripping his side waists in the splashing water.

She stroked his hair. "Thank you," she said.

"For what?"

"For making my father love you, too."

"You love me?" He angled his face to her.

"I do."

"Me, too," he said.

She slipped her hand slowly down his belly, then lower, the gift of her pleasure to him sincere and heartfelt.

———~~~———

There was a barbeque at Will's rented house in Whitefish Bay to say good-bye to her brother and Alisa before they left for L.A. Will's place was white clapboard, set against the side of a wooded glen, huge cedars and Tamaracks towering over the cottage. Dory had always liked it. It felt cozy inside, with hardwood floors and slip-covered furniture in cream tones; a giant deck opening out from his bedroom, the thick-girthed, exquisitely tall trees towering overhead. He had a log picnic table and benches on the deck, and a shiny stainless steel barbeque sat out from the arms of one of the mammoth trees. It was May, early, the weather wavering upon warmth and getting its early sea-legs of rising temperatures, and the still-moist earth under the trees felt, to Dory, like it was fertilizing everything.

Inside, there were labeled boxes piled neatly against all the inside walls, the movers due any day.

All three couples were there: Dory and Cord, Bertie and Chaska, and, of course, Will and Alisa. There had been a family gathering with her older brothers and father a few days before; a separate dinner for Will with their mother and her new husband Jerome.

It was obvious to Dory that Will and Alisa were in love. Will often stroked Alisa's cheek with the back of his hand, speaking to her softly and humbly—a face of her brother she'd never seen before. Will was six-foot-two and Alisa was barely five-foot-one—"As long as it works out horizontally, who gives a shit about the rest of it," Alisa had said, laughing.

Dory thought they looked completely adorable, Will always bending his large frame to her body to kiss or touch or hold her. He was happy. It was as if love had made him pliable and physically flexible, as if he was dancing with it. Dory hadn't realized how *unhappy* Will had truly been until he and Alisa fell in love. Her brother shined now—smiling, laughing, telling jokes and being more helpful and chivalrous than she had ever known him to be.

"Beautiful girl," Will said to Alisa in his kitchen. "Can I get you a beer? Some wine? Here–I've got a glass for you right here in my hand." He set the glass down and wrapped his arms around Alisa, kissing her ear, then bent over and grabbed her bare knees below her denim miniskirt.

To Dory, he said, "God help me. Even her kneecaps make me crazy."

Alisa shook her mane of wild red hair and laughed boisterously. "Nothing like the real thing to make every corner of your heart and body turn into *mush*."

Will grinned. "Any time we start making you all nauseous, just let us know." He was proud of being in love, Dory could tell.

When they moved outside to the deck, Chaska stood next to Cord placing Bratwurst on the barbeque.

Bertie pulled a bottle of good Bourbon out of her huge patchwork purse and set it on the log table. "Tonight, we're toasting!" She grabbed a handful of plastic cups from a pile and poured out small amounts of the rich brown liquid, then leaned into Dory.

"First toast is ours," she said under her breath. "Mm-hm. Yep. Look right there at those two at the barbeque. Nothin' like a good hunk of man a handful of years younger than you to tick your clock and make it purr, right Dory?"

"I heard that, Bertie," Chaska said, flipping Bratwurst.

"What're you gonna do about it, is what I want to know, you handsome devil." She opened her wide mouth in mock-surprise, taunting him.

Chaska coolly handed the barbeque fork to Cord, then stepped to Bertie, leaning over to give her a wet kiss. "Objectification," he said to Dory. "Works on me every time."

They all laughed.

Chaska and Bertie headed back, but Dory and Cord spent the night in Will's guest room. Dory had said her goodbyes to her brother and Alisa the night before.

"You text me and call me just like you do here or I'm gonna have Cord come out there and hogtie you right there at your agent's desk."

"I promise," Will said, holding her close. "Thank you, Dor," he whispered. "None of this ever would've happened without you. You're my angel."

"I love you, Will," Dory said.

That night, in Will's guest bed, she pressed her back and limbs into Cord, and he wrapped his strong body around her, pulling her in. She smelled the sandy scent of his hair next to her cheek (it always smelled like hay, even when he had just washed it), felt the ticklish bit of his belly hair against her warm back. She was grateful for love; for its intimacies, surely–for the winding around each other it had brought her with Cord, for his kindness and his willingness to come to know her, for the against-the-grain surprise of finding him. But, more than that, she was grateful that love had touched the people she cared about most: Will, Alisa, Chaska, Bertie. They were–all of them–uncommonly mismatched by any measurement or standard she was raised to believe in. Yet the turn in her road, the veering off and the unraveling, the disappointments and the disappointing, had brought her what she loved best about life: unexpected and unlikely joy. The surprising gifts of not knowing, and then *finding*.

—᠁—

In the morning–she knew Cord would be up at the crack of dawn, his habit–she tiptoed around Will's place making coffee before they hit the road. As they sipped in her brother's kitchen, Dory sat on the tiled countertop with her legs apart and feet dangling, Cord in front of her, leaning his back into her chest. She felt it. The gifts that Chaska, Bertie and Cord, in her first bits of time in Kewaskum, had awakened in her.

It was the *calm* of living, the ability to welcome in the unformed and bare spaces. Knowing that life, in all of its "fucked-up and imperfect glory," as Bertie would say, could fill the empty spaces, and then level out again, lovingly. Should she have courage–real and genuine bravery–love would find her, beyond the bounds of anything she could hope for.

I will let it, she thought. *For the rest of my life, I will let it.*

She reached up and tousled Cord's hair with her left hand, her coffee cup in the other. He turned around, put his own cup down, looked into her eyes. His hands landed lightly on her thighs. "What?" he said.

She opened her mouth to speak, then paused.

"What're you thinking, Dor?"

She smiled. "I'm thinking that we're *blessed*. All of us."

His face went soft, his eyes suddenly wet. "Blessed to have *you*," he said.

She reached her arms around him and pressed her head to his chest, holding on tightly. ᜒ

Acknowledgements

Always, first, I thank my husband Michael, a superb writer and editor who lives with my written words every day, then helps me shape my themes, arcs, characters and lyrical lines on the page. You are my rock and my center, and these stories are made so much better by your expert hand and loving heart. I love you.

Then, to my wonderful writing group–Holly Brady, Julia Erwin-Weiner, Scott Gordon, Ron Ost, Marcia Sterling Kemp and Richard Abramson. You read and edited, supported and suggested week by week all along my writing path, and each of you helped me craft these stories. I am deeply grateful.

To my trusted readers–Jaime Love, Julia Maffei, Rose Whitmore, Kris Cannon, Deb Sotka and Scott Lubbock. Your commentary enriched each page and I am so thankful to you. To the women friends who have my back while I walk this courageous writer's walk, and who talk me down off the wall when I need it–Stefanie Morse, Michelle Flynn, Claudette de Carbonel, Barb Drye, and Elizabeth Evans. Your support and love means the world to me.

To Polly McCann at Flying Ketchup Press–thank you, sincerely, for every moment of editing, discussion, bantering, theme conversations, and of course, for believing in these stories with a driving confidence. The days we spent pouring over my fiction were so very lovely, and to get to spend my writer's days with you is a joy and an honor.

I thank the Burlingame Library and its staff, where my husband Mike spends much of his time on the board of trustees and working with the library's foundation, and where I often hide out in an upstairs alcove, put my feet up, and write. You are a welcome place for a writer, and I thank you all.

And lastly, to the teachers in my life–the ones who taught me how to live, how to offer my heart to my art and not stop offering it, no matter what the results–I send up a prayer of thanks to you. You fire my courage in the world and hold me up while I work, and I sing out a song of praise and thanks to all of you who have crossed my path.

About the Author

JoAnneh Nagler is the author of three nonfiction books including *Naked Marriage* (Skyhorse Publishing); *How to Be an Artist Without Losing Your Mind, Your Shirt, or Your Creative Compass* (W.W. Norton); and *The Debt-Free Spending Plan* (Harper-Collins), two of which were Amazon Top-100 titles. Her books have been featured in *The New York Times, Cosmopolitan, The Huffington Post, Essence Magazine, U.S. News and World Report, LiveStrong Magazine* and many more media outlets. Recently awarded the National League of PEN Women Achiever Award (2020), she wrote and directed the play *Ruby and George in Love* (Sonoma Arts Live Theatre Company), and composed two singer-songwriter albums, *I Burn* and *Enraptured*, available in all outlets. Her work has been published in the literary journals *New Haven Review, Glimmer Train, Mobius* and *Gold Man Review*. She is a founding member of The Pacific Coast Writer's Collective, and has just completed her first novel, *Key West*. Find more at www.AnArtistryLife.com.

Design

—⁓—

This book uses the font Garamond, a beautiful typeface with an air of in-formality. Its smooth curves and simple serifs have classical roman style form based on a cut by Jean Jannon, 1615, inspired by the designs from Claude Garamond in the 1500s, who in turn took inspiration from Aldus Manutius in 1495. The heads are in Didot. The word/name Didot came from the famous French printing and type producing Didot family.

Fonts like good stories inspire a long tradition of beauty and creativity. The embellishments in this book were chosen with green leaves because of a single green leaf that inspired the first story written for the collection and because of their closeness to arrows. The arrow symbolizes great fiction pointing the way for creativity and the sojourner's direction of the heart-led journey.

Stay with Me, Wisconsin was designed by Kēvin Callahan in Kansas City, MO for Coyote Point Press in 2021.